TENEBRASCO

BOOK 1: THE PEARL WIELDER TRILOGY

HANNAH REED

Independently published

Cover design by Keve Szatmari

ISBN: 9781072360155

For everyone pursuing their dream

PEARL GUIDE

Seven original pearls existed, wielded by the mer long before they knew humans shared the planet with them - Assurgere, Communico, Curo, Essentia, Factus, Tempus and Tenebrasco. Members of the royal mer family were the only ones who could transform into the mystical beings with two legs. Until one day an ancient King combined the powers of the Curo and Essentia pearl to create the Commutavi pearl – so all mer could transform. The final pearl is a recent invention by scientists, the mer solution to instant connectivity – the Iris pearl.

~

ASSURGERE
Power: The ability to grow and manipulate plant life
Colour: Green, the colour of green fleece seaweed

COMMUNICO
Power: The innate knowledge of all the tongues under the sea
Colour: Red

COMMUTAVI
Power: The transformation pearl from mer to human form
Colour: Purple

CURO
Power: The healers pearl
Colour: Sky blue

ESSENTIA
Power: The life force of the mer
Colour: Rose pink

FACTUS
Power: The ability to control water
Colour: White

IRIS
Power: The ability to manipulate the water
Colour: Cream

TEMPUS
Power: The gift of manipulating the weather
Colour: Navy

TENEBRASCO
Power: Unknown, long since believed to have died out
Colour: Onyx

PROLOGUE

April strained to keep up with her Dad. She put her arms out in front of her with one hand on top of the other and tried to swim faster. Kicking her tail rapidly, she sped forward with a burst of energy.

"Slow down April," her Mum Freya called from behind. April ignored her Mum and dashed on ahead through the tunnel. It was a perfectly smoothed cylinder of reddish brown rock.

"Daddy, are we almost there yet?" April asked, huffing out of breath as she reached him. She beamed in triumph having caught him up.

"Almost," Nathaniel said. He stopped swimming and grabbed April in mid-sea to spin her around. "The Ula caves are going to be very excited to see you."

Their Ula cave attendant swam them to the end of the tunnel. The attendants were stereotypically bookish mer, the sort you might find in a museum. But this attendant mer was huge with tattoos covering the breadth of his chest. Freya thought he could have at least worn a shirt for a royal appointment.

"It's my job Princess April to act as a gatekeeper of the pearls. We guard them and nurture them and help young mer select their own set of pearls."

April looked around confused as the attendant continued to float in front of the bare wall. He pointed upwards with a conciliatory wink. April's eyes followed and saw an intricate design of shells inlaid around a handle. Freya and Lorelai joined their party as he started talking again. The Queen's best friend Lorelai was also April's pearl guardian. It was a tradition that pearl guardians guide young mer to the caves and help them through the selection process. But, for a royal pearl selection, the process was kept private.

"Now above us, April is our most sophisticated pearl cave at the Ula Caves."

The cave attendant floated down so he could talk directly to the young princess. "First you will present yourself to the pearls. They will test your abilities through your Essentia energy - your life force if you will. All the pearls will light up in response as they decide if you are worthy to wield them. Then the winning pearls will stay lit and they will be yours to wield."

April's smile faltered. "What if none of the pearls want me?" she asked looking from the attendant to her Dad.

Nathaniel chuckled and bounced April on his hip. "I promise you April, all the pearls will be competing for your attention."

Freya gave her husband a stern look.

"Well, all the pearls that you have the ability to wield," he said his smile faltering too.

"Are you ready to go in, your majesties?" the attendant asked.

"I'm afraid this is as far as I can go April. Good luck and remember you can always ask me anything," Lorelai said as she kissed April quickly on the forehead.

"Thank you." April smiled shyly. Lorelai winked at her.

"See you later Freya." The two hugged before Lorelai swam back down the tunnel. April turned to the Ula Cave attendant and nodded at him. The attendant grasped the handle in the ceiling and twisted. Looking up April's eyes widened. A round disc opened and spiralled into the stone creating a hole in the ceiling. The attendant motioned for the Meridian Royal Family to swim up into the Royal Ula cave.

April looked around mesmerised by the cave before her. She glanced at her Mum and Dad to see if they were seeing what she was. Across the cave's walls were thousands of glistening pearls undulating light. Suddenly she could feel her whole body glowing, she looked down and raised her arms in amazement. Blue, pink, and green - every colour of the rainbow swam across her body from the pearls' light and her powers glowed in response. Waves of coloured energy poured out of her body and sparkled across her diamond coloured tail.

The attendant held out his hand to April and together they swam to the podium in the centre of the cave. April dropped his hand so she could swim closer to the podium, its energy beckoning her forward.

"Right, now April, I want you to swim down into the podium and let your tail fin brush up against the Essentia pearls."

April looked closer and could see the inside of the podium was inlaid entirely with rose coloured Essentia pearls. They were glowing in a rhythmic beat fading and dimming as one. She looked back to her parents and they nodded at her in encouragement. Letting go of the attendant's hand, she swam down into place. The moment her fins brushed the surface of the Essentia pearls she could feel a buzzing across the cave. She looked up in panic. About to swim out of the podium, April stalled as the whole cave burst into light. She screwed her eyes shut tight to block out the light. She heard the attendant and her parent's gasp in shock. Eventually, the light started to fade through her eyelids and she cautiously opened her eyes.

"Well, that was..." the attendant said pausing. He bobbed in the water as he tried to compose himself. "That was incredible," he said simply and sagged for a moment. Then, he hurriedly swam forward.

"You can swim out now April," he called.

April swam out slowly and moved to float by the attendant. She was careful to avoid eye contact and instead focused solidly on the ground. Freya and Nathaniel swam over to her and Nathaniel scooped her up in his arms.

"You did excellently April!" Nathaniel said. Tickling her stomach, he was rewarded with a tentative smile.

"She really did," the attendant said. "I've never seen all the pearls shine so brightly."

"Our merita is destined for greatness. Right darling," Nathaniel said.

"Yes dear," Freya said smoothly. She swam down to head height with her daughter. "Are you ready to collect your pearls?" she said softly to April.

April nodded into her Dad's warm jumper before swimming into her Mum's open arms.

"Would you like us to help you?" Freya asked. April nodded again, now more excited to seek out her new pearls.

Together they swam towards one of the remaining glowing pearls.

"Now April, we keep the pearls in these caves because they like to grow in darkness. Young pearls have soft shells so the sunshine can penetrate their core," the attendant said. "In this cave, we house all the pearls except the Iris pearls and the Commutavi ones."

"Why?" April asked.

The attendant chuckled at her tenacity. "Because the Iris pearls are manufactured. And the Commutavi pearls prefer a warmer climate so we keep them in separate caves."

April nodded knowingly, her eyes wide as she took in all the information.

"We'll collect your Commutavi pearl afterwards. Every mer, has a Commutavi pearl to help them transform into a legged."

"Do I need one?" April asked.

Nathaniel laughed, "Not everyone can transform without their Commutavi pearl."

They stopped at the top of the cave where three different pearls were lit within a metre radius. April could make out a blue, black and green glow shining from each. Freya lifted April up towards the pearls so she could get a closer look. April swam free and darted to the closest pearl.

"Right, now pull it down gently," the attendant said. The pearl's glow was so intense April could feel the heat radiating from it. She swam a little closer and plucked the pearl from its position. With a big grin, she swam back down to her parents.

"Mummy, Daddy look!" April said. She cupped her hand and held it out to show them her glowing blue pearl. It was an averagely sized pearl, smaller than a marble but bigger than a pea. It was almost spherical for all but a small dip on the top - to April it was perfect.

"Ohh the Tempus pearl," Nathaniel said in excitement peering over to look at the pearl.

April turned to the attendant expectantly.

"A rare pearl indeed Princess. This is the Tempus pearl; a wielder like you can manipulate the weather. And with enough practice one day you will control it."

"That explains the rainbows and hailstorms," Freya said laughing. Whenever April was excited rainbows would appear in the sky but when she was particularly grumpy, as four-year-olds often were, it started hailing.

April's excitement grew and the glow across her tail intensified. She looked down at her pearl in wonder.

"Let me hold your pearl while you get the next one," Freya said. April turned around and placed the pearl carefully in her Mum's hand before swimming off. Less timid, she plucked the green one quickly from the surface. Then she swam a little to her right and grabbed a third darker one that was pulsing a steady black. This time she swam straight to the attendant.

"What do these ones do?" she asked, her voice high with excitement.

"This green one is the Assurgere pearl. It means you can wield your powers to grow plants."

"And this one?" April said holding out her black pearl expectantly.

"That one..." the attendant paused. He leant in to inspect it further. "Well it can't be."

Freya and Nathaniel leant forward to see the pearl in their daughter's hand.

"That's a Tenebrasco pearl," Freya said, her face paling.

"I suppose it runs in the Royal family," the attendant said looking first from Nathaniel to Freya for reassurance.

"Yes," Nathaniel said. He held April's shoulders protectively as she looked up at the three adults.

"The Tenebrasco pearl is a special pearl. We don't know what it does because the powers have been lost," the attendant said.

"Do I have the powers?" April asked furrowing her eyebrows. She looked to her Mum and then the attendant for an explanation.

"Maybe," Freya said with a strained smile. "Why don't you go and get your next pearl."

April hesitated for a moment looking between the adults. Then she dropped her pearls into her Mum's hand and swam down towards the next glowing pearl. This one glowed a bright red; it reminded her of the ruby necklace Lorelai wore. She picked it up and swam over to where her next pearl glowed. No longer worried about hurting them, she grabbed the pink pearl. Then she swam to collect her last shining pearl. This pearl was glowing the brightest of them all. As she swam closer she could see it was buried under a group of other pearls. Moving them to the side she picked up a bright white pearl. Underneath her white pearl was a smaller pearl glowing a faint blue. She picked it up too.

Swimming back up to the adults she ran her fingers over her pearls. They were all smooth but they weren't perfectly spherical. As she traced the lumps and bumps of her pearls with her finger she could feel them warming to her touch.

"Hello pearls," she said quietly.

"What have you found now?" Nathaniel called to her.

"I have a white one, a red one, a blue one and a pink one," she said holding her pearls up with a flourish.

"Excellent work," the attendant said smiling, but his eyebrows didn't move. "That means you wield all seven of the original pearls."

"All seven!" April cried in excitement. She swam up to her Mum and pouring the last of the pearls into her Mum's hand, April counted them quickly to double check.

"What do these four do?" she asked bobbing up and down.

"The white one is your Factus pearl, it allows you to move and manipulate water. The red one is the Communico pearl. It means you can speak and understand all the languages of the animal kingdom. The Essentia pearl is the pink one and it allows you to monitor mer life force. And finally, you have the Curo pearl. It helps you heal other mer when they are sick."

As the attendant listed the powers of each pearl he pointed to them in turn.

Freya glanced up at Nathaniel.

"That's a lot of power for one merita," she said. Her hand was frozen in its cupped position.

Nathaniel shook his head slightly at Freya before he bent down and picked up April.

"Well done darling. You wield all the pearl powers," he said nuzzling his forehead against his daughter's.

"I do," she said smiling. "Just like you."

~

"Now Kayla," April said very seriously "watch what I do and repeat."

April curled her tail underneath her and focused on the potted plant in front of her. At ten years old, she was prone to experimenting with her powers. She brought her hands up and started to make weaving motions as she twisted her wrists. Her little hands glowed green and the plant started to grow. Its tendrils twisted together while April weaved and soon the plant was as tall as the ceiling. Kayla clapped her hands hard together. At age seven everything her sister did was cool. Kayla was always a willing participant in April's experiments.

"Do it again!" Kayla called.

April grinned and focused her attention on the other potted plants in the room. Her whole body glowed a deep green with Assurgere power as she swirled her hands in the air. The seaweed grew and grew twisting through the sea. Kayla laughed and started swimming through the tendrils.

"This is so cool!" she shouted, dashing in and out of the seaweed.

April screwed her face up in concentration and held her hands up in front of her face. She held her hands apart as if she was holding a ball. An orb of green and white light grew in front of her. Then suddenly she twisted her hands. The seaweed tendrils knotted together forming a tight ball. The writhing mass of seaweed started to expand as it grew with April's power. She pulled her hands apart and created an opening.

"Let's swim inside," April called to Kayla. Kayla quickly swam ahead of April and dashed into the entrance. April flicked her hand and the seaweed latched onto Kayla's tail.

"Not so fast!" April laughed.

"Hey, no fair!" Kayla said, but she still made it into the orb first.

"What is going on in here?" Freya said from the doorway. April turned around slowly.

"April made us a seaweed den," Kayla said excitedly swimming over to her Mum. Freya grabbed her in mid-sea and placed her on her hip fins. She stared at April until she averted her gaze.

"It was just for fun," April said avoiding looking at her Mum. Freya sighed and swam over to her daughter.

"April one day you will be the ruler of the seven seas. You can't wield your pearl powers for fun. You have a responsibility to learn control and use your powers to help merkind."

April looked up at her Mum. "But I am in control."

"No, you're not."

"Yes, I am," April glowered at her Mum.

"Then why are you glowing, and the seaweed still moving?" Freya said eyeing the seaweed behind April.

April turned around quickly and looked up at the seaweed. She closed her eyes and tried to stop the green glow. Concentrating hard she focused on the Assurgere energy absorbing back into her.

"April!" Freya said her voice rising. The seaweed tendrils were starting to expand at an alarming rate.

"I'm trying," April said, her eyes wide as she looked at the mass in front of her. "Stop pressuring me."

"Kayla swim out of here," Freya said releasing her. Kayla looked from her mum to her sister and then sped out the room weaving through the seaweed. Freya swam up to April and placed her hands on her shoulders. She tried not to look at the ever-growing seaweed mass around her.

"Listen to me April, you can do this," Freya said staring into April's eyes. April nodded. Tears were starting to spill down her cheeks. She looked down at her hands and focused her energy. The glowing dimmed. She strained against her powers and the seaweed stopped writhing. April closed her eyes and the seaweed unravelled. Freya hesitated for a moment before straightening up to her full height. April looked up at her Mum with a small smile until April saw how her Mum was floating.

"You almost destroyed the lounge, you put your sister in danger and you lost control."

"But, I stopped it, we were just having fun," April said throwing her arms down.

"April, you never stop and think about your actions," Freya said. She swam around in a tight circle. "I don't know what I'm going to do with you."

April floated in the middle of the room watching her Mum. Freya sighed and swam away leaving April alone with her withered kelp creation.

It wasn't so much the telling off that left April deflated it was the truth behind her Mum's words. She couldn't help it; her emotions ruled her powers. April swam over to the seaweed while clasping her still glowing Assurgere pearl. Through her fingers she could still see its green light. Closing her eyes April slowly breathed in and out and imagined the seaweed gently unfurling and returning to its pots. With her final exhale, she opened her eyes to see that order had returned to the lounge.

~

April idled in the dining room of the Pinkouinos Palace. The waters were cold in the Kara Sea so April was wrapped up snugly in a thick jumper. This palace was an odd assortment of extensions all jumbled together to create the Royal Palace in the sixth sea. It was a quiet place so April presumed that the royals before her entertained themselves by remodelling and adding extra wings to combat sheer boredom. Right now, her own boredom led her to practice her sculpture making. Inspired by the myth of Circe she lazily waved her hand and froze another sheet of water above her. Her whole body glowed white with Factus energy as she wielded her powers to move different ice sculptures around the room. The Great Pearl floating above flickered with Factus energy in response to April's wielding. She was getting quite good if she did say so herself. It calmed her to be in the presence of one of the seven Great Pearls. They made her powers feel more manageable. The size of a large sea turtle, the Great Pearl's presence was undeniable.

"Princess April. Your Mother is coming," one of the palace maids informed her quickly before swimming off.

"Thank you!" April called. She hurriedly started melting the figurines she had created. Focusing on her Factus energy she raised the temperature in the room. The ice sculptures of humpback whales, tiny krill and giant Emperor penguins melted back into the ocean. Just in time the room was back to its boring stately self and April stopped glowing white with Factus energy. April floated down and settled back into one of the large grey dining chairs. She leant forward and grabbed the book she was supposed to be studying and opened it to a random page.

"April," Freya said, her voice sounding flustered as she swam into the dining room. "There you are."

"Here I am," April said. She casually turned over to the next page. Freya swam to April's side of the table and placed her hands on her hip fins.

"Why aren't you in class with your sister?" Freya asked dryly.

"Because I'm studying in here."

"You won't be able to do this at boarding school April," Freya said. She pulled out a chair and perched in front of her daughter. Freya clasped her hands on top of her bent tail.

"I wish you would take your studies seriously. You have a lot to learn."

"I do take my studies seriously. I have A's in all my subjects. I have an A in Oceanography, Linguistics, Pearl Metaphysics, I even have an A in Pinkouinos which is a dying language in my opinion."

"I meant your pearl wielding classes," Freya said eyeing her daughter sternly.

April sat up and thrust her book down. "What's the point in them? You'd rather I never even used my powers."

"To learn control," Freya said sitting upright.

"I am in control," April shouted. But, as she raised her voice her whole body started to glow.

"Then why is the Great Pearl pulsating?" Freya said. She looked upwards and April's eyes followed her gaze.

April took in a deep breath and tried not to let her Mum get to her. She closed her eyes for a moment and concentrated on her breath. The Great Pearl stopped pulsating and resumed its steady white glow of Factus energy.

"I want you to use your powers only when you have learnt control."

April scowled. She swam up and headed for the door.

"You could be so talented April. If only you learnt to control your powers."

"How can I learn to control them if I'm never supposed to use them?" April shouted as she swam out the door.

Freya was left alone in the room. She tapped on her Iris pad to call Lorelai. Only two more weeks and April would be at boarding school.

CHAPTER 1

5 years later

Queen Freya turned the final page of the Peace Treaty. For years Nathaniel had been working to broker peace between mer and humans. Finally, it was coming to fruition. She picked the document up from her desk in the library and swam to her husband's study. She knocked lightly on the door before swimming in. Nathaniel sat at his desk reviewing his speech for the ceremony next week.

"It's finished," Freya said with a trace of giddiness in her voice.

"Finally," Nathaniel said and rushed forward to hug his wife. He spun her round in the water their tails entwining for a moment. Emerald green and navy blue shimmered across the smooth stone floor.

"You've done it."

"We've done it," Nathaniel corrected. "After all these years, we will have peace at last." He released his wife and they floated in the water. Freya wielded her Factus powers and sent the document to her husband's desk with a flourish. Nathaniel raised his eyebrows in mock horror.

"I can use my powers frivolously if I want to," Freya said smiling coyly. "How is the speech going?"

"I want it to be perfect."

Freya swam over to the desk and skimmed the first few paragraphs of her husband's speech. It hadn't changed much since she last read it. A few phrases had been added, a couple of words strengthened, but otherwise, it was the same.

"April returns from boarding school tonight," Nathaniel stated floating behind his wife.

"...Yes."

"As it's the end of her exams I thought we could have a little celebration."

"Like a party?" Freya asked without bothering to look up from the document. Nathaniel noticed his wife's slender shoulders stiffen.

"Yes, she deserves it after her hard work."

"I don't think that it is appropriate. We should be concentrating on the treaty Nathaniel."

"I haven't planned anything yet," Nathaniel said. He tried to find the excitement that was in his wife's eyes a moment before. But, it was gone.

"Good," Freya said her shoulders relaxing. "Maybe we can at a later date. But for now, there is simply too much to finalise."

Nathaniel paused looking at his wife's back and opened his mouth to try again.

"Have the legged confirmed that their blockade on the Chukchi Sea is over?" Freya asked without looking up. Legged was the slang word mer used for humans.

Nathaniel sighed, "Yes, first thing this morning."

The Peace Treaty was undoing years of hatred. It was not easy but slowly; step-by-step everything was coming back together again.

"Remind me to ask April to look after the weather," Nathaniel said, rubbing his forehead.

"Are you sure? What about Shaman Tate?" Freya asked, quickly swimming over to the other side of the room.

"Shaman Tate is already busy making sure everyone is relaxed with her Curo powers."

"I suppose the weather is simple enough," Freya said abruptly turning around.

"Freya, she is more than capable."

Not for the first time, Nathaniel wondered if there was truth in April's insistence that her Mother didn't like her. Freya was always so austere whenever their eldest daughter was concerned. But, that was his wife. She followed her head over her heart in all matters.

"I have arranged for the Jet Stream to take us to the Summerland Palace on Friday," Freya said as they glided through the corridor. The royal family were currently based in the underwater Hanarian palace. Each sea had at least one underwater palace and a corresponding land palace. The Summerland Palace was positioned just off the Bahamas not far from where the Treaty would be signed on the Otter Cliffs.

"Good morning," Nathaniel said to a group of passing squid wielding his Communico pearl without thinking to slip into Cephalopodlian. A slight red glow was the only evidence he was using his powers.

"Morning your Majesty," they responded in unison.

"Excellent Freya," Nathaniel said in English once more. "I feel like something big is about to happen. I can feel the pearls stirring."

"Well, something big is about to happen. You're about to broker peace with the legged. This day will go down in history," Freya said a smile on her lips. Nathaniel murmured inaudibly in response.

The mer stewards glowed white with their Factus energy as they swung the dining room doors open for the King and Queen. The dining room was one of the oldest settlements in the seven seas. It was a simple room with a large circular table in the centre. Directly above the table floated one of the seven original Great Pearls.

"Nate, it's black," Freya said as she swam into the dining room and floated stock still staring at the Great Pearl.

"The Tenebrasco energy," Nathaniel said swimming up to it. He touched it and his own Tenebrasco pearl glowed in response. "I can't remember the last time this happened."

"I much prefer when it is Factus or Curo, white and blue go so much better with our décor in Hanaria," Freya said lightly. She lowered her gaze from the pearl and sat at the table.

"I'll be sure to tell the pearls that," he said, but quietly enough so Freya wouldn't hear.

The two royals sat down to their breakfast. Nathaniel spread his speech papers out in front of him. There was only a week to go until the Peace Treaty and he needed to concentrate but his eyes kept on flickering up to the Great Pearl.

"Nate," Freya said sharply.

"Yes," Nathaniel said shaking his head and bringing his gaze back to his wife.

"You've been staring at the Great Pearl for the past seven minutes."

"Seven minutes," Nathaniel laughed. "Were you timing me?"

Freya rolled her eyes and turned her attention back to her documents.

"Can you remember any of the Great Pearls ever glowing with Tenebrasco energy?" Nathaniel asked.

Freya looked up slowly and placed her pen down on the table.

"I don't pay attention to the moods of the pearls," she said. "But no."

"Neither can I," Nathaniel said ignoring Freya's tone. "Maybe I should look back through the Great Pearls' history."

Freya rolled her eyes and resumed eating her breakfast.

~

Two weeks later

"Help! Come over now Setha, I have no idea what to do with these things."

"It can't be that bad April, they're just clothes."

"These aren't clothes, I can't make head or tail of it. I'm starting to regret dismissing Mum's advice."

Setha made an inelegant harrumph, "What do you need a dresser for when you have me!"

"Thank you so much."

"I'll dive round now," Setha said.

"See you soon," April smiled as she heard the tap of Setha's Iris pad disconnecting.

Sitting on her bed April went through her checklist of everything she needed to remember for the Peace Treaty. The names of all the legged dignitaries drifted through her mind, the order of ceremony, the correct bow for the different legged royals... She was bored with the treaty though and her legged bed was too comfortable for concentrating. Her palace beds were always a novelty compared to her bed at boarding school.

A soft summer breeze blew through her open balcony doors. It lifted her golden hair from her shoulders and dropped it down again in time with her sigh. This was another novelty of being on the surface. A cool breeze was something she missed under the sea. April shivered and surveyed the lavishly wrapped perfumed box she had just torn into. She had thought it was a present from her Dad, a little good luck something for the evening ahead; or a bribe from her

Mum to remind her to be on her best behaviour and to follow her instructions. She read again the gift tag that was attached to the box.

'*Dear Princess April,*
Please accept this outfit as a welcome present from our nation. I look forward to meeting you tonight,
President Darius.'

The friendly tone made April shudder involuntarily.

She started rifling through the box once more. She lifted out an ornate bracelet and fastened it around her wrist. The navy gems matched the ones surrounding the Tempus pearl on her necklace. Next, she took out the perfume, sprayed some on her wrist and inhaled deeply. She was surprised at its light floral fragrance. April held the dress at arm's length. She couldn't work out which way was up. It was exquisite with lots of fabric in complimentary shades of blue with the occasional flash of silvery pink. But if she couldn't figure out all the straps and loops it would be useless. April flicked her long hair behind her shoulders and walked away from the mess.

April walked barefoot onto the balcony and leant on the cool stone ledge and looked out to the open sea. The sun was still high in the sky and it made the rippling sea glisten a sharp blue. Her blue eyes reflected back the colour of the sea and her hair shimmered with the light of the sun. It was breath-taking to see her home from above. She felt an overwhelming desire to dive off the balcony and hide in her favourite coral cove for the evening.

The Summerland Palace stood proudly on a private island in the Pacific Ocean. It was made out of creamy bricks with pale brown and red spirals dancing over the bricks' surface. In comparison to the Hanarian Palace in these waters, the Summerland Palace was rather bulky. But, the squat structure strangely made April feel safe. Her bedroom looked out onto the back of the castle. From her balcony, she looked onto a stretch of garden, then golden sand, and after that all she could see for miles around was the sea. The view made her ache to be back in the water.

For now though, she had to behave like an ordinary legged. She reached up and held onto her pearl necklace for comfort. Her Mum had all but banned her from wielding her powers during the Peace Treaty weekend. Apparently, it would appear 'rude and insensitive'. April could feel her powers building within her, itching to be free.

She could expend some energy at least ensuring clear skies and sunshine, but that was the forecast today anyway. If she wasn't careful she would be glowing for the entire weekend.

Control, April thought wryly, was not her strong suit. Although April could tell her Dad was happy to have her for support, her Mum would prefer that Kayla was the daughter to represent the family. Unfortunately, April would have to do. With one final longing glance at the sea, April pushed off from her balcony and walked back into her room. She slipped on the heels President May had sent. Bending down to tie them up she determined to master them before Setha arrived.

April took a tentative step forward. If she were to face the legged without the support of her sister, she would do it without falling over. She placed both feet together and tried to not look down as she took another step forward. Standing seemed to be okay, it was moving that was the problem. Distracting her for a moment she saw her Iris pad glow, tapping the Iris pad she read the message, *'First dance, centre of the floor, see you there.'*

"Eurghhh," April fell backwards onto her bed, she had forgotten about the dance aspect of the evening. Never before had an item of clothing caused her so much annoyance. At this moment Setha opened the door and raised her eyebrows at the spectacle before her.

CHAPTER 2

"Go on then, throw the disaster at me," Setha chuckled. Without looking over at her, April threw the contents of the box in the general direction of the door.

"Having a hard day are we?" Setha smirked at her best friend. She leant down and picked up the crumpled mess from the floor. She walked over to the mirror and shook the dress out in front of her. Shaking her curly hair, she turned the garment around trying to decide which was the top or bottom. She could see that it was intricately made and without a doubt incredibly expensive. But, none of that would matter if they couldn't work out how April was supposed to wear it.

"Ethan just reminded me about the dance, how am I supposed to dance in these?" April stuck her legs up in the air. She resumed her previous activity of angrily glaring at the shoes.

"Oh my," exclaimed Setha as she glanced at the shoes in the mirror. She turned around to admire them. "They must be at least 12 shells high, and so pointy!" she said as she grabbed April's leg. "How the legged come up with these things I don't know."

"It's because they want to break their legs." April swung her legs down and stood back up.

Setha looked her up and down and her smile took on a sarcastic glimmer. "Ethan will be there to catch you at least."

"Oh, ha ha Setha, you know nothing is going on between us."

"But maybe, whilst signing the World's Peace Treaty, your eyes will meet as you both reach for the same pen," Setha sighed dramatically.

"You do realise that I won't actually be signing the Peace Treaty, right?" April asked to change the subject as she sat up and hugged a pillow. "I'm merely there to look '"pretty and harmless.'"

"Your Mum's words?"

"How did you guess?" April said with mock shock.

"Well, as soon as we figure out this dress, we can work on making you look so stunning that the legged men and women will be dying to live in a world at peace with you."

April stood up and spun around, flinging her pillow behind her. She caught her heel on the bedspread and collapsed in a heap on the floor, she looked up laughing.

"This might take longer than you thought."

Setha stifled a laugh. She pulled April up saying, "Why don't you practice walking?"

"Not spinning?"

"No. If you break your ankle on my watch your Mum will feed me to the sharks."

"This is true," April nodded "but only baby ones." She set about walking up and down her room. She took tentative steps on the plush carpet; it was certainly not the best terrain to be learning to walk in the devil shoes. She manoeuvred herself back to her balcony, hoping that the wooden decking would be more manageable. April couldn't help feel that these shoes were a test. It was as if the legged wanted her to slip up and reveal herself as the uncivilised 'mermaid' they thought she was. This thought caused her to wobble fractionally. She straightened herself up and determinedly stepped forward, April would represent the mer flawlessly tonight. She would not let the mer down.

Setha was applying the finishing touches to April's make-up. It had taken April several hours but she was now able to walk in her shoes. She looked at the flat surface of her Iris bracelet. The timer was counting down, only twenty minutes left until a helicopter would pick up the mer entourage. Not that April knew what a helicopter was. She was pretty sure that one of her Dad's advisors had tried to compare it to a hummingbird that they'd seen in the Hasani Palace garden in the Indian ocean. The noise from downstairs drifted up to April's suite. April knew she was supposed to be mingling with the mer attendees of the Peace Treaty but Setha wouldn't let her go until she was perfect. Setha stepped back to take a look at her handiwork.

"Can I see yet?" April implored while trying to look as cute as possible to win Setha over. Setha was not easily won over.

"No," Setha shook her head and walked out of the dressing room and into the bedroom. April reached up to itch her face then scowled as she remembered she couldn't. She took off her Iris bracelet and replaced it with the bracelet the legged President sent her.

"We have one final piece to put into place," Setha walked back with the bejewelled hair ornament that had baffled April earlier. Setha skilfully pinned it into April's hair allowing the jewels to cascade down her neck and fall gently over her shoulder.

"Done," Setha pronounced with a flourish and stepped back to admire her handiwork once more. "You can look now," Setha said smiling.

April stood up and walked slowly and carefully to the mirror. Setha followed behind her and she beamed with pride. April's golden wavy hair was now braided into an elegant chignon. The dress' blues and pinks reflected against each other, as she swished the dress from side to side. It glimmered the same diamond colour as her tail. April watched the delicate ruffles move with her as she did. It reminded her of the surface weed swaying in the water. April smoothed her hands over the bodice and reached up to adjust her pearls, each one glowed warmly against her skin. They were behaving now and their persistent hum of energy quietened.

~

Ethan ran up the hallway taking the stairs two at a time. He swung himself around the bannister and strode towards April's room.

"Wow," Ethan exclaimed as he walked through the door. "You look beautiful."

April turned to smile at him, "Thank you."

"Well... I mean wow; it took you all day to look like this. No wonder you look so awful on a daily basis."

Ethan laughed and walked over to give April a hug. April rolled her eyes.

"Thanks Ethan."

"And what about me?" he said with a flourish as he turned suavely on the spot. "Don't you think I look rather dashing tonight?"

"You look wonderful Ethan," Setha said sarcastically from her position in the corner of the room.

"Oh Setha, I didn't see you there, pleasure as always," Ethan turned and gave her a mock bow. Setha blushed slightly but managed to roll her eyes.

"Are you ready?" Ethan asked moving over to the bed and picking up pieces of packaging.

"I'll be ready soon," April said. "Can you take a photo of me Setha?"

"Sure," Setha said. She moved to April's bed and, avoiding Ethan's gaze picked up April's Iris pad.

April moved over to the balcony.

Setha held up the Iris Pad and started laughing, "April relax."

"Okay," April said shifting. She tried a new position, looked down at her feet, and then looked up again smiling.

"You're the most awkward person I've ever seen," Ethan said striding over. "Come on."

"Thanks for the motivational speech," April said dropping her gaze, "Let's just forget it." She made a move back to her bedroom.

"No, come on."

Ethan grabbed her arm and dragged her back to the balcony. He held April's hand and raised it above her head twirling her. April tripped and fell into his arms and pushed herself back laughing.

"Much better," Setha said quietly. April walked over and looked at the photos.

"Thank you so much Setha, they look great. I will tell everyone I meet tonight that I was styled by Setha Moretta," April said empathically as she hugged her friend.

"Don't worry about it. Enjoy yourself tonight, you're making history and you'll do us proud," Setha said.

"Umm April, we'd better be going," Ethan said looking at his watch to avoid Setha's gaze.

Setha squeezed April's hand before letting her walk towards the door.

"Bye Setha, say hi to your Dad for me," April said as she and Ethan left the room.

"Will do, break a leg April," Setha laughed.

The door shut, leaving Setha alone in the plush room. In the absence of April's kinetic energy, an eerie stillness fell over her. Without it, the air felt flat. Setha walked over to the dressing room and started tidying up. She had spent many a night here during the summer holidays with April but the room always had the impersonal feeling of a hotel suite. Watching April and Ethan walk off together into their own private world, Setha couldn't help but feel a little lonely. She sighed as she pulled out her Iris pad and checked to see if there was a message from her Dad. She smiled and her shoulders relaxed as she read his message, 'Can't wait to see you tonight!'

Setha gathered her things and made her way through to April's private staircase. The stairs led out into Setha's favourite part of the Summerland palace. The garden Setha stepped into was immaculate. Whenever April stayed she wielded her Assurgere powers to help the gardeners. The colour scheme at the moment was white and yellow. Arches had been decorated with tiny flowers that grew in delicate patterns. She inhaled as she walked, her shoulders relaxing at the scent. Setha reached the water's edge and prepared to enter the transformation bubble. When suddenly she heard a loud whirring. She looked up and was pushed backwards by an unexpected wind. She tripped and thudded to the ground. The helicopters had arrived.

Setha groaned as she stood up, she was not looking forward to the bruise that would no doubt appear on her tail. She brushed the dust off herself and frowned at the monstrosity that was slowly lowering itself onto the beach in front of the palace. Her tranquillity ruined, Setha walked into the sea and slipped down to the guest transformation bubble. In front of her were neat piles of legged clothing and a selection of lockers. Setha quickly unlocked her locker and took out her clothes. She swapped from the borrowed legged clothing into her outfit and put her borrowed clothing in the laundry basket. She adjusted herself in the mirror and then tapped the release button to let the bubble fill itself with water. With a glow of violet Commutavi power, she transformed.

She swam towards the ray stop a little way away from the Summerland Palace Island. The island was a hub for tropical fish and corals. Swimming slowly, she took in the vibrancy of the surrounding ocean until she reached the open sea. She waited for a school of yellowfin tuna to pass, then continued on her way to the ray bus. Setha waited patiently at her stop. The ray bus, painted a lurid green to promote the Peace Treaty, glided towards her. Setha swiped her Iris card and settled herself into a seat by the window.

CHAPTER 3

"Your Royal Majesties," the guard made a low bow to King Nathaniel and Queen Freya before turning to the rest of the hall. "Will you please step this way now that the whole company is gathered." The guard's eyes flickered to April and Ethan who were making their way down the stairs. April was still not 100% convinced that the shoes were actually intended for moving in. She held firmly onto Ethan with one hand and held her train in the other. Walking slowly, she tried not to look down at the staircase. Everyone started to exit the sumptuously decorated ballroom and moved into the entrance foyer.

April looked around in awe. The decorators had outdone themselves for this event. Sand dollars seemed to be the overriding theme of the evening. They were the snowflakes of the sea April had heard her Mum explain to a legged decorator. Each one was unique and very delicate. Sand dollar lanterns hung from the ballroom ceiling casting rays of soft light onto the crowd below. The bar tables were made out of creamy marble columns of stacked sand dollars and the glasses were blown with the dollars delicate markings imprinted around them. The whole effect was calming. April suspected her Mum chose this theme specifically for its tranquillity. She tripped and grabbed onto the railings with both hands.

April shooed Ethan's help as she righted herself and followed the gathering through to the entrance foyer. The large double doors, which were double Ethan's height and twice as wide, were opened fully for the occasion. The party walked out onto the beach to wait for the helicopters. April looked around at the most influential mer of the seven seas. She smiled at the different political party leaders, waved at the invited military powers and avoided the pearl shamans. Weaving her way through the crowd she looked down at her dress and was reminded of when she and Kayla used to play dress up. April would never say she didn't enjoy being a Princess but having to live up to the scrutiny of the world was not an easy task. April wondered if this was why her Mum always seemed in such a bad mood.

Queen Freya was the most elegant hostess. She was the beloved Queen of the seven seas who was always in control. April only got to see this side of her Mum. At home, Freya only truly relaxed when she was alone with her husband. April could remember as a merita wanting to swim into the snug to cuddle with her parents. But she had known that the second she entered the room the warmth would fade out of her Mum's face. And so, April contented herself to watch from the doorway, before swimming upstairs to her bedroom.

"April… April," Ethan said while waving his hand in front of April's face. April stared into the distance, her gaze unfocused.

"Oh sorry," April said shaking her head slightly.

"Are you okay?" Ethan looked down at her in concern.

"Yeah, I'm fine, it's just..." April looked down and fiddled with her necklace. "It's like a wall has broken down in my mind. I feel like the pearls are trying to communicate with me," she said in a rush.

"The pearls. As in like pearl blackouts? Have you spoken to anyone about this?" Ethan leaned forward instinctively.

"No, not yet. It's no big deal," April said gesturing flippantly with her hand.

"Are you sure, pearl memories aren't supposed to happen until your powers go through the Kallion."

"I'm sure Ethan," April said with force. "It's probably just an heir thing." She put her drink down signalling the end of the conversation. Ethan looked at her warily.

"You can always talk to me April," Ethan said moving her away from the crowd. April stared up at him.

"I know," she breathed deeply. Ethan was her oldest friend and apart from Setha her closest. It wasn't that she didn't want to tell him. She didn't like talking about her powers with anyone.

"Do you remember when I refused to take pearl wielding classes anymore?"

"Yes," Ethan laughed. "Your Mum was furious."

April fiddled with her glass momentarily before looking up again. "I refused because they were testing me."

"Testing you?" Ethan said furrowing his brow.

"They would weigh me to the ocean floor and see if I could use my powers to get free, or they would throw attacks at me and I had to fight them off. Once I was abandoned in a cave and sealed in. My Mum just chatted above with Shaman Tate as I cried for them to let me out."

Ethan stared in shock. "That's barbaric. Are you sure?"

"Yes. All she wants is to keep my powers under control," April said quietly. "But, the pearls they're a part of me." April waved her hands more as she spoke.

"April no one can control you. You need to have more confidence in yourself, take control of your life," Ethan said.

April smiled at him. She took a sip of his drink and looked down to the bar table and traced the lines of a sand dollar. A flicker of dark light followed her finger. She gasped in shock, but it disappeared so quickly she wasn't sure if she'd imagined it. About to say something April looked back up but Ethan interrupted.

"Look!" he pointed outside.

A huge roar and a gust of wind came from behind them as the final helicopter landed.

"Come on," Ethan smiled at April and took her hand. She followed him and tried to ignore the black light she thought she had seen. Together they walked across the sand towards the helicopters. As they reached the helicopter April couldn't help but look back. She was suddenly filled with a sense of nostalgia for the Summerland Palace. More pearl memories she presumed and tried to push the feelings away. The guard was standing impatiently at the helicopter's stairs as by now everyone else had made their way onto the aircraft. April was glad that her Mum's helicopter had already taken off and she couldn't possibly know who was causing the delay.

The helicopters were nothing like April imagined. They were big, noisy and unsightly things; they did not resemble hummingbirds. Still, a thrill of excitement shot through her, she had travelled a lot but never by air. She hastened up the steps at the thought of being able to see her home from above and, to the guard's great approval, finally made it on board the helicopter. A guard helped them into their seats and with great difficulty, because of the many accoutrements to April's dress, fastened them in. She smiled apologetically at the guard as he walked off the helicopter shaking his head and gave the pilot the all clear.

"This is exciting!"

"What is?" Ethan replied distractedly looking in the other direction.

"Flying! I've never been up in the air before."

"Oh... yeah." Ethan pulled his gaze back to April. "It's kind of nauseating."

"You've flown before?" April said incredulously but she had lost Ethan's attention again. "Ethan." April tapped him on the arm. While doing so she leaned forward and strained against the straps to try and see what Ethan was staring at. The object of her friend's attention soon became clear.

April tapped Ethan on the shoulder.

"So, do you think he's cute?" she said with a smirk.

"Well, I did when we were dating," Ethan said with a wry smile. "Am I that unsubtle? It's amazing no one else has cottoned on yet."

"You two dated! Is this the mystery guy?"

"Shhhh, yes," Ethan said sagging slightly in his seat. "The guy up there is William. We just went on a couple of dates when I went to help my Dad draft the order of ceremony."

"Ohhhh," April said leaning over, it wasn't often Ethan was forthcoming with information about his love life.

"Yeah, he was really nice. I didn't realise he was even flirting with me at first. I never thought that a legged would look my way," Ethan said.

"I would look at you," April widened her eyes at Ethan jokingly, "You're a catch."

"Thanks, but it turns out I was right. He hadn't realised I was a mer. On our third date he figured it out."

"Had the blue tongue not tipped him off already?" April said raising her eyebrows.

"Apparently not, turns out old William is colour blind. Anyway, we were taking a walk along the beach and he suggested that we go for a swim..."

"Oh, so it was a bit of a shock."

"Yeah, you could say that. Things got a bit nasty from there, so I just swam around the coast and made my own way back to the hotel." Ethan sunk even further into his seat.

"Maybe he feels bad about what he did," April said placing her hand on her friend's shoulder, wishing she could hug him. She could see a slight sheen appear across his blue eyes.

"I doubt it, just was a bit of a shock seeing him again, I didn't even know he was a pilot, I thought he was in the military."

As if on cue William's voice boomed out over the speakers – "Good Evening Ladi... umhem Mera and Mer. I'm William your pilot for this evening. The trip will only take thirty minutes ..."

April zoned out and started to think about Ethan's experience with William. It didn't sound like the sort of attitude that came from someone who was facilitating the Peace agreement. She hoped that he was an anomaly. April sneaked a peek at Ethan who was looking determinedly at his hands. He was tracing the lines on his palms. April had a feeling this was more to do with the impending nausea of flying than to do with William's presence. She reached out for her healing Curo pearl power and sent calm and reassurance to Ethan. She felt rather than saw her pearl light up a pale blue. The warmth moved through her and she watched the colour flood back into Ethan's face. Ethan stopped tracing his hands and looked up at April in surprise.

"Hey... did you just do that?" Ethan asked.

"Maybe," April shrugged.

"Well, I was wrong April Meridia, you do have your uses."

"Thanks Ethan, I'll keep your glowing praise in mind on our return trip."

Ethan put his arm over April's shoulders.

"What do you think tonight will be like?" he asked.

"Strange," April said. "I wonder how much things will change once we're at peace again."

"Who knows," Ethan said. They lapsed into a comfortable silence.

"Are we going out tonight?" April asked suddenly.

"Oh," Ethan said reddening slightly. "Can we look like we could be going out? But, that it's not a definite thing."

"Okay. Once again you seem to be forgetting my horrendous acting skills. I will do my best though."

"Thank you, April," Ethan said sincerely. "So how are you at the moment?" Ethan asked.

"Love-wise?"

"No, I mean with the pearl blackouts," Ethan laughed.

"Is my love life so funny to you?"

"Nah, I just know that no one has stolen your heart yet," Ethan said seriously.

"I'm fine," April said looking straight ahead.

"Excellent, just the amount of detail I was looking for."

"My powers are getting stronger I suppose. But, it's weird. My pearls are definitely trying to tell me something," April said in another rush. She massaged her temples to try and keep the memories at bay.

"And you really think talking to someone is a bad idea?" Ethan asked.

"No. Everyone is too busy. I can handle it." April caught Ethan shaking his head. But, fortunately, he dropped it.

CHAPTER 4

The first helicopter touched down on the peninsula where the Peace Treaty would take place. The finest mer and human architects had been constructing the peace building for the past 10 months when the arrangements for the Peace Treaty were finalised. The peninsula was chosen, as according to mer legend, here the last human and mer were married. Their marriage was symbolic of the two worlds uniting once more. Its design was agonised over by architects and designers but the result stood before the Mer Royal Majesties now as they disembarked from their helicopter.

Freya and Nathaniel looked up at the building.

"It looks like it sprung from the ground," Freya said looking up sceptically.

"Try and hide your disdain," Nathaniel said with a chuckle. He extended his arm and the two followed their guide.

"Good evening your majesties. Would you like to hear the history of the Ainomrah?"

"How can it have history when it was only finished a couple of weeks ago," Freya whispered up to Nathaniel. He ignored her and said, "We would love to."

The guide straightened up importantly. He was short for a legged and had a surprisingly deep voice. His navy blazer and turquoise chinos were immaculate. He beamed at them before launching into his speech.

"The Ainomrah was inspired by Aino and Mrah the legendary couple who were last united from land and sea. To commemorate their union the design incorporates an element of balance between land and sea at every level. Thus, the building is in the shape of the mighty oak tree but is made out of glass and titanium to mimic the water. Whereas the waves circling the building are carved out of wood – the land and sea, working in harmony."

"Are you counting how many times he is saying land and sea?" Nathaniel asked quietly looking down at his wife pursing her lips. She rolled her eyes up at him.

"If you look closely, you can see animals from the land and sea carved into the building. Bats, narwhals, elephants and eels, so many animals can be found. Artists and architects from both land and sea were involved in creating the Ainomrah and we hope it will stand forever as a symbol of peace. This summer the Ainomrah will open as a summer school for mer and humans to attend together. This is part of a cultural enrichment programme for the young that the Peace Treaty council are funding. We aim for a long-term peace not one that will wither away with the next generation," their guide finished with a flourish.

King Nathaniel and Queen Freya continued to follow their guide who had finally lapsed into silence. He followed the maze of shell paths that weaved through the grasses and wildflowers that had been encouraged to grow naturally along the peninsula.

"The shells we're walking on, you will notice, swirl in spirals towards the Ainomrah. They represent the waves. The wildflowers and grasses bordering the shells show how the land is welcoming back the sea. All the paths eventually lead to the Ainomrah."

Freya looked ahead while Nathaniel nodded politely to the attendant.

"Good evening your majesties," the Chinese ambassador said bowing low as they met on the path. "It is an honour to meet you."

Nathaniel reached forward and shook the ambassador's hand and then embraced his wife.

"Thank you, it is wonderful to meet you both too."

Their guide swiftly moved them on and chose an empty path to continue their journey to the entrance of the Ainomrah.

~

As the final helicopter neared the peninsula, April and Ethan leaned forward to see the Ainomrah. From above, the intricate paths created a mesmerising pattern in the ground. April wondered whether the effect would be as magnificent from ground level. She could see floods of people all making their way down the paths, each accompanied by a footman with a lantern. The picture was indeed magical. The cultural centre, however, was one of the most hideous buildings she had ever seen. Its sheer size seemed to oppress the surroundings.

"Do you think they're trying to compensate for something?" Ethan whispered over the headset. April choked on her laughter. Ethan was right, the closer they were getting to land the sheer size of this monstrosity was becoming apparent. By the time William finally landed the helicopter, the building dwarfed them. April shifted in her seat as William wished the passengers a pleasant evening. Flying had been an experience, but not necessarily one that April was keen to repeat. Swimming would always be her favourite mode of transport, and travelling through the currents was far more comfortable, and a lot less noisy.

Mer could swim at great speeds for short bursts of time. April once managed to maintain 50 knots for an hour when she was rushing to make the palace curfew. April checked her hair in the window as a footman opened the door and started beckoning the passengers to exit. April and Ethan quickly unclipped their harnesses to depart the helicopter. Ethan stood up and forgetting the low ceiling of the helicopter, hit his head on the roof.

"Owww."

In searing pain, Ethan closed his eyes and staggered forward. He reached out to steady himself and grabbed onto the back of April's dress as she began to descend the steps. Ethan fell backwards unbalancing April on her precarious heels. April's shoes slipped out from under her and together they fell unceremoniously down the helicopter steps.

The footmen rushed to Ethan's and April's aid, disentangling them from the floor and setting them both straight again. April clutched the back of her neck and stared down angrily at the shoes. She knew it was unreasonable to hate shoes, but for these ones, she was willing to make an exception.

"Princess April, are you okay?" One of the footmen enquired scanning her up and down.

"I'm fine, thank you for your help," April smiled through the pain at the footmen as they bowed and walked away with nervous smiles.

"Where's the personal inquiry about my health?" Ethan said from behind her still holding his head. "I'm so sorry April. Are you okay?"

April assessed her body and dress patting herself up and down. Both seemed to be intact, it was just her neck that hurt. She ran her fingers along the hemline feeling where the dress had torn when Ethan grabbed onto it. She reached up to itch her neck. She brushed over the zip and immediately winced. The zip had caught her skin and was making her necklace and the now frayed fabric agitate the cut.

"Don't worry about it Ethan, accidents happen," April said trying to relax her face.

Ethan stepped in front of her to observe for himself that she was okay. His eyes jumped to the cut on her neck.

"April your neck is grazed."

"Oh shoot, I didn't realise it was that bad." She drew from her Curo powers again to heal herself. Breathing in, her Curo pearl glowed a sky blue and the light wrapped around her neck.

"There we go," she smiled "all better."

But, as she said this, her arm reached back to itch her neck again. The fraying was now chafing even more against her necklace. An irritating itch could not be healed away. The constant draw on her powers to solve such a small problem would also be frowned upon greatly by her Mum. April reached up to unclasp her necklace and immediately the itching lessened. But, the moment the necklace left her neck, heaviness settled within her. Feeling deflated she looked down at her necklace in a daze.

April's powers and pearls were an extension of herself and on an evening like tonight, she couldn't imagine facing the world without them. Ethan watched April for a moment then instinctively removed his watch and fastened it around April's wrist. Immediately the colour washed back into her and her spirits rose. She looked down at her wrist and saw Ethan's watch inlaid with his pearls. Ethan wielded the Essentia, Commutavi and Assurgere pearls. His watch face doubled up as an Iris pad. The watch was a twenty-first birthday present from his parents and was one of his most prized possessions. The comfort the pearls provided and the warmth from Ethan's body soothed April after her momentary feeling of emptiness.

"April are you okay, you zoned out again?" Ethan said his voice higher than usual.

"Thank you, I'm okay now," April looked up at Ethan and smiled with gratitude. "I think, because my powers are playing up my connection to the pearls is more delicate and vulnerable than usual."

"Will my watch be enough for the evening?" Ethan said looking at her intently.

"Yes, it's perfect. And it means that when I have to be on the stage alone I will have a piece of you with me."

Ethan took April's necklace from her and pooled it in his pocket.

"And I will look after this for you until you can get that wretched dress off."

The dress and shoes had caused more harm than they were worth. She knew that President May couldn't have planned Ethan's head bashing and the consequential tripping and ruining of her dress. But, his gift was not putting her mind in the most peaceful of frames. Peaceful thoughts, happy thoughts April thought in an overly optimistic voice. This evening she was going to have to channel her mother.

"Right, let's go. It's time to look pretty and harmless," April said.

Ethan looked at April but chose not to question her. Instead, he linked arms to steady her in her shoes and off they walked. They followed their footman along the twisting shell paths towards the looming architectural structure. Despite her distaste for the building, she could not deny that it made an impressive first impact for the evening. Tonight, land and sea would be united once more.

CHAPTER 5

The ray bus dropped Setha off outside the hospital. With everyone watching live screenings of the Peace Treaty there hadn't been much traffic, which meant she arrived before visiting hours started. She hovered momentarily in the foyer wondering if it was worth going back out for a swim. But, there were only five minutes to wait so she floated down onto one of the large sea sponges.

It was such a miserable place. Setha tried to avoid the foyer. Too often she saw family's breaking down over a loved one's illness or accident. She plugged in her eardrops and turned up her music to try and block out the sounds of everyone around. The clock hands slowly ticked. Setha tried to stop her eyes from flickering to the clock. She took out her Iris pad and scrolled through her updates to pass the time. Finally, the visitor light flashed on and Setha swam out of the room as fast as she could.

Setha sat beside her Dad's bed in the Catfish ward. She was worried that the water was too warm for him. He seemed to be tossing more than usual in his sleep. His face was flushed but the rest of his body remained a ghostly, unsettling white. Setha itched to wield her Factus powers to cool down the room, but the last time she altered the climate the nurses kicked her out. She stretched her hands out in frustration. Rocking back and forth she continued her vigil studying her Dad. The vulnerability in her Dad only showed when he was asleep. It proved to her how much her Dad was feigning optimism when he was awake.

Now in front of her, his face looked tense, his tail was limp and his whole body sagged into the bed. She could see that his bright red scales, which Setha had inherited, were becoming clouded and turning black at the fin. She needed a distraction. She mindlessly plaited her hair and un-plaited it again. Suddenly she kicked up out of her seat and floated for a second looking around the room. Setha spied the bedside table and swam over to it. She routed through the contents to see if there was anything to occupy her mind until he woke again. Anything would be good at this point. She found some Jelly Sea Cucumbers and started chewing on them while continuing her rummaging.

What was that? She thought and picked up a small book. She hadn't seen this notepad before, and she felt she knew the tiny room very intimately by this stage of her Dad's treatment. It was small, a perfect fit for her hand. The binding was made from crushed blue coral and it had a strong burgundy seaweed string tying it shut. Setha turned it over in her hands about to put it back, when she found herself swimming back to her chair. She undid the string and started flipping through the pages. Setha gasped. There were sketches of her receiving her degree. There were drawings of her and her Dad on her wedding day, ones of her Mum and Dad at Christmas with friends and family. The sketches went on and on.

The pictures brought tears to her eyes. But, Setha couldn't pull herself away from the little sketchbook. With each drawing, a little piece inside of her broke. He was drawing a future. A future he would never get to see. Setha looked over to her Dad. She knew that the cancer was terminal, but a part of her never really believed it. She had heard all the miracle stories, her own grandmother's next-door neighbour was given two weeks to live, and she was still alive 30 years later. Besides, he was her Dad. He couldn't die. What would she do without him?

For the next hour and a half, Setha sat by her Dad's bed absorbing every detail of the drawings. Not once did he stir during her vigil. At the end of the visiting hours, she slipped the notepad back into the drawer. She made a mental note to buy more Jelly Sea Cucumbers and she wrote a quick note to her Dad on the memo pad promising to return tomorrow. With one last look at her Dad, she swam out of the Catfish Ward. It had just gone nine o'clock and the ray bus would be here soon. Setha wondered what April was doing at the Peace Treaty. Surely it must be signed by now.

CHAPTER 6

"We are gathered here today…" King Nathaniel addressed the crowd. Ethan thought it sounded more like a wedding ceremony than a Peace Treaty. He could see April standing a little to the left of her father surrounded by the President of America's three tall sons. April was tall for a mera and even taller in those killer heels, but next to these three she looked tiny. Her ever-changing blue eyes were currently clouded over, deep in thought. Despite the sons' looming presence April stood proud. But, Ethan was pretty sure he could see April minutely fiddling with the frills on her dress.

Ethan was proud of his best friend. She had been preparing for almost a year for the Peace Treaty. She went to legged language lessons, legged etiquette classes and dance lessons. Then her Mum forced her to memorise the order of ceremony, all the speeches and the names of everyone attending. April was a walking, talking trivia set with her specialist subject being the Peace Treaty. Only April's presence had made the reception bearable.

Ethan was usually comfortable at important events because everyone knew him. There were always questions about how he was doing at school or whether he had finally asked April out. He had never really been interested in politics but it had always been an option that his family encouraged. However, after his awkward attempt at mingling, he was pretty sure that politics was not a profession he would be pursuing. April was able to make conversation with everyone. Tonight, she was the perfect princess, even if she did have to grip his arm to stop herself from falling in her legged shoes.

Ethan scanned the rest of the gathered dignitaries. His Dad looked very serious and was nodding every few sentences. The Queen however didn't seem to be following the King's speech at all. Instead, she was scanning the crowd. Watching her, Ethan felt nervous. Freya was like an aunt to him, but she was the sort of aunt who knew when something bad was about to happen. She was probably preparing for damage control in case anyone took offense at Nathaniel's speech. That was Freya, she was the backbone of the royal family and without her, Ethan doubted that King Nathaniel's reign would have been quite so successful. Ethan turned his attention back to the King, as he seemed to be wrapping up his speech.

~

It's over, that was quick, April thought. Admittedly she hadn't really been concentrating on what her Dad was saying as she knew his speech off by heart. Her Mum had forced her to memorise the speech, in case people questioned her about it later. April was also versed in pre-approved satisfactory answers to any questions people might have about the treaty. April resented the parrotfish fashion learning at the time but now she felt begrudgingly grateful.

April continued clapping with everyone on the stage as the footmen below started to manoeuvre the crowd and tables into a circle. At the back of the room, an orchestra was starting up. April recognised the music from her dance rehearsals. She groaned internally, it was now time to dance. Her parents had been part of the music selection process and from the sound of the orchestra the music was worse than she remembered. The dancing tonight was reminiscent of the style of dancing typical of courtship back in the days when their two worlds lived in peace. But, instead of matching potential suitors together, this dance signified the end of mer and legged separation. April had pointed out Ethan's dance partners to him earlier after his Dad handed him a pre-filled dance card. Ethan was not very good with names or faces.

April sneaked another look at her dance partners. If peace had come a hundred years earlier, one of these legged brothers would likely have been her future husband. She was sure one of the gossip magazines would claim she was dating one of them. They might even say she was stringing Ethan along at the same time. The tabloids would have a field day if they discovered the truth about her and Ethan. She imagined they would be furious learning that they had been leading them along and tricking them for all these years. April wondered how they would represent her, a fool, a fellow conspirator or a woeful casualty.

President Darius' three sons were all somewhat of a mystery to April, she couldn't put her finger on it but there was something off about them. Then again, she was probably a bit off herself that evening. They probably understood more than anyone else the stress that her parents placed on her. But, still April thought they were a bit weird. Even the way they clapped felt regimented as if they were trying to clap in time. Between her shoes and their robotic movements, she didn't hold much hope for dancing with any of them.

The applause was finally over and her Dad and President Darius were inviting the guests to gather for the ritual dances. April followed suit like a fish swimming in formation. There was a lack of females in Darius' family so other members of his Bureau were stepping into place. The head of finance, Georgiana, took the honour of dancing with her Dad. Her Mum was with President Darius himself and April got the pleasure of first dancing with Frederick, Darius' eldest son. The younger two seemed to disappear for the first dance. Lucky them, April thought.

The music swelled and April felt the steps rush to her feet. Her Mum's insistence that she learn the dances by heart meant April could relinquish herself to muscle memory. Dancing on land was not natural for mer who were used to whirling under the sea. She caught Ethan's eye across the dance floor. He was spinning a pretty redhead under his arm. Ethan winked and made a face behind Frederick's back. April almost chuckled but, could feel her Mum's stern stare admonishing her to do nothing of the sort. Really it was not her fault though, Frederick was not the dancing sort. Fortunately, their regimented, slow pace was a perfect speed for the precarious heels.

"Nice watch."

"Oh, thank you, I mean, it's not mine, it's a friend's."

"I thought as much," Frederick replied smugly.

"I tripped in these shoes, and my neck got scratched," April responded. The conversation starters her tutor had drilled her in were not paying off well. They were dancing so close to one another she tried to avert her gaze from his eyes as she continued.

"I tried to heal it, but for some reason, it wouldn't work. My necklace was irritating the cut, so my friend, Ethan, swapped with me."

Too much detail thought April. But with Frederick's curtness, one of them needed to do the talking.

"Ah. That would be the fabric," Frederick replied staring down at her.

"Pardon? The fabric, what has the fabric done?"

"Some of our fabrics are poisonous to mer."

April could swear she heard a satisfied smirk in his voice.

"Oh…goodness, we'll have to get them to discontinue the line or change the fabric dye."

"I suppose we shall. It was an honest mistake though," Frederick replied in a monotone voice as he dipped April with a flourish. The music stopped and Frederick pulled April to standing with a jolt.

"A pleasure dancing with you April," Frederick said as he fixed her with a steely gaze. A flicker of a smile crossed his lips. He bowed low and then walked off before April could utter a word in response. She checked herself. She felt as if she had been pounded by a wave and had suddenly popped back up to the surface.

CHAPTER 7

April walked over to where Queen Freya was standing with a group of legged officials. Keeping her head held high and a smile planted firmly on her face she tried to push down the worry building inside her. She recognised the Prime Minister of England and the French President talking to her Mum. April approached and they bobbed a bow to her as she stood patiently next to her Mum waiting for their conversation to tail off.

"Mum," April whispered.

"Yes, April," Queen Freya turned to her daughter. The Queen of Meridia was striking. Her long golden hair was elegantly twisted up into a low bun and was dotted with jewels. Her dress was a rich emerald, the colour of her tail. It was fitted but allowed for dancing. Practicality was one of Freya's specialities.

"I'm feeling really light-headed."

Freya motioned to one of the staff to bring a chair over discreetly.

"Take a seat."

"Thank you," April said as she sat down. The waiter passed April a glass of cool water.

"Do you feel better?" Freya asked.

"Yes," April said slowly. "Mum, something weird just happened. Frederick, the President's son, I think he said my dress is poisoned."

Her Mum looked at her with a withering glare.

"That is absurd April."

"But..."

"No buts. Now if you have nothing sensible to say you can go and introduce yourself to the British royal family."

"Mum, please."

"April."

Wanting to storm off as she did after most conversations with her Mum, April instead focused on her glass. Suddenly, a black flicker shot over her fingers. She splayed her hand and watched another black tendril dart its way across her knuckles and seep back into her.

"Mum," April said alarmed. She looked up to find her Mum stony-faced above her.

"April, control your powers," Freya said in an even voice. It was pitched so low that only April could hear it.

"But, I didn't do it."

"You understand the importance of today don't you?" Freya said her lips forming a hard line.

"Yes, I…"

"Good," Freya cut her off. She looked back down apprehensively at April's fingers but the black light seemed to have disappeared.

"Now, go outside and get some fresh air," Freya said, her facial expression relaxing slightly. "I'm sure you'll feel better soon."

"Okay."

April got up slowly and thanked the usher who efficiently came to remove the chair. Her Mum nodded at her, before moving towards a different group of leggeds to continue mingling. April stood for a moment rooted to the spot. She checked her fingers again looking for a hint of the lingering darkness. She folded her hands in the frills of her dress. There were no pearl shamans to be seen and her Dad was occupied in the centre of the room, so she did what she was told and moved outside onto the balcony for some fresh air.

~

"Would you like a drink?"

Ethan turned around and saw the redhead he danced with earlier. She was holding two flutes of champagne and several people were openly admiring her around the room.

"Uh, no thank you," Ethan said gesturing with the full glass of wine he was already holding.

"No worries."

The woman placed the extra glass down on the poseur table and leant in towards him.

"You're the Mer Prime Minister's son, aren't you?"

"Yes, I am and you are..." Ethan hesitated. They were partnered together for the first dance but he couldn't remember her name.

"Darcy Gray," she said offering her hand with a smile. "We danced together earlier."

"I remember."

"You're an excellent dancer."

"Thank you."

"Maybe we can dance again after the treaty is signed," Darcy said.

"Yes, maybe." Ethan looked past Darcy trying to find a polite escape. He spotted April outside on the balcony.

"Sorry, you must excuse me. I need to pay my dues to the mer crown." Ethan bobbed a small bow and strode towards the balcony. He always felt uncomfortable when women flirted with him. Especially someone like Darcy who was used to getting what she wanted. He breathed a sigh of relief as soon as he passed through the door to the balcony. Ethan made straight for April.

"Thank goodness I've found you," Ethan said. "This stunning legged woman was trying to make a move on me."

"How terrible for you?" April laughed.

"It really was. She was beautiful and confident and sexy and I just felt like a clam."

"Well you do look a bit clammy," April said with a straight face.

Ethan frowned at her and continued his standard speech about the awkwardness of women flirting with him.

April was half listening to Ethan as she continued to marvel at the sky. The moon was high in the sky tonight and cast a soft pearlescent glow over the water. The sea, to April, seemed to be reaching up toward her as the stars twinkled on its surface. It gently lapped against the cliffs coastline sounding like peaceful sighs. The balcony was huge. It stretched out like a plate-shaped branch extending from the tree. The designer for the balcony seemed to have dismissed the idea of combining land and sea and had instead gone for a deep black marble. April imagined that in broad daylight, the floor would look as if it was going to swallow you and send you down into a dark abyss. But, in the dark April felt as if she was standing on the night sky amongst the stars.

"Ethan?" April asked disrupting his dialogue. "Do your pearls ever... misbehave?"

"Misbehave? I don't think so," Ethan said laughing. "Why?"

"Well, this energy just flickered across my fingers," April said and her vision clouded over. "And it was like this dark light was coming out of me." She shook her head and brought herself back into the present.

"Could it be your Tempus powers?" Ethan said, glancing over at April.

"Yeah," April said. She looked out across the dark night sky. "It might be, it's just it was like nothing I've ever seen before," she said quietly.

"It's probably part of your powers maturing or the stress of the treaty getting to you. You need to talk to someone."

April dropped her head.

Ethan and April lapsed into silence together. As they stared out across the sea a cool breeze swept over them. April shivered and Ethan reflexively put his arm around her shoulders.

"Ethan." April pretended to push him away. "We can't show the world such a public display of affection. We'll be engaged in the magazines tomorrow."

Ethan laughed, "Well we need to keep the tabloids in business with more facts to work with."

"I wonder how they're going to describe tonight."

"Yeah, how many epic romances can they find that are more important than the trivial, basically insignificant event, that is the World Peace Treaty," Ethan said turning around to lean against the glass.

April screwed up her face and pretended to think seriously, "Ten."

"Twelve," he countered with an eye roll. Ethan adopted a faux high-pitched accent. "I saw them under the stars and the sexual tension was rife. Then next thing I knew he was on one knee and April was crying."

As they dissolved into laughter a gong sounded indicating there were only five minutes left until the treaty would be signed.

"Right, me lady, that be our cue." Ethan extended his arm to April to escort her into the Grand Hall.

"Ethan, your arm, you're bleeding." April grabbed his arm and turned it back and forth. She rolled up his sleeve.

"Steady on April, now you're trying to undress me," Ethan chuckled

"No, seriously, look. You're bleeding." Ethan inspected his arm for himself.

April was right; there was blood but no bleeding. He looked back up at April confusedly and he spotted a tiny smudge of blood at the nape of her neck. He leaned forward and swept her hairpiece aside.

"April! Your neck! The cut has deepened. It's you, you're bleeding."

April looked at him in shock her arm reaching to feel her neck. As she touched her skin it seared in pain. It was so cold out here she hadn't noticed how hot her skin was. Frederick was right. The dress was poisoning her. Whilst April was inspecting her hand that came away glistening in blood from her neck, Ethan had already spurred himself into action.

"Right, you stay here, I shall run and get some towels to clean up the bleeding and a plaster to cover the bits your hairpiece doesn't hide. I'll be as fast as I can." Ethan started retreating. "Just stay there."

April focused her Curo power on the wound. It wasn't difficult to close but with the fabric constantly irritating her it was impossible to heal it fully until she was out of the dress. April looked through the glass doors to see that almost everyone had gathered on the stage by now. She shifted anxiously, not wanting to be late. She tried to wipe the blood from her neck.

"Urghh," she groaned in frustration. Now she had two bloody hands and nowhere to wipe them. She was just contemplating summoning up some water with her Factus powers to clean her hands when she saw Ethan kind of trotting towards the doors. Not running, but certainly not walking. If this was his attempt to not attract attention then he was failing April thought as she rolled her eyes.

Then in an instant, everything was different. Ethan wasn't trotting; he was being thrown into the air. It was no longer music and chatter April could hear but screams and crashing and the smashing of glass. All this she absorbed in an instance as she was lifted into the air and thrown back, and down into the sea.

CHAPTER 8

Warm sea streamed through Setha's bedroom window as the tides changed and brought the shallows towards her. She rolled over and stretched out leisurely. She knew it was one o'clock but she couldn't care less. Her Grandmother was at a painting class all morning and wouldn't be back until she had had afternoon tea with her friends. Grandmother Jocelyn was a mera of habit. Sometimes her strict schedule irked Setha but in times like these, she was appreciative of her Grandmother's reliability.

Leaning over, Setha stretched to grab her pearl earrings from the nightstand. As she popped them in her ears the sea lifted her body up as the Factus energy pulsed through her. She checked her Iris and was surprised to see no messages from April about her evening. Maybe April was sleeping in too she thought. She quickly responded to her Mum.

"Next weekend's great, see you then." Her body was heavy with sleep and she yawned wide as she swam down to the kitchen in search of breakfast. Her Grandmother's mansion in Hanaria was really too big for one person. Setha was surprised that her Grandmother enjoyed living on her own in such a large house.

The upper level spiralled down into a large foyer that was weekly themed with different corals and shells. Setha found herself matching her wardrobe to the different themes when she first moved in and now made a concerted effort to dress as contrastingly as possible. She did not need her wardrobe to reflect a 70-year-old mera's taste in coral. She could smell something good coming from the kitchen. She swam to the kitchen and saw a freshly baked tray of crab cakes, perfect for breakfast Setha thought. Her Grandmother routinely baked things and left them on the side for people to take as they fancy. Setha grabbed a few, rifled through the post until she found her weekly subscription to Tailspin, poured herself a glass of the orange juice purée April had given her from her last visit to the leggeds and moved into the lounge. The silence that emanated from the mansion when she was alone was creepy, so she switched on the TV for company and began to eat her crab cakes.

There was nothing of interest on TV so Setha decided to watch her favourite film. It was a remake of the Shakespearean classic Much Ado About Nothing set underwater. Beatrice had long been Setha's favourite fictional character. She often tried to maintain the same levels of aloofness.

"Nobody marks you," Setha dramatically intoned with the actress on screen. She popped another crab cake in her mouth as Beatrice continued to tear into Benedict. Checking her Iris again she huffed in frustration at the lack of information from April.

"Hey! How was last night??" she typed and sent off.

Ten minutes later there was still no reply. Queen Freya rarely allowed April to sleep in; she deemed it a waste of one's precious life. Setha started to worry. They had messaged each other every day without fail for the past four years.

"Hey, how was last night? Just wondering if you know where April is?" Setha paused in indecision she hated contacting Ethan. No one else knew about her crush on him and that was the way she intended it to stay. She swiped the message off before she could change her mind. But, it immediately bounced back.

"Message unable to send." Setha tried again. But, the message bounced back once more. Setha tried to stop herself from imagining Ethan in bed with a fancy legged woman he had just met. She swam off the couch and went to fetch a snack to improve her mood.

"Setha? Honey are you home?" her Grandmother shouted as the door swung shut. The formidable Mrs Moretta swam into the kitchen before Setha could reply. As usual, she was impeccably dressed. A tight fitting yet modest bolero in a dark navy was the jacket of choice for today's luncheon. Setha saw that the Atlantica summer handbag had made its first outing too. After assessing her Grandmother's outfit Setha quickly realised that something was not right. Firstly, her Grandmother shouldn't be home yet, and secondly, her well-rouged face was white in shock.

"Is everything okay?" Setha asked, her body suddenly tense.

"Have you seen the news today?" her Grandmother asked as she dropped her bag down onto the counter.

"No, the news? What's happened?" Setha asked, though she instantly relaxed in relief that it was nothing to do with her Dad.

"Honestly Setha, what have you been doing with your day. It's everywhere," Jocelyn said swimming agitatedly around the kitchen.

Setha waited impatiently for her Grandmother to inform her what this shocking news was.

"Can you boil this for me please?" her Grandmother asked. Setha wielded her limited Factus powers to boil the flask of coffee presented to her.

"There you go."

"Thank you dear." Her Grandmother took a sip and her face instantly relaxed. "Now as I was saying. It's everywhere. The Peace Treaty last night. It was a disaster."

"A disaster? As in it wasn't signed?" Setha asked as she helped herself to one of the cookies her Grandmother had brought home.

"Setha, no it wasn't signed, a bomb went off! The entire building was destroyed," she said exasperatedly as she swam into a chair.

"What! Is everyone okay?" Setha asked as she followed her Grandmother.

"They don't know. Lots of mer are injured but many are still trapped in the wreckage. They won't release official figures and details until they have more information."

"April, Ethan. They could be, could be…." Setha stuttered. Her annoyance that neither replied to her instantly replaced with fear.

"I'm sure they're okay Setha," her Grandmother said kindly. "We just need to wait for further news."

"Okay," Setha said in shock. She didn't know what to do with herself. She swam hurriedly into the lounge and switched on the news, a story about the Peace Treaty bombing was on. She sat down and hugged her tail to her chest as she watched. An enthusiastic reporter was recounting the details. Most of the information washed over Setha. She just wanted to know if April and Ethan were okay.

CHAPTER 9

The sun was rising as Alex bent down to tie up his shoelaces. He jogged on the spot inside the doorway, then with a grin he sprinted off. The island looked magical first thing in the morning. But, this particular morning it felt like it was buzzing with extra energy. The flowers stretched wide open to show off their bright petals and there wasn't a cloud in the sky. It was the perfect start to summer. Alex finished his sprint through the thigh-high grass meadow to the top of the hill outside his house. Bending to his knees, he panted from the exertion of the near vertical slope. He mopped his brow and looked up, with a view like this it was easy to get up early in the morning.

Stretched out in front of him like a sheet of glass was the sea. Sometimes, if he was lucky, he could see dolphins playing in the surf. He hoped that one morning he would see a pod of whales breaching out in the distance. Alex presumed they loved the island and its surroundings as much as he did. The unblemished sea reached out until it joined with the sky. The view was peaceful but he could still feel the island's tangible energy all around him. It was as if the sea was alert. Beneath the glass like water, he could feel power radiating from the ocean. Alex set off again now pounding down the hill, weaving his way through the trees of the mini forest. With his calf muscles burning and sweat gathering on his forehead, he headed directly for the sea.

Alex and his brother had only been on Shell Island for a week since flying to the island after Connor's high school graduation. He had finished his own training at the Omega Military Facility last month, but the early morning starts were still an ingrained habit.

Alex had been making use of his early morning wake-ups to explore the island. Their house was nestled in a clearing on the North of the island. One side of the house looked out onto a meadow and the other the beach. The first portion of his morning run was always the beach. Beach, then round the back of the house, through a field of grass which reached up to his waist, then back down the hill to go home ready for breakfast.

Alex liked his routine on Shell Island and unlike his brother was in no hurry to leave. The Omega Military had been the last item on a long list of things he had done for his Dad. And now, there was nothing. He had jumped the final hurdle. For once it was nice to just breathe. He burst through the trees, onto the seashore and set off at a steady pace. A slight sea breeze cooled his calves and whipped through his hair. The sea air had done wonders for his breath control. He could now keep a metered breath for his entire circuit. Whereas back home in the city, his breathing went up and down with the smog levels.

The beach was full of debris today. How bizarre Alex thought. Derek, their caretaker, would be down later on to clean it up. He slowed his pace to look at what was washed up on the shoreline. Dodging the treacherous chunks that threatened to send him flying, Alex tried to figure out what was going on. There were large bits of wood, some sculpted animals and chunks of coral all clumped together with shells. It was an odd collection, there were even a few chair legs and if Alex wasn't mistaken there was part of a helicopter wing sticking out of the sand. What could have happened? He slowed to a jog as his path became more perilous. A large branch blocked his way and as Alex went to hurdle over it he glanced down and stopped in his tracks. Consequently, hurling him to the ground. He rolled over and scrambled towards the branch. What he had presumed was a solid object actually resembled a hollowed-out canoe. It was closer in size to a tree trunk than to a branch and inside this obstacle was a young lady.

First instinct, mouth-to-mouth resuscitation. Alex carefully manoeuvred her onto the sand and checked for a pulse. Thank goodness, she was still alive. Her skin felt too warm for someone who had been washed up on the shore and she was covered in angry looking sores, but otherwise, she seemed okay. The girl could almost have been sleeping. He leant down to check she was still breathing. She was issuing a slow steady breath and he could see her chest rise and fall. Debating on whether or not to move her, he quickly checked over her body. He was certain nothing was broken and so Alex scooped her up in his arms to carry her back to the house for help. As he lifted up her torso he noticed a pool of blood previously obscured by her hair. He carefully touched the back of her neck and his hand came away sticky with blood. With more urgency than he previously intended he positioned her head against his shoulder, slid his arms under her legs and set off quickly for the house shouting for help as he moved.

He reached the door that opened up onto the beach and called loudly hoping that Rosetta would hear him from the kitchen. The panic in his own voice alarmed him. "Rosetta!" he called even louder. Peter one of the chefs heard his call instead and came to open the sliding door. His eyes jumped down and he hurried Alex in.

"My heavens Master Alex! Quick come inside, bring her into the guest bedroom." Alex followed Peter through to the downstairs guestroom and lay the girl on the bed careful not to jostle her. Now that he was here he didn't know what to do. He had been to military school since he was five and yet all his training deserted him on the spot. Alex started pacing by the bed casting anxious looks at the girl. Peter disappeared to find help and returned with Rosetta and a new female member of staff Alex hadn't met. Rosetta took charge immediately. She was a robust middle-aged woman who took everything in her stride.

"Where did you find her? In what state was she in?" Rosetta calmly asked as she started to check the girl's pulse and assess her body.

"She was washed up on the beach, inside a log," Alex explained. He paced by the bed while he spoke. "She was unconscious when I found her. The back of her neck... it's bleeding, or it was bleeding. Is she going to be okay?"

Rosetta stood up from leaning over the girl and turned to smile at Alex in reassurance.

"It was risky moving her but she's going to be okay, her breathing is fine." Rosetta checked the girl's throat and closed her lips. "She must have choked up any water she swallowed. I will take care of her."

"Thank God." Alex exhaled in relief. "Is there anything I can do?"

"No, you have done enough, why don't you go and shower and you can check on her later." Rosetta started waving him out of the room.

"Okay, thank you Rosetta." Alex moved as he was told while still staring at the girl. Dragging his attention away from her just in time, he narrowly missed walking into the doorframe. He hoped she would be okay. For the first time in his life, he felt responsible for someone.

As Alex left, Rosetta turned to Peter, "Peter tell the other members of the household to not come into this guest suite. Megan and I will stay here and look after the girl. I trust you can take care of the house for the time being."

"Yes," Peter replied eyeing the girl on the bed with concern. "I'll get right on it." Peter left the room closing the door with care behind him. Rosetta sprang into action. She gathered the girl up in her arms and carried her into the wet room. She laid the girl on the floor with smooth efficiency. Megan followed.

"Shouldn't we call someone?" Megan asked worriedly.

"This is a private island, we only call sea rescue if there is an emergency. I'm first aid trained and I think she is okay."

"Oh," Megan said uncertain of how to reply. Rosetta turned to Megan with a cold stare.

"I trust you Megan not to say a word to anyone of what I'm about to tell to you."

Megan nodded timidly. She liked Rosetta and was glad to have finally found a job, but her boss was acting so covert.

"This girl, Megan, is a mermaid. I need you to fetch me some scissors so I can cut her out of her dress." Rosetta turned back to assessing the mermaid. She undid the ridiculously complicated ties that did up her shoes and placed them to the side. She looked back up to see Megan standing and grinning like a fool. Rosetta scowled at her and Megan scurried off. Seriously Rosetta thought, this mermaid needed help not ogling. Rosetta shuffled up to inspect the girl's neck. Alex was right it had been bleeding and a deep red rash extended in hexagons from the cut. The rash seemed to follow the outline of the girl's dress. It was deepest at the seams and blossomed out getting gradually pinker. At the darkest red areas of the rash the girl's skin was burning to touch. Rosetta had never seen anything like it. Megan returned with the scissors.

"How do you know she is a mera?" Megan asked.

Rosetta shot her a look but proceeded to answer the question. She tilted the girl's head so her jaw gently opened.

"Her tongue," Rosetta said by way of explanation. Megan leant closer and noticed that inside the mera's mouth was a navy-blue tongue.

"Oh."

"Can you get me some ice please?" Rosetta said calmly. She didn't know a lot about mermaids but she presumed water would help and with this thought she stretched up and turned the shower on above them.

Oh, my goodness Megan thought, a real-life mermaid or a mera to be correct. Inside her head, she was squealing with excitement. Megan loved the merfolk. She grew up with her Grandfather telling her stories of the young mera he fell in love with. And now, one week into the job, a real-life mera had appeared. Megan couldn't help but feel it was fate. Then again, she had thought that about the job too. Clearly, she was just lucky. Megan located the ice in the freezer and wrapped it in a tea towel. She resolved then and there to befriend the mera.

A deep shiver ran down the mera's back as her eyes fluttered open and the room zoomed in and out of view. Darkness descended and she blacked out again. Rosetta had removed the dress and undergarments and managed to pull the mera into one of the boy's t-shirts. Since removing the clothing the rash had remained as vivid but the burning temperature of her skin had reduced. Rosetta couldn't afford to spend all day in the wet room. She returned to her duties and left Megan in charge of checking on the mera every half hour for any signs of change. The mera's brief resurfacing was missed by Megan. And since then the mera had remained unconscious. Freshly showered Alex returned to inquire after the mera, but Rosetta managed to steer him away saying that the girl needed rest and time to heal. By nightfall, the mera had still not woken and Rosetta sent Megan to bed. There was no point them both staying awake worrying. But, the stress of hiding the mermaid and keeping the house together had taken its toll and by 11:30pm Rosetta also retired to bed.

CHAPTER 10

Water lapped at the sides of April's waist. She stretched out her fingers expecting to feel her smooth seaweed silk mattress cover underneath her. Instead, her fingers met a slippery surface with ridges. Where am I? April thought. She started racking her brain for the last thing she could remember. The Peace Treaty, the party. April lifted her hand to her forehead without opening her eyes, was all this aching merely a bad hangover she mused. As far as she could remember though she only drank one glass of champagne at the opening reception. She rubbed her eyes and brought her hand down to her neck to feel the calming smoothness and power of her pearls. Her fingers searched her neck but to no avail and with the shattering realisation that her necklace was gone she sat bolt upright.

April's eyes were wide and frantic as she looked down at her neck trying to see what she could not feel. My pearls, where are my pearls, April internally panicked as she reached her hands up and tugged at her hair in frustration. April looked around the room as she tried to fathom what was going on. The shower had been running all day and the wet room appeared to have finally given up on draining the water. Water reached up to her mid-thigh and was gently rocking. The room was tastefully decorated but showed no signs of a personal touch. April closed her eyes and rubbed her temples trying to draw up some memory of what had happened. The water splashing down onto her head soothed her headache.

"I was at the party, I drank too much? And I passed out in a bathroom," concluded April. She groaned out loud. Her Mum was going to be so angry. April may have been less than cautious with some of her decisions but she had never done something as stupid as this. April started talking to herself as she always did when she was stressed.

"I'm probably in a hotel nearby or maybe still at the Ainomrah conference building. Yes, that's it, I'll get up, find an Iris and Setha can come and bring me clothes." April looked around for the door ready to exit the room. At this point April noticed what she probably should have realised upon her first inspection of the room. Where is my dress? April internally groaned. She grasped at the t-shirt she was wearing. Inspecting it she realised it was a man's, and that she was wearing some baggy shorts as well. Her clothes and necklace were gone. April jumped to the worst conclusion.

"Okay April, calm down. Maybe you changed yourself. This doesn't mean anything." April reached out to the wall to help pull herself off the floor and out of the water. As she noticed Ethan's watch on her wrist a searing hot pain burnt into her skin. April staggered towards the large modern wall-length mirror and looked at her reflection. She gasped. Her skin looked as if a hexagonal pattern had been painted on. Now out of the water, her skin started to burn more fiercely. She rolled the sleeves of the t-shirt up to her shoulder where the pain was most potent. Here her skin was bright red with almost black hexagonal markings. As she turned around to inspect the rest of her body her eyes caught sight of a bloodstain at the collar of her shirt. She stepped closer to the mirror and lifted up her hair. Someone had bandaged her up but the water had lifted the plaster away from her skin at one of the edges. April saw a small cut that seemed to have stretched open and from it the hexagonal rash spiralled out.

What had happened? April thought. She needed to sort this out before her Mum saw her. Fortunately, strange rashes were nothing new to April. None ever hurt quite like this before, but during her Assurgere pearl classes she frequently had allergic reactions to different corals, flora and fauna. Even without her necklace the task would not be taxing. Ethan possessed the standard Essentia, Commutavi and Iris pearls as well as an Assurgere one. It was far less energy than she was used to but she didn't really need the pearls, they were more like a support. April took a deep breath and visualised her Curo energy, then with a deep exhale she wielded the sky-blue energy across her skin. Looking in the mirror to admire her handiwork, April watched as the red marks faded into her skin and the hexagons slowly disappeared. She turned to inspect her neck and pulled off the bandage, the cut was no more than a distant memory.

Although feeling remarkably better, April felt troubled that there was something about the rash that was out of the ordinary. However, she had more pressing issues on her hands. Such as, figuring out what on earth had happened? April tapped on the watch face to bring up Ethan's Iris pad. She clicked into messages and scrolled down until she found Setha's contact. "Hey, it's April, having a disaster – do you know where I am?" April hit send. There, that is done she thought. Setha would be able to help. A small vibration alerted her of the reply and she looked down at the watch face in relief. Annoyance rose as she read "Message unable to send."

"Great," April muttered. She circled her hand to focus her Factus energy and stop the water running out of the shower. Next, she turned her attention to her clothes and with a downward flick from the neck she banished the water from them too. Looking slightly more presentable she was ready to face the world, or at least April mused some sympathetic hotel staff. April had not been to a legged hotel before but how different could it be?

Slowly, April pushed the door open and was surprised to see that it was pitch black in the adjoining room. With no windows in her beige tiled wet room she had presumed it was late morning. The artificial light disoriented her usually decent night vision. April cautiously stepped out into the room and quietly closed the door behind her. Now, out of her tiled cell, she could feel the pull of the ocean. Thank goodness April thought, being too far inland always made her nervous. The sea was the source of April's powers and without her pearls she appreciated the sea's comfort even more.

April felt her mind go blank as a wave of pearl memories surged over her. She was young, maybe five and was locked in a door-less room. The darkness overwhelmed her and only the lapping of the sea above her cell kept her from unleashing her powers and breaking free. She lay motionless curled up on the floor, worn out from crying and beating her hands against the walls. April fought her way back to consciousness. These debilitating memories were really starting to irk her. When she was back home she would see a doctor and pearlist about them. Some of the shaman's attempts to assess her powers and control when she was younger haunted her. Fear filled memories flooded back to her now.

Shaking her head to bring her back to the present, April followed her senses and moved towards the sea. She wasn't a merita anymore; she was in control. In the dark, her arms stretched out, she walked straight into a door. April muffled a groan as she stubbed her toe. In a breath, she wielded a glow of sky blue Curo energy around her big toe and the pain was gone. Groping around she located the handle, slowly opened the door and slinked out into the adjoining room. Moonlight spilled into a large open plan room. In a quick swoop April could make out a large lounge that opened up into a kitchen to the right and a conservatory to the left. This did not look like a hotel April thought. Maybe she was in a private suite or in someone's house. She turned to the left and followed the moonlight towards the glass doors.

April's shoulders relaxed as she spied the sea. She tested the doors that led out onto the beach and was relieved when she heard a faint click. Without making a sound she carefully opened the door and shut it behind her. The soft sand felt wonderful between her toes. April broke out into a run towards the sea. The stars above her shone brightly and sparkled on the tranquil water. As April neared the ocean she started to feel a tugging inside of her, the same tugging that happened when her pearls warned her she was about to overexert herself. April started to slow. What had always been a sanctuary now radiated ominously.

Pulling to a halt, April tripped over a piece of driftwood and sprawled across the sand. A gentle wave rolled up and over her. She sighed in relief. She had made it. But then, an intense pain spread across her body, the water was burning her skin. April scrabbled out of the water as fast as she could. Quickly wicking the water away from her body with her Factus powers she momentarily relaxed. But the pain took its toll on her newly healed skin. She wielded a wave of sky blue Curo energy across her skin and April knelt down into the sand as the soothing feeling spread throughout her body.

She stared out to the sea and forced herself back up to standing. She took a step into the water and ignored the pain. She kept on walking until she was thigh high. The pain was tearing through her and she gritted her teeth and tried to force herself to submerge. But it was too much. She shot out her Factus energy and pushed herself back to the shore. She hurriedly turned around at ankle depth and ran from the water. She wielded another wave of Curo energy over her. Her legs felt as if they were on fire and she stumbled to the ground.

She looked down and saw the same rash as before covering her skin. It was as if the sea was poisoned. April looked back up to the house she had run from. She didn't know where to turn. The surrounding area was entirely foreign to her. April held her head in her hands and started to sob. Right now, all she really wanted was her Mum.

Too overwhelmed by shock April failed to notice a young man open the conservatory door. He ran down to where April was huddled on the beach and approached her carefully.

"Excuse me, are you okay?'"

April jumped startled by his appearance. She hurried to a standing position and looked him in the eyes. April scrabbled to think about where to start, what to ask first. Suddenly, a second wave of the rash pain surged over her body as she started to cry once more she uttered the word, "No."

The young man looked horrified at what was happening before him.

"I'm Connor, my brother Alex found you on the beach yesterday. Would you like to come back inside?" he asked.

April looked out to the sea one last time. "Yes please."

Connor smiled at her kindly and together they walked slowly back up to the house. As they walked she took a closer look at him. She definitely recognised his face. Could he be from the Peace Treaty? Her Mum had made her memorise hundreds of names and faces for the Peace Treaty ceremony. But, for the life of her, she couldn't recall this one.

CHAPTER 11

The microwave pinged and Connor brought April a large mug of hot chocolate. With a flourish, he sprayed some whipped cream on top and then poured on some mini-marshmallows and chocolate sprinkles.

"Be careful, it's hot!"

"Thank you," April said without making a move to pick up the mug.

Since bringing April inside the two had become acquainted. Feeling completely out of his depth, Connor had opted to lead a sobbing April back into his house. The girl seemed crazy. He found her a large dressing robe and wrapped her in it before seating her down at the breakfast bar. Despite her burning hot skin the girl shivered with cold so he continued his efforts to warm her up.

Why on earth she had gone outside he didn't know. It looked like she was in a trance. He happened to be awake, video chatting one of his school friends holidaying in Scotland when he saw her walking down the beach from his window. He watched her in surprise as she tried and failed to go for a swim. She had looked like a crazed person. When he approached her, he was perturbed to find her crying. Women were not really Connor's forte.

After more in-depth introductions, April had started to feel safer. Connor was younger than she had first presumed. He was eighteen, just finished high school and on summer holiday before he went to university. The mer education system worked differently so April, aged nineteen had also just finished her secondary school education and was applying for colleges. He looked very friendly. His hair was an unusual red-brown colour and he seemed to be both tan and freckled at the same time. His movements around the kitchen were awkward and jerky. He still moved like someone who had not fully grown into their body. He towered above April though so presumably his gangling height was causing these issues. His easy-going manner soon relaxed April. His smile was infectious whenever he forgot to be nervous. She felt ridiculous for bursting into tears. Nothing like moonlight and missing pearls to make a mera go crazy she thought. Now safely wrapped up in a warm home she felt her panic subside.

April had managed to paint a vague story of who she was while neglecting to mention that she was a mera. She drew on her Commutavi powers to make sure that her tongue remained a pinkish red colour and not her mera blue. Whoever lived by a sea that was poisonous to mer was worthy of being a potential threat in her mind. She was currently trying to gather as much information as possible from Connor.

"So how did you find me?" April asked while she watched Connor.

"Oh, that was my brother, Alex," Connor said. He seemed to go red as he said this.

"Our housekeeper has been looking after you. She's highly trained."

"I must thank her when I see her," April said smiling tightly.

"Do you ...?" April started.

As Connor said, "How did you...?" They both stopped and smiled.

"After you," April said.

"How did you come to be washed up?" Connor asked.

"I don't know. I've been trying to remember but I just can't figure it out." At this point a memory surge would be rather useful April thought ruefully.

"You must have hit your head pretty hard or something." Connor walked over with his mug of hot chocolate.

Connor smiled at her and went about drinking his own hot chocolate. He spied April staring oddly at her drink out of the corner of his eye. She seemed apprehensive about drinking it. He watched her grasp the mug in both hands and take a big gulp. Pulling it away he saw her smile in surprise with a large dollop of cream on her nose. Connor hid a smile - he liked this girl. She may be completely crazy but she had a sparkle about her that most people seemed to have lost upon hitting double digits.

Considering all she had been through she seemed remarkably chipper. Connor would have expected more panic from someone who had no idea where they were or how they came to be here. Connor reckoned she must be either hiding something, or she really had incurred some form of memory loss, or she was actually a crazy person. Connor decided to probe a bit further. He looked at April over his own mug of hot chocolate. "So, what is the last thing you can remember?"

~

"Ummm... I'm not sure." April scrabbled to think of a semi-normal response that didn't make her sound ridiculous. "I was at a function with my parents on a boat, and there was lots of alcohol and one thing led to another and now I'm here," she said.

"Wow, that must have been one crazy evening."

"It was."

"I didn't realise boats were allowed anywhere around here," Connor pressed.

April paused for a moment. She had forgotten about the boat restriction laws. "Yes, we have a small private island."

"I see. I don't know any other private islands around here."

"Where is here?" April asked

"This is my family's private island. My Dad moved us here for the summer."

April noticed that Connor averted his gaze from her while he said this and proceeded to take a very long gulp of his hot chocolate.

"That must be cool," April smiled. "Living on an island," she qualified. "Where about is it?" Usually April could tell wherever she was as long as she was near the ocean. But, the poisoned waters were interfering with her internal compass.

"It's just near Florida but quite far out. We're pretty isolated here."

"Ah okay," April knew these waters well, but the Peace Treaty was a reasonable distance away. How on earth did she get here?

"Would you like to call someone? Let them know you're okay?" Connor asked.

Shoot April thought. "Umm no, that's okay, I don't know any of their numbers."

She could have contacted Ethan or Setha to come and get her out of this mess but neither of them would be able to get through the poisoned waters easily. Her Dad would be the obvious person to contact but then that would mean letting her Mum know. But, she had no idea how to contact anyone without a working Iris pearl. Silence fell between them while April mulled over her options.

~

Alex jogged down the stairs whistling to himself as he went. It was a beautiful day and he couldn't wait to start on his morning run. He swung himself down the stairs and into the kitchen where he stopped abruptly. Connor and a girl, a very attractive girl, were sitting at the island together. Alex was impressed and stunned all at once. His brother was never usually good with the ladies, how on earth had he managed to find one on a private island? Alex approached his brother ready to pay him back for a lifetime of early morning tormenting when he had had a girl over and was trying to smuggle her out of the house. Connor never failed to embarrass him.

"Good morning, you two. Had a good night did we?" Alex proclaimed in a stage voice as he approached them. Connor jumped spilling his drink and the girl span round in her chair standing up in alarm.

As the girl stood up Alex realised his mistake.

"Oh my goodness, I'm so sorry," Alex flustered. "Are you okay?"

From smooth arrogance into concerned waffle in under a second, Connor had never seen his brother so ruffled. He was usually the cool, popular, charming type; clearly this girl had shaken him.

"I'm okay thank you," April replied.

Connor interceded, "This is Alex, my brother. He rescued you," Connor added reluctantly.

"Thank you for helping me. I'm April." Once again April's manners kicked in and she extended her hand to shake Alex's. Alex reached out and shook her hand not stopping to think about the oddity of shaking hands at six in the morning.

"Nice to meet you, I'm glad you're okay." The awkward silence that Connor and April had been in the midst of was only exacerbated by Alex's arrival.

"Ummm would you like something to eat maybe? Some breakfast?" Alex asked. April hadn't realised how hungry she was but at the mention of breakfast her stomach lurched in response.

"Breakfast would be great, thank you."

"The chefs have the weekend off, so I hope you don't mind my cooking."

Alex busied himself around the kitchen gathering all sorts of utensils and ingredients. Connor smirked as he watched Alex fluster. He walked over to the wall and brought up the TV panel and turned it onto the news.

~

"Are pancakes okay?"

"Pancakes sound great," April smiled. What on earth are pancakes? She wondered.

"Thank you for rescuing me," she said again. She took a closer look at Alex as he started weighing out ingredients. He looked nothing like Connor. Alex was not as tall as Connor but he seemed to take up more room. His tanned and obviously muscular body was barely concealed under a running top. He had golden hair much like hers but coupled with warm coffee brown eyes. Although she knew she should not trust a book by its cover she instinctively trusted him. Her shoulders relaxed for the first time since she woke up in the bathroom.

"So where did you find me, how was I? Did I look like I had swa... washed up on shore?" Somehow, she needed to find out if this Alex knew that she was a mera.

"You were washed up on the shore not too far from here, inside some sort of hollowed out branch. Your skin was burning hot to touch and yet you must have been out there for some time as your skin and clothing were dry." Alex paused for a moment to consult a tattered recipe book. It was the one his Mum kept all their favourite childhood recipes in. "Do you have any memory of how you got here?"

"None." April shook her head. "What was I wearing when you found me?"

"I didn't really notice to be honest with you... sorry about that, Rosetta our housekeeper will fill you in though."

"Do you remember anything?" Alex asked. He was whisking together a large bowl of milk, eggs and flour.

"No, nothing," April said. She didn't want to go through this again.

"We should alert the coast guard now you're conscious. You know, try to find something out."

April's smile froze and she mumbled something non-committedly. Alex was so focused on his pancakes he didn't seem to notice.

"You're of course welcome to stay here as long as you need. Rosetta will settle you in," Alex said.

"Oh, umm thank you," April said.

"Is there anyone you can call for help?" Alex asked.

"She can't remember anyone's numbers," Connor answered for her. April felt a flicker of annoyance at Connor answering for her.

"Ah I see. Maybe we should go to the mainland to get a doctor to check your head," Alex said as he started ladling the mixture into a pan.

"Oh no, it's fine. I'm sure my memories will come back to me soon," April said.

"Would you like blueberries with your pancakes? The chef usually stocks blueberries for us..." Alex said routing through the fridge.

"Wait a second," Connor had moved to stand in front of the TV and was turning the volume up.

A whole day has passed since the Peace Conference and finally information has been leaked as to what happened on that monumental day. What was thought to be a tactical media launch was in fact a terrorist delay.

Alex and April were now focusing their attention on the screen too.

The final signing of the treaty was about to commence when a bomb was set off in the ground underneath the building. The positioning of the bomb sent tremors throughout the massive structure and the entire building exploded outwards. Highly trained military professionals were on hand immediately to help the occupants out of the building. The concealment of this violence has been maintained until the correct party was found guilty of the attack. It is with great regret that President Darius had this news to announce just moments ago.

The broadcast cut to a film of the legged President standing outside the white house.

"The mer never wanted peace, or if they did those in power chose not to give it to them. This attack has destroyed everything we fought for and tried to build over the last few years. Instead of peace, they brought us war."

The news lady reappeared and continued to discuss the bombing but April stared at the images flashing up on the screen. She saw photos of herself dancing and standing on the stage. The photos of festivity transformed into clips of the wrecked building. Had anyone survived was April's first thought. She felt sick. Her eyes were trained on the flashing images. She tried to comprehend the wreckage she was seeing. A photo of her Dad appeared on screen and April snapped her attention back to the reporter's voice.

King Nathaniel managed to escape the military's grasp and his location remains unknown. It is believed that he was the leader behind this massacre. The King has currently remained silent but we wait for his inevitable response to President May's message. From peace to war in one day.

It all made sense now April thought. She tried to think back to the last thing she remembered before waking up in the bathroom. Blood, she remembered blood. Instinctively she moved her hand to rub the back of her neck. As she rubbed the faint scab, the evening started tumbling back into place. The fall from the helicopter, the necklace-watch swap, the blood and that final image of Ethan jogging towards her, all of these images swam in April's vision. She gripped the table edge in panic. Another photo of her Dad came onto the screen. April breathed a sigh of relief, at least her Dad was okay. He would fix everything.

There was no way he masterminded the attack. The Peace Treaty was his baby. So, it must have been the legged then? There was so much security. It seemed impossible that an outsider could have successfully launched an attack without it being foiled. She thought back to the Peace Treaty, her dress, and the poisoned sea. It must be the legged. Her Dad had been fighting for peace ever since he ascended to the throne and campaigned for it long before that. April's expression hardened. She needed to go back home and help her family. Without realising what she was doing she had already stood up and turned to go towards the conservatory.

"Well at least we know where Dad is then," Alex shrugged.

April span around. "That's your father?" she said incredulously. She was in the octopus's den.

"Yup, President Darius is our good old Dad," Alex joked uncomfortably as he turned his attention back to the pancakes. April felt herself shifting her position as she nervously scanned the room. Get a grip she told herself. She must act composed, clearly they had no idea who she was and she needed to keep it that way. April lifted her head up and smiled towards Alex and Connor hoping that she was portraying a calm and completely unruffled disposition.

April rapidly ran through her mental memory from her Peace Treaty preparation. Darius May was President of the legged's most powerful nation. He had three sons, Frederick whom she had danced with and of course, Alex and Connor. His wife had died when the boys were young. The Alex and Connor April was introduced to at the treaty were definitely not these two. As she tried to maintain her stance she noticed that she was not the only one who was struggling to keep their cool. Connor was wringing his hands beside the TV as he swapped the channel onto a random film.

"I can't believe this," Connor muttered under his breath. "I'm going to go and freshen up," Connor announced to the room. He gave a tight smile to April and then suddenly departed.

"Don't mind him," Alex said as he flipped yet another pancake. He was creating three perfect stacks of pancakes and seemed intent on continuing until they were each 10 high.

"He isn't a fan of Dad's political agendas," Alex continued.

"Oh," April said not sure what to reply to that, "And you? Do you...care for his political agenda?" April asked hesitantly, hoping that Alex would say no.

"Honestly, I've never paid much attention to politics. I didn't want to be known as the President's son so I invested a lot of time in trying to avoid becoming anything like him." With a final flip, Alex placed the last pancake onto the stack, "And the pancakes are ready!" Alex beamed looking proud of himself. "Sorry if I sound completely politically ignorant but I never saw why my Dad's career should impact who I am."

Alex busied himself pulling out a wide assortment of condiments onto the breakfast bar. April got the impression that Alex was slightly embarrassed by his admission. She knew exactly what he meant, in fact, he reminded her of Ethan. Between them they had had many a conversation about refusing to comply with everyone's predetermined ideals of the King and Prime Minister's children. There was no reason to fear these two even if their Dad was the President. April walked around the bar and picked up two plates of pancakes.

"I think politics is boring too," April smiled, "Where did you want me to set these?"

Alex's mood visibly relaxed as he picked up his tray laden with condiments and a third stack of pancakes.

"Follow me, we can eat out on the veranda and enjoy the view."

"Sounds good to me," April said as she followed him. The veranda was large and spacious with wooden slats. The glass table glinted in the sunlight as April placed down the plates. She sat down and looked out to sea, from a distance she could almost forget that it was poisonous.

"Do you think the news reporter was right?"

"Right?" Alex asked through a mouthful of pancake.

"About war I mean. A war starting between leg...uh I mean humans and mer," April asked.

"Personally, I reckon this is some radical group who are going to cause some fuss and eventually everything will calm down. Just hopefully there weren't too many serious casualties."

"Yeah, hopefully."

"Trust me April. Being the son of the President makes you realise that disasters like this happen every day."

"I suppose," April said while thinking that her Dad must have shielded her from many such disasters. Once again, she thought of how much better equipped Kayla was to deal with these situations.

"Don't worry about it April. These things are always painted worse by the media than what they really are."

As they ate their pancakes in silence April's worries overwhelmed her. She was trying to figure out how to get home and make sure her parents and Ethan were okay. She focused on her pancakes and tried to stop tears from welling in her eyes. Suddenly her finger tips started glowing a faint blue. She hurriedly hid them in her lap. She could feel her powers welling within her. If she cried then she wouldn't be able to hold her powers in. She tried to focus on Alex and his pancakes. But, looking at him it reminded her of one of her most pressing concerns. If these were the President's real sons, who were the boys she had stood with at the treaty?

"We can take a boat to the mainland and hopefully figure out how to get you home," Alex said with a smile.

"Thanks, that would be great," April said, trying to keep her voice upbeat. Her stomach dropped. She didn't want to go home and face war. She didn't want to be told what to do and what her role in the war was. But, she couldn't stay here.

"Is this your summer home?" April asked trying to change the subject.

"Yes, sort of," Alex said and put his fork down. "We used to come here with my Mum, it was her favourite place in the whole world. But, she passed away when we were young and I think it was too difficult for my Dad to come back."

"I'm sorry," April said.

"It's okay. I'm just glad to be back. We'll have to show you around before you go."

"I'd like that."

They both lapsed into silence.

CHAPTER 12

Ethan woke up and stretched his arms above his head as he did every morning. He had hoped yesterday was a bad dream but as he opened his eyes the stark reality hit him once again. When the bomb exploded he was inside the main hall. His hands were full of tissues and plasters to help April. When he replayed the scene in his head it happened in slow motion. He shut his eyes and saw April's look of horror as she was lifted like a doll up, into the air and slammed outwards away from the glass wall. As the ceiling-high glass doors collapsed, Ethan was thrown into a pile of broken glass and debris from the building. Everything fell down around him. All he could hear was crashing and screaming. The scene made no sense, all around him was utter chaos. However, the chaotic images didn't last for long as from above one of the many ornately carved animals dropped down and buried Ethan underneath it. From there his mind went blank.

He didn't know how many hours he was unconscious for but when the army came in to help shift the debris he was awake and in an agony that felt like he had been stuck for weeks. His whole body screamed in pain. He wasn't sure what was wrong but he was certain that several bones were broken. Luck was on his side at least as an elephant sculpture had fallen to his left and the legs and trunk saved him from being crushed to death. Ethan lay still and called for help intermittently. He was too tired to even thank the soldiers who eventually found him under the rubble. As he was pulled out he could see several other groups roaming through the chaos to try and help the trapped. Some were barely recognisable from the night before.

Everyone was covered in a thick coat of dust. It clung to their bodies, hair and clothes. The brown dust was only absent where it congealed with blood to form a sticky burgundy clump. Ethan remembered being supported out of the rubble to a van of sorts. He was handed over to the doctors. The fresh air gave him enough energy to open his mouth to thank them when one of the nurses calmly noted. "He's one of them." Next thing he knew he woke up in this hellhole.

From the guards' chatter he knew that the peace conference only took place two days ago. He had been found yesterday. In opening his mouth to say thank you, Ethan revealed his tongue and unwittingly exposed himself as the enemy. So much for peace, he thought despondently. From a throbbing on the back of his head that he didn't remember yesterday, he presumed he was knocked unconscious by a blow. Other than that, he seemed to have been patched up by the doctors before being locked away. This disconcerted him more than anything else. If he was the enemy then why did they want him healthy? There were no casts on his body or any other signs of legged medicine. He felt as if he had been healed by Curo energy.

Yesterday his numb body stopped him from standing as he regained consciousness. The darkness outside meant he couldn't take full stock of his surroundings. He stood up now in his 'room.' He felt surprisingly well, but he was acutely aware of the absence of his pearls. He reached down into his pocket and confirmed what he already knew. April's pearls were gone too.

Three stark white walls surrounded him. No other furnishings were in the room other than the bed. The fourth wall shimmered. Ethan stood up and moved towards his transparent wall. Inspecting it closely he slowly reached out to touch it. His hand was confronted with a hard force field. In hindsight, he realised that he was lucky that it was not electrified. He pushed against it with all his weight and deduced that this wall would not be granting him exit from his room any time soon. Sighing he leant against the invisible barrier. If only he could just fall through it he thought. He willed himself to slide through the invisible wall. But, to no avail, today was not the day he developed a superpower. He turned around and looked up and down the hallway. All he could see was a white corridor with several closed doors and some similar looking cells to his own. None of which appeared to be occupied. Excellent Ethan thought worriedly.

With nothing better to do Ethan decided to take stock of his body. Stretching from side to side to test the damage of the explosion he winced in pain. He rolled his shoulders back and forth hearing them crunch from lack of movement. Then he leant over to stretch out his legs. As he did a door at the end of the corridor opened. Cautiously he rolled upwards. He could hear several people purposefully striding down his corridor. Somehow, he just knew they were coming for him. Doing what all Vale men did in the face of a threat Ethan stood tall and braced himself. Whatever he had landed himself in he did not have a good feeling about it.

Ethan stepped back as three military men stopped in front of his cell. The leader of the group pressed his hand against the transparent wall and a blue light dashed around his hand, a quick beep later and the wall was dividing in two, granting the two other men access into the cell. Ethan stepped back in surprise at the wall's separation. His momentary lapse and current state allowed the two men to quickly restrain him. One fastened his hands behind his back and the other attached a collar around his neck. The leader lifted up his right hand and with a tap of a button the cuff around his wrist shot out a blue light to Ethan's collar. Ethan felt a small tug emanating from the collar on his neck. As the leader started marching back up the corridor Ethan found himself pulled along behind him, with the other two men flanking him. The entire procedure was performed in complete silence. Ethan held his tongue. His questions could wait. He was taken through a menagerie of corridors and staircases. Ethan monitored his surroundings trying to decipher where he was, but the stark whiteness remained disorientating.

The man leading Ethan slowed and scanned them into another room. This room was, if possible, even brighter than the others. The opposite wall to the door was a giant window. Ethan was glad it was not another force field. The wall was perfectly still and didn't exude that strange hum. Bright sunlight pierced through the room. Ethan blinked, it had been a while since he was exposed to natural light. He was marched further into the room and his guard shot the blue beam of light from his cuff to attach it to a chair. Ethan scrabbled forward as his neck became attached to a high-backed chair in front of a glass tabletop. His eyes finally adjusted and Ethan peered up into the piercing eyes of the woman sat in front of him.

"Hello Ethan, how are you? I trust you've found yourself in good health?"

"Ummm," Ethan was lost momentarily for words. There was something startlingly familiar about those eyes. And why was this woman being so nice? Ethan decided to go for feigned confidence, he had nothing to lose at this point.

"I'm good thank you. Who are you?" he said with as little feeling as he could muster.

"Hah, my brother said you were a gentleman. I'm Lydia. This is my research facility."

The game Lydia was playing was not one Ethan fancied entertaining at the moment.

"I know your brother?"

"Yes, an unfortunate and brief liaison but, you two knew each other none the less."

"Right..." This was getting him nowhere, Ethan was trying to maintain his bravado but internally he was becoming more and more apprehensive at this woman's familiarity. He wiped his hands tentatively on his trousers. Her eyes pierced into him and suddenly it clicked where he had seen them before. William.

"William is your brother," Ethan said in mild shock. Lydia let out a sharp bark of laughter.

"Figured it all out now have you." She leant against one of the high lab tables. "Poor old Will, I think he really fell for you. Until of course the swimming incident."

"Where is he?" Ethan demanded.

"Will is off flying his plane somewhere I'm sure. He has no idea I have you here in my facility."

Ethan was quiet for a moment. He felt used. William may know nothing but he clearly came from a mer hating family. He caught onto the last part of Lydia's sentence.

"Facility? What are you doing here?"

"All in good time Ethan. I'm afraid I'm the one who will be asking the questions."

The fixed smile slid from Lydia's face. The sinister smile that replaced it was, if possible, even more uninviting. She stood up from her desk and walked towards the window. She tapped her metal wristband as she moved and Ethan felt a jerk at his neck again.

As Lydia walked she dragged Ethan along behind her. Lydia stopped and gazed out of the window. Ethan's electrical tether was kept at a restricted length, just out of arms reach he noted. The sun was setting and Ethan couldn't help smirking again as he thought how romantic a location this could be and yet here he was electrically tethered to a crazy woman's wrist. They were overlooking the ocean and Ethan felt a pang of longing to be swimming in the sea and not looking at it. Glancing down he could see the sea gently lapping at a rugged cliff face. He was trying to work out whether he had seen this shoreline before when Lydia snapped him out of his reverie.

"Do you know where Princess April is?"

Ethan froze. They didn't have April. That meant there was hope.

"Pardon?"

"You heard me, where is Princess April?"

"I don't know. I've been unconscious. Had you not noticed?"

Choosing to ignore this Lydia continued, "This necklace was found in your possession." Lydia tapped her control cuff and a projection of April's necklace appeared circling in front of them. "This necklace is Princess April's is it not?"

"It might be? I don't know?"

"Well it certainly isn't your necklace, is it? And I know that you prefer the company of men so it's not a present for a lady friend."

Another tap on the cuff and April's voice echoed through the room, 'My necklace was irritating the cut, so my friend, Ethan, swapped with me.' An image of his watch appeared on April's dainty wrist.

Ethan stared blankly at Lydia as he tried to remain impassive. All the while his brain was going into overdrive.

"Are you willing to play with me now? I know you know this is April's necklace and I know you know where she is." She turned to the door. "Are you going to tell me, or will Frederick have to force the information out of you."

With her final words a man walked into the room.

"Why hello Ethan, I'm not sure we had the pleasure of being introduced at the Peace Treaty. I'm Frederick. I danced with your friend Princess April at the …"

"I remember," Ethan said curtly.

"Frederick here has kindly been helping me with my research. We've been collaborating together on a little project. However, your friend April, her powers… Well she could make our operation so much simpler. Help me with my research, and help Frederick remove a potential obstacle and we'll send you home. We're both very interested in finding her. Finding her for..." Lydia paused and smiled, "research purposes."

"We think you know where she is, and I will do whatever is necessary until you tell us," Frederick said.

"You're always so serious Frederick."

"What do you want with April?" Ethan demanded.

"Wouldn't you like to know?" Lydia said her eyes gleaming.

Ethan instinctively leant away from her. Frederick tapped on his wrist cuff and Ethan felt himself jerk towards him. With a look back at Lydia, Ethan shivered at her cold smile fixed on him. He wasn't sure which one of them unnerved him more.

CHAPTER 13

"Silence." An authoritative voice rang through the cave. Kayla entered. She let the boulders roll back into place, creating an impressive dome behind her before she proceeded into the cave. She swam slowly and in a controlled manner. Now more than ever she needed to impress upon these mer that at seventeen she was their senior and their leader. At 5ft this was no mean feat, her armour that usually made her feel powerful, now made her feel like she was playing dress up. A strand of hair floated in front of her face her eyes focused on it for a second but she resisted the temptation to brush it away or blow it from her face. Nothing would faze her now. As she reached the end of the cave she turned and swam upwards to the royal throne. She floated into her seat and surveyed the faces she had impassively swum past.

The war council was assembled. Yelta's War chamber was located in the centre of the Yeltan whirlpool in an ancient cave that was buried deep within the corals. It was only used for highly confidential matters because of its sheer depth. Spending too much time in the cave was incredibly claustrophobic as the water pressure mounted upon you. This cave was believed to have been where the original pearl wielders first mined for the black Tenebrasco pearls. Those hungry for their destructive power had mined to the death according to mer legend. The cave interior was smooth and rounded, and glistened as black as the pearls it was rumoured to hold. Kayla had never liked the cave. It echoed horribly. Sound was thrown back aggressively from every surface and voices were distorted into sinister mimics. Not to mention it was freezing.

The stern faces around her were looking up expectantly. They waited for her to lead them, but their expressions revealed their doubts. Kayla knew that they chafed under the authority of a seventeen-year-old. In mer culture you weren't considered an adult until you turned twenty-five. At that point, a mer's powers were fully realised. But, with her Dad otherwise occupied she was the only royal trained and available. At least she wasn't April she mused. Right now, all power plays would involve her sister and how best to utilise her power. Kayla was often thankful that she at least had been asked if she wanted this role. For April, there was no escaping hers. Kayla turned to the war council leader Demetrius. He gave her a small, but encouraging smile. Demetrius was her father's best mer and had served as a father figure for Kayla since she joined Yelta three years ago. After his smile, she gave him the nod and allowed Demetrius to start the session.

"Welcome Princess Kayla. The war council has convened after the Peace Treaty attack. You have all been briefed on the current situation. I shall now update you on the most recent developments." At this Demetrius took a deep breath. He glanced in her direction before continuing. Kayla stared forward impassively as if immune to the cold and critical stares of her council.

"The update I received this morning detailed the tragic news of Queen Freya's death." He heard a sharp intake of breath from Kayla but continued on before she could react further.

"We will hold a minute of silence at the end of our session in respect of her Royal Highness." The heads of the war council simultaneously bowed in respect. "The second critical update we received is that there are several bodies of water that are reportedly poisonous to mer. Each of these poisonous waters surround islands or coastlines that are controlled by the US military and navy services. It is believed that these areas hold captive mer and house plans of the next assault. Unfortunately, we have no lead as to which location holds which information, if any," Demetrius continued.

Demetrius spoke and drew images up out of the Iris platform. He showed the locations of the poisoned areas on the water map for the council to see. The mer dignitaries captured at the Peace Treaty bombing were thought to be held at these locations. Kayla took it all in. Her training had taken over. On an emotional level she was devastated. She wanted to break down and dive out of the room. She wanted to scream at her Dad for not being the one to tell her and she wanted to wield a tidal wave through the room to knock everyone who doubted her out of their seats. However, her rational side was already devising a strategy to see if there was a way around the poison. She would need to decide which team would be best equipped to deploy a neutraliser for the poison once one was found. Demetrius continued speaking detailing the location of each of the areas and the circumference of poison that surrounded them. As he concluded his report Kayla felt all eyes shift back to her.

She leant forward and squashing the emotions surging through her she began to speak.

"Demetrius, thank you for the update." She swallowed, the lump in her throat. "The time has come for us to make our move. My Father, King Nathaniel, has entrusted me with the leadership of Yelta's forces. I trust that you all support my father's decision and in turn show the Meridian crown unwavering fealty. We have already lost my Mother and I doubt this will be the last of our losses. It is time for us to fight." Kayla finished her speech. She discussed with the council members her plans and after some minor alterations everything was sorted. But, in reality she wasn't there. Kayla could feel herself looking in on the situation as if she was floating outside of her body. The confident war commander she saw scared her. Calm and efficient with an iron will that was the leader everyone needed. But, in reality she was devastated and vulnerable. To do this she was going to need an ally. Someone, the mer could rally around.

"Demetrius, has there been any news on April?" Kayla asked quickly, her voice hitching with emotion. "As the most powerful wielder of the pearls she is an imperative piece of the rescue effort," she continued more composedly.

"Your Highness, I thought you had been informed. As of yet there has been no information on April's whereabouts." Demetrius pulled up an image on the Iris platform. "This is the last time your sister was sighted."

Kayla leaned forward and watched the ragdoll figure being lifted into the air and thrown backwards into the sea.

"None? And what is being done to rectify this? Can't my Dad or the Shamans locate her?"

The war council ministers shifted uncomfortably. Kayla eyed them coldly.

Gregor spoke, "Your sister."

"Her Royal Highness," Kayla interjected

"Princess April has not been considered a high priority rescue Your Highness. Considering her age and lack of training, we felt it was better to focus on the missing members of the mer court, the Pearl shamans and pearlists, and our own missing mer warriors. As a member of the royal family she will be used as leverage and won't come to any harm."

The glare Kayla directed at the minister caused him to tail off as he reached the end of his excuses. She turned to stare around the rest of the table.

"Your father has tried to find her, as have the shamans but something is blocking them from locating her," Demetrius intervened. Kayla paused for a moment then straightened herself up again.

"The loss of Queen Freya, my Mother, will have a devastating effect on the King. At this time, he will need my sister to bolster his own powers. We do not want a war." At this she paused to stare them down again. "What we need is to reveal who was behind this attack. We will punish them and continue on our path to peace."

Most of the ministers were nodding along, however, she could see a few of them frozen in place. She fought hard not to let their disapproving gazes falter her resolve.

"Your Highness, we cannot sit back and let this attack go without a retaliation. We will look weak," Gregor countered.

"What we are attacking is the accusation that it was mer who launched the attack. We do not look weak, at the moment we are the threat," Kayla argued.

"Kayla is right," Demetrius stepped in again. "Our main aim is to prove our innocence and prove to the legged who was behind the terror attack."

"Thank you, Demetrius," Kayla smiled in approval. "Now you all have your briefs, I would like you to initiate our plans among the departments. We will meet again tomorrow to comment on your progress." She stared around the circle to make sure no one undermined her rule.

"Perfect. We will now hold a minute's silence for her Royal Majesty Queen Freya Meridia, my Mother."

Kayla bowed her head and wielded her Essentia pearl, willing it to glow with her heart's energy. The rose pearls of the war council lit up the dark cave. The Essentia pearl was the 'life' pearl. During a period of mourning the Essentia pearl was lit to celebrate the life lost as a sign of respect. The pale pink light revealed everyone's faces in a warm glow. Kayla took this moment to look around the mer gathered before her. Sometimes she forgot that they all had lives outside of Yelta. Some of them had been present at the Peace Treaty. They may have lost loved ones too. After a minute, she let her Essentia pearl dim. Before anyone could say another word, Kayla pushed upwards with a powerful stroke of her tail and addressed the entire chamber.

"The council may be dismissed." And with that she swam slowly from the room, desperate to flee but managing to muster enough control to compose herself for her final moments in the chamber.

Upon leaving the council cave Kayla fled. She didn't wait for questions or for anyone to offer their condolences. Right now, she wanted to be alone. She swam straight to her bedroom. She sunk to the floor and curled in on herself. All the emotions she suppressed throughout the meeting came rushing forth. Her Mum. She hadn't seen her properly in over two years. And now, now she never would. She couldn't think straight. Crying was beyond her. Huge sobs shuddered against her armour. She started stripping off the stiff material and threw it onto the bed. Hugging her tail, she rocked herself backwards and forwards. She tried to comprehend the news. Why did no one warn her? Why didn't her Dad or April tell her? Although she had lived alone for over three years it was only now that she felt isolation press against her.

Kayla and her Mum had been close, really close. They shared the same determination to succeed no matter the cost. Both were resolute and found it easy to let their heads govern their hearts. With grief still heavy in her heart Kayla slowly sat up and swam towards her bookshelf. She picked up a large green leather book the same colour as her Mum's and her tail. They both had dark emerald tails that glistened like the gemstone. She heaved the book into her lap. It was a photo book that April made for her as a leaving present when she moved to Yelta to complete her training. Kayla turned the pages and now the tears came thick and fast. She paused on a photo of her and her Mum. Strength and determination was what Kayla learnt from her Mum. She knew that her Mum would tell her it was okay to grieve. But, she would remind her that she had a duty to her mer and she could not let them down.

She flipped the pages until the book fell to the centre page. It was a photo of her Mum and her with seaweed goo all over their hands, a disaster of a kitchen all around them, and the world's most hideous looking cake sat in front of them. April bet that neither of them could make a cake. She reckoned they were so focused on success they were incapable of making something which was frivolous and fun. Her Mum gave the kitchen staff a day off and they spent the whole day together just the two of them. April and her Dad popped down to taste the final product and snapped this picture. It had tasted horrible. But, her Mum pretended to love it and ate her entire slice. When April and her Dad left incredulous, her Mum broke down laughing. Laughter was what she remembered from that day, so much laughter. Hysterical laughter started to bubble out of Kayla now as she stared at the picture. Picking up the book she hugged it to herself and resumed her rocking back and forth. "Mum," she sobbed.

CHAPTER 14

Setha's crab cakes were left after one bite. The news unfolding on the TV stopped all ideas of food. Newsflash after newsflash, each showing more horrid images than the next kept her mind occupied. CTV footage of the Peace Treaty had been uncovered. April was shown being blasted from the building and King Nathaniel was pictured shielding the people closest to him with his powers. But, the attack had come too quickly and as too big a surprise. His attempts saved many, but in the initial blast Queen Freya was crushed immediately. The scene was horrific.

Setha was horrified watching the footage but she couldn't look away. As the news reporter started reading the names of the dead Setha hugged her tail even tighter. When she moved onto naming the missing mer Setha was relieved to hear Ethan and April's names on the list. At least there was hope that they were both alive. Setha tried messaging and calling them again and again. But, to no avail. Now she was receiving error messages from both of their Iris'. It was while watching the news her Iris pad rang.

~

Setha floated awkwardly in April's living room waiting for the royal family's Head of Operations. Setha was not entirely sure what his job was. The King liaised with so many officials it was hard to keep track. April would have been able to tell her. Hundreds of times, possibly thousands Setha chilled in this lounge. It was huge.

Once, when April was upset about a grade, Setha convinced April to wield her Assurgere powers to grow a seaweed forest in the room. For the whole afternoon, they played hide and seek amongst the weeds to cheer April up. Setha could still remember chasing the flashes of April's diamond coloured tail. But, all the fun memories had been wiped. The windows were shuttered down and no natural light permeated the room. The palace was in lockdown. All the large entrances were blocked and security was tripled around the border. Setha underwent rigorous screening to enter even the palace grounds, which were usually open to all.

Setha drifted around the cavernous room. Summoned to give information on Ethan and April's activities before the Peace Treaty, Setha felt gloom seep through her. She knew she had nothing of use to say. How could she let King Nathaniel down again with even more bad news? Setha tried not to think about the alternatives of what could have happened to Ethan and April. A thud sounded behind her and she whipped around. Galloping towards her were the King's two pet giant seahorses, Tarzan and Titan. They raced at her in excitement completely oblivious to the sombre atmosphere in the living room. The two whizzed round her twirling Setha in their tail stream. She calmed them down so she could stroke them.

"Hello Titan," Setha said stroking him on the head. Titan gleamed a deep purple flecked with gold. He was shyer than Tarzan and intuitive to people's feelings. He nuzzled against her tail. Tarzan tried to butt him out of the way. He was like a great black bulldozer. He was a deep shiny midnight blue and constantly excited.

"And hello to you too Tarzan," Setha said. Moments later King Nathaniel, and presumably the Head of Operations, swam into the room. Setha straightened up flustered. Tarzan and Titan swam back to Nathaniel. From then on Titan didn't leave the King's side. The first thing Setha noted was that the King looked a sallow grey colour, one that was not too different from her Dad's. However, despite his colour, he still floated tall and seemed even more imposing than usual.

"Hello Setha, thank you for coming to help me in these troubling times."

"Your Majesty," Setha bobbed a bow and the King inclined his head. Nathaniel floated over to the settees and gestured for them both to sit down. At this point Clyde took over. He leant forwards.

"Good afternoon Setha, I'm Clyde, Head of Operations." He shook Setha's hand firmly and then got straight to business. "The Meritia are interested in only one thing. They want to prove the mer's innocence and punish those who incriminated us." Setha nodded and tried to look like she was in the know.

"But, this is only half the story. My job is to find out why they attacked us from the crown's perspective. This set up was a very clever scheme, years in the making and we need to know what their end game is." Clyde was no longer really talking to Setha but seemed to be voicing his own internal thoughts.

"And you think I can help?" Setha inquired.

"Yes, all information is vital!"

Setha glanced confusedly at the King but he was staring across the room. He absent-mindedly stroked Titan who floated by his chair.

"Umm okay," she started hesitantly. "What would you like to know?"

"I need to know if anything unusual has happened to Princess April or Ethan recently, something out of the ordinary. The bomb went off when they were both isolated from the main chamber and each other." Clyde leant further forwards. "We have reason to believe they may have been targeted. At no other time during the ceremony were those two alone together." With this revelation, he gave a satisfied flick of his tail.

Setha rarely felt the social differences between herself, April and Ethan. At school Setha was the popular one in their year, Ethan had been too before he graduated. April always invited Setha to the royal functions and Setha made sure April attended all the parties at school. Money wise Setha was never without anything she needed, and Queen Freya always kept April to a strict budget. It was only times like this when Setha was reminded that April and Ethan were of mernational importance and she was just one of the masses. And yet, it was in these instances that she didn't feel any jealousy for the spotlight the two possessed.

Setha racked her brain for Clyde. But honestly, she couldn't think of anything.

"Well I'm not really friends with Ethan, so I'm not sure about him."

Clyde looked at her obviously disappointed. Setha couldn't help but hope he had more leads than her to work with otherwise his intelligence was going to be minimal.

"He did start dating a legged!" Setha blurted out. Why on earth did she say that she mentally scolded herself, but Clyde perked up.

"A legged? And how did this come about?" he said clapping his hands on his tail.

Setha blushed automatically. She developed a crush on Ethan when she first moved to Hanaria. He was charming and perfect, and that was also why she hated him. For the first two years she admired him from a distance. As she rapidly became one of the most popular meras at school she hoped that he would pay attention to her. And she hated herself for this weakness. Setha was someone who took what she wanted. She didn't sit around pining after some mer. Yet, here she was multiple opportunities missed over the years and Ethan was still none the wiser of her crush. Setha had never spoken about it with April, but she hoped April was completely oblivious too. When she wanted, Setha could conceal her feelings pretty well. One of the main reasons she didn't tell April was because she felt stupid that she once believed the rumours surrounding April and Ethan, and so actively avoided April's advance of friendship. Thankfully that was behind her. Not telling her also meant saving April from being in an awkward position between her two best friends. It was this crush that meant she had kept tabs on Ethan's whereabouts for years. However, information on Ethan's love life wasn't what Setha thought Clyde would want to know.

"It was about a month ago. Ethan was keeping it secret. I just saw a message on his Iris." No need to mention how she had been looking at the messages appear on his watch when he left it at April's one evening.

"The legged was angry at him for not mentioning that he was a mer, and so Ethan broke it off." Setha twisted her bag on top of her tail. "From the messages, it looked like Ethan was shocked at the legged's anger."

Clyde seemed overly interested in this information. Even more interested than Setha had been when she peeped at the messages.

"And anything else?"

Setha thought intently once more. Had anything else unusual been happening…

"April's powers have been intensifying. She doesn't like to worry anyone by talking about it, but they've been progressing at an alarming rate."

King Nathaniel looked up at this.

"How exactly are they manifesting?" Clyde asked.

"Well, they aren't changing too much at the moment. Her wielding control is getting worse when she is emotional," Setha said looking down at her bag. "Oh, and she is experiencing more and more pearl blackouts, uh when memories resurge in her brain brought up by the pearls." Her hands were gesticulating now. "And her Tenebrasco pearl keeps on glowing for some reason. But we aren't sure why that is and all her pearls glow a lot."

Setha felt like she was waffling but the King was giving her his full attention now. He seemed to be concentrating hard on something. His hand paused in mid-sea above Titan who looked up reproachfully at the pause in his petting. Setha was worried that she had spoken out of turn. Before she could apologise or change the subject Nathaniel spoke.

"How old is April?"

Setha stared blankly, blinking in surprise before answering, "She's nineteen Your Majesty."

"I thought so, I just wanted to confirm," Nathaniel said. "Then April should not be experiencing these changes yet. Her powers shouldn't fully mature until her twenty-fifth birthday."

"Maybe she is advanced for her years Your Majesty," Clyde offered looking between the two.

"No. That is the way the pearls work. If April's powers are maturing early something is making this happen. Or something has gone horribly wrong," Nathaniel said his voice trailing off at the end.

"Your Majesty I'm not sure I understand..." Clyde started but Nathaniel cut him off mid-sentence, talking as if he was reminding himself.

"The powers of the firstborn are governed by the same rules of the original pearl wielder. The process has never changed. April is showing the early signs of intensification, which should only happen two years before her twenty-fifth birthday. During this period, the firstborn is at their most vulnerable. Until they are able to access the full range of their powers the pearls have more control than at any other stage."

"The pearls have the power?" Setha asked.

"Yes, the pearls we wear are not merely wells of power, they are balls of energy and sometimes they like to expend their own influence."

Setha stared in confusion. She had never heard the pearls spoken about in this way.

"The pearls are alive then?" she asked.

"Yes and no, different pearls have different intelligence and conscious levels if you will."

"Oh…" Setha tailed off. Clyde looked between the two again not sure who would say something interesting next. He seemed to be vibrating with energy as he jogged his tail up and down.

"And back to April Your Majesty. So, the convergence of early powers has never happened before? There have been no exceptions?" Clyde asked.

"No," King Nathaniel answered. Clyde beamed looking positively delighted at such grave news.

"Then this must be the key?" exclaimed Clyde. Setha had no idea what the key was, and she was almost certain Clyde didn't know either. At Setha's blank look the King explained.

"The twenty-four hours before the firstborn turns twenty-five are the most dangerous. The heir becomes completely incapable of control. A special cave has been used for millennia. It is inlaid with Tenebrasco pearls. As long as the firstborn is in the cave they are protected and their powers are kept at bay." Clyde raised his hand but Nathaniel continued before Clyde could interrupt him again. "While they are in this state of 'uncontrol' a Tenebrasco pearl wielder could control them. There are horrible myths, awful legends which detail the horrifying actions of a controlled first born."

"The city of Atlantis?" Setha asked without thinking.

"Exactly, to get revenge on his brother's advanced nation, Galatia took control of the first born and commanded him to wield the vines to grow and wrap around the inhabitants so they were tied down and then sink the island. An entire nation was wiped out in under an hour."

Setha sat in shock. Clearly, that wasn't true it was just a myth. Clyde seemed to be experiencing the same issues.

"Surely, surely not. April couldn't do all that."

"No," Nathaniel started and Clyde visibly relaxed "Not for another six years," King Nathaniel finished.

"But, there aren't any Tenebrasco wielders left, there haven't been any for centuries?" Clyde said.

Nathaniel sighed, "Theoretically April and I could wield the Tenebrasco pearl power, but I've never connected with it and neither has April. The power remains dormant."

Clyde nodded unsure of what to say. The three sat in silence for a moment. The large room seemed to grow even larger.

"Right...Thank you Setha for shedding light on this situation," Clyde eventually said while floating into an upright position. He seemed determined to find a positive conclusion to this meeting. Setha followed suit, she looked over at the King who was looking into the distance.

"Sorry I couldn't be of more help," she said turning to shake Clyde's hand.

"You were a lot more helpful than you think Setha, thank you for coming in," Clyde said.

Then unexpectedly the King floated up and shook her hand too.

"I'm sorry about your loss King Nathaniel. I hope April is found soon," Setha said trying to stop tears from clouding her eyes.

The King nodded kindly. "I hope so too, thank you Setha."

Setha swam out of the room with Titan and Tarzan following in her wake. Patting them at the entrance she shooed them to head back towards the King. She left feeling confused. April clearly didn't know that her powers were behaving out of the ordinary. Setha supposed that if April were more willing to learn about her powers then maybe a shaman would have discovered these abnormalities. Setha swam to the gates and was swiftly ushered out. Setha mentally recapped the conversation with Clyde and the King. Trying to think if there was anything else she should have told them, she almost swam into a school of grumpy mahi-mahi. She didn't need Communico powers to understand they were annoyed. She made her way to the ray stop. Tapping her Iris, she checked once more whether April had contacted her, or if even Ethan had messaged her. But, there was no word from them. There was only a message from her Grandmother asking if she would be back in time for dinner. The ray bus appeared and Setha swam on and took a seat at the back. She leant her head against the window and put her ear drops in. With the volume up high she tried to forget the pressing feeling of uselessness closing in around her.

CHAPTER 15

The rain poured down outside splashing onto the veranda. April felt like kicking herself for not taking up Alex's offer to go to the mainland yesterday. She was so tired she thought that one-day to relax would be okay. But, now looking at the weather she didn't need to be a marine expert to know there was no way a boat was sailing. She focused her Tempus energy and tried to calm the waves. But, the toxins in the water started stabbing her brain. Pressing her hands against the window she screwed up her forehead and pushed harder against the waves, forcing them into submission. Beads of sweat gathered on her brow from the pain.

"Argh."

She collapsed her head forward onto the window. Her breath came in shallow gasps. April straightened herself up and opened the door. She strode outside towards the sea. The rain stormed down but she ignored it, she came to a stop at the edge of the ocean. April breathed in deeply and raised her hands in front of her. She channelled her Factus and Tempus energy. Pushing the deep navy energy out of her hands she pushed the waves flat. The sea roared in response but started to calm under her pressure. April started shaking from the toxins. She looked down at her hands in shock. Her arms were leaden but she strained to keep them strong. The poison started to sweep through her system again. She clung to her focus but she could feel herself losing her hold over the waves. A searing pain stabbed her brain again and she dropped her arms.

April stood looking out at the sea. Her arms heavy she wrapped them around herself. Suddenly she shivered. The rain seeped into her skin and she looked down at her bare feet white against the sand. A moment too late she stepped back from the oncoming tide. She doubled over lifting her feet up in agony. Gritting her toes in the sand she tried to ignore the pain. With one last look at the sea she walked away back to the house. Derek, the caretaker, shouted something at her through the rain. She smiled, but couldn't hear him. She opened the door and made her way to the shower.

The lock clicked shut as she turned the handle, her hand dropped and she just stood there for a moment, her head hanging forward. Tears slowly streamed down her face. Threading her fingers through her hair she stepped away and moved under the shower. She slid down the wall and waved her hand to start the shower. The water rushed down and she let it soothe her. Her Factus powers flooded through her and she glowed a faint white.

"Stop it," April said to herself. She opened her eyes, wiped her tears and stretched out her legs. Leaning forward she massaged her sore feet. There had to be another way off the island she thought. But, she couldn't swim, the weather was too dangerous for travel and she had no way to communicate with another mer. April wandered if anyone was looking for her. Surely her Dad would be able to find her. Maybe he was the cause of the storm April thought. She looked around nervously and then dipped into her Commutavi powers, a glow of purple later her tail appeared. Concentrating on the sparkle of her scales she ran her fingers over them. It felt wrong to be on land in her mera form but it comforted her. She would just have to make the most of being a legged and hope no one found her out until the storm passed or the mer found her.

~

The next morning, April snuck out of the guest room early and treaded carefully into the lounge. She paused to feel the fluffy rug between her toes. Although she was getting used to being on land long term, shoes were still not to her taste. Settling onto the couch she located the remote and turned on the TV. This had become her routine for the last few days. Megan, the friendly housemaid, had lent April a selection of her clothes. April wore these with a couple of extras supplied by Rosetta. Today she was wearing her favourite outfit. It was a grey t-shirt dress with tassel fringing. April thought it was hilarious. When she first tried it on she twisted from side to side in the mirror to see the tassels splay out. She felt like a squid and it was so comfortable. The legged fashion was so similar yet so different from mer tastes. April couldn't quite put her finger on it. April preferred wearing dresses and letting her legs be free. Her land wardrobe at home consisted mainly of tunic dresses. As a mera, she dressed quite conservatively but with lots of colour. She had never gotten into the 'Tail Tight' trend of tail covers. They made her feel so restricted.

She pulled a blanket over her bare legs and hugged her knees into her chest. She was avoiding wielding her Factus powers to heat the air in case people noticed that there was always a bubble of warmth around her. But, it was very tempting in the air-conditioned room. Staring at the TV she waited impatiently for an update on the 'Mer Terrorist Attack.' She fiddled with the tassel fringing on her sleeves. So far it seemed like the news reporters had nothing to go on. They kept on repeating the same news and revealing more CCTV footage. April sighed in frustration. She jumped back as the curtains rustled from the wind emanating from her. She breathed back in and the wind calmed. She looked around to check no one had seen her Tempus outburst. Her powers were getting restless and all she wanted was the news.

"Good morning!"

April turned around in surprise, "Connor!" she exclaimed. April gathered the blanket around her. "I didn't hear you come in."

"Are you okay?" Connor said, standing awkwardly in the archway.

"Oh, I'm just umm frustrated with the lack of information."

Connor looked quizzically at April and came and sat down next to her.

"Are you still frustrated at the loss of your memories?" he asked sympathetically.

"Umm, yes..." April said while shifting slightly further along the couch. She fiddled once more with the tassels. She was frustrated at a lot of things, at this very moment she was most frustrated that Ethan's Iris was still not working. She presumed it was the poisonous water surrounding the island. But, she was hoping she would find a signal somewhere.

"I feel like we should be doing more to help you April," Connor said staring at her intently.

"Connor, you've already done too much. You're letting me stay here until I get my head figured out," April smiled kindly at him. "You heard what the coastguard said on the phone. Until I can remember any details of my life they can't help to relocate me. And I don't want to make a fuss when all I need is time."

"It looks like the weather has calmed down today. Maybe we can try the boat again."

"Maybe," April said non-committedly.

"I suppose after your last boat venture you're not super keen to get back in one," Connor laughed.

April meekly laughed too.

"But there must be a way to trigger your memories." Connor grabbed his tablet from the coffee table and started pulling up quizzes again. April groaned internally, not this again. He kept on finding more quizzes or experiments to try and draw the memories out of her. It was really sweet, but it was getting more and more difficult to keep track of her fictional half-remembered life. Part of her wanted to just tell them the truth. But, she continued with her memory-loss story to help explain why she couldn't contact anyone for help.

"It's fine really Connor. Maybe we should do something fun and see if we can trigger the memories through emotions...." April trailed off, as she had no idea what she was talking about.

"Hmmm, yes that could work," Connor said excitedly. "We should go to the beach, play some volleyball or go for a swim with the dolphins, oh or maybe some jet-skiing now that the sun is coming out."

April nodded in agreement until he reached swimming.

"Uh no, I don't think the beach is a good idea. How about somewhere inland."

"There is a natural pool which I think is fed from a little estuary from the sea, we could go there. Have a picnic. There is a rope swing into the pool," Connor said in a rush. He was leaning closer towards her with each of his suggestions.

Did all his ideas have to involve seawater she groaned internally. She tried a different tactic.

"That sounds like an excellent idea. But, what I mean Connor is that I don't have a ... swimsuit." Is that what they're called? Swimsuits. Connor didn't question her so she mentally high fived herself.

"Oh, I didn't think of that."

April actually felt rather sorry for him. He looked so deflated. She was just about to console him.

"I spoke to Derek, the boat needs some repair work after the storm, but it should be ready to take April to the mainland tomorrow. I could lend you a bikini for today though."

April and Connor turned abruptly at the voice from the archway. Standing there was Megan, Rosetta's assistant.

"Megan, that would be very helpful. Thank you," Connor said.

"That's excellent news," April said standing up in excitement at the prospect of no longer having to feel guilty about enjoying herself on Shell Island. Wait a second no, April realised as she clocked onto the second part of Megan's sentence. April rushed to speak, "Oh no Megan there is no need for you to go to more trouble, thank you for the offer."

"I don't mind, really. It's no trouble," Megan said helpfully "Come and try some on."

Connor was already standing and ready to follow Megan out of the room. April didn't know what to say to stop them.

"Wait," April called frantically. They both turned and stared at her.

"I… ummm…I can't swim. I don't know how to swim." There we go, that sounded plausible she thought. For some reason Connor's face fell. What had she done now? April struggled to see where she went wrong this time.

"You can't swim. April. No wonder you're in shock." Next thing she knew he was back across the room holding onto her hands. She looked up into his eyes and was scared at what she saw there. He was focused on her with such intense care. April had never seen someone look at her like this before. She opened her mouth but didn't know what to say. Just then Alex walked into the room.

As Alex walked in April jumped away from Connor. 'Great' Connor thought, just great. Why did Alex have it so easy with girls? Maybe it was how oblivious he was to awkward situations.

"Wow, we're all up early today. What's the occasion?" Alex asked

"We…we were just planning what we were doing today!" April said.

"April can't swim," Connor provided dejectedly.

"You can't swim, how on earth did you survive?"

"Don't worry about it Alex. I survived and that is all that matters," April said kindly, but her impatience was growing thin with the brothers' attentiveness. She hated feeling helpless or being insinuated that she was. At least Alex hadn't rushed to comfort her.

"I know what we could do today. I could teach you to swim. We can do it in the pool here. I'm a trained lifeguard," Alex said.

Why didn't I think of that Connor thought as he took a step away from April so they were at a normal distance from each other. From here he could still smell the sweet yet salty smell of her hair. It was very distracting. It reminded him of popcorn.

"That sounds fun, do you fancy that April? Everyone should know how to swim," Connor said trying to pull April's attention back to him. She was fiddling with the tassels on her sleeves.

"Yeah, that sounds like fun" April said.

"Cool, I'll ask Peter to make breakfast and then we can head down," Alex said.

"April do you want to come and try on the swimming costumes?" Megan asked from the doorway. She had retreated further out of the room since Alex arrived and was trying to shield her face from the blush that was rapidly spreading.

"Okay, I'll see you guys at breakfast," April replied and followed Megan up the stairs.

Since April's arrival Megan hadn't seen much of her. Rosetta was giving her lots of work in the linen room and the rest of her days were spent preparing the President's suite of rooms for his return. She couldn't believe her luck when she was passing through this morning and overheard Connor and April's conversation. As April followed her into the staff's section of the house she struggled to contain her excitement. Should she come straight out and say, "I know you're a mera," or should she wait and build a friendship with her first? Megan grinned to herself. A real-life mera! It was too exciting. She turned back to smile at April and noticed April was eyeing her oddly before she hastily returned the smile. Clearly, she needed to tone down the excitement.

"My room is just here," Megan said as she gestured towards the door at the end of the hallway.

"Thank you so much for this Megan." April stepped into the room and was warmed to see such a normal bedroom. April was growing restless in the emotionless guestroom she was staying in. It felt like she was intruding on the room's orderliness. By contrast, Megan's room was nice and homely. The window was east facing so Megan's room was lit with natural soft light at this time in the morning. April looked around the room and was surprised to see pictures of the sea from all over the world tacked to the walls. She recognised most of the shorelines, many of which were about an hour's swim from the Hanarian Palace. As Megan busied herself pulling out the swimming costumes, April walked over to her bookcase. Almost all the books were mermaid fictions or factual books about mer. It was astounding. April had never thought that some legged might be fascinated by mer life. She always presumed that most legged hated the mer or simply had no interest at all. She scanned the books and briefly touched their spines. Legged books always fascinated April. The texture was so different from those she read under the sea. April loved to read, it was one of the few things she had in common with her Mum.

"Is there anything there you would like to borrow?" Megan asked,

April jumped around. She paused and looked back at the bookshelf. "I think I would actually, if that's okay. You've already been so generous."

"It's not a problem," Megan said standing awkwardly behind April. She wanted April to know she could trust her. April continued looking across the different titles until she saw one that made her smile. Pulling it off the shelf she flicked through the pages.

"Mer Life for Dummies?" Megan asked.

"Yeah," April said. "Is it okay if I borrow this?"

"Sure."

April continued to flick through the book laughing every so often as she saw some of the chapter titles, 'Breathing Under Water: Not as hard as you think.'

"So here are the swimming costumes. The ensuite is in there if you would like to try them on," Megan said. She gestured towards the door next to her wardrobe. April closed the book, put it on the bed and gathered up the suits Megan had laid out.

~

April made her way to the pool. The beauty of the island impressed her for the first time. The sun was starting to shine and she could feel its warmth seeping into her skin. For a moment she relaxed, then panic and guilt tightened her shoulders. She knew she should be trying harder to get home or at least contact home. But, she was scared. The footage from the bomb kept on replaying in her mind. On repeat she saw herself being picked up and thrown down into the sea. April just wanted to know if her friends and family were okay, but she was equally scared to find out otherwise. She thought of her Dad and imagined his devastation at this terror attack against peace. Everything he believed in had been blasted to pieces in one evening. Looking out at the sea she tried to live in the moment and focus only on the beauty before her.

The pool area was stunning. She suspected that the architect had studied the rock pools of Lakkada. The layering of the pools was very similar. The pool was spread over three levels, the water constantly running towards the sea. She stepped towards the top pool and slowly dipped her foot in the outer rim. Thank goodness, she thought. Her skin remained its normal colour and there was no burning feeling. The water must be fresh for the pool. That solved that problem at least.

About a mile out to sea she could see a pod of dolphins playing in the waves. April grinned in amusement. If the sea wasn't poisonous she could dive in and be with the dolphins in a few short seconds. Yet, here she was about to get swimming lessons from a pair of leggeds. April walked back into the house and through to the conservatory. Alex decided it was best to eat there today. She sat down and waited for the boys to arrive. The front door slammed and a moment later a very sweaty Alex appeared.

"Excellent timing, I think the food is coming shortly," April said smiling.

"Perfect," Alex said. He sat down opposite April and tried to stop his panting.

"Good run?"

"Honestly, it was excellent," Alex grinned. "You sure you don't mind the smell?"

"No, it's fine, you just smell salty to me."

The smell didn't bother April one bit. It reminded her of certain tides.

"Urgh, you smell disgusting," Connor said wrinkling his nose. He walked around the table and pulled up a chair next to April. Connor thought exercising was only worth it if you didn't break out in a sweat.

"Thanks for that," Alex said.

The boys continued to bicker as one of the staff brought breakfast through. The brothers had the same argument every morning.

"Why can't you shower first?"

"Because I'm hungry."

April had learnt to leave them to it. She thanked the server and helped herself to a *pain au chocolat*. They were still warm.

"So, have either of you heard any news about the Peace Treaty bombing?" April ventured.

Alex chewed through his *pain raisin* before answering.

"No, not really."

He was useless when it came to deciding what was interesting information. Connor had reluctantly admitted one morning that Alex was a borderline genius. Therefore, his opinion on what was important differed to most other people. It seemed that Connor doubted his brother's intelligence though.

"Connor?" April asked.

"Not a lot. The news reporters don't seem to have any concrete answers yet. The mermaids haven't done anything further and we haven't retaliated."

"Mer." April couldn't help but correct him. "I see," she said. "Have you spoken to your Dad?"

"Not really, he checked in to say he couldn't come over during the storm. I mentioned you were staying," Connor said.

"You did," April said, her *pain au chocolat* paused in mid-air.

"Yeah, he didn't seem that bothered," Connor said munching again. "Selfish bastard."

April watched Connor carefully then resumed eating her pastry when he didn't say anything further.

"He's got the doubles with him anyway for his appearances," Alex said.

"Doubles?" April asked.

"Exactly, he doesn't need us," Connor said.

"As in body doubles? Don't the public realise it isn't you?" April asked. April had forgotten her confusion that the brothers she met at the Peace Treaty were not the real Alex and Connor. Body doubles would explain the situation.

"I presume so, but after our Mum died they understand Dad's precautions."

April nodded before asking, "Are your Dad and Freddie okay?"

"Yup, they were fine. Really lucky actually, Dad stepped out to make a call five minutes before the bomb went off and Freddie was with him," Connor said.

"That is lucky," April agreed but her tone fell flat.

"I'm just glad we weren't there," Alex chipped in. "Without the mermaid powers, I doubt many people would have survived."

"The mer powers were a blessing," April said.

They lapsed into silence over breakfast. The brothers ate pastry after pastry. Even if she couldn't trust the President, Alex and Connor had done nothing to make her doubt them.

After breakfast, they all went their separate ways to get ready for April's 'swimming lesson'. April sat on her bed and tapped Ethan's Iris in frustration. She oscillated between wanting to know everything that was going on back home and being thankful that she was apart from it all. Ethan's watch sat heavily on her wrist but she was starting to get used to the weight. His pearls were less responsive than hers but she could sense their eagerness to be wielded. April leant out of her open window and looked from side to side. Certain no one could see her; she focused her energy on the ground.

Instantly, her Assurgere powers responded, she located a seed and started to imagine its growth. Soon a sprout sprung from the grass, April fed it more energy her fingertips glowing green as she gripped the ledge. By now her seed was a small sapling. Little flowers started to bud on the end of the branches so she seized her flow of energy before it could become fully grown. Surely no one would notice one more tree in the forest. Ethan's pearls hummed contentedly. "Happy now?" April asked. She walked out of her room and headed down to the pool.

It was already hot outside. April was thankful for the sunglasses and suntan lotion Megan had insisted on lending her. She could feel the sun beating down on her gathering a light sweat on her skin. April made her way down the steps to the lowest pool, her breathing more laboured than she was used to. She claimed a sun lounger under an umbrella and spread out like a starfish to try and cool off.

"There you are!"

April snapped out of her reverie by the voice shouting out the top window.

"I'll be down in a second."

She squinted up but couldn't work out which brother it was. Minutes later Connor walked out onto the pool's patio and started making his way down.

"Hello, are you ready?" he smiled. April could see him trying and failing not to look at her in her bikini. She was in shock herself. The amount of material used on these things was laughable. When she came out of the bathroom she double-checked with Megan that this was the normal amount of skin shown. April also never realised how much hair leggeds grew. She queried Megan about this as well. Fortunately, April had perfected creating a water slice many years ago so that was dealt with quickly. From Connor's facial expression it seemed that she was good looking enough for a legged.

"I'm ready for my lesson."

"Lovely sea isn't it." Connor turned dramatically to the ocean.

"It is lovely," April said trying not to chuckle. As Connor tried to look away while maintaining a conversation, Alex appeared. He reminded her a lot of Ethan. They both seemed to possess the same quality of looking effortlessly confident. But, it was how he made her instantly at ease that really reminded her of her best friend. Alex ran towards the pool and dived straight in.

"Right April, there is nothing to be scared of let's start at the shallow end."

April followed Connor towards the pool. She stopped at the deep end to double check that the water wasn't poisonous. She dipped her foot into the pool and was relieved when it didn't burn.

"Be careful April." Connor warned.

April rolled her eyes. She straightened and stepped forward. Her foot slipped out from underneath her.

"April!" Connor cried.

Then, splash. The moment she hit the water her whole-body tingled. Ethan's Commutavi pearl glowed in anticipation. It ached to not transform back into her mera form. She fought the instinct with every fibre in her body. While she was concentrating on this Alex swam up behind her. He grabbed her around the waist and swam her to the surface. As they broke the surface together, April tried to look scared like someone who couldn't swim but she couldn't help grinning. It may not be the open ocean, but she was back where she belonged.

An hour later Connor and Alex were still marvelling at how quickly April had learnt to swim. She gloried in their praise, not admitting to any slight advantage. She walked down the steps carrying three tumblers of lemonade. She had developed a taste for the stuff. Lemons were a rarity under the sea. Her senses tingled; it was so quiet she could practically hear them plotting something. Sure enough, she rounded the corner and was confronted by two guns. Fortunately, the grins on their faces reassured her that this was all still a game.

"Put the glasses down and we promise we won't hurt you," Connor said.

"It's cold water," Alex said mock seriously.

"Fine," April replied raising her eyebrows over her sunglasses. She walked over to the table, placed the lemonade and her sunglasses down, and then, she suddenly spun and dove into the water without making a splash. The boys jumped in after her. April mused that theoretically she could just stay down here. However, that might reveal her secret. Instead, she went for a sneak attack and swum quickly round them whilst all their bubbles hid her. She waited a moment then kicked upwards and splashed out at them with her arms. She wielded a little of her Factus energy to give momentum to the splash and the result was marvellous. The brothers were swept backwards and lost hold of their guns. While they were underwater April quickly seized the water guns.

"What?" Alex spluttered as he surfaced and got his bearings.

"How did you do that?" Connor asked. Instead of answering, April pulled the trigger and laughed as she blasted them both with cold water.

"That's for throwing me in earlier," she said. At least Connor had been right about one thing, having fun was definitely the best way to distract her.

CHAPTER 16

The heat glared down and Alex rolled over onto his back. He glanced at his watch; it was already 2pm, where had the time gone he thought. He sat up slowly and looked at the other two also zonked out after their hard-core water fight. The heat was really getting too much for him. About to drag his sunbed over to the parasol he spied the water guns abandoned by the pool. Seconds later he was standing at the head of April and Connor's sun beds.

"Sneak Attack!" he shouted and fired.

"Ahhhhh!" April and Connor shouted, both raising their arms to protect themselves.

"At least I cooled you down, you two were in danger of burning!"

"Pfft," April laughed. She actually looked surprisingly dry Alex thought. Connor, on the other hand, was soaked and did not look impressed.

"What did you do that for?"

Quick to relieve the tension Alex announced his new plan.

"How about we go to Beaulieu Falls? I could do with some shade."

"Is the pool filled with fresh water?" April asked.

"Ummm yes," Alex said. "Why?"

"Just wondering. Sounds good to me," April answered brightly.

"Yeah, I'm up for it," Connor said. He leaned over and grabbed a towel to dry his face.

"Meet out front in ten?" Alex asked, he offered his hand to April and pulled her up from her sun bed.

"Sure thing," Connor said as he watched Alex and April make their way back into the house.

Connor and Alex stood in the foyer waiting for April. Connor shuffled from side to side. He was anxious to see April and show her Beaulieu Falls. It was just a shame Alex was coming with them.

"When do you get your grades?" Alex asked.

"18th August," Connor said.

"Then where are you going?" Alex asked leaning against the pillar.

"I want to go to the University of St Andrews," Connor said. He was sure he had told Alex this all before.

"Where is St Andrews?

"In Scotland."

"Scotland?" Alex said. This was the reaction Connor had been receiving for months. Every time he told people he was planning on studying outside of the States people seemed to think he was crazy.

"Yup," Connor said. He could see Alex waiting for further clarification but he stubbornly maintained his silence.

"Why?" Alex eventually asked. He was flicking the car key in and out of its case. He always fidgeted when he was thinking.

"Because."

"Because… right. That clears it up," Alex replied. Connor rolled his eyes at him.

"Because I want to learn about the world. Not just this egocentric version Dad presents to us."

"Right, I'm ready! Sorry to keep you waiting," April said as she wandered into the foyer.

"Are you ready?" she asked looking between the two brothers, her eyebrows lifting. Connor and Alex were standing oddly far apart.

"Yes, we are," Connor replied. He opened the garage door in the foyer and the three made their way inside. Darius kept an assortment of cars on Shell Island. It was one of the few places he could drive in peace without a security detail. Alex beeped open a large, black, open top jeep.

"I'll sit in the back," April said as she clambered in. Connor followed her into the back. He caught Alex smirking in the rear-view mirror. Connor kicked Alex's chair and received a short laugh that annoyed him further.

While Alex drove them towards Beaulieu Falls, Connor turned his attention to April.

"So, what are your plans for after school?" Connor asked in an incredibly chipper voice that earned him a muffled laugh from Alex.

"My plans… eurgh," April paused "I'm weighing up my options at the moment." April gestured vaguely with her hands. "What about you?"

"He wants to go to Scotland," Alex answered. Connor was about to inform Alex he could answer for himself when April said enthusiastically.

"Oh, I love Scotland,"

"You've been?" Connor said leaning forward.

"You're remembering," Alex said excitedly.

"Yes, snippets," April said. She kept on forgetting she was supposed to be suffering from amnesia.

"It's only recent memories I'm struggling with really," she said avoiding their eyes. "My family have a house near the Isle of Skye. Where about do you want to go?"

Connor grinned. This was the most positive anyone had reacted to his Scotland plan. His mind started racing forwards. Maybe he and April would end up there together. They could live in Scotland together.

"St Andrews, they have an excellent international university there."

"The East Coast. Very nice, the seas around St Andrews are stunning. Cold but stunning," April said. She loved the time she spent exploring the British Isles.

"Do you stay in Scotland often? I thought you had a British accent?" Alex said.

"Yeah, I'm kind of from all over the place. My Dad travels a lot for work. He visits all the different…" April paused. "Ummm companies. And stays there for a while to see how they're operating. Moving around so often is probably why I'm struggling to remember the details of where I was," she said trying to cover herself.

"That's so cool," Connor yelped as the jeep went over a hole in the road. Connor fell towards April, his hands landing on her legs. He removed them quickly as if he had been burned. Feeling sorry for his brother Alex intervened.

"Sorry guys, that is amazing though April. I would love to travel the world," Alex said. He slowed down the jeep as they approached a clearing.

"It is exciting. When I was young I loved it. But after a while it does get lonely. I've been in boarding school since I was fourteen."

"Same," Alex said. "Military school from age five. It sucked."

Connor watched April and Alex share a small smile in the mirror.

"Right, we're here," Alex said.

The three took off their seat belts and exited the jeep. They were standing in a clearing of tall, thick grass that went up almost to their knees. Connor caught April looking in bewilderment at all the foliage as she lifted her legs up and over to walk out of the grass. He smiled involuntarily.

"Follow me," Alex said as he started to traipse through the clearing.

"Close your eyes April," Connor said.

"Is this necessary?" April laughed. Alex rolled his eyes up ahead but Connor persevered. He stood behind April and put his hands over her eyes. He was careful to not let the rest of his body touch her.

"Yes, it is." He walked her through the undergrowth from the small clearing. His hands were starting to get clammy and he willed them to not sweat onto April's face.

April tread carefully but she was confident that Connor wouldn't let her fall. In front of her she could feel Alex moving the plants out of her way.

"Okay, you can open them now," Connor said as he gently lifted his hands away.

The sight before her compelled her to move further into the heart of Beaulieu Falls. Trees towered around a natural pool and let in shafting rays of light. Light glistened off the water and then reflected back onto the glossy grey wall of stone that the waterfall thundered down. The pool was large and they had come out at the farthest end from the falls but the tumultuous roar echoed through the clearing. Surrounding the pool were patches of brightly coloured wild flowers. The scene was straight out of one her mertale books. April stood and stared, taking it all in. She just about noticed Alex setting up their towels and chairs for the afternoon.

Connor stood back watching April marvel at the pool. He stepped forward to join her when Alex called.

"Can I get some help over here?"

Connor shook his head and turned around scowling. But, April didn't hear Alex. Eyes trained on the pool she ran forward and dived seamlessly into the water. It was deliciously cool after the humid car ride. She hovered underwater for a moment taking in the clarity of the pool. Then she swam down into its depths. Her every fibre was intent on reaching the bottom. The water was crystal clear and a beautiful storm cloud blue. The pool was deeper than she first presumed, she feared this was an inappropriate amount of time for a legged to be underwater but her compulsion to reach the bottom quelled her fears.

Consumed with her task April lost all other thoughts. Deep within her was a hum as if her heart was trying to escape from her chest. The humming was getting stronger and stronger as she swam deeper into the pool. She pushed through the plant life wielding her Assurgere and Factus powers. She frowned in irritation as she swept her arms in an arc above her head and wielded a white light that shone around her as a protective orb of Factus energy. Something glittering caught her eye and she was drawn further down towards it. It was like a magnet drawing her in. Without thinking she reached out to pick up the shining black stone. The second her fingers made contact, everything stopped for a second and her white Factus orb absorbed back into her. Her brain cleared and she was transported to the deep sea.

She treaded water in a moment of perfect stillness. For miles around she could see nothing, just an endless stretch of ocean. Then a swirling mass began to form in front of her. The sea grew darker and began knitting together until a dark figure appeared before her. Its form kept shifting as the tendrils of the dark sea writhed. April could just make out the form of a Merdevil as the wisps of darkness came together. It towered over her easily as it grew to the size of a killer whale. Yet, she felt oddly calm. She tried to swim towards the Merdevil but was unable to move. She stayed perfectly in place before the giant. Tilting her head, she tried to fathom why it was there.

Then suddenly, a deep cold washed through her, the chill felt sinister. Dark tendrils of energy were writhing towards her. Panic flooded into her brain and the compulsion to reach the Merdevil was broken. She tried to drop the stone but it clung to her hand. Her panic levels increased and April thrust all her powers outwards. She propelled herself upwards and the Merdevil dissipated as she found herself back in the lake.

Finally, she broke through the surface and hurriedly clambered onto the grass. Clouds had gathered overhead and all the waterweeds had shot up. April looked around in alarm. The beautiful flowers were now overgrown with grasses. She looked to her hand where she was still gripping the black stone. A dark flicker ran across her fingers, she blinked and it was gone. April shook her head trying to make sense of what had happened. She felt cold, very cold.

~

Connor and Alex were frozen ten metres away from April. Their faces mirrored the horror of the other's expression. Silence settled over the pool. Even the sudden clouds froze in place hanging ominously above. Only a few seconds had passed but it felt like everyone had stopped for several minutes. The cold was slowly seeping into April's skin. She looked up towards the sky and wielded her Tempus powers to part the clouds and let the sunshine back through to heat her up. April turned to assess the damage she had caused, but the pool area had reverted back to normal. She stood up and whipped the water from her body with her Factus powers as she walked through the grass. A glow of white Factus and navy-blue Tempus energy surrounded her. As she wielded her pearl powers she heard an intake of breath to her left. Suddenly she remembered who she was with. Alex and Connor still hadn't moved. Transfixed by April's actions they were both utterly still. April took a small step towards them and as if the power had been turned back on, they both abruptly burst into life.

"What was that?" Alex said.

"What's going on?" Connor asked.

"Who are you?"

"Are you okay?"

Their questions and exclamations continued and April patiently waited for them to get it out of their system. Her shoulders relaxed slightly and she sighed in relief. Relief that they had not run away and that they seemed to still care about her. She wondered if that would change after she told them the truth. While they continued their shocked ramblings, she tried to figure out the best way to explain everything. Not that she knew how to explain what had just happened. Her pearl glow dimmed and she felt warmer from the sun's rays. The two brothers reached the end of their stream of questions and both said in uncanny unison, "April?" as they beseeched an answer from her.

"I'm a mera," she said simply. "When I swam into the water I was drawn to an object down there." She produced the stone to show them. Their eyes flicked from the stone then back up to her face.

"When I touched it my powers went haywire, it was like I was in the middle of the ocean with a great Merdevil. I'm sorry, I didn't want to lie to you, but I was worried after the Peace Treaty terror acts and with your Dad being the President, you would hate me, or turn me in, and I didn't know what would happen."

The two brothers continued to stare at her expectantly; apparently, this wasn't enough of an explanation. April sat down on the towel Alex had laid out for her and waited for the brothers to join her. They sat but kept their distance. As April explained how she came to be there the brothers' faces swelled with different emotions. April was desperate to find out how they felt about her, but she continued on with her story.

"… When you wanted to go to the beach I panicked because of the poison in the seawater and that's why I pretended I couldn't swim, which led us to here." She finished lamely. April had kept her eyes trained above their heads throughout the story; she lowered her gaze to see what the brothers were thinking. Connor and Alex continued to stare at her in silence. Connor kept on opening his mouth and then closing it again. Alex, on the other hand, remained frozen. April was not sure whose reaction she feared most.

It was Alex who moved first. He came and sat next to April.

"I thought I recognised you," he said.

Connor shifted further forward.

"You're the Princess aren't you?" Alex asked.

"Yes," she said confused that this was what he wanted to discuss.

"April, I have something to tell you. I would have mentioned it sooner but obviously I… we didn't know. In the explosion," Alex paused awkwardly. "Your Mum, she died."

In a million years these would not have been the words April expected Alex to say after she revealed she was a mera.

"No," she said. Her eyes searched his face willing him to tell her it wasn't true. An ache tore through her body; her powers were welling up inside of her, trying to escape, trying to fix the unfixable.

"No," she said again shaking her head. Her pearl powers were overwhelming her as she absorbed what Alex had said. She leant forward and gripped the blanket trying to ground herself.

"April?" Alex asked. Her body was pulsing with different colours and she trembled uncontrollably. With a scream, a stream of energy shot out of April like a wall of light and lifted her into the sky. The power shooting out of her pushed Alex and Connor from her side and they tumbled to the ground. As April cried the light spread out amongst the sky and it started to rain. The winds picked up and the waters started to toss and turn. Her powers sought to mirror the turmoil in her heart. Her body floated in an orb of pulsing light, flickering from pink to yellow, black to blue, green to red. Alex pushed up from his fallen position and crawled his way through the energy radiating from April. The light, wind and rain forced him back but he fought his way towards her. He knelt at the foot of the energy stream. Connor struggled to stand from his position. The wind was racing around Beaulieu Falls and the foliage was growing out of control. He tried to shield himself with his arms from the thundering rain and join Alex, but he kept on being pushed back. "April," Connor called but his voice was lost in the wind.

"April," Alex managed to shout over the storm. "April, listen to me." He pushed up from his knees and succeeded in standing as the wind and light emanating from April sent him backwards.

"April, I'm here for you." His voice seemed to finally get her attention as he noticed her blink. Alex reached up and gently grabbed April's shoulders.

"I know what it's like to lose your Mum," Alex shouted through the noise trying to get April to listen to him. "It's awful, you feel like a piece of you has been lost forever. But, I promise, I will help you get through this." Alex felt April's shoulders shake.

"Alex," she said. Her voice sounded like it was coming from far away.

"April, I'm here."

For a moment, everything froze then the light relocated back into April. The storm stopped, the wind quietened and the waters calmed. April collapsed to the ground in exhaustion bringing Alex down with her. Alex managed to sit up. He pulled the unconscious April onto his lap and gathered her in his arms.

"You're going to be okay April. I'm here for you okay." Alex checked that her breathing was steady. Connor looked around in shock.

"What are we going to do?" he asked.

"What do you mean?" Alex asked.

"How are we going to protect her? All the staff on the island will have seen that explosion."

"Just calm down okay, no one will think April's involved."

Connor continued to stand and stare.

"Calm down Connor."

"I am calm," Connor said as he dragged his hands over his head.

"What's your problem? April is your friend. We can't let her down now. I don't believe a word Dad has been saying."

"No, you're right, neither do I." Connor started pacing. "I'm just scared." He walked towards Alex and April and stopped at an awkward arm's length distance. "Is she okay?" he asked more tenderly than he had meant to.

"Yes, I think she's just exhausted. That was a lot of power she just released. And she might be in emotional shock," he said looking down to study her face.

"I can't believe she's a mermaid," Connor said. Alex shook his head not taking his eyes off April.

"Shall we head back to the house?" Connor asked looking around.

Alex adjusted April and stood up in one fluid movement while carrying her.

"Let's get out of here."

CHAPTER 17

"Arrghhh!"

The scream echoed through the underwater maze of the Yeltan caves. Across every department mer stopped what they were doing and swam towards the noise. Guards abandoned their posts to investigate fearing a potential security breach. The echoing made the screams sound as if they were coming from all different directions. Mer swam about in disarray trying to find the source. The security team near the Royal chambers were first to feel the pulsating water coming from the inner sanctum of Kayla's quarters. They swam against the current as it continued to surge towards them. Then suddenly the screaming stopped. Finally, the security team made it to the door of the Royal suite. They entered and followed the rolling waves to the kitchen.

"How do we get in?" one of the guards asked clinging to the cave wall to stop from being pushed away by the current.

"The waves are too strong," another guard said. The guard glanced at the mer who had joined them. None of them wore the white stripes that distinguished the Factus pearl wielders.

"Stay back," a voice boomed. Suddenly the water stilled and the ends of the surging waves crashed into the walls of the hallway. Demetrius swam through the entrance.

"You two guard the doors. The rest of you follow me." Demetrius swam forward towards the kitchen door, and carefully opened it. His fingertips glowed white in preparation. He took in the disturbing scene, table overturned, chairs shattered, cutlery floating around the room and at the centre was Kayla. The debris around the room floated in an orbit around her. The princess jerked with pulses of light and with each shudder energy ripped through her body and manifested in the waves surging through Yelta. Demetrius kicked his tail hard to try and reach Kayla. His powers were useless now he was in the room. He scanned the area trying to find a way to Kayla's side when suddenly she stilled. Everything hovered in place for a moment.

"April," Kayla uttered still pulsing with light. Then suddenly the glowing stopped and Kayla gasped in pain as she collapsed to the ground.

~

For over two hours Kayla lay awake in the infirmary. She maintained her stillness. The bubbles issuing from her mouth kept a regulated slowness. It was times like these that she was incredibly thankful for her military training. Control in all things was necessary. She couldn't lose control again. But, the problem was, that it hadn't been her. It was April. It was crazy and unexplainable but April took over her body. The pain had been excruciating. Kayla was certain April didn't survive. Pain was something Kayla was used to dealing with. She had held out through all the pain and allowed April to channel the energy through her body. Until in an instant April's presence vanished. The emptiness and sudden loss of energy still made her feel weak. She was down two family members in one week. It was just her and her Dad now. Kayla lay in her bed and tried to feel nothing.

Another hour passed and then another and she continued to feign sleep. Lying in the hospital bed she could pretend that everything was okay. She didn't want to get up and face reality. Right here and right now nothing was wrong. Pressing the button beside her bed she waited for the blissful numbness of her sedatives to run through her veins and send her back to sleep. But, when another morning came the numbness began to fade and what was left was pure anger. Whoever had done this to her family was going to pay. She raised herself up and flicked the covers off with her tail. Without a backward glance at her hospital bed, she swam out of the room and headed for the Intelligence Department at the centre of Yelta. There were some perks to being in charge she thought as she swam past the nurses and guards with no questions asked.

Kayla made her way to the ID. She floated in place while the guard scanned her tail fin. The guard's mouth opened as if to question her but Kayla silenced him with a scowl. Swimming past Iris pads of all shapes and sizes that displayed endless charts and graphs and reams of text, she made her way to the centre of the room. She silently drifted round to the energy map. It charted mer power usage and helped to keep track of potential new pearl sources. But, it also read large energy readings from pearl wielders. April's lack of emotional control over her powers caused many false alarms. April's level of control had never been great. She expended vast amounts of power performing some of the simplest of pearl commands. The intensity of her power the other day must have been off the chart. Kayla shook her head and rubbed her eyebrows, she didn't want to think about her sister.

She approached the Iris Map and started flicking through the accompanying chart until she found this week's energy listings. She tried to tap through the water screen to make it appear in descending order. Scanning in frustration for the right button she drummed her fingers. Yes, there we go Kayla thought leaning forward. An energy reading of 87% was at the top. The next highest reading came in at 30%. What had happened to April to cause her to unleash so much energy, Kayla thought. Questions and suspicions pulsed through Kayla as she swallowed back the sob that had formed in her throat. Double tapping on the energy reading to pull up the statistics, she streamed the information onto her Yelta Iris.

The corresponding map zoomed into the location of the power surge. The island was not far from the Peace Treaty peninsula. A message popped up on her Yelta Iris informing her that the Junior War Council was assembled and awaiting her orders. As the data finished downloading she swam from the room, making a mental note to berate the ID later for not paying more attention to what critical information mer were accessing.

~

Sitting at the head of the strategic table in the cave, Kayla realised that for the first time in this room she wasn't nervous. For once she felt in complete control. She was the best mera to lead this fight. Kayla was going to fight this war to reinstate peace for her Dad and avenge her Mum and April. She flicked the downloaded images from her Yelta Iris into the water so everyone could see. She floated down into her chair and waited for the tips of her golden hair to float down onto her shoulders. Everything in order, she began her meeting.

"Do we have any details about who owns this Island?" Kayla asked and silenced the table. This team were far less informed than the leaders of the War Council but their methods and ideologies were more aligned with Kayla's.

"Not yet Your Highness. How would you like us to proceed?"

"I .."

A junior member of the team interrupted her, "Sorry, Your Highness. I think I have found something." He looked apologetically up at her before continuing to speak. Kayla nodded at him. Never had she felt so powerful. Not even when she took on the master meritian warriors.

"I was running the location coordinates through all the departments across government to see if they had any information. And, the environmental department does." As he spoke he flicked a revolving picture of the island from his Iris pad into the water.

"See these purple lines surrounding the island? This represents a toxic gulf of water. From here to inland the water is poisonous to mer. According to these figures they have been poisonous since one month before the Peace Conference. And it doesn't stop there." He zoomed out on the map. Kayla shared a look with Demetrius. The poisoned waters were all around American government-owned land. Kayla zoned back to what the junior member was saying.

"You see, several of these islands and coastlines they have the same purple lines. They thought it was some mutant coral. But..."

"But, it could be a weapon. A weapon against us," Naomi one of the strategic experts interjected.

"All of these areas should be investigated. If April is held in one of them all these areas could be headquarters or prisons," the junior said.

Kayla nodded impressed. These juniors had jumped to the heart of the problem in a matter of minutes.

"The poisoned waters surround areas controlled by the US military and government," she said slowly. "The leaders of the War Council are monitoring them. However, I would like you to investigate this Island please," she paused for a moment smoothing her hair behind her ear.

"We will launch a scout group on Island X to find out whether there are any prisoners there, or if April washed up there or ...." Kayla paused unsure of what she was saying. She took a deep breath. "In the meantime can you, Naomi, look into what inhabits this Island? Give us as much information before we reach Island X. And..."

"Jared," the junior member supplied as Kayla paused.

"Jared, can you contact the development team. I want them to know that they have Yelta's support. We need them to analyse the poison, find its source and create a neutraliser so we can safely reach the islands."

Jared nodded as he typed quickly on his Yelta Iris, his fingers flying over the screen.

"Let's start planning then," she said with a tight smile.

At Kayla's words the table burst into action. Logistics planning commenced immediately. Her grief had intensified her interest in authority. It was a lot easier to work with the Junior War Council. She interjected once or twice to make sure she was leading the reconnaissance into Island X but other than that she was happy to let these council members do their job. Her mind drifted to her Dad. Should she tell him about April when she had no concrete proof? The more Kayla thought about it the less certain she became. Now that her body had had time to recover from the extreme pressure she could not be sure. The great emptiness had disappeared. She was thinking logically again. As the council meeting came to an end Kayla came to a new conclusion.

"The mission to Island X is going to be a rescue mission. We will save her Royal Highness Princess April and bring her home to join the fight."

"Sorry Your Highness, but how do you know April is there?" Kayla recognised the voice even though he didn't bother to assert himself. Gregor, one of the longest-serving members of the War Council, never failed to doubt her plans. He swam through the entrance to the chamber.

"The disturbance which I'm sure you all felt recently was because of a power surge from my sister. She channelled some of her energy through my body." As Kayla spoke she flicked the data from her Iris pearl onto the screen. "As you can see these mer power readings are astronomical and coincide with the time of April's distress. The location…" she said while scrolling down to the map "of this burst is the same as one of the island's surrounded by poisoned waters. I know that my sister is on that island, and we will rescue her," Kayla said definitively to Gregor. She was not ready to face her sister's death so soon after losing her Mum. She was on a rescue mission. Kayla put aside the terrifying thought that it might be her sister's body she was bringing back. She stared down Gregor until he nodded his approval. Gregor swam around the table looking over the notes the Junior Council had in front of them.

"Was there anything you required?" Kayla asked her eyes unblinking as she focused on Gregor.

"No," Gregor said with a smile raising his head. "Your Highness." He bowed minutely still smiling up at her.

"Meeting adjourned then." Kayla swam from the chamber without another look at Gregor.

CHAPTER 18

Frederick enjoyed inflicting pain. That was the first thing Ethan learnt as he was marched through the facility by his leash. Frederick took no care to stop Ethan from being bounced from corner to corner of the corridor. If he fell Frederick kept on walking. When Ethan finally stumbled into the laboratory of choice for today he squinted. The bright light seemed to permanently stream through the windows in this facility. Ethan mused to himself that he had probably never seen so much white in his life.

"Arghhh," Ethan screamed mid-thought as his neck was wrenched to the right. Frederick had sent the leash's electronic connection to the head of a chair. Ethan twisted in the chair until he found a somewhat comfortable sitting position.

He sat and watched Frederick move around the room. He was well built but there was a reptilian quality to his features and movements that hindered him from traditional handsomeness. He flicked his eyes from object to object with cold calculation. Frederick moved out of Ethan's sight as he disappeared into a back room. Ethan tried to get his bearings. He hadn't been in this lab before. He looked around at the equipment to see if anything was familiar from Flotsam College. He saw drilling tools of some form and laser machinery. But most of the equipment was well beyond his knowledge. Lydia hadn't been lying - this was an experimental lab. Every time Ethan was dragged to a different lab he was shocked at how much equipment Lydia and Frederick had access to. Before Frederick returned to the room Ethan could feel a shift in the air. His hands relaxed in his lap and his leg stopped twitching. His senses were heightened and a feeling of warmth and strength washed over him. Immediately, after relishing in his new health a sense of dread sunk through him. Ethan turned his head toward the door. He knew what had created this feeling; it could only be April's pearls.

"Your flushed appearance betrays you," Frederick laughed as he walked into the lab. He placed a box in front of Ethan just out of reach.

"We've been successful with our pearl tests before. But, with the acquisition of this piece." He gestured at the box. "Our efforts have become futile. I'm hoping you can help."

Frederick moved to lean against the window. Ethan's sense of dread increased. What were they going to ask of him? He had a pretty good feeling he was incapable of helping regardless of whether he wanted too or not.

"You see, the mer have an unfair advantage. You stole all the power for yourselves, and Lydia and I are working to readdress this imbalance. We plan to make your powers accessible to all."

"They aren't accessible to all," Ethan interjected. Frederick's head snapped around in obvious anger. "It's a unique gift. Everyone has different abilities and capabilities when it comes to wielding the pearls."

The glint in Frederick's eyes darkened but Ethan ignored him.

"Even, if I did help you, which I presume is what you need. Right, help."

Frederick's eyes narrowed.

"Only the first born in the royal bloodline has ever been able to control all the pearls. You have the wrong mer. Aghhhh!"

Bright red spots burst into Ethan's vision. His head felt like it was exploding. What was happening he panicked? He tried to bring his hands up to cradle his head but his wrists were tethered to his armrests with another blue laser. He squinted up to look at Frederick's smirking face and the stabbing vanished leaving a dull ache in its place.

"You will help," Frederick said striding over to the table. "You think you know it all don't you," Frederick said as he leant against one of the lab tabletops.

"'It's a unique gift'," he cruelly mimicked. "Well, we've harnessed it. You're not the only mer to come through here."

Ethan's face betrayed his shock as Frederick laughed again. "We've already experimented on you," Frederick said. "Your injuries from the bombs were healed by energy extracted from the Curo pearls."

"No," Ethan said. He struggled to recall if he had heard of such a thing before.

"Yes," Frederick smiled.

Frederick moved his fingers minutely to press on his control cuff. With a smile, he sent another shock through Ethan. Ethan writhed in pain in his chair. His wrists strained against the lasers holding him down until red welts appeared.

"You're going to find a way to release the energy inside these pearls," Frederick said. "I suggest you get to work."

He turned and exited the room. Ethan put his head into his hands, relieved to find that he had full movement of them again. What was he going to do he thought. He couldn't release the powers. He wouldn't release them even if he could. He leant forward to test his neck leash. Standing carefully, he moved over to the box. He lifted the lid and there, nestled inside the box, lay the most beautiful pearl necklace. All nine pearls glimmered with diamonds, sapphires, emeralds and rubies linking the pearls together. He picked up the necklace and walked over to the window. His electronic leash at least allowed him this privilege. He looked down at the pearl necklace in his hands and leaned his head against the fortified window.

"Where are you April?" he whispered.

~

The sunrise today was unbelievable. Ethan had to hand it to Lydia, she couldn't have chosen a more beautiful location for her scientific experiments. The light glistened off the waves and the pale pink rays mixed perfectly with the new blue of the sky. Ethan reckoned he'd been returning to this lab for over a week now. He couldn't be sure though. Often Frederick became so frustrated with a lack of results that the ensuing torture meant Ethan passed out in pain. He had no idea how long these bouts of unconsciousness lasted. He looked at his reflection in the window. His naturally tanned skin looked pale and dark circles under his eyes were now a permanent feature. Bruises spread out across his arms in varying shades depending on their age. Despite this, Ethan felt relatively healthy. He was given regular meals and was forced to exercise often. He almost laughed at the thought. He was living in hell and was scared to the point of numbness, but at least with some make-up on, he would look right as rain.

He looked down to April's necklace wrapped twice around his wrist. It went some way to making up for the lack of his watch. He looked around the room. Knowing that other mer had been through this same hell made the lab seem even more sinister with its clinical cleanliness. There was no trace of the previous mer. Once again, he focused his energy on the Curo pearl. Straining every fibre of his being he tried to connect with its energy.

"Urghhhh!"

This was futile. What did they want from him? He couldn't even wield the Curo pearl to stop his headache. He started to wander aimlessly around the room, opening drawers and closing them again. He had given up hope that he would find anything of use. But it gave him something to do. Wandering around agitatedly he eventually made his way to the window again and slunk to the ground. He went over his options of escape again and again but unless he could break the electric tether he could see no way out. A door slammed outside the room and Ethan sprang to attention. Moving up from the floor he strode over to one of the lab desks so he could look like he was doing something. A polite knock on the door sounded. That was odd thought Ethan, he hadn't been granted the dignity of a knock before. After no one entered Ethan jokingly called, "Come in?"

In marched a young man dressed unsurprisingly all in white saying, "Your presence is requested at breakfast with Frederick. He asks that you follow me."

"He asks?"

Before Ethan had finished the question, his electric leash had attached itself to the server's wrist cuff.

"Right, I see."

Ethan slid off his chair and made his way towards the door.

"So where are we going?" Ethan asked. "Does Frederick have something special in mind? ...Is this his idea of a date?" Ethan laughed. The man stood still and minutely raised his eyebrows. Great, no information was coming out of his escort. Their journey was made in silence. Ethan was pretty certain that they were going somewhere in the facility that he hadn't been before. He followed obediently. He wiped his sweaty palms against his white uniform and continued his mental mapping of the corridors.

"Pancakes? That is your breakfast food of choice?" Ethan said stepping into the room. 'Room' was probably a bit of an understatement. It was a vast kitchen into lounge area tastefully decorated in duck egg blue with subtle touches of lemon yellow. Never before had Ethan been so grateful to see some colour. The white was beginning to oppress his spirits.

"That will be all Oliver." Frederick gestured and Ethan was immediately attached to the chair opposite Frederick. He took this as a gentle suggestion and went and took his seat.

"Thank you for joining me Ethan," Frederick said.

"As if I had a choice," Ethan muttered.

Frederick continued, ignoring him. "Please have some breakfast." He waved at the heavily laden table.

Ethan turned his eyes back towards the table, other than pancakes there were waffles, strawberries, an array of sauces and the traditional lemon and sugar. When he visited legged hotels with his Dad he always ordered the waffles. They possessed a crispness that was difficult to achieve underwater.

"Thank you," Ethan said.

Frederick took his time eating breakfast and Ethan started to get nervous again.

He cautiously helped himself to a plate of waffles and tried some of the different sauces. Frederick ate in silence. Ethan looked around the room, at his food, in his lap anywhere but at Frederick whose silence was unnerving him. Subconsciously, he started to pick at the skin around his nails.

"So, I suppose you're wondering why I brought you here Ethan?" Frederick said. Ethan looked up startled.

"I brought you here because we have decided to change tactics." Ethan felt the leash release him.

"Guards."

CHAPTER 19

"Your Majesty?" Clyde stuck his head around the door into the King's study. "May I enter?" The King put down the papers he was reading and looked wearily out at the darkening waters beyond his window.

"Of course. What can I do for you?" Nathaniel asked. Clyde swam through the door and clocked the exhaustion on Nathaniel's face. The room was immaculate as usual but the photos of Freya were hidden from sight. He didn't want to add to the King's pain, but he couldn't delay this conversation any longer.

"Your Majesty, I've been looking into April's early displays of power. And I think I may have found something," Clyde said.

Nathaniel looked up, his face was composed but the fear in his eyes was real.

"I don't want to dredge up the past considering your recent loss, but..." Clyde continued with determination. He swished his tail in the water as he bobbed from side to side.

"I understand," Nathaniel replied. He rubbed his forehead and gestured for Clyde to sit down in the chair opposite his desk. "What have you found?"

"Thank you. You stated yourself, sire, that nothing of this kind had ever happened before. But, none the less I felt that the Royal Archive was the place to look. What I didn't expect was that I wouldn't have to look too far. Do you remember the Tale of the Twins Your Majesty?"

King Nathaniel stiffened. "The old fish tale? Please tell me you're not wasting my time with a merita's story?" Nathaniel said, a touch of anger seeping into his voice.

"I promise I'm not Your Majesty. That story, however, holds the key. I tracked down Queen Freya's maid and she showed me something." Clyde's tail started to twitch. "I think your wife was hiding the truth from you."

"How dare you?" The water chilled in the room, as Nathaniel floated to his full height. "How dare you accuse the Queen?"

"Please Your Majesty, were you aware she kept a diary?"

"A diary?" Nathaniel hesitated.

"Yes. She started one after her post-natal depression with the twins, to help her gain some perspective."

Nathaniel's face darkened at the mention of the twins. It was an unwritten rule that no one mentioned them. But, Clyde pressed on. "She didn't write in it often. It reads like short fact sheets as if..."

"You read it," Nathaniel accused coldly his eyes unblinking.

"Only parts of it Your Majesty, and I think you should too. Please, I have the papers here. Just take a look through them." Clyde swam to his full height and produced the seaweed press papers. He placed them onto the King's desk.

"You need to read these. I will report back in the morning and see if you reached the same conclusion I did," Clyde hesitated and opened his mouth to say more, but instead he swam to the door. "Goodnight Your Majesty. I hope you sleep well."

Left alone Nathaniel swam up from his desk. Since the loss of Freya, he avoided anything that could remind him of her. All his efforts were invested in finding his daughter and uncovering who was behind the Peace Treaty bombing. He floated over to his windowsill and looked out. The palace was in lockdown but he insisted that he still had access to his window. From here he had the best view of Hanaria. At this late hour, the dark waters were spotted with light from the city below. A song reached his ears. Nathaniel looked into the distance. A pod of male humpback whales were swimming towards the city. He let their melody wash over him as they sang in a round. His Communico pearl hummed as it joined in with the melody.

And we dance together through the sea,
By your side I am free.
Blue skies above and darkness below,
By your side wherever you go.

Nathaniel floated in the windowsill with his eyes shut. The timelessness of the humpback whales reminded him of his insignificance. One day, all this would be gone. The humpbacks soon passed over and Nathaniel opened his eyes. He turned away from the window and swam back over to his desk. The papers stared up at him. He immediately recognised the elaborate swirl of his wife's handwriting. His heart clenched as he took in her favourite butter yellow ink on the dark green paper. Even this evidence of her existence threatened to overwhelm him. But, he couldn't fall apart. April, Kayla and the seven seas depended on him. He grasped the papers and left his study.

Swimming down the corridor in the top west wing turret, he swam towards the east wing. Not wanting to be disturbed he was thankful he didn't bump into too many members of the palace staff. He stopped outside Freya's library. It was her favourite place in all of the seven seas. Without hesitating he pushed open the door and swam in. He wasn't sure what he expected to find, maybe some physical sign of his wife's absence. But, nothing had changed.

The floor to ceiling bookshelves still stood in place. The elaborate paintings on the floor were still as bright. They swirled around the library showing montages of different mer myths and legends; quotes brought the images to life. He swam into the centre of the room and could almost feel his wife's presence there with him. He remembered the numerous occasions they fell asleep in front of the warm water stove back before he ascended the throne, back when life was simple. This library had been their haven. Nathaniel moved slowly through the library making his way to the balcony doors. Outside their bench sat waiting for him. He lowered himself down and stared out to sea. Finally, he lifted the pages and began to read.

13ᵗʰ July 1995

Another question to you diary - what do you do when you are scared for your children? The birth of the twins was stressful enough. The pressure of producing the royal bloodline, and somehow, I managed to mess it up. Having twins in the family is so rare no one knew what would happen. I was determined, however, that they would both thrive. Anthony and Julia are inseparable. They function as two halves of one whole. I hoped they could share the position. They share the powers of the pearls each showing unique abilities even at their young age. I presumed that they would share the throne. But, now I'm not so sure.

April is scaring me. I am scared for the twins and I am scared for her and of her. From birth, she was clearly a powerful pearl wielder. She and Nate had an instant bond, unlike the slow process he went through with the twins. Surely, she can't command them all. But, when April cries it starts to rain, if she is angry the water boils and if you get her giggling a rainbow appears. When she is happy random plants start flowering, and her favourite game is to manoeuvre the water in her air bath so none of the air touches her. All the animals love her and she never becomes ill. She is a protégé. She is a mini Nathaniel. Every day I watch them together and I resent her. I resent my own daughter, am I an awful mum for begrudging the connection they share?

Nate's Mother warned me about the bond between firstborns. Was this what she was talking about? My fears are mounting for the twins. Is April a threat to them? But, the twins dote on April. They are the only mer she behaves for.

Today while visiting the Kara Land Palace, Anthony and Julia ran into the sea and shot off. April crawled in after them and was swimming under the watch of her nanny. According to Perdita, April suddenly popped to the surface and started crying. Perdita stood up and called to her trying to encourage her to come ashore and explain her problem. The screaming continued and the clouds were gathering. Perdita said she quickly dove into the water to calm April before she caused a storm. Perdita reached April and cradled her in her arms. She could feel a weird heat surrounding April. April continued to cry so Perdita swam deeper into the sea to calm April and surround her by the soothing water. As she swam deeper April's screaming lessened to sobs. She wielded her Curo powers, but weak as they are, she couldn't detect anything wrong with April. Apparently, if anything, April seemed stronger than her last check-

up. April started to look happier and her sobs turned into hiccups. Perdita said that by then the sun was shining back down through the sea and the clouds had parted. April suddenly wriggled out of her arms and darted into the rocks. Perdita followed her good-naturedly. April is, according to Perdita, the most temperamental merita she has ever looked after. As Perdita neared April, who was merrily prodding a sea cucumber, she noticed that the twins were lying on the seafloor. Perdita called out to them. They didn't respond. There was something unnatural about their stillness. Perdita swam towards them and shuddered as the water turned colder. She reached them and saw they were unconscious with a slow stream of bubbles issuing from their mouths. Perdita gathered them into her arms and said she was shocked to feel that they were both ice cold. Perdita poured her Curo power into the twins trying to warm them up.

Holding Anthony and Julia, she swam towards April. As Perdita swam towards her, April swam up to her brother and sister and touched them to see what was wrong. Blue Curo energy flowed from April to the twins. Only one year old and her power was far superior to Perdita's. Almost instantly, the twins started blinking their eyes open and colour and heat returned to them. As they opened their eyes completely, April uttered one word 'play?' When Perdita recounted this to me I was concerned about the twins' health. But, after seeing them myself they seem completely fine. The twins don't recall what happened. They just remember feeling really cold. They wanted to know if April was okay as well. I went to see April and I could tell, that in one short day apart she had grown stronger. I fear for the twins. What is happening?

Nathaniel buried his head in his hands unwilling to continue reading. What had Freya kept from him? He scoured his brain trying to remember any conversations they had concerning April. April and he had always had a closer relationship than she and Freya. Was this why? All those times April had cried to him claiming that her Mum didn't like her. Perhaps there was some truth to it. Freya could never forgive the mer who she believed was a danger to her firstborns, even if it was her own daughter? The strictness and insistence on control with April, was it all to stop her from gaining more power?

His head swam with memories from when Anthony and Julia were discovered dead. He had always presumed, as horrible as it was, that it was because they were twins that their pearl powers consumed them. It was like the mertale. Twins weren't able to fulfil the first-born destiny. April had been born with access to all the pearls from the beginning. Clyde was right. With the fresh pain of Anthony and Julia's death in his heart, Nathaniel reached out to his own Curo pearl. One night won't hurt he thought as a sky-blue glow spread out from his medallion and into his heart.

CHAPTER 20

The drive back to the house was long. April drifted in and out of consciousness. Each time she went under again rapid, vivid pearl flashbacks blasted through her mind. It was as if her powers were struggling to remember every pearl command she had ever performed. Connor kept a tight hold of April as Alex drove the car back to the house. Her twitching body pulsed with changing colours of light.

"What's going on back there?"

"I don't know," Connor replied looking to Alex in fear, "I think these are the colours of the pearls. She's burning up."

Connor grasped April tighter.

"Please be okay," he whispered as he leant down and kissed her on the forehead. "Please." He studied her face and noticed a sheen of sweat gathering at her hairline.

She was a mermaid. He couldn't believe it. All his life the mer people had fascinated him. The mer stories his Mum told him as a child were his favourites. Black Pearl, The Three Whales, The Tale of the Twins, Prince Triton, he could still remember them now. His favourite subject at school was marine biology and now he could actually meet someone from the ocean. April could answer all his questions. Together they could unravel the mer and human divide. Connor stopped himself mid-thought. April. She seemed so fragile in his arms, but he didn't know how to help her.

"Alex, how did you calm April down?"

"Ummm, I spoke to her and I rubbed her back. That stopped the storm at least." Alex gripped the steering wheel; he was trying to avoid the many potholes in the dirt track.

"I think I should try and keep her awake. The light intensifies when she goes unconscious," Connor said.

"Good idea. We're almost home. You're going to be okay April," Alex said confidently. But, his eyes kept on darting to the rear-view mirror to check on her.

"April, can you hear me?" Connor asked. April stirred slightly and gripped onto Connor's arm. "April, it's going to be okay. I'm going to look after you. We don't care that you're a mermaid. But, you need to help me. You need to tell me how I can help you. How to stop the flashing lights?" He gave a feeble laugh. "I'm not very good at this I know," Connor said.

April opened her mouth but her words came out as a whisper.

"April?" Connor leaned down closer towards her.

"Tell me a story, please," April murmured.

"Oh okay," Connor looked down at April as she nestled her head into his chest. Another shock of light pulsed through her body and she grimaced in pain.

"I need something to concentrate on," she said through gritted teeth. "Help me."

"I love mermaids," Connor started dropping his voice.

"Mer," April interrupted.

Connor chuckled; even in intense pain, she was still sassy. "Right sorry, I love mera and mer for that matter. We have lots of myths and legends about your people. My Mum, she used to tell us the stories when we were younger. Alex loved the Prince Triton stories, I thought they were a bit too far-fetched, to be honest."

"Heyyy," Alex interrupted as April choked out a small laugh. Connor ignored Alex and continued trying to occupy April's attention.

"I wonder if they're the same stories as the ones you would have been told as a child. Do you want to hear my favourite?" Connor asked. April smiled with her eyes still shut. Connor took this as a sign to continue.

"Once upon a time there was a beautiful young maiden. She grew up on her Father's farm high up in the mountains. Every day she would go out and take the sheep across the meadows and see them safely to their different pastures. But, one day a horrific storm hit the farm and her Father was killed as a tree struck by lightning fell. A fire raged destroying the farm and killing off all the sheep and goats. Shella was left alone. A week passed as she sobbed in one of the mountain caves. What was she to do next?"

Connor looked down at April as he gained confidence. He felt awkward holding her in his arms, but at the same time, he never wanted to let her go. Her eyes were now open so he continued.

"Shella plucked up the courage and decided to explore the remains of the farm. But, there was nothing left. Filled with despair Shella determined to leave and never return. Strengthened by her newfound freedom she started walking. She walked and walked down the mountains. Two weeks later she stumbled across a town. Knocking on the first door she came to she collapsed on the porch. Next thing she knew she woke up in a warm, cosy bed. Too exhausted and sad to care where she was, she just lay there. 'Hello,' a voice said. Shella was startled. A man had been there all along. Shella looked up and instantly fell in love. The man was the owner of a seaside pub and she was asleep in his bed. After a brief courtship, they married. In a year she gave birth to a set of twins, two beautiful baby girls. One day when she was down by the sea the twins disappeared. Shella shouted and looked everywhere. Then out of the sea walked her husband holding her two babies, but they had tails. She fainted in shock."

April chuckled. "So dramatic," she said faintly with her eyes half closed.

"May I continue?" Connor asked indignantly. He caught Alex rolling his eyes in the rear-view mirror. April nodded with a small smile.

"So yes, she fainted and when she came around her husband explained everything. He was a banished mer Prince. His Father had tried to force him to start a war against the neighbouring mer tribe. When he refused he was exiled. Shella was confused but she loved him no less. She also loved her two baby mermaids, I mean meras. Watching them play with their waterpower's was one of her favourite activities. The next year she fell pregnant again. This time she gave birth to a baby boy. Right from the beginning, his powers were extraordinary. They were unlike anything Shella had seen before. When he fell asleep by the sea the waves moved in and out in time to his breath. Father and son bonded instantly, they adored each other. The baby boy loved to follow his sisters around too and tried to join in their games. But one day, down by the beach her son fell and hit his head. Shella panicked as she crouched by him, he wasn't breathing. Her husband wasn't near so Shella called to her girls to help. As the twins approached him they used their healing powers to help. But, suddenly the light drained out of them. Her daughters started crying in pain, and in horror Shella pulled her girls away from her son. But it was too late. As their eyes closed and they turned cold, her baby boy awoke and started crying. Her husband was the heir to the throne, and thus he could only have one true heir. The twins were too weak with the powers of the pearls divided and so the baby boy's powers, with a life of their own, fed off the twin's kindness to ensure his own rule. Shella was grief-stricken. She was never able to look at her son in quite the same way again. But, she knew, that one day he would be an almighty ruler of the seven seas."

"What do you think? Pretty dark and mysterious eh."

"Come on, it's only a children's story," Alex said, but he looked over at April and noticed that she was even paler than before.

"I know that story. We tell it differently. The Tale of the Twins," April said her voice weak with exhaustion. It was as if she had been drained of all energy and all care. All she wanted was to sleep and feel nothing.

"Oh," Connor said deflated, worried that his story-telling had not been up to par.

"Oh no, it wasn't your fault. It's just the way I was told the story. The reason for the draining was never explained as a matter of legitimacy, just powers gone rogue, the baby mer prince is evil in our version."

Connor and Alex exchanged confused looks in the front mirror.

"It's only a story April. Don't worry about it," Alex assured her.

April tried to smile. She closed her eyes, leant back into Connor's shoulder and fell into a restless sleep.

CHAPTER 21

A bobbing motion jolted April to consciousness. Panic gripped her. Then the realisation came crashing down around her - her Mum, her home, her skin. April's breathing got faster and faster and she tried to move. Then she felt the warmth around her and the soft fabric rubbing up and down her back. Looking around she realised she was back in Alex's arms. It was dusk. The trip back home must have taken longer than their initial journey. The safety and comfort of Alex's arms made her reluctant to tell the brothers that she was awake. For now, it was a relief to just be looked after. It was a relief that he was still there holding her after all he had learned.

"I could have held her," Connor's petulant voice piped up.

"But you didn't. Now stop whining and open the door."

April smiled at their bickering.

"Thank you," Alex strode into the room while Connor followed behind him.

"I wasn't whining. I'm merely saying you don't have to leap in and play the hero every time. April is just as much my friend. Ouch. Why'd you stop?" Connor rubbed his head after walking straight into Alex and looked up.

"Dad!?" Connor said.

"General Tarn, umm the rest of the council." Alex nodded at the group of people assembled in the conservatory. A large table had been set up in the middle of the room and their Dad was sitting at the head.

April locked eyes with Connor and he stepped forward instinctively to protect her.

"Boys, pack your bags. We're leaving," President Darius said. April recognised his melodic voice from the Peace Treaty.

Alex and Connor stood bewildered in the doorway. April tensed and made to get up but Alex shook his head in a minuscule motion so only she could see.

"Dad, April is staying with us at the moment. Can she come too?"

Darius, acknowledged April in Alex's arms and gave him a disapproving look.

"Very well. The jet leaves at 8pm sharp."

Connor nodded. The President and the assembled committee resumed talking and ignored the three in the hallway. Connor paused for a moment. He looked to Alex who flicked his eyes towards the stairs. Connor turned on his heels and led them up upstairs.

"Megan?" Connor called out. He needed to find out what was going on. "Megan?" he moved from room to room trying to find her. At last, he stopped outside her room and knocked, "Megan?" Connor called. No answer.

"Alex, have you found Megan?" Connor shouted out to no reply. Connor frowned in irritation. He stalked down the back staircase and stopped at April's door. Checking his reflection in the hallway mirror, he ruffled his hair and did his best to fix his features into a relaxed and composed expression. He knocked on the door and entered. The colour in his face drained as he paused in the doorway.

"Hey," Alex flushed and pulled his hair uncomfortably. Connor glowered at him and quickly shut the door.

"I was just coming to check on April," Connor said.

"Same," Alex said.

'Where is she then?'

"Just in the bathroom getting changed,"

"I see."

The atmosphere between the brothers was tense. Connor had never cared much for Alex's lifestyle before. Girls flitted in and out of Alex's life like butterflies. But, it had never affected him. Now he was invested, he cared about April and didn't want her getting hurt. He wanted Alex to stay the hell away.

"Maybe you should leave then?" Connor suggested tersely.

"Why?" Alex countered.

"April is my friend. She doesn't need you hanging around here bothering her."

"Whoah, hold up." Alex stood up. The two brothers stood facing each other. Connor's hands curled into fists. Alex raised his eyebrows at the movement. Connor took a step towards him.

"Alex?" April called.

The brothers turned around in unison as they heard April's voice. "April?" They both responded.

"Are you two okay out there?" April asked.

Excellent, Connor thought, he came to check if she was okay and instead they were making her worry about them.

"Everything's fine," Alex replied, shooting Connor a look. "We were just wondering where Megan was?"

Once again Alex had gotten there before him. Connor was starting to notice a pattern developing.

"Megan went to see if she could find me a suitcase for the journey. She has pulled out more clothes for me to borrow. She is so kind. Will she be coming with us?"

"Ummm I don't know?"

"Do you think your Dad recognised me?" April asked.

"I don't think so April," Alex said. "He is too consumed with his own agenda to worry about anyone he deems insignificant."

"Right. I just feel that maybe I should have been taking getting home more seriously," April said.

"You can come with us to Rushton and then we will find a way to get you home April," Connor responded as April walked through the door. He couldn't help it but his face relaxed into a smile the second he saw her. Megan had chosen a floaty white dress for April to wear and it suited her perfectly. Connor wanted nothing more than to take her into his arms and protect her from…from everything.

Alex took stock of April as she walked into the room. She looked ethereal. He could tell she was still shaken up from the earlier events. However, her eyes had turned a dark blue with steely resolve. April was ready. Alex didn't know what for, but April looked determined and Alex was willing to help her achieve whatever she needed. April was someone who gave him hope for the future. And hope was not something Alex felt often.

"Can I come in?" a voice sounded from outside. Shaking his head Alex brought himself out of his reverie. As he looked up, Megan was poking her head around the door. She brightened red when she saw that he and Connor were there too.

"Oh sorry, I didn't mean to interrupt," Megan said.

"It's fine Megan we were looking for you," Connor replied.

"You were?" Megan asked shocked.

Alex looked from a blushing Megan to an oblivious Connor. Connor was hopelessly clueless to the musings of women.

"Thank you for the suitcase Megan," April said as she walked over and helped Megan with the bag. "I feel so bad about you lending me so many of your clothes. I promise I'll pay you back at some point."

"It's no problem. Honestly," Megan said as she hovered awkwardly in the doorway. Looking anywhere but at Connor, she moved over to the bed. Reverting to her duties she started folding clothes for April and neatly placing them into the suitcase. With her hands busy she felt more emboldened to address the boys.

"You were looking for me?" Megan asked tentatively into the air, just as April remarked how pretty one of the dresses were.

"It is pretty," Connor replied eagerly while Alex more sensibly turned his attention to Megan. Megan looked crestfallen as Alex replied and she immediately turned red again.

"I... We were wondering whether you had any idea why Dad has the entire board sitting in the conservatory and is ordering us off the island?"

At this question, Megan's blush deepened.

"Umm, well. I was in the utility room at the time. I was asked to make them all drinks, but Derek had run out of ice in the kitchen," she said trying to justify herself. "I couldn't help but overhear."

"Overhear what?" Connor interrupted impatiently. Alex shook his head. Connor really was obtuse. April and Alex looked at Megan encouragingly.

"Apparently, there is going to be an attack on the Island. They say it's a counter attack from the mer." As Megan concluded her sentence she involuntarily looked at April.

April looked stunned. "Who is attacking? Why?"

"Counter-attack? Were those the exact words they used?" Alex asked.

Megan nodded. "Definitely a counter-attack. They mentioned it coming from someone called Yelta."

"That means it was them. Us I mean," Alex said looking directly at April. "If it's a counter-attack then the humans must have attacked the mer in the first place. What is Dad playing at?"

"Kayla," April said. Connor looked up. He wouldn't have even heard April if he didn't pay so much attention to her.

"Kayla?" Connor asked, but before April could open her mouth to speak a voice sounded behind him.

"Kayla's your sister, isn't she? The second in line to the throne." Connor and Alex whipped their heads round to look at Megan. She was still carefully folding the clothes and packing them into the suitcase.

"Yes," April said.

Connor and Alex were dumbfounded. Their unspoken questions were so apparent on their faces that Megan answered them.

"I saw April when Rosetta first brought her in. We left her in the wet room and she was unconscious so couldn't hide her tongue. I follow the mer news and I recognised her."

Alex was impressed. He learnt all about the mer royal family when he thought he was going to the Peace Conference, yet he didn't recognise April.

Connor looked angry but before he could shout at Megan, April stepped in. "Thank you for not telling anyone Megan."

Megan broke into a smile. "Don't worry, I would never." Silently she was jubilant. Her first step of friendship had been made.

"What do you mean your tongue?" Connor asked.

Alex muttered something about irrelevancy as April started to explain, but Megan's voice overrode them all.

"Mer tongues are different colours. Greens and blues of all shades," she said.

"Yup." April stuck out her tongue and let it return to its usual navy blue.

Connor visibly recoiled and April hastily changed it back to pink.

"That's so cool," Alex said.

"I've never heard of that before," Connor said defensively.

A silence descended upon the group. April gripped her arms around her body. Alex took a step towards her and, to Connor's annoyance, she instantly relaxed.

"So, Kayla?" Alex asked trying to move over Megan's revelation and bring the topic of conversation back to where they had started.

"Yelta isn't a person. It's a place. It's our highest-ranking military facility. Kayla, my sister, she's there to train, to become the royal meritia leader."

"And Dad thinks they're launching an attack here. Why?" Connor asked.

"If it's anything like our secret services then Yelta must know where government-owned land is, they're probably coming for information, or to force a confession," Alex said.

"I need to go home and help sort out all this mess," April said.

"Wait, why haven't you just swum away?" Megan asked momentarily stopping her packing.

"I tried, you know that night you found me on the beach Connor," April said.

"I thought you were a crazy person."

"The seawater around this Island is poisonous to me, poisonous to mer," April said.

"What?" Alex and Megan said in unison.

"Yeah, I thought you would have known, I mentioned it before," April said.

"No, I mean the salt levels are high so I always feel a bit tingly!" Alex said. "That's," he paused failing to find the word necessary "that's awful."

"I know," April said. "I thought the owners of a place guarded against mer must hate us."

"I'm starting to think maybe they do," Alex said putting his hands into his pockets.

An awkward silence descended across the room. Megan continued packing April's things and then dismissed herself. Alex and Connor left shortly after. April was left alone. She tapped Ethan's Iris pad futilely. Not ready for bed yet, she got up and walked onto the veranda from the guestroom. It was a perfect summer's evening with a mild sea breeze. April gazed at the tranquil sea. However, despite her calm surroundings, on the inside April was far from perfect. She gripped the balcony railing and started to cry.

CHAPTER 22

It was 6:30am in the morning and April was leaning on Alex's shoulder in one of the President's private jets. Her second-time flying was far more luxurious than the helicopter. The seats were plush and there was no need for one of those dreadful harnesses. While Connor and Alex discussed what their Dad's ulterior motives were April pretended to sleep. She knew they didn't believe that Darius was merely fleeing, but right now April didn't care. She was trying to keep her mind occupied.

The knowledge that she had lost her Mum hadn't fully sunk in. It was as if her mind was refusing to accept the information. She wanted to hear it from her Dad, to see it in his eyes that her Mum was gone forever. April always believed that one day her and her Mum would connect and move past their struggles. If her Mum was truly gone then April didn't know what she was going to do. She tried to keep her spirits up last night, but the episode at the lake had terrified her. It was as if she had been possessed. The Onyx coloured beast still flashed through her mind. The more she focused the more she thought it looked familiar, like something from a dream that had been long forgotten.

April gripped the stone she had been drawn to at the bottom of the pool. She tried to put it down, but then without realising she would find it back in her hand again. Even now when April turned her attention to it she realised that she was subconsciously caressing it with her thumb. It brought her an eerie sense of calm. April would ask the pearl shamans what it was when she returned to the sea. Maybe they could explain her uncontrollable power surge too. She should ask her Dad as well she thought. He would know what was going on. But, April was more worried about her Dad than she was for herself. How was he coping without her Mum? These thoughts went around and around in her head. She wanted to be back home. She closed her eyes and willed herself to drift to sleep. The sounds of Connor and Alex's conversation soon became dull background noise.

"Do you know what Dad's doing?" Connor asked in a hushed voice.

"Me? No," Alex replied in confusion. "Do you?"

"No," Connor replied quickly. "I just thought maybe you still hacked into Dad's systems."

"Oh, no. I used to do that for fun. I've been away so long everything's probably changed." Alex looked down at April to see if she was asleep.

"But you could?" Connor asked. His eyes followed Alex's. Once again Connor had been in the wrong place at the wrong time. That could have been his shoulder.

"I could," Alex said slowly. "We could help April, help the mer." Alex raised his eyes to study his brother's expression. He couldn't tell if Connor was on the same page as him.

"Dad would kill us," Connor replied quietly. His gaze was now firmly fixed on April's golden head.

"But, it's the right thing to do," Alex replied.

"It is, and April needs us."

Alex nodded solemnly.

Connor and Alex's conversation drifted to a halt. Alex looked out of the window in quiet contemplation. He could commit treason and help the mer. It would mean going against all his training. All those years of learning to be an Omega Warrior, being taught his duty was to his country. But, here was an opportunity. He could forge his own path. He could be who he wanted to be. He could do something real and not follow the narrow path set out for him.

"I don't think April should be on her own," Connor said. "Just in case one of the staff recognises her."

Alex turned towards Connor and was jolted out of his reverie. Disturbed by the movement, April woke up.

"April can sleep in my bed and I'll sleep on the floor," Alex offered.

"Why am I sleeping in your bed?" April asked in indignation as she raised her head off of Alex's shoulder.

"You don't need to sleep in his bed, you can sleep in mine," Connor replied before Alex had a chance.

"Pardon?" April said.

"We think it's safer that you're not alone," Connor explained.

April glared at Connor. She knew he meant well but the fussing was too much. Too many other things were vying for attention in her brain. There was no room for amorousness.

"This is nonsense, we're on a plane," April said.

"For once I agree with Connor," Alex said shifting slightly to the left.

"Why?" April said glaring at the brothers. She spotted Megan walk in from the other side of the room.

"Megan, can I share your room tonight?" April asked.

Megan who was serving tea and coffee beamed.

"Of course you can."

"Well that's sorted then," April said brightly. She avoided looking over at Connor's crestfallen face.

The plane journey was a long one. The pilot announced they would be taking a routine detour to fill up on fuel and then another diversion for supplies for the President. April groaned internally at the thought of spending almost two days stuck in a metal box hanging in mid-air. Although better than the helicopter, she was still not entirely comfortable with the concept of flying. She wandered back into her designated cabin and rifled in her bag until she found the book Megan leant her - Mer for Dummies. She brought it back into the lounge area and curled up onto one of the plush, brown leather sofas. The book was surprisingly fat and covered many aspects of mer life. April flipped through the pages until she landed on an interesting chapter. 'Where do mer live?' It was accompanied with a picture of a cartoon mer poking his head out of a cave. April skim read the chapter chuckling every so often.

Connor's eyes flicked up as April giggled. He tried to focus back on his own book. April chuckled again.

"What's so funny?" Connor asked edgily, worried she was somehow laughing at him.

"This," April said waving the book. "The mer don't like to live deep underwater as it's too far away from the surface." She read aloud in a mock serious voice. "I mean seriously, not that it would be freezing and dark if we all swam around at the bottom of the ocean."

"I've always wondered what a mer city looks like," Alex piped up.

"You haven't seen one?" April asked, putting the book down in her lap.

"Well no, not a recent one. We only have photos leftover from before the Great Divide."

"Oh." April tapped on Ethan's Iris pad that was still useless for contacting anyone while they flew so high above the sea. She wielded water out of the jug on the table with her Factus powers and created an iced screen. Alex and Connor watched on in awe.

"Come and have a look," she said. The two brothers moved over to join her on her couch.

"I'm sure Ethan has some photos on his Iris." She flicked through images on Ethan's Iris then tapped to project them onto the ice screen. She was hoping to find an aerial shot of Hanaria.

"Here we go." April smoothed the frozen water so the picture was crystal clear. Alex leant forward and touched April's instant ice screen in wonder.

"See, so I think he must be quite close to the surface here. And this is a photo looking down onto the western part of Hanaria."

Connor moved closer to the screen but as his arm touched April's he recoiled. Thinking he didn't have enough room April instinctively moved closer to Alex. Connor, for what felt like the hundredth time since meeting April, mentally kicked himself.

"This is the main shopping area really." April pointed to a circular arrangement of buildings. "And this over here is one of our national beds, I think you call them parks."

"So, this isn't the bottom of the ocean?" Connor asked.

"No." April looked at him incredulously. "It would be so dark!"

"How does it work then?"

"Most of our cities are built on floating islands within the ocean. Then most of our high-speed transport happens below the city."

"How does it float?" Alex asked.

"Umm, I don't know the exact science, but it is like a series of giant weighted bubbles," April said and received confused looks from the brothers. "They were invented by a powerful pearl shaman. They need to be maintained every day."

"I see," Connor said.

"So, there you go, that is a mer city," April shrugged.

"It would be cool to see one in real life," Alex said. His eyes glued to the screen.

"You should come and visit," April said smiling up at him.

"That would be cool," Connor replied.

"You can kind of understand the initial hatred can't you," Alex said quietly.

"Hatred?" April asked her voice rising.

"Yeah, imagine no longer having access to the sea April, but knowing that a whole world continued without you," Alex said. "It must have been maddening."

"I suppose." April nodded, staring at her home. "But, it doesn't warrant these attacks."

"No, it doesn't," Alex said. April looked up again at the tone of his voice. Alex seemed to be on the verge of saying something.

"Alex…" April started.

"Right, I had better get back to my programming," he said and pushed up from the couch and went back over to his laptop.

"Are there any more photos April?" Connor asked.

"Umhmm," April handed the ice block to Connor and pulled different images out of Ethan's Iris for him. She looked over at Alex and saw the tightness in his shoulders. Instinctively she sent a wave of Curo energy over her friend. She smiled as she saw his shoulders drop and heard a sigh escape his lips.

CHAPTER 23

After a late dinner, April made her way to Megan's room. She was still not impressed with being babysat but making a fuss didn't seem worth it. She changed into pyjamas and crawled into bed ready to fall asleep. Just as her eyes closed a purposeful knock sounded on the door.

"Can I come in?"

"Umm-hmm," April said. She tried to lie in bed with her eyes closed as Megan entered the room but after ten minutes of Megan clattering around, she finally opened them.

"How was your day?" she asked sitting up.

"It was good thank you," Megan beamed. "Just organising the kitchen for our new supplies tomorrow."

"Excellent," April nodded and pulled the duvet up around her. Her plan to fall asleep fell apart as Megan proceeded to bombard her with questions about mer life.

"So, when you hear an animal and you can understand what they're saying, does it sound like a human?"

April stared at Megan for a split second before responding to check she was being serious.

"Well no, it sounds like that specific animal."

"Oh, then how do you understand them?"

"I don't know. It's like being born with the ability to understand all the animal languages. Each one sounds different."

"That's so interesting." Megan's mindless chatter and probing questions about mundane merness at least temporarily distracted April from thinking about her more pressing issues.

"What's that?" Megan asked. She gestured at April's hands. Without realising it April had picked up the shiny black stone once more. She was repeatedly turning it over in her hands. It felt cool to the touch no matter how long she held it. The cold was soothing though.

"This? This is the stone I found at Beaulieu Falls," April said. She didn't feel like going into the details now and had avoided talking about it with Alex and Connor. It felt like a dark power had consumed her temporarily.

"Can I see?" Megan asked her face lighting up. April leant forward and passed it to her.

"Oh, it's surprisingly heavy," Megan said.

"Is it?" April asked incredulously. She thought the exact opposite. April watched as Megan turned the stone over in her hands. She was mesmerised, and as she watched the stone rotate dark flickers rippled over April's fingers.

"You know, I think I've seen something like this," Megan stepped around the bed and went over to her suitcase. Suddenly, the dark energy in April's fingers darted towards Megan.

"Here it is," Megan said. She stood up and turned back towards April. "Your hands," she gasped and gripped the book.

"What?" April looked down to her hands. She turned them over but she couldn't see anything.

"Your hands," Megan repeated. Her feet stayed firmly rooted to the spot with the book now raised like a shield.

"There's nothing here," April reassured her confusedly. Megan didn't move.

"I promise." April held up her hands as evidence. She twisted them around. "See."

Megan visibly relaxed. "I must have imagined it," she said and climbed into bed. "It looked like black light was weaving out of you." Megan giggled nervously. April buried her fingers in the duvet self-consciously.

"Anyway, look." Megan flipped through the book to a page titled Devil's Hole. She pointed to a picture of a collection of large, slightly disfigured spherical stones. They were all completely black like April's. There was just something different about them. Even in picture form, they seemed to radiate energy. They looked more like precious gems than stones.

"I think I'll sleep now," Megan said. She handed the stone back warily and turned off her light.

"Goodnight," she said while rolling to face away from April.

"Night."

April dimmed her bedside light and sat and read the book.

"Devil's Hole or Le Creux de vis is located on the North Coast of the largest of the Channel Islands, Jersey. Devil's Hole is a natural crater with a blowhole. The crater is 100ft wide and the blowhole 200ft deep." April read the summary and felt a chill along her arms. It sounded like a Tenebrasco pearl cave. She put the stone down and turned off the light. She was determined to sleep.

But, while Megan's breath deepened and slowed April was alert. She lay in the small cabin bed and listened to the buffeting of the air against the giant plane as they hurtled through the night sky. She turned over and puffed up her pillow. Could she join Kayla at Yelta and lead the fight? Should she find her Dad and assist him? April had no idea how wars were fought. Was this a war? Should she just focus on learning to control and wield her powers? Her confusion jumped her back and forth between half-formed and seemingly impossible solutions. Eventually, she lay still staring up at the ceiling, her entire body aching with indecision. By morning she was exhausted. It was still early but she decided to give up on sleep. She slid out of bed quietly so as not to wake Megan and slipped out the door. April moved over to the window in the hall and saw a wall of grey cloud. She summoned her Tempus energy and wielded it to part the clouds. All it revealed was another layer of dense grey clouds. April focused harder and tried to push through that layer too, but only more fog appeared. With a disparaging look, she walked away.

April slid the doors open into the main cabin and was glad to find Alex sitting there with his laptop.

"You look exhausted," he said.

She smiled at him weakly. "Are you okay?" he asked. "Do you want to talk about anything."

"Not right now," April said. "What are you working on?"

Alex was sat on the floor leaning against the sofa while he typed away. He hadn't stopped typing while talking to April.

"It's a hacking software I'm developing," Alex said. April came and sat down beside him while he showed her page upon page of code. He tried to explain his years of work.

"It's almost sophisticated enough to hack into any database now," he said proudly. April rested her head on Alex's shoulder while he continued to talk about his programme. When he put his arm around her shoulders and started subconsciously fiddling with her hair she was surprised but comforted. Like this, she could almost pretend she was back home nestled on the sea sponge watching TV with Ethan.

A tall man was standing over her. April looked to his hand and was alarmed to see an electric leash. He snatched it back and she fell down onto her knees. As she raised her head pain pulsed through her body. She noticed blearily that the leash was emitting electricity. With each shock she arched her back and screamed. But, it wasn't her voice. Suddenly, she was outside of her body looking on. It was a man on the floor. She would recognise him anywhere. It was Ethan.

"Ethan," April cried. Alex jumped up. April's lips had turned blue and she was shivering. She cried out once more. "Ethan!"

Connor ran into the cabin and knelt beside her.

"April, April. Can you hear me?".

"Connor, go and get Megan and bring some blankets to cover April. She's freezing," Alex said. He tried to reposition her so she was lying down against the couch. Connor looked torn, not wanting to leave April's side. "Go!" Alex said.

"He can't, he can't!" April screamed. Her eyes were wide open but she stared past Alex.

Alex shifted April's head onto his lap. She was starting to emit a faint blue glow. He recognised her lack of control from the oasis clearing. He rubbed her forehead and spoke calmly to her. "I've got you April. You're safe. Come back to me."

The man with the leash was bearing down on Ethan. "Use the pearls," he shouted "Go on, I know you can do it. Is that not enough pain for you?" Suddenly he lashed out again across Ethan's back. As his howl of pain curdled April's blood she ran at the man, trying to force him to stop. But as she reached out to grab his arm she found herself powerless like a spectre looking on at the horror. As she turned back to face Ethan she sobbed in apology. Then she saw her pearls wrapped around his wrist. Instinctively she let her powers reach out to him. Doing what she did best she wielded her Curo pearl energy to reach out and cover Ethan whole. His screams stopped and he looked up and smiled. "April" he whispered as he collapsed.

"Ethan!" April blinked and was shocked to find that she was still on the plane.

"April? What happened are you okay?" Alex asked

April stared up straight into Alex's eyes. He looked bewildered. But, looking into those eyes she made the connection.

"Frederick," she whispered.

Alex laughed nervously in relief. He couldn't help himself. "My brother this time?" And April started laughing too. There was nothing funny about the situation, but once again Alex had been there for her and managed to bring her back to reality.

"Frederick, your brother. I met him at the Peace Conference. He danced with me."

Connor passed April a steaming mug of hot chocolate while Megan tucked a blanket around her. April could feel her cheeks going red. The most powerful mera in all the oceans and she was reduced to a shivering child by a mere dream.

"He was threatening Ethan in the dream. No … he was punishing him or attacking him. Shouting at him to use them." April said her voice cold. Every time she thought about it she wanted to attack Frederick for what he was doing to Ethan.

"Who is Ethan?" Alex asked.

"Ethan is the mer Prime Minister's son. Ethan's Mum and April's Mum are best friends as they grew up together." Connor explained. "I read up on the emails we were sent for the Peace Treaty," he said shrugging his shoulders.

April nodded, "Yes, Ethan's like a brother to me."

"And what did Freddie want him to use?" Alex asked.

"Describe the vision fully April," Megan said crossing her legs over.

April looked up at Megan. "Vision?" she asked.

"Well yes. It sounds like you were having a vision. Don't powerful mer experience those when their power develops?" Megan stated looking between the three of them.

Alex looked deeply impressed at Megan's knowledge.

"April's powers aren't ready to develop. She's too young," Connor responded condescendingly with his newfound mer intel.

"Then what's going on?" Alex interjected.

"You're both right. And, I don't know. Maybe something is wrong with my powers. I don't know. The dream felt so real, but I couldn't do anything. They couldn't hear me I couldn't stop him."

"Is there anything else you can remember?" Megan enquired. Her thirst for mer knowledge was insatiable.

April's hand reached for her neck. She usually tugged on her pearls when she was stressed. And it hit her "My pearls," she said. April's head swam, could she have accessed her pearls at this distance? How was it even possible? The others were looking at her expectantly to explain.

"The night of the Peace Conference I tripped, Ethan and I swapped pearls." She held up her wrist to show them Ethan's watch. "I had to give him my necklace... In the vision, he was wearing my pearls. And when I saw them, I reached out to my pearls and I... I healed him. But I can't have. I'm so far away." But, even as she questioned its plausibility she was certain it wasn't just a dream. It had been real, she was sure of it.

"You glowed kind of a blue colour, that's the colour of the healing pearl right?" Alex asked.

"How did you know that?" Connor asked in surprise.

"The Lost Prince in Prince Triton, his sword was inlaid with sky blue pearls," Alex said.

"So he could save a life for every one he took," April finished smiling at him.

"You used your power through a vision. That's incredible April," Megan said looking on in awe. Alex noticed how much more confident Megan seemed whenever mer were the topic. Maybe Connor would finally take notice of her.

"The real question is why did Freddie have your friend?" Connor asked.

CHAPTER 24

Swimming through the streets of Hanaria, Setha stopped and stared at the magazine display window. There on the cover of some trashy tabloid magazine was a photo of Ethan and April. Setha recognised the outfits immediately. It was a photo taken of them the night of the Peace Treaty. They were pictured hand in hand in a bizarre shell garden maze. Laughing together in a candid shot they looked like the perfect couple. The unimaginative title splashed across the bottom of the page read 'How far will you go to get your true love?' Setha swam into the store and purchased the magazine. It had been a week now and there was still no news on either of them. Well, no real news she thought ruefully. Once seated on the ray bus to the hospital, Setha shook out the magazine and started reading. Her face was set firmly in a grimace of disgust.

Two weeks after the bombing at the Peace Conference and, although tensions are high, nothing is happening. As each side waits patiently for the other to make the first move it's advised to stay safely in deep waters as much as possible. This is not the time for a legged fling!

However, one couple we suspect might be benefitting is Princess April Meridia and the Prime Minister's son Ethan Vale. The two deny any such liaisons at the moment, but you know old corals have a habit of re-growing. Neither has been sighted since the bombing and the extremists are jumping foolishly to the conclusion that they've been kidnapped. But, we here at TIDAL WAVE believe differently. Anonymous tips have been sent in from mer who have spotted this fabulous couple at remote locations across the oceans. Could the bomb that has been a catastrophe for many be the ultimate excuse for a couple in the limelight to escape... But, they won't be able to escape us for long. Message our TIDAL WAVE Iris if you have any sightings of the gorgeous couple and we shall be sure to keep the rest of our readers updated.

In the meantime... Take our quiz, how far will you go to spend some private time with your lover - would you set off a bomb or merely hide in a shell closet?

Setha closed the magazine. She did not need to take the stupid test. How ridiculous could some mer be? Rolling the magazine up in her gold seaweed tote she angrily swam off the ray bus as it pulled up outside the hospital. Setha had filled her Dad in on the events of the past week. He seemed to be recovering at the moment and she looked forward to seeing him react angrily to such an article. Cooper was passionate about the privacy of individuals. He himself endured many a scandal when her Mum was being accused of affairs in different tabloids over the years. On second thought, maybe it was better not to tell her Dad about the article. Her musings on the subject brought her right outside her Dad's door in the Catfish ward. Suddenly, a tremor shuddered through the water. A hiss followed shortly after. Setha looked around in alarm and entered hurriedly into her Dad's room. He was sitting up in his bed.

"What was that Setha-Bella?"

"I don't know Dad. Maybe something is wrong with the energy supply?"

Setha was on edge. Hospitals were creepy enough, let alone when something went wrong. Then suddenly a shock passed through the water pushing her to the ground.

"Setha," Cooper shouted.

The alarms in the hospital sounded. They didn't sound like power failure alarms. This was a red alert. Another shock went through the water forcing Setha down again. Suddenly a voice sounded over the hospital horn shells.

"Please remain calm. The surrounding sea has been contaminated. For the safety of all, we must evacuate the hospital. Those who need help will receive it. Please remain calm..."

The monotone voice continued and continued. Setha tried to force herself up off the ground but the water felt so heavy. She wielded her

Factus pearl to jet hot water out of her hands to leverage herself off the floor. Her powers may not be strong but heat was her speciality.

"Dad we've got to get out of here."

"Setha-bella…" but Cooper's words were lost in the next tremor. Setha was prepared this time and held tightly to the bed frame. As the pressure subsided she swam to the back of the bed and collected her Dad's breath regulation machine and his drip. Detaching them from the wall she let them float next to her as she turned her attention to her Dad. Another shock passed through the building and Setha refused to let the panic rising within her take over. She helped her Dad put his arm around her shoulders and in the other arm she held onto the breathing equipment. Incredibly thankful that her Grandmother had insisted on a private room with a window, Setha forced open the glass with a blast of her Factus energy. The hot water hissed as it slammed the window open. At the last moment, she reached over to her Dad's bedside table drawer and grabbed his notepad. She stuffed it into her bag and together they swam out the room.

In her head 'evacuating the hospital' was all that was necessary to escape the danger. But, the fear in her heart was confirmed as she looked up to the surface as she exited through the window. A dark shadow was directly overhead; it looked like a huge hexagonal grid had been laid out across the ocean. As the shadow receded Setha breathed a sigh of relief. But, as she continued swimming it smacked back down into the water causing another tremor. Its force sent Setha and her Dad spinning deeper into the ocean.

"Setha," Cooper said while pointing upwards. A thick purplish smog was permeating down through the sea. Squinting up carefully Setha could see that it was forming hexagons across the water. At the highest levels, everyone was swarming down away from the thick smog. The chaos around them was intensifying. One mer swam past her with his skin bright red with burnt hexagons forming a shining welt. He screamed in pain as he rushed away. In no control of his movements, he cut a thrashing path through the crowd of hospital evacuees.

"Come on, let's try and get out from under this," Setha shouted. She tried to sound calm for her Dad's sake but really she wanted someone, anyone else to take control.

The meritia on scene were doing their best to control the smog or at least stop it from permeating any further into the water. As Setha swam along she thought that their attempts were making some impact. The smog was not descending any lower. But, still she kept swimming.

"Come on Dad," Setha said. "Just a bit further."

Her heart pounded in her chest but she looked straight ahead not wanting to be distracted by the chaos.

Up above, the meritia were using large metal plated shells to scoop the smog up and out of the water. The wielders of the Factus pearl were forcing the infected water upwards. Setha spotted several mer swimming upwards to help their efforts. Setha's powers were not strong enough to help though and besides her Dad needed her most right now. She kept on swimming glancing upwards every so often to check that the hexagons were not going to slam into the water again. Their shadow floated ominously above. A group seemed to have gathered in front of her and she headed towards them.

"We'll be alright Setha-Bell," Copper smiled weakly as he hung from her.

"Sorry Dad, I don't want to hurry you I just want to get you out of here."

A hospital nurse swam over to Setha, "Are you okay Miss? Do you need help?"

"We're fine thank you," Setha said.

"Keep heading towards that group. Transportation to alternative hospitals is arriving momentarily," the nurse said and she swam off to speak to other patients.

"Right, we're almost there," Setha said. The panic in her own voice scared her.

"Don't worry Setha, we'll make it," Copper said as he sagged against her.

Setha kept on swimming them forward. The panic around them was still rife. Mer were swarming towards the alternate transportation. Setha tried to keep her Dad from being knocked by all the mer darting around them, however, the panic had sent everyone into a frenzy. A red tinge floated in front of her. As she swam through it she detected the metallic taste of blood. Opening her mouth to ask her Dad what he thought, Setha was stopped mid-sentence. Instead, she screamed. The chaos around them meant that no one noticed Setha's world imploding around her. The breathing equipment floated innocently beside her Dad while his head lolled in the water. His face calm as if he slept, but Setha knew the truth.

CHAPTER 25

"King Nathaniel, King Nathaniel. We have an emergency. Your Majesty."

A knocking on the door and some inane harassed chatter woke Nathaniel up from a night of disturbed sleep. What was going on he thought. Sunlight poured through his window and he raised his hand to deflect its painful glare. Nathaniel allowed himself to float off his bed and slowly bring himself back into the now. He was the King of the Ocean, the ruler of the seven seas. He was not allowed to fall apart. Kings did not break down at the loss of their wife. They were not distraught at the news of a missing daughter. And they certainly didn't fear their other daughter leading a meritian attack. Bringing himself into the now was not a fun task. He reached for his Curo pearl to soothe his permanent headache. A slight glow around the temple and all was better.

"Move aside, move aside!" Nathaniel heard the distinct tones of Clyde's voice. The ornate doors to Nathaniel's bedroom swung open.

"Oh! Your Majesty, my deepest apologies. I feared you may have been ill. You didn't attend breakfast or lunch or the war council meeting," Clyde said hurriedly. He hovered in the entrance of the doorway while Titan and Tarzan dashed into the room. Nathaniel mustered his face into an expression of authority and swam himself into his armchair. Clyde's role in his cabinet seemed to have altered so that he was now Nathaniel's personal babysitter. The King was in a way thankful. Clyde was a lot better than others would have been.

"My absence was on account of a headache." That was close enough to the truth he thought. He started to stroke his overexcited pets. "Now that you have disturbed me, what is the emergency?"

~

Nathaniel kept imagining the atrocities at the hospital as he was sped to the surface. The shellpedo was hurtling along wasting no time at all. But, the chaos in Nathaniel's mind moved at a snail's pace. He knew that his Curo indulgence last night had not caused the attack. Yet, had he been awake could he have stopped this toxic substance before it hurt so many of his mer? Clyde seemed to think that the hexagonal pump, as he described it, had been targeting the palace. The attackers' information was clearly wrong. Perhaps it was out-dated, believing the palace to be the tallest building in Hanaria and not knowing of the newly built hospital which towered above all the other buildings.

Nathaniel brought up his mail on his Iris pad. Alert after alert was being posted to him- updates of the wounded, updates of the infected area, updates of the attackers, update, after update, after update. He had wanted 'a hands-on' approach to ruling. But, he hated to admit it, perhaps he was now unfit to rule. As this sobering thought settled within him the shellpedo came to a smooth halt and the door released open. Without waiting for the formalities of being called and escorted, Nathaniel swam out and broke through the surface.

"Your Majesty. You're currently in a cleared area. We have sent test tubes of the hexagonal poison to the labs for a thorough analysis. Our main concern at the moment is this." The general speaking to Nathaniel gestured rather unnecessarily to the hexagonal tubing that was floating ominously to their left.

"We were hoping that you, Your Majesty, would be able to assist us in dismantling the infrastructure. We have yet to decide whether it would be better to sink the object or to try and move it to one of our land bases. Whatever we do we hope to minimise the chance of it pumping any more toxins into the ocean." The general finished rather pompously Nathaniel thought and he had to restrain himself from rolling his eyes. Of course, the aim was to stop the lethal weapon from causing more harm. He simply nodded at the mer and swam towards the structure. Assessing it from this angle he saw that it could be easily sliced apart at the welded edges. However, would that release the toxins?

Nathaniel reached out with his Essentia pearl. For regular mer the pearl merely reacted to the life of the mer who wore it; staying at sea temperature when all was well and then soaring in times of fever and cooling at death. Those blessed with the Essentia gift were able to extend the pearl's powers to other objects and assess their life source. Nathaniel was particularly adept at doing it with the sea. Normally he could sense when something was wrong just by a slight shift in the chemical components in the water. However, with his recent reliance on the Curo pearl to ease his troubled mind his senses were dimmed. Reaching out to the water inside the hexagonal structure Nathaniel immediately recoiled. A burning feeling added to his persistent headache. Pure poison rested inside those hexagons.

"We can't dismantle the hexagons," Nathaniel stated as he submerged underwater to see the bottom of the metal tubes that held the intricate wires in place.

"Pardon? We must Your Majesty," the General stuttered as he caught up with him.

"The tubes are still full of poison," Nathaniel said turning to the General. "They need to be drained first. If we drill a hole I can remove the toxin but then we would need another container. Or if the labs have already created one, an antidote can be poured in to neutralise the poison."

"It's still full of poison?"

"Yes," Nathaniel said.

"We had presumed that the structure was empty Your Majesty," the General said shifting slightly. "My apologies Your Majesty. I will contact the lab now." With a bow, the General swam off.

~

Since he had sent the most senior and experienced meritia to aid Kayla he was surrounded by incompetence. War was not his expertise. But, at least he possessed some common sense. When Kayla returned to Hanaria after her mission he would make her the official head of the meritia and not just a figurehead. She would do a better job than he; she had the aptitude and the training. He swam down to the shellpedo and went into the comfy saloon area. Relaxing into one of the chairs he started to read through the correspondence on his Iris pad. Hopefully, there would be no more attacks today. He wanted to make sure that all the hospital evacuees were being properly looked after in the pop-up meritia medical facility. Swimming into the next room he informed Clyde that he planned on spending the day helping to heal the infirm.

~

What time is it Setha thought as she opened her eyes? Her room was pitch black and her whole body felt empty. Then it hit her. Flashbacks of screaming, her screams flooding the water, a member of the meritia swimming to escort her and her Dad. Then seeing his realisation, she lived through the shock again. Setha lay in bed numb. With all the chaos surrounding her, all she could do was contact her Grandmother. Never had she been more thankful to see someone before. Her Grandmother had given Setha some sleeping tablets and sent her to bed. Setha didn't remember falling asleep. Yesterday's events blurred until all she could remember were the sounds of her own screaming. Setha pulled her Iris pad to her and pressed three. She waited while it rang and then the door burst open.

"Mum," Setha said in shock. Her Mum floated in the doorway her eyes welled up in tears. She swam over to Setha's side and collapsed onto her daughter. Together they started to cry.

CHAPTER 26

The jet took off once more and they continued to sail smoothly through the sky. Megan brought the last of Darius' supplies into the kitchen area. Over a day's detour had been made for specific types of tea, seasoning and wine. She mused that maybe their detour had been more to postpone the brothers' arrival than to stock up on the President's essentials. She looked out the window as she started to sort the boxes. Megan stared at the stars shining outside; it was one of the most startling sights she had ever seen. Soaring above the ocean watching the starlight sparkle across the clouds she felt exhilarated. How had she become so fortunate?

When Rosetta had informed her that she was to travel with Alex and Connor to Darius' safe house she was so excited. Apparently, there weren't enough maids at Rushton to cater for the two boys. And, as Darius' decision had been so last minute there was no time to arrange for different transport for her either. Thus, here she was. Megan Charles flying on a private jet, with a mera and the guy she had fancied since she started work a few weeks ago. Never in a million years would she have imagined this happening. Since her parents had refused to pay for her to go to university she had been worried she would be stuck in the same place forever, destined to become miserable in a dead-end job. Yet, here she was, her first job and it was as a maid to the President.

~

Connor couldn't sleep. He lay in his cabin staring up at the oak wood cupboards. Once again he had lost the girl. Once again Alex had won. He didn't understand. Connor was the one who originally befriended her. Connor knew all about the mer. He loved the mer. Alex was ambivalent to most things except women. Maybe, Connor mused, that was the point. The only thing Connor had never excelled at was women, well, women and sports. And now he was lying here moping like a love-struck teenager when the world was potentially on the brink of war. How pathetic.

"Connor," a whispered voice came from outside his cabin door followed by a gentle knock. "Connor?" the voice came again. He couldn't tell over the sound of the jet if it was Megan or April. Only one of whom he fancied talking to. He lay still while he weighed his options.

"I'm awake," Connor replied nonchalantly.

"Can I come in?"

"Yes," he said and the door slowly inched open.

"I couldn't sleep. Megan disappeared so I thought I would go for a wander. What are you doing up?" April said as she clambered onto the end of the bed. She was wearing nothing but a long white shirtdress. April should always wear white Connor mused.

"Connor, are you sure you're awake? I can leave if you want." April made a start to get off the bed.

"No no!" Connor replied, perhaps a little too quickly.

"Oh okay."

They sat in an awkward silence, for a while. Well, it felt awkward to Connor. He wanted to say something, casual but intelligent and perhaps deeply insightful. What this was, he had no idea.

"Connor."

"Umm hmmm."

"I'm scared."

Talking to Connor was not as easy as talking to Alex. But, she needed someone now and there had been no response from Alex's room. It felt good to finally get it off her chest. She was scared, and that was okay.

"Why do you feel scared? I will protect you," Connor replied and instantly regretted it.

April couldn't help but giggle, though she stopped abruptly at the crestfallen look that Connor tried to hide. April shuffled forward on the bed and held out her arms. Maybe all they both needed was a hug.

"I'm scared because I don't know what I should do next," April said looking down at the duvet. "I know what I want to do. I want to help broker peace between mer and the legged. But how do I do that? I can't even control my powers," she said and moved out of the hug.

Connor started stroking April's hair as he had seen Alex do, hoping it would soothe her.

"Well, maybe that is the first step. Learn to control them. You have so much raw power April," Connor said speaking faster and faster. "I could help you to study. Dad has so many books on mer. He removed all Mum's from the house. I bet they're at the safe house where his office is."

"I suppose it's a start," April agreed shifting slightly on the bed. "Maybe I should reveal who I am to your Dad and talk to him about peace. Surely he wants peace as much as we do?" April said looking up as she fiddled with the duvet.

Connor looked sceptical at this suggestion.

"Perhaps it would be better if your Father or the Prime Minister were the ones to talk to him. No offence April."

"April!" Alex's concerned whisper was heard down the hall.

"I'm in here."

Alex sauntered into the tiny cabin. "Nice and cosy in here," he said glancing at Connor. "I saw Megan's door was open and you were both gone. I was worried about what had happened to you?"

"On a plane Alex? You're beginning to sound like Connor," April joked.

"We wouldn't want that now would we." Alex leaned in to ruffle Connor's hair. Connor dodged him grumpily but was then appeased when April went in to hug him again.

"Is everyone okay?" Megan said appearing at the door.

"We're fine Megan, though a cup of tea wouldn't go amiss," Connor said flippantly. April and Alex rolled their eyes then smirked when they caught the other doing it too.

"Ah okay. Tea coming up," Megan said retreating from the cabin.

The jet landed with a jolt. Looking out of the window she could see them rolling slowly into an air locker in the side of a vast cliff face. It was just like a film Setha's Mum had been in. She missed her best friends, Setha and Ethan. As soon as she was back home she would tell them everything that had happened. Between them, they would know how to help her. She was excited to read the books Connor had mentioned too. Maybe the legged had access to some lost mer knowledge. She wanted something to explain this odd stone. The onyx stone was resting in her shirt pocket at the moment. The weight comforted her. Finally arriving at their destination, a sinking feeling settled on her chest. The danger she ignored while on Shell Island was becoming harder to deny. She hoped that Freddie would not be at the Rushton facility to recognise her. Though, she wondered if he would even recognise her in shorts and a t-shirt compared to the ball gown she wore for the Peace Treaty. A voice over the intercom announced that the jet was now safe to depart. April tried to sit up but the dead weight of Alex's legs and Connor's arm weighed her down.

"Guys! It's time to get up now."

An incomprehensible grumble reached her ears. She kicked out with her legs.

"Ow, whaddya do that for?" Connor mumbled sleepily.

"Oh sorry, April," Alex said shifting himself then offering his hand to help pull her out from under Connor. His strength pulled her straight into his arms. Connor blanched as he fully opened his eyes and saw April and Alex in such a close embrace. April moved away and prodded Connor to cajole him out of bed in an attempt to recover from the awkwardness.

"Right, I'll quickly get changed and meet you both on the platform," she said.

April rapidly exited the room and returned to the cabin she was sharing with Megan.

Megan's stuff was already gone as was their luggage. But, a new outfit was waiting for her laid out on the bed. April still didn't like flying but private jet was preferable to helicopter. She got changed and hurried to join the boys. She descended the steps to the platform carefully, not wanting a repeat of the last time she fell out of an aircraft. The second her feet hit the surface a heat flushed through her. Her hair lifted slightly from her shoulders and she stood up a little taller.

"You just glowed," Alex hissed at her as Connor moved to block her from anyone's view.

"My pearls," she whispered in shock. But, a broad smile broke out across her face. Her pearls were close. She could feel them.

"Greetings Master Alex and Master Connor and this must be Miss April. I'm Taylor," President Darius' personal assistant announced as he strode towards them his arms open wide. "Your Father asked me to come down and greet you all as he is busy. I'm here to escort you to your rooms and show you the safe areas of the building to visit and the exits into the forests. Please follow me." Taylor gestured to a door and turned with purpose.

"Yeah, right he's busy. Can't be bothered is more like it," Connor muttered.

Taylor showed them around the facility not needing much more than an affirmative when he pointed to an out of bounds area. Completely ignoring Taylor, April chose to quiz Alex and Connor instead.

"So, what is this place?"

"Umm," Connor said.

"It's a state of the art facility for science and military ventures. It also acts as a safe house for the President. The entire area is heavily guarded. As all three units are top security and often interact, Dad decided to unite the three. It was one of the pet projects Freddie was assigned. He is probably around here somewhere," Alex said.

"Oh," April replied as Connor continued where Alex left off.

"Mum couldn't stand the place. She refused to come here; she didn't like the work of the science laboratories. What was the name of that psychopath?"

"Lydia?"

"Yeah, that's the one," Connor said.

"She's the Head of Scientific Research and Advancement," Alex explained. "Our Mum hated her. Shell Island was used as more of a safe house than here. You won't have noticed but it's heavily guarded. Mum had it built so that the safety elements wouldn't intrude on our summer holidays."

"Shell Island was Mum's favourite. She always told us about hidden underwater passages she had built under the house to hide treasure in when we were younger. I loved those stories of the black pearl rooms and the secret meetings of the mer and humans," Connor said.

"This place though. Well, you're about to see. Let's just say it is very white," Alex said.

April looked between the two brothers to see if they were over-exaggerating. But, they had tuned back into Taylor's diatribe as he typed a code into the security pad and huge metal walls slid open.

"Welcome to Rushton," Connor said with a bleak smile.

Very white and very black, that was April's initial impression of Rushton. It was as if the designer of the strange facility had no knowledge that other colours existed. There weren't even any grey tones to soothe down the stark white and pitch black. It made April feel on edge. In a way it was striking, but also terrifying. It reminded her of the Orca. They looked so beautiful and yet they were some of the most efficient killers she had ever seen. April walked into the cavernous reception area of Alex and Connor's apartment. A geometric staircase made its way around the rectangular room with several plateaus jutting out as entrances to the different floors. Taylor led them through one reception room and into another.

This room instantly became April's favourite at Rushton. Blackwood covered the floor and in one corner of the massive room was an island kitchen with sleek white marble surfaces. Directly opposite the reception room entrance were several white leather square couches facing an enormous window. The window took up the entire wall. April couldn't help walking towards it.

"Magnificent isn't it." April heard Taylor start up again on his incessant monologue. Ignoring him she placed her hand on the glass and looked down. She was surprised to see that they were on the edge of a cliff face still. After walking for so long with Taylor she presumed they would be somewhere deep in a forest or deep underground. But no, dark blue seas churned beneath them with a smattering of treacherous rocks. The sky above was equally dark, mirroring the water below. She wondered if the sea was poisoned as it had been around Shell Island. It looked so inviting. April tapped Ethan's Iris pad to see if it worked. She pressed send on one of her countless messages. Moments later the error message appeared once more. April longed to smash the window and dive through. She could swim home. Reaching for her powers she knew she could do it. At least, if everything went wrong, here was her escape route.

CHAPTER 27

How long does it take to assemble a small elite unit to ambush an island and perform a rescue mission? - Half a day. How long does it take to plan the mission? - One day. How long does it take to convince everyone that it's suitable for her to lead the attack? - Forever.

"I'm the Princess in charge around here, it's my sister who needs rescuing and I'm the one who has a special connection with her." Kayla realised that she was sounding whiny, but the time for a mature and well-argued debate had ended half a week ago. Why would no one listen to her?

"Princess Kayla, you are set to be the new commander in chief of the meritia. It is not prudent for you to be on the front line. Please stay behind the attack and use your knowledge to relay information." Gregor tried to reason with her.

This was useless; they were going around in circles she thought. At this rate, she would have to wait until she was the meritia commander before the mission could happen, then she wouldn't need permission.

"How about we set out and then reassess upon our arrival?" Kayla suggested.

Demetrius smiled. Kayla had always struck bargains when she was younger.

"Okay then," Gregor finally acquiesced. He huffed and pulled out his Iris pad and typed away.

There was no way she wasn't going on this mission Kayla thought. At least this way everyone could stay happy for another day or two.

~

The shellpedo fleet they were using for the Island X mission was Kayla's favourite. They were modelled on the skin of a shortfin mako shark and known for their impressive speed and ability to change direction quickly. Inside the shellpedo, Kayla felt like she had the power of that awesome predator. They tore through the sea at alarming speeds with only their tailspin to show that they had been there. In homage to the mako shark, this particular model had a slash of silver painted across the top and the metallic casing gradually grew lighter and lighter as it rounded towards the bottom.

Looking back out the window Kayla could see her fleet behind her, moving in synchronisation like a school of sharks. It was sleek but chilling. She remembered when she was first shown the design. The skin casement surrounding the metal was incredible. It was an extremely thin material layered like rows of pointy teeth to minimise the drag in the water. Soft to touch, but it was practically impossible to tear through. Not many things made Kayla feel old enough for the role she undertook but the sight of her fleet following her lead was one of them. Moving to the upper level of her shellpedo, Kayla went to inspect their current progress through the ocean.

Flicking the map up into the water in front of her, Kayla studied their position. Richard, her most experienced navigator, was steering them to the most eastern bay of the island. Here they were able to get closest to Island X without coming in contact with the poisoned water. Even if the water corroded the outer skin of the shellpedos they would still make it onto dry land before the inner shell was damaged.

"Where is Gregor?" Kayla asked.

"He had a last-minute emergency," Demetrius said from the back of the shellpedo.

"Look at this Princess," Richard called from upfront.

Kayla swam forward and instantly chuckled at Richard's screen. Instead of blobs on the map small sharks were gaining on the island.

"Excellent Richard," Demetrius said behind Kayla, his voice dripping with sarcasm. Kayla was very proud that she didn't bob up in surprise at his sudden approach. Sometimes he needed to lighten up.

"We'll be reaching the infected area within the next hour. How would you like us to proceed?" Richard asked.

"Take us to the surface when we arrive, but inform the other shellpedo's to stay below. I'll take a look to check that our information is correct before we proceed," Kayla said.

"As you wish Princess."

Kayla sat down in her designated chair and let her steely resolve calm her. The chair was a dense floating bubble, waiting to be moulded to your desired seating position. Kayla closed her eyes momentarily as she remembered when her Mum finally gave in and let April and Kayla have bubble chairs at their breakfast bar. April was so excited that she accidentally burst hers. Not long now, and they would be reunited Kayla thought. Kayla opened her eyes and turned her attention back to the impressive display in the front window as the shellpedo stormed through the water.

The hour passed quickly enough with various generals messaging through to check their plans with Kayla or ask for advice. Many of which she diverted onto Demetrius. Kayla wanted to be leading the frontline; she was not ready to have a desk job in the meritia. She jogged her emerald green tail up and down in anticipation.

"Princess, we're about to take her up," Richard said.

Kayla floated into an upright position ready to swim out of the shellpedo.

"There we go Princess. The blowhole is open."

Demetrius gave Richard a disapproving look but Kayla was certain she saw a glimmer of a smirk on his face. The panel above swirled in a circle receding into the shellpedo. Kayla swam out quickly with Demetrius following more composedly after her, along with one of the operation generals. Breaching the surface, Kayla wicked the water from her eyes so she could survey Island X.

"It's exactly as our models showed. This should be easy," she said comparing the landscape with her Iris pad.

"I wouldn't be so optimistic Your Highness," The operation general commented. He pointed to the sky. "I think we've been spotted."

Demetrius forced Kayla under the water and back into the shellpedo.

"Let go of me," Kayla said, shoving Demetrius' arm off her. About to express her anger she was suddenly stopped. The entire shellpedo was rocketed backwards. Flung against the side of the wall Kayla knocked her head against one of the low hanging shelves. The horror on Richard's face at the front of the shellpedo forced Kayla to ignore the pain and swim forwards.

Everything was in disarray floating within the shellpedo. Kayla noticed faintly that a strange ringing was coursing through her ears. Shaking her head nothing changed. Swimming through masses of tiny bubbles within the shaken-up water, Kayla eventually made her way to the front. The view on Richard's map was horrifying. What had once been an island was now a bright orange scar. Kayla slammed down on the blowhole-opening button. Frantically swimming to its entrance Kayla knocked the floating instruments out of her way as she hastened to exit.

She swam up as fast as she could and the sound slowly started to return to her. All around she could hear mer emerging from their own shellpedos. They wondered loudly what had happened and started supporting the more dazed members of the team. Fortunately, no one seemed badly hurt. Yet, Kayla didn't stop. Surging upward she finally broke the surface. Her heart tightened, and she opened her mouth wide in shock. She jerked forward then stopped, looking around for a solution. But, there was none. Island X was covered in fire. A huge mushroom cloud of smoky ashes and flames hovered in the air, while down below fire was growing and spreading across the island.

"April!!" she screamed. "April!" Then with a feral scream drawing all her energy she forced every last drop of her power through her Factus pearl. She glowed like April did when emotion overrun her. With April fixed firmly in her mind, she wielded the water up around her. It grew and grew as Kayla glowed even more ferociously until a towering wall of water stood 50 ft. high. It thundered and curled at the top like a wild animal waiting to explode. It was doubtful who was in control at this moment - Kayla or the pearls. The mer below scattered in fear of where Kayla's wall of water was going to come smashing down. The wall grew until it was as wide as the island itself. The shadow cast by the wave sent the sunny day into darkness. But, the fiery island tinged the shadow an ominous red.

Kayla hovered supported by the wave. Her arms raised above her strained under the Factus energy. Kayla shook in anger until suddenly the power became too much and with one final cry for her sister she released the wave. It roared forward as Kayla sank beneath its power. No longer under control, the wave moved like a solid wall. The unstoppable force grew and gained momentum as it neared the island until it smashed down engulfing the fire. The orange tower of flames was devoured instantly. With no one summoning more power to sustain it the seas became eerily calm. Only a small ripple coming from the centre of the island gave any evidence of the wave that had just appeared. Smoke and steam rose up from the battered island. First burnt to a crisp and now smothered with water; nothing on the island could have survived. No one could have survived. The young Princess sank down into the darkness of the ocean letting the cool water soothe her. Unable to move she let herself be swallowed by the sea. She had failed. April was gone. What was the point anymore?

CHAPTER 28

A private island in the Pacific Ocean has just suffered a brutal attack. First being consumed by fire and then snuffed out with a tidal wave. Footage of the destruction was captured by a chance pleasure plane flying over the area. The scenes unfold as you would only expect to see in a movie...

The voice droned on and April and Megan held their spoons in identical positions inches away from their mouths.

"Gormless expressions, what's with you two? ... Oh my...." Connor had turned to look where the transfixed girls' eyes were trained.

"That's Shell Island," Connor said.

"Yup," April said.

Several hours later April and Megan waited tensely in the main lounge. Megan reading a newspaper, the pages of which she hadn't turned for the last 20 minutes, and on the other couch, April twitching in and out of restless sleep. Megan noticed that every so often April glowed. Her hand was still tightly gripping the odd onyx black stone.

"Arghh," April gasped waking out of a fitful dream.

"Are you okay?" Megan said lowering the newspaper. April rubbed her forehead, the stone still clasped in her hands.

"Yeah, just a nightmare," she said crossing her legs on the couch.

"Do, you want to talk about it?" Megan asked hesitantly.

"Not really," April said with a rueful smile. "I want to be distracted."

Megan smiled and turned back to her paper.

"How did you get the job on Shell Island?" April asked. Megan looked back up to see April staring at her. She was still fidgeting with the stone and the blanket that covered her. Her eyes were puffy from crying. Megan was reminded that the girl in front of her, no matter how powerful, was still miles from home dealing with the knowledge that her Mum was dead. Megan put down her paper and started to talk.

"I applied for a private maid's role. It was advertised in our local paper."

"Very mysterious."

"Yeah. I went for it because it mentioned that the residency was beside the sea. I like the sea," Megan clarified.

"I noticed," April forced a laughed. "In your room, all the pictures. It was weird, I never knew some legged were fascinated by the ocean."

"Yes," Megan said moving closer to April on the couch. "My Grandfather fell in love with a mera. He was sailing one day and got caught in a rip so had to go out of bounds. She saw that he was in trouble and so helped move his ship. My Grandfather said she was a powerful Tempus wielder. But, their parents found out. She was banned from ever setting foot on land or she would be stripped of her pearls and my Grandfather was moved inland by his parents."

"That's awful," April said.

"Yeah, he married my Grandma but, I think he still always loved the mera so eventually their marriage broke down. My Mum blames him for her Mum leaving. We aren't allowed to discuss the mer at home. But, my Grandfather always told me stories about the mera he loved when I visited. Every time the wind touches his cheek he says it is like a kiss from the past."

"Did he ever get to see her again?" April asked.

"Nope. I'd never even seen the sea before moving to Shell Island."

April tried to imagine a life without the sea. But, she couldn't, it was intrinsically linked to her.

"Well, I'm glad you got to see the sea," April said.

"Do you want to talk about your Mum?"

April stiffened. Her heart rate spiked. Megan shivered involuntarily as electricity crackled through the room.

"I don't think I can yet," April said quietly.

"Okay," Megan gave her a small smile.

"Thank you."

The two sat in silence for a moment then both started reading.

After a further half an hour of waiting, Alex and Connor finally re-entered the room.

"What did Darius say?" Megan asked before they were even seated. Megan moved to make room for them both on her couch. Alex sat and Connor moved to sit by April.

"Dad was quite excited," Alex said running his hands over his jeans.

"Excited?" Megan asked.

"Yeah, apparently his intelligence team hacked into the mer military database. And looking at the information they deduced that a recon sort of mission was being aimed at Shell Island," Alex started.

"That was why Dad moved us so suddenly from the island. After we left a team came in and removed anything of value and evacuated everyone. The mermaid mission was delayed though for some reason," Connor continued. Both brothers seemed reluctant to continue.

"Mer," April said tersely.

"And? That doesn't explain the fire and tidal wave?" Megan pressed.

"Well, Freddie suggested that Dad bomb the island. Demoralise the mer and provoke them into an attack," Alex said.

"Darius bombed his own island. That's absurd," Megan interjected.

"The tidal wave was a mer retaliation then," April said quietly.

"I'm not sure," Alex said "Why would you attack an island when it is clearly already destroyed?"

"Did your Dad mention what the mer were after?" Megan asked.

"He didn't say," Connor replied.

"Only an incredibly powerful mer could wield such a wave. And usually only after drawing as much energy as possible from your Factus pearl," April mused.

"Maybe it was an emotional response? Like you April, when you found out about…" Alex trailed off.

"My Mum," April finished. She took some deep breaths to try and bring her heart rate back down again.

The other three started talking earnestly about the reason why the mer would be looking for something on Shell Island. Something that was clearly removable or Darius wouldn't have set fire to his own island. Darius himself perhaps Megan supplied. Information kept in his office maybe. None of the options seemed like they would provoke such a response. As they talked April's mind slipped into a pearl blackout.

She was seven and she had swum out of her window. She was dashing through the open sea testing her full speed when she came across a loan manatee. The calf was abandoned. April slowed down to approach it. "Hello," April said using her Communico powers. She waved her hand in a circle wielding her Assurgere powers to grow some kelp and offered it to the calf. "I won't hurt you. I can be your friend," she said.

The manatee swam over and ate the kelp. April started to stroke the manatee, "What's your name?" she asked. The calf looked at her quizzically. "I shall call you Maxi." April hugged the manatee. She looked all afternoon but couldn't find a herd for Maxi so she snuck him back into the royal stables. In her minds' eye, April saw her silvery tail and Maxi's grey fin slip into the barn. The seahorse handler who worked there promised to look after him if April came and exercised him every day while she was staying at the Hanarian Palace.

Suddenly April was eleven. After, a particularly boring lesson with her Mum on pearl mining, April rushed to the stables. Maxi usually returned from his swim to greet her there. As she approached his favourite stall the smell hit her. Swimming faster and faster she called out to him, "Maxi!" She reached the stall and found Maxi floating at the top of his pen, a bleeding gash across his belly. His body already starting to bloat. April swam and hugged him trying to see if he could be saved. He had been one of her best friends, never treating her differently because she was a Princess. Without her realising the tumult in her mind radiated through her powers. A cyclone whirled all around her. The stables were torn apart and dragged into the storm. Her cyclone grew until it reached the surface of the water drawing sea creatures into it as it built. Eventually, it towered high into the sky rooted to April as its base. Finally, after expending so much energy, April collapsed to her tail and the water crashed down.

April came back to reality with a start. None of her friends noticed that she had slipped into a pearl blackout. It was always the death of a loved one that provoked someone to unleash uncontrollable power.

"Me, they were looking for me."

Megan, Alex and Connor acknowledged April for the first time in several minutes. Before they could interrupt her April continued.

"If the mission was to save me, then that fire would have signalled my death," April said definitively. "And," April realised, "if my Dad was on the mission. Then he could have summoned the wave. It wasn't retaliation. It was mourning and grief. Returning me to the water and releasing my body from the flames," April said.

"That actually makes sense," Megan said. April restrained herself from rolling her eyes.

"Does that mean that Dad did know then?" Connor asked leaning forward.

"Know that they were looking for me? Probably," April asserted. "It will be seen as a direct assault against the mer."

"Forcing the mer to retaliate. With your presumed death April, Dad could have started a war," Alex said.

"I need to go home," April stood then promptly sat back down. "But first, I'm going to get my pearls back."

"Do you think Dad knew you were on Shell Island?" Alex asked slowly. "If the mer authorities knew, then I wouldn't put it past him either."

April sat in stunned silence, "I don't know."

"Surely, he didn't," Connor interjected. "Otherwise why would he let you wander around freely?"

"Unless this is all a trap," Alex said warily looking at April.

CHAPTER 29

Sitting and spinning in Darius' chair April felt incredibly comfortable. Yet, you wouldn't think this when looking at her. Her eyes kept on darting between the two doors that allowed access into the room. Her hands gripped the armrests tightly and her legs were folded at an odd angle. But, the soft leather that moulded to her body was wonderful. Alex had been relegated to a standard chair while he was at the computer typing furiously. April had never really come across a computer before, apart from Alex's laptop, and she was fascinated by it. Alex's laptop seemed so small compared to this massive screen. She was used to flicking images in and out of the water from the different Iris pads. Iris pads let you pull data straight from the Iris pearls and onto other Iris pads. But, she felt like the computer was practically alive with its knowledge of everything. Alex had told her what he was doing but after staring blankly at him for several seconds he summarised - "I'm copying everything."

Everything sounded like a lot in April's mind. As she had been no use to Alex she started helping Connor select books from his Dad's library. But, apparently, Connor could "copy" them too so she was leaving him to it. April flicked through each book he passed her to confirm that it was useful before Connor whisked it away again to copy it. Her thoughts were preoccupied once again with all the problems and obstacles that seemed to be mounting against her. She twisted the cool black stone in her hands for comfort.

Darius' study was the last place she felt safe. The windowless room made her feel trapped. The wall-to-wall bookcases felt ominous as if they were watching her and may tumble down upon her at any moment. It was also the only room April had seen so far, which was allowed a break from the white and black design of Rushton. The dark, oak, wooden desk was formidable and adorned with green leather inlays. But the ornate rug depicting a battle scene was what unnerved April the most. April stared at it now trying to decipher what the image represented. It looked like men in the sky were attacking those down below. But, in the centre was a great ship breaking up the crowd. Around the edges were smaller scenes all depicting different battles. The rug was a fascinating yet, grotesque piece of art. The entire room felt like it was bearing in on her. The land-based materials were intimidating and foreign in a way April had never experienced before.

The brothers led April through a series of white corridors to access Darius' private study. Although there was a quicker route through the brother's apartments they wanted to check where their Dad was before breaking in. When they knew he was occupied elsewhere they slipped inside his office and locked the door behind them. It was the only old-fashioned door with a key that April had seen in the entirety of Rushton. April was shocked at the lack of security the legged President had to get into his inner sanctum. Didn't he realise how easily his teenage sons could access all the information the President was privy too? Then again April thought, she and Ethan had done similar things before. Once when Ethan had a particularly annoying bodyguard, April and he used the King's private mer mail to get the mer reassigned. It had been child's play April remembered. Those in power often underestimated those closest to them.

April closed her eyes for a moment and reached out her Essentia energy. She let her consciousness move through Rushton.

"April, you're glowing," Connor said while copying the books.

"I know." April opened her eyes and span round to face him in the large spinning chair. "I'm trying to find my pearls."

"I thought you couldn't," Connor said.

"I am trying though. I thought maybe I would be far enough away from the poison here," April said tossing the stone back and forth in her hands.

"And?" Connor asked.

"What do you think?" she said raising her eyebrows. "The sea is calling me, but the poison is like a constant pain stabbing me when I use my Essentia powers," April said rubbing her forehead.

"Is this the longest you've ever been on land for?" Alex asked without looking up.

"Yes, actually it is," April said turning to him in her chair. "Why?"

"I was wondering if that would have an effect on you?"

"I don't know," April said. "There are stories of mer going land crazy, but I don't think they're true."

She spun around in the chair again, deep in thought, while keeping up her post as sentry. Fortunately, Alex hadn't found any information to suggest that a full staged war had been waged against the mer. But, April was certain it was only a matter of time. And what then, whose side would Alex and Connor choose? This was something to discuss with them. April didn't want either of the brothers to put themselves in danger to help her protect her mer. They were risking enough already. Darius would guess how the mer acquired all this intelligence. April was about to open her mouth when she heard a disturbance outside.

"Guys!" April hissed.

Alex and Connor immediately stopped what they were doing and listened. There were definite murmurings coming from outside the door to their right.

"April, I need 40 more seconds, then I have almost all the useful information. Can you hold that door?" Alex whispered.

April nodded and Connor proceeded to organise the books neatly away. Focusing her Factus powers April closed her fist and hardened the moisture around the lock freezing the mechanics in place. Alex was drumming his fingers at the keyboard while April quickly manoeuvred all the furniture around him so there was no trace of them being there.

"Got it," Alex grinned; he quickly shut down the computer and deleted any evidence of someone accessing the cloud or the hard drive. Connor nodded in agreement and the three slipped quickly out of the alternate door. April released the moisture on the lock once they were a safe distance away from the study. This door conveniently led into Darius' private rooms that eventually connected through to Alex and Connor's living quarters.

"Dad is such an arrogant arsehole," Alex said as he flopped onto the couch. April sat down next to him hoping that Alex's chilled out attitude would rub off on her. She ignored Connor's hurt expression as he sat on the couch opposite on his own.

"I mean the man's security is ridiculous. Just because he's in his own private fortress he seems to think there are no threats. I have half a mind to inform Freddie. He would flip if he knew."

"You got it all though?" Connor questioned trying to bring his brother back to the seriousness of the situation.

"Yup, and now any information dear old Dad is privy to I am too." Alex smugly waved his phone in the air. "One day he is going to regret my unconventional education."

Alex's good humour was infectious and April couldn't help laughing.

"Did you copy all the useful texts Connor?" April asked

"Everything," Connor said finally relaxing his facial muscles.

"Let's hope there is something in there to explain my power surges..."

At that moment, the door swung open. Before she had a chance to realise what was going on, Alex started kissing her. Although utterly confused, she was aware of Connor exiting the lounge area quickly.

"Hey!" Connor said.

"Alex, nothing has changed then," a chilling drawl sounded through the room. As the footsteps retreated and the chatter of Connor and the man receded into the kitchen, Alex pulled away - his face scarlet.

"What the hell was that?" April stared him down.

"Sorry! I didn't know what to do. I thought it was best to go with what Dad told him."

"Told who?" April demanded.

"That was Freddie."

April's mind whirled. Freddie was here. She was going to be caught. There was no way he wouldn't recognise her.

"Alex, I need to leave now," April said.

"April, calm down," Alex hissed. "You're making the water in the vases start to rise. Come on, let's go upstairs and wait until he's gone." April sat rooted to the spot.

"He expects the worst of me anyway."

"I can't stay here forever Alex," April whispered.

"You need your pearls, and you need to learn any useful information that will help your Dad."

About to protest April quickly stopped herself. Following Alex out of the room, she suddenly said, "Alex! If Freddie is here, do you think Ethan might be too?"

CHAPTER 30

Pearls, Ethan, pearls, Ethan. Pushing aside her worries about her Dad and her shock about her Mum, all April could focus on was finding Ethan and her pearls. She needed to find them. If she found the pearls first, obviously she could help Ethan. But, so far her searches had been futile. Hopefully, Alex had found the information on the prisoners of war by now. They may have been able to copy Darius' intelligence, but it was a lot of information to sift through. Lying in Alex's bed she wished she was back home. The black and white interior was driving her crazy. The sparseness of the Ruston suite made her feel claustrophobic unless she was sat by the window in the lounge. Her brain kept flicking from coherent plans to frantic worry, with alarming speed. She felt so useless. Kicking her legs in frustration and anger she yielded to the Commutavi energy. With a purple glow, she transformed her legs back into her tail. It made her feel more powerful. In the sea, she was a force to be reckoned with. On land, she was Alex's latest conquest. She tossed her stone back and forth. Her eyes followed the stone mesmerised by its energy, like slipping into a current, her mind was swept away.

Darkness swirled around her and the water was ice cold. But, despite the burning freeze across her body, April felt alive with heat. She swam forward but couldn't tell if she had actually moved. The black tendrils enveloping her made it impossible to see anything but them. Subconsciously she was aware that she should be scared. Yet, her heartbeat remained even. A sudden surge and she was pulled down further into the depths of the ocean. Her body stayed calm and in control. No fear permeated through her. Finally, she was back in the sea.

"Follow me." A voice echoed through the darkness.

April calmly looked behind her to where the voice came from. The black spirals had formed themselves into an immense tunnel. Finally, able to use her tail she pushed off deeper into the darkness.

"We've been waiting for you."

Yes, April thought. A throbbing hum travelled through her body. She could feel power emanating from the end of the tunnel. Just a little bit closer and she would be there. Just a little bit further. She kicked her tail with more vigour.

"Not long now." The voice grew louder and she strained to decipher if it was many voices all speaking together as one. The power of the voice resonated deep within her. This is where she belonged. The further she swam the more her head cleared. Thoughts of her pearls, her Mum, her escape all became faint. She was the ocean. Welcoming the tendrils as they slithered to her, they started to wrap and entwine like slippery black gossamer around her arms. Fusing into her skin the black swirls imprinted themselves into her veins. She was part of the power now. It was hers to control.

"Connor," Megan screamed. "Connor!"

The note of panic in Megan's voice sent Connor flying up the stairs. Before he reached Alex's room he could feel something was wrong in the air. It radiated cold raw power. Racing towards Megan's screams Connor came to a stop at the door. Cowering on the floor, Megan hid from the black light pouring out of the room. It moved as if it was searching for something. Black tendrils were reaching out in all directions, climbing through the air. Connor's face fell. Careful not to let the black light engulf him, he moved into the room.

Shock registered on his face as he saw April floating mid-air supported by an undulating sea of black light. He had never seen anything like it. At first, he stood stunned yet mesmerised, until he saw that the darkness was not merely supporting April, it was consuming her. Dark marks were blossoming under her skin as the light pulsed through her. He stepped over the dark light and heaved himself onto the bed. He stood up and careful not to touch the energy pulsing around her, cupped her face. He fought to stop his hands from shaking. He didn't know if she was in immediate danger.

"April? April please? Can you hear me," the desperation in his own voice shocked him. He grabbed her hand and had to stop himself from recoiling. Ice-cold skin greeted him, but her hand pulsed with energy. It sent a shiver through Connor. This was not like the usual glow April emitted. Connor had no idea how to help her.

"April, can you hear me?" Connor paused clearing his throat. "Come back to me." He pushed her hair away from her forehead.

"Please April. You're the most powerful mera in the world. Only you can stop this." Connor swallowed the fear lodged in his throat. But, he felt alive with power. He could feel the darkness radiating through him.

"April, listen to my voice. You need to fight this. Follow my voice."

Connor? What is he doing here? April thought. Connor, where are you? She looked around in the darkness

"Don't listen to him," the dark voices surged again. She was flooded with darkness, the energy filling her lungs. April gasped.

April's back arched and the darkness surged out from her with more intensity. Connor looked around the room in desperation to find some way of helping her. The darkness swarmed towards him lifting him from the bed. He grasped April's hand firmly once more. The tendrils of dark light tried to smother him out of the door. The room's temperature plummeted once more. As it intensified a cup of water on the bedside table froze and shattered the over-expanded glass.

"April," Connor shouted in earnest as he struggled to remain in contact with her. His teeth started chattering and as he looked back down he cringed in fear. Cocooned in a web of dark light the only parts of him left unwrapped were his head and outstretched arm. Kicking out with his legs, Connor attempted to break free. But, the light only tightened further around him.

Currents shifted below April as she swam further into the swirling tunnel. She was close now. Flexing her arm she brought a cascade of darkness in front of her so she could slide down to the voices.

"Arghhh," she exhaled in frustration. Something had grasped her hand. Pulling at her. A whirlpool of black tendrils whipped themselves in front of April. The warmth in her hand started to spread through her body. As she started to come back to consciousness she looked blindly around in panic. As she focused on the warmth in her hand, the whirling blackness around her went into a frenzy. Remembering the power she felt earlier, April slashed down at the darkness. Slicing through the tendrils she swam free. She sped up into warmer waters. The darkness started to recede and April instinctively swam upwards toward the light.

In a panic, April awoke and immediately fell. She screamed in surprise and sat up and looked around.

"Connor? What are you doing down there?" April asked. She shivered as she looked over the side of Alex's bed. Transforming back into her legged form she swung off the bed to help lift Connor up. "What's going on Connor?" she asked. Connor stared dumbfounded.

"Connor? What is going on?" April said again. She started fiddling with her nightdress, its length making her feel exposed.

"You really don't know. Do you?" he replied and April noticed for the first time that Connor was ashen-faced with a sheen of sweat across his brow.

"Are you okay? What's happened?" April asked. At this moment Megan burst through the door. April took in her dishevelled hair and tear streaks running down her face. Without thinking she went to give Megan a hug. Before she could reach her Megan recoiled and took a lunging step towards Connor. Taken aback by the quivering mess in front of him, Connor automatically reached out and Megan sunk into his arms.

A blush reached April's cheeks. She didn't know where to look and took a step away from them.

"Umm Megan, Connor, what's going on?" April asked hesitantly. She felt like the guilty party but had no idea what she had done.

"April. You were covered in darkness. No... you were exuding black light. It was coming from you," Connor stammered unsure of how to explain it. Now that April was back to her normal self, it seemed absurd.

"The whole room went cold. These black fingers were working their way into your skin..."

April dropped down onto the bed. She didn't need to hear the rest of the story. All too clearly, she could picture Connor's words now that he was saying them. It hadn't just been a dream. April's mind sped through all the mer knowledge she had, but she could only come to one conclusion... and it didn't make any sense.

Tilting forward she grasped her head in her hands. None of this made sense. She was too young. These powers weren't hers to control. They shouldn't be anyone's to control. It was supposed to be a legend. Looking up at Megan she knew she was right. April shook her head in confusion. Without thinking she flexed her arm as she had done in the dream and watched mesmerised as dark spirals danced around her wrist.

~

Alex arrived late that evening. He had been summoned by his Dad to lend advice to one of the research teams trying to crack a code. Reading between the lines Alex had gathered that the code was April's pearls. His phone ran out of battery around lunchtime so he raced upstairs to tell April the news. Alex was pretty sure he knew where her pearls were. Perhaps if April channelled her energy she could confirm the location before they planned a rescue.

"April? Are you decent?" Alex called as he knocked on the door. Now that Freddie was around, Alex and April had been sharing a room. They were enacting their fictional fling to make sure he wasn't suspicious. After an awkward couple of days, following April walking in on him naked, Alex had learnt to knock. Alex chortled again at the thought. April had turned bright red in embarrassment. She was such a prude. He knocked again to no response. Alex opened the door slowly, expecting to see her asleep in bed. But, there was no April. A shiver of worry ran through him. He wandered around the room getting ready for bed when he realised he could hear the shower running. He knocked on the bathroom door to no response. He opened the door slowly giving April time to shout at him if she wasn't decent. There in his bathtub was a sleeping mera with a cloud raining above her.

Alex smiled. He walked over and bent beside the bath careful not to sit under the rain cloud. He was thankful that her long hair and the copious bubbles protected her modesty.

"April, sweetie, it's time to wake up," Alex said in a faux motherly voice. April's arms splashed down into the water as she woke with a start. Jumping back Alex laughed shaking the water off of him. The cloud instantly vanished.

"Alex!" she protested. Quickly folding her arms over her chest.

"Sorry I couldn't resist," Alex said. "Don't worry you're all covered up. I was worried you were drowning."

"Yes, a mera drowning in a shower…"

Alex barked a laugh and sat down on the bath mat.

"I guess I must have fallen asleep," April said self-consciously. "What time is it?"

"It was eleven when I made it back to the apartment. Come on let's get you out of there."

Alex bent over and scooped her out of the bathtub.

"Alex!" she protested, her hands scrambling to protect her modesty.

"Ouef! You weigh a tonne April!"

"Rude. My tail is all muscle."

Alex settled her down on the fuzzy bath mat and fetched some warm towels from the heated rack. Wrapping them around April she sat in front of him like a giant crystallised caterpillar. A glow of violet light later and ten toes poked out of the end of the towel.

"Shall I give you some privacy?" Alex smirked. April gave him a pointed look. As Alex retreated back into his room she called through the door, "can you throw me some pyjama's please?"

Walking into the room April sunk into the bed and pulled the duvet high up around her. Alex switched the TV on and they started the next episode of the series they were watching. Alex had learnt early on that April struggled to sleep, and that he couldn't sleep when she kept on waking him up. So, their routine had slowly developed. He would never admit it but his favourite part was combing her hair. There was something satisfying about combing out all the knots. He liked being friends with a girl and having someone to hang out with. Pulling the comb slowly through her damp hair one last time he placed his hands on her shoulders. He would miss her when she was gone.

"There you go."

"Thank you," April smiled as with a swish of her hand she wicked all the moisture from her hair and transferred it into a plant pot. April shuffled back under the covers and rolled over to face Alex as he too snuggled into the mattress.

"How was your meeting today?" April asked.

"I think I know where your pearls are," Alex said sitting up. April sat up instantly.

"What? You know where they are? Can we get them?" April asked. She thrummed with energy and didn't even attempt to stop the white glow permeating from her.

"I think so," he leaned over and grabbed his laptop. He started typing and pulled up a map of Rushton.

"So, we are here." He pointed. "And here, five levels down, but almost directly below us... I think are your pearls," Alex said, highlighting the place on the map. April stared at it. All this time, they were right below her.

"How do we get there?" April asked.

"It's not easy, but I think with some careful planning we can get in and out using one of the all-access wrist cuffs," Alex said.

'How long will it take to get one?' April asked.

"I don't know, I will need to either swipe one or think of a way to convince Freddie to give me one," Alex said.

"Okay."

"April, we can do this. We can get your pearls back." He smiled at her encouragingly.

"Yes, but then what?" she said. She hugged the duvet around her. Alex noticed goose bumps break out across her arms.

"Then, it's up to you," Alex said. "I presume with your full powers you can make your way back home?"

"Yes, but then, what if I'm damaged," April said, pulling her legs up to her chest.

"Damaged?"

"Alex, I should be able to break free from here even without my pearls. But, my powers, I can't control them," April said.

"April, over the last week you've been bombed off an island, washed up on another, been poisoned, found out your Mum has passed and had to trust two complete strangers for help when you have no idea where you are. Of course, your powers are out of sorts," Alex said.

April looked up at him, her blue eyes shining with tears. He could feel the energy rolling from her as if she was projecting her emotions.

"I mean it April. There is nothing wrong with you," Alex said. He leant in and hugged her around the shoulders.

"Thanks Alex," April murmured into his shirt. The energy bubbling within her abated slightly. "It's late we should probably sleep."

"Okay," he paused wanting to say more to help her, but instead he leant over to turn off the light.

"Goodnight."

"Night Alex," April said rolling away from him.

CHAPTER 31

"Is she stable now?"

"Yes. I think we're out of the danger zone. Her body recuperated remarkably after the King came to see her. The powers of the Curo pearl are awesome." The female nurse shook her head in awe while she swam out of the room chatting with the junior doctor. The movement of the water ruffled the sheets covering Kayla. Stirring in her sleep, Kayla opened her eyes consciously for the first time in a week.

Not again was her first internal groan. What had happened this time? Kayla slumped her body further into the bed. She tried to sit up but it felt as if the water was heavier. Raising her arm to her head Kayla flexed her fingers. Something was wrong. Thrusting her tail and ignoring the frailty in its stroke she forced herself into an upright position. Summoning her Factus energy she pushed her hand upwards. Nothing. Kayla repeated the movement. Again, nothing, again... Nothing.

"No," she said quietly as she looked at her hands in bewilderment.

She tried to swim but her heaviness sunk her to the floor. Feebly she thrust her arm forward. Tears spilling down her cheeks, she rested her head against her bed. She resolutely stared upwards not wanting to look down at her bracelet. Choking back a sob she steeled her expression. Finally, she brought forward her pearl bracelet scared to see what she already knew. Bringing her finger forward to touch her Factus pearl, she felt a lump form in her throat. Instead of warming and lighting to her presence, it lay lifeless.

~

"What happened?" Kayla demanded.

Sitting in the family suite of the private hospital that her grandparents sponsored, Kayla stared impassively at her Dad. The soothing abstract paintings and floating petals drifting around the room were wasted on Kayla and Nathaniel. She noticed the dark circles under his eyes and she saw how his hands shook. But, none of this mattered to her. Answers were all she required. Maintaining her stare she posed her question again.

"What happened?"

"Kayla, dear, you aren't..." the King was silenced by the cruel look his daughter threw at him.

"You look so like your Mum," he sighed. Kayla felt her heart soften a little. But, it didn't weaken her resolve. She had lost everything. No longer could she afford weakness or leniency or dependency. In Kayla's mind, she was alone and that was the best way to be. Summoning a word, she had not used in years she asked the King one more time.

"Dad? What happened?"

Looking around as if hoping someone else would rise and takeover this summons, Nathaniel tried and failed to find the words necessary. Where was Freya? His eyes glistened once more with tears. Reaching for his powers he wielded his Curo pearl to soothe him. Kayla noted the sky-blue glow and her eyes hardened once more.

"Dad?"

"You were tricked. The legged's intelligence system infiltrated Yelta's systems. They knew about the raid on the Island," Nathaniel finally said.

"It was all for nothing," Kayla said quietly. Memories of planning flooded back to her.

"What about April?"

"You believed your sister was held there because of the energy surge. It's not yet known whether..." at this Nathaniel paused. He pulled his blazer closer around him. "Whether she was present on the island at the time of the bomb." He stopped and stared at his daughter trying to convey to her the pain that telling this story brought. Kayla stared impassively at him. He couldn't tell what was going on behind those deep green eyes.

"As the island went up in flames, you released your powers. But, they weren't yours to use. You tapped into the pearl's core. And now, they're... free." Nathaniel finished sadly.

"Free?" Kayla grasped at the only positive information she could glean. "So, they haven't disappeared."

"The power hasn't vanished, it still exists," he hesitated not wanting to anger his daughter further. "But it has returned to the ocean. Your powers, your ability to wield the Factus energy is gone," Nathaniel said.

Kayla visibly blanched. Seeing the pain on his daughter's face, Nathaniel reached for his Curo pearl once more to send its relief across them both.

"No!" Kayla shouted swimming upright, her tail twitching in anger. Nathaniel's blue glow faded immediately. "You might want to hide from reality, but I won't." Looking down at him she bowed marginally and swam from the room. The doctors had told her to return to her bed at once. But, she turned away from her door at the last moment. Kayla wanted fresh sea.

Outside the hospital the water was cooler. Its movement across her skin was more effective than any treatment she had had so far. She swayed in the current and relished the feeling. Being supported by the sea allowed her body to finally relax. Closing her eyes, she imagined herself far out in the open ocean, just her, and no responsibilities. A whooshing sound above made her look up. A new ray fleet was arriving with patients for the hospital. The floating poison still lingered at the public hospital in Hanaria so all patients were being transferred to private and pop-up hospitals. Kayla felt bad taking up a whole suite of rooms. She didn't deserve it.

Shutting her eyes briefly, the tidal wave loomed back above her threatening to collapse. She understood her dream now. The wave had been her. That was how she had lost her powers. All her energy had been sent out into the ocean. And now it was gone. Sagging against the wall she didn't feel much like the meritia leader of the mer. She couldn't do this. She wanted her sister. She needed her Mum. Kayla fought to stop herself from thinking about them. Did she trust anyone else? Her Dad was clearly losing control. Demetrius would help her. What was her next step? Kayla thought over all the actions and decisions she had made over the last few weeks. Despite Yelta's strategy the leggeds were gaining more and more control of the sea. The public relations departments were getting nowhere.

Legged media seemed hell-bent on blaming the mer. Suddenly it hit her. They wanted war. They wanted war and would not stop until they won. This wasn't some terror attack that would go away with careful manoeuvring, this was the beginning of a war. She'd tried to deny it, perhaps wishing that it wouldn't come to this. But, if it was war the legged wanted... it was a war that Kayla would win. Kayla tore off her pearl bracelet and let it fall. Watching it sink, Kayla let her fear drown too. Only she was capable of protecting the mer now.

CHAPTER 32

Setha floated in line to shake hands with the mer at her Dad's Reflexus. She put a smile on her face and thanked the countless mer swimming past, each one with their Essentia pearl glowing brightly. In honour of her Dad's flamboyant artistic style, everyone was dressed gaudily as the invitation encouraged. Setha spotted one woman wearing a rainbow Tail Tight and another head to toe in pink seaweed. Shaking hands, saying thank you and nodding occasionally she couldn't even remember who had floated past her in the reception line. She had dreaded this day ever since her Mum and Grandmother set the date. But, now numbness settled over her.

Last week the nurses told Setha and her Mum that the meeting scheduled the afternoon of the poisoning was to warn Setha that Cooper was terminal. Within a week he would have suffered a rapid decline that would have most likely been the end. Her Dad's death was a shock, but Setha knew he would have chosen this death over one in his hospital bed. He hated being cooped up in the hospital. And, at least she had been with him. This was what she kept telling herself, that really it was all for the best. She had been preparing herself for this moment for years. All that time and yet she was still robbed of the chance to say goodbye.

"Setha honey," Roxana Moretta called. "It's time to go to the reception now."

Setha smiled and swam towards the shell shuttle that was taking them back to her Grandmother's house.

"What a lovely Reflexus," Jocelyn Moretta, Setha's Grandmother stated. "It was nice that so many mer came to say farewell to Cooper."

Setha nodded at her Grandmother. She looked across at her Mum who was uncharacteristically silent.

"Mum, are you okay?" Setha asked.

"Yes, yes I am. I was just thinking about your Dad and what will happen now," Roxana said. Her make-up was still immaculate but when Setha looked into her eyes she could see the film of tears waiting to flow.

"I should have come home," Roxana said quietly. Setha and Jocelyn looked at each other across the shell. Roxana was not one for showing emotion; she kept that for the cameras. When her husband became sick she couldn't deal with it. It simply did not fit in with how she saw her life.

"Mum it's not your fault," Setha said.

"He wanted you to be happy and live your life Roxie," Jocelyn said. There was little love between Roxanna and her Mother-in-law. Jocelyn decried Roxana's lavish lifestyle and love of attention. Roxana looked up in shock and nodded in thanks. Jocelyn turned away to stare out the window. She was wearing the rainbow-speckled dress she wore for her son's wedding. They had picked it out together and she was glad it still fitted. As she stroked the fabric she tried to hold back her own tears.

Setha tapped on her bracelet hoping against hope that April had finally been rescued and had messaged her. She needed her best friend more than ever now. But, there was still an error message attached to April's Iris. She bowed her head in defeat. Her mass of curls swung forward and floated around her face.

"Setha?" Roxanna said "Are you okay honey?" She leant forward and flicked the tip of her tail on top of her daughters.

Setha looked up slowly, tucked her hair behind her ears and gently lifted her tail in response to her Mum's.

"Yes Mum. I'm okay."

CHAPTER 33

Kayla thought that adapting to life without her powers would be easy. Although her Factus pearl energy channels were nowhere near as powerful as April's she hadn't realised how much she used them in everyday life. Even swimming was more arduous now. After her Dad's revelation that her powers were 'free', Kayla spent the majority of her time in physiotherapy. She had to learn how to swim again without the pearls aiding her and adjust to the new weight of the water. Everyone focused on her physical recovery. Yet, no one seemed to care about the chaos raging within her. Frustration grew and grew like the wave she had released but now she had no way to expel it.

She snuck into the reception to find out when she would be allowed to leave the hospital. The man at the desk was one of Kayla's favourite wardens. He wasn't nearly as surly as the others.

"Hello Jenko, having a good day?"

"Hello Your Highness. It has been a quiet morning thankfully. How are you?"

"I'm good, just ready to go home now. Do you know when I can go home?"

A disapproving tut behind her caused Kayla to swivel in mid-sea. There, floating before her, hands on her purple tailfins was her grandmother.

"Kayla, what are you doing down here? You should be resting," Clarry said.

"Hello Grandma." She swam forwards and kissed her Grandmother on each cheek.

"Come on Kayla, back up to your room." She ushered Kayla towards the water shoot. "Jenko, some tea would be greatly appreciated."

Clarry joined Kayla at the water shoot and together they floated up to the top floor. Clarry wandered through the suite and opened up all the blinds. She fluffed the pillows then made the bed and finally sat herself down on the sponge. Kayla watched her grandmother tending to the room. That she wasn't saying anything was highly unusual. When Clarry finally sat, Kayla joined her on the other side of the sponge and hugged her tail into her chest.

"You look so like your Mum," Clarry said her stern facial expression finally softening. "How do you feel about... about losing her?"

Kayla sat in silence. She hadn't discussed her Mum with anyone yet. She stroked the beading on her waist wrap.

"I miss her."

Clarry moved over to Kayla's side of the couch and put her arm around her shoulders. Kayla stiffened for a moment before dropping her head down onto her shoulder.

"I just, I can't afford to lose control Grandma," Kayla said her voice thick with her unshed sobs. "So many people are counting on me, and I can't take the hope anymore. The pain, it's too much."

"Shhh," Clarry said and gently stroked her Granddaughter's head. Wielding her Factus energy she floated over a blanket and tucked it around her.

"You need rest my dear," Clarry waited until Kayla's breathing evened out before continuing. "You can't shut everyone out. Needing help is not a weakness."

Kayla blinked away her tears before looking up. Clarry was staring down at her.

"True strength is admitting you cannot succeed alone."

"But..." Kayla started but she was silenced with a look.

"Use your connection to the pearls. Through them we are all connected. They unite us under the sea."

Kayla averted her gaze from her Grandmother's.

"Kayla?" she enquired. A knock at the door stopped her from questioning Kayla further.

"Come in please," Clarry called. A mer swam in with a bubble tray laid out for tea. "Perfect, let's eat, you will feel better with some food in you."

Kayla swam up from the couch with her Grandmother. She tugged on her sleeve to cover her bare wrists.

That afternoon Kayla was to endure another session of physiotherapy.

"Thrust your tail forward with determination to then swivel yourself around ready to fire." The physiotherapist of the day intoned. Kayla obediently thrust forward. The dull room was becoming the place that haunted her dreams. Considering they were in the middle of one of the most beautiful oceans, the designer had lacked inspiration. The rehabilitation rooms looked out onto a bleak stonewall which blocked out all natural light. The room itself was filled with practical chairs and patient beds. There was nothing to inspire her while she endlessly drilled tail lifts, balance reconfiguration exercises and swim patterns.

"Eurgh," she vented in frustration. She thrust out with her arms instinctively but was annoyed when the bubbles did not immediately dispel as they used to under her command.

"Princess Kayla it's okay..." the therapist started before Kayla cut her off.

"It's not okay!" she shouted. Meeting with her Grandma this morning had disturbed her calm facade.

"Everything is not okay," she repeated again more quietly. Letting herself sink to the floor she curled her tail towards herself and squeezed hard. All she wanted was to not feel angry and upset and confused. The therapist floated down towards her and settled herself on the ground. Keeping a respectable distance, she asked the Princess the one question no one else had.

"Would you like to talk about it?" she asked hesitantly. Kayla looked up. Instinctively, she opened her mouth to say no. But, something stopped her. The mera said nothing and remained sat on the floor. Kayla hesitated and then smiled.

"What's your name?" Kayla was ashamed to admit that she didn't listen to the mera's introduction at the start of their session. Insignificant details had stopped mattering to her days ago.

"I'm Fallon Your Highness. I attended the same boarding school as your sister. I heard that it is, well rumoured, that she... Have you, are you..." Her sentence hung in the water around them.

"I thought she was dead once. Now, I know she is. I can't bare feeling hope anymore, it's too painful to have it torn away again."

"Hope? How can you not have hope?"

"Because," Kayla paused "I gave up."

The silence settled around them and Kayla started to relax. There. She had said it. She had given up hope. Maybe not the hope for her mer, but hope for herself. Happiness was no longer within reach.

"I miss my Mum. I haven't, I mean, I hardly saw her for three years. And now I never will. I threw myself into proving that I could be worthy of my station. That even without impressive powers, I was still a royal. But, what was it all for. I didn't see April for three years. She wrote to me every month and I barely ever replied. Countless messages asking how I was, saying she missed me, and that she needed me. I wasn't there for her," Kayla said folding her hands in her lap.

"You can't blame yourself. You shouldered a great responsibility. You are worthy. Power doesn't make you special."

"I want to scream and then I want to cry. Repeat. Instead, here I am planning a war in-between physio sessions." At this Kayla started laughing. Aware that she probably sounded like a crazy mera she abruptly stopped.

"Thank you, Fallon. I will be back tomorrow." Uncurling herself from the floor she swam with as much dignity as she could through the door. Before it clicked shut behind her she heard Fallon whisper, "Good luck."

For the first time in a long time, she felt like just maybe she might have found a friend.

CHAPTER 34

Pain, boredom, pain, boredom. That was Ethan's routine now. Nothing else entered his day. He wasn't sure what was worse at this point though. It was debatable what lasted longer the pain or the boredom. He had long since stopped counting the days. What was the point? It didn't make anything happen any quicker. If anything, the snail pace passage of time was more depressing. It was easier to not give up hope this way. He was still certain that someone would find him sooner or later. He just had to make sure he was still in one piece when he was found.

The latest additions to Ethan's day were Lydia's scientific experiments. Some of these were almost fun in his dull environment. At least he got to swim. Security guards would strap him up and he would be wheeled down to a huge swimming pool. It wasn't salt water, but it would do. He was then upended into the pool and shouted at until he transformed. Not that much encouragement was necessary. Once in his mer form the electronic tasers lashed out and fastened themselves around his neck, wrist, torso and tail. Lydia would then command him to swim up and down while she changed the temperature of the water and added different chemicals. She did all this while clacking up and down the poolside in her razor-sharp heels. Clipboard in hand she made her notes. Ethan admired her for reverting back to pen and paper. This was old school research and he could tell she loved it. While Ethan swam he was entertained with Lydia's never-ending commentary.

"Do you like being released into my fish tank Ethan? If you're lucky I will keep you as my pet. I wouldn't mind taking a ride on you."

Ethan learnt early on not to bother replying to these comments. Lydia enjoyed being the wittiest person in the room.

This afternoon was one of his swimming opportunities. Being kept in this white prison was starting to mess with Ethan's head. He looked forward to his swimming sessions more than he would ever admit to Lydia. They kept him sane. He could have sworn that some of April's pearls had started to look like they were glowing. Ethan was worried he was going mad. Strolling up and down the length of the lab, Ethan tried not to think of the monotony of his day. He dared not use his Assurgere powers in case Lydia or Frederick were monitoring him. He didn't want them to try and harness his power like the mer captives before him. To keep himself occupied, he refined his escape plan. With time still to kill before someone would come to collect him Ethan practised once more. Reaching the end of the room he turned and ran. Then just before he reached the other side he jerked to the left and threw himself to the floor.

"Eurgh," he groaned as he rolled on the tiles. He looked down and saw that the blue laser was still glowing happily around his neck. Ethan sat and leant against the lab desk and banged his head against the door.

"Why won't you snap?" Ethan grimaced at his neck restraint. At some point, he theorised, if the laser was strained it would have to retract or recoil, and if he got far enough away, the retrieval motion would spring back the laser and reverse its current, thus releasing him. Ethan had no idea if this would work, but he had exhausted his other escape options.

He had tried dismantling the chair to short circuit the laser. But, he didn't understand the legged electricity. It was entirely alien to him. After one very painful electric shock, he decided to take his chances with Lydia and Frederick over being electrocuted. Ethan had been tempted to try and shatter the window and leap through. But, a grotesque image of him hanging in mid-air being strangled above the sea plagued him too much to try. He knew the only way was to either gain access to a controller or for someone to forget to re-tether him to his chair. Unfortunately, neither of these options seemed likely.

"Throwing yourself around the room again I see," Lydia said as she walked into the lab. Ethan didn't even bother to get up off the floor. He just sat and waited. She would move him when she needed him.

"Today we're going to run some fun little tests," Lydia said. She placed her case on the centre tabletop and started removing lots of little vials. Ethan tried to not look too interested. But, anything with the word 'fun' involved was not going to make for a pleasant afternoon.

"No swimming?" Ethan asked.

Lydia smiled maliciously at the disappointment in his voice. She pressed her cuff and Ethan was jolted until he made his way to stand beside her.

"Right, chop chop Ethan. I haven't got all day."

His wrists and ankles were safely cuffed together with new lasers as he reached her.

"Excellent, now roll up your sleeve and let's get started," Lydia said. She inserted one of her vials into an odd contraption. Ethan made no move to obey. Lydia smiled and tapped her control cuff. Pain lanced up Ethan's arms blinding him in pain. An attendant strode over and roughly rolled up his sleeves. The pain stopped and Ethan was left with a dull ache across his arms.

"What are you doing?" he panted. Lydia ignored him and continued to twist and turn her vial in place. Then she turned around and smiled. Ethan looked down at her warily. Then suddenly, squirt. With one swift movement, she sprayed a cold liquid onto his arm. Ethan looked down in bewilderment. She was going to spray him with different liquids? He caught the smell of salt water. Looking down at his arm he was glad to see that nothing sinister was happening. Lydia was busy making recordings out of his line of vision.

"Right, next one," she said with another spray. This one tingled slightly. It wasn't unpleasant, just odd. Lydia continued with her observations. The spraying continued for over an hour. The tingling sensation turned to itching, and the itching turned to burning. A weird hexagonal rash spread across Ethan's forearm. He winced each time she sprayed a different concoction on his arm. The pain from the last now blending into the next, until eventually he started to bleed. His corroded skin gave in and he was desperate to plunge it into the water or scream out in pain. Instead, he stood resolutely still and refused to give Lydia the satisfaction. Trapped like a prisoner in his own body he tried to focus on the sea through the window and remember who he was protecting.

"And that is the last one," Lydia said with a flourish as she squirted a final solution onto his skin. "Wasn't that fun." She smiled at him with a glimmer in her eye. Ethan refused to rise to her challenge.

Lydia started packing away her tools and left Ethan rooted to the spot.

"I'll see you tomorrow," she said with a smirk. As she left the lab a faint click signalled his leash returning to normal. The second he was released he ran to one of the sinks and fell over it. His eyes blurred over from the pain. He tried to breathe in deep gulps of air to stop himself from passing out. Slumped over the basin he ran the cold tap and lay his burning and bleeding arm in the sink. The soothing effect was instantaneous. Clouds of noxious smoke were released from his arm as the water cleansed him. A sheen of sweat covered Ethan's body. He dampened a towel and carefully sat on the floor cradling his arm with the cold, wet towel wrapped around it. It looked like Lydia was done testing the pearls Ethan thought ruefully.

CHAPTER 35

Dispatched from the hospital, Kayla was being forced to wait until the weekend to return to Yelta. Her Dad wanted her home to have a chat. Yet, after two days at home, she had barely heard more than a 'Good Morning' and a 'How are you?' from him. Kayla was worried. The staff were starting to realise something was wrong as well. The other day she spoke to the palace manager and asked him to make sure word of her Dad's condition didn't leave the palace walls. Fortunately, the palace staff were fiercely loyal to the royal family. The Curo addiction was starting to take hold as he glowed a faint sky blue at most times of the day. Whenever they tried to talk the glowing intensified. She couldn't tell if he was aware he was doing it anymore. Kayla so wished to be a merita again so she could sit on her Dad's lap and let him solve all her problems. The distance that had been growing between her and her Dad had only increased with the loss of her Mum and April.

As she prepared to leave the palace Kayla sat on her bed and actually looked around her room. Four years had passed since she called this room hers. While everything around her had changed, this room had stood still. Her old clothes still hung in the wardrobe waiting to be worn. They looked like they belonged to a completely different mera. Kayla felt like a stranger in her own bedroom. She couldn't be the mera who proudly displayed all her fighting medals, or the mera who experimented with fin dye, or the mera with seahorse print curtains... that mera was gone.

The palace was too quiet and too empty. No wonder her Dad was going crazy she thought. Being in her silent room made her miss

April and her Mum even more. They both possessed an energy that influenced everything around them. She left her room without looking back. She would ask Clyde to place her in a guest room if she ever visited one of the palaces again. Kayla swam through the corridors absent-minded. The Hanarian Palace was never a favourite of hers. She preferred the colder seas style of architecture. This one was too big and open. She shivered even in the warmth as she looked up at the high ceilings. All this space made her feel exposed. She stopped to admire the wall towering next to her. This one was inlaid with thousands of little shells swirling out to make a mosaic of one of her ancestors.

A large mer king was bare-chested in the middle holding his hands out before him. Kayla's eyes followed the curve of the arc above his head. He looked like he was juggling the pearls, the first eight arrayed before him. Essentia, Commutavi, Factus, Assurgere, Curo, Tempus, Communico and Tenebrasco. Within the giant representations of the pearls were small mosaic figures to resemble their power. Kayla leant closer to the Tenebrasco pearl depiction where a Merdevil face glared out at her. She shuddered minutely. The pearl powers had never appealed to her. There was too much uncertainty. She didn't like trusting a faceless power. She liked to be in complete control of everything she wielded. Moving away from the mosaic she swam to the end of the corridor. The final door on this floor was April's room.

Kayla hovered outside the silver door. A group of small fish popped out through the keyhole startling her. Shaking her head, she stopped her hesitation and opened the door. April's distinct smell hit her. The sweetened salty smell made April's absence even more real. Kayla swam into the room and perched on the seaweed silk bed. It was a new one since Kayla had last been here. She ran her fingers over the silken fabric. April's room had the most windows in the palace as it was placed in one of the turrets. Where Kayla liked a house to feel secure, April always wanted to feel as free as possible. Her walls were still covered in the smooth inlay of mother of pearl that April insisted on having when she was thirteen. The room shimmered exactly like April's tail.

Kayla could feel her chest constricting as memories threatened to overwhelm her. Bringing her hand to her chest she mentally scolded herself for coming in. She made to swim from the room when a flutter from April's dressing table caught her attention. She swam over to the ornately gilded, coral dressing table and mirror. Strung across the top of April's mirror was a piece of simple seaweed string with photos clammed to it. Kayla swam up to them. There were photos of Setha and Ethan, some of April on her own, one of Maxi, one of Grandma and Perch on a swim with Titan and Tarzan and there in the centre was their latest family photo.

It was one she didn't have in her photo book. April liked candid photos. In this one April was smiling into the distance, her Mum was in the process of criticising someone, the photographer most likely, Dad was looking at his watch, and there she was obediently looking straight ahead at the camera. Kayla un-clammed the photo and held it tightly. She swam out of April's window in a hurry. Not knowing where to go, or what to do she floated in the garden and tried not to think.

CHAPTER 36

"Your Majesty, we must. There is no time now. We must discuss this with Kayla. She might know something. Freya may have confided in her," Clyde implored with Nathaniel.

"Maybe," he answered his eyes struggling to focus on Clyde.

Reaching the end of his tether, Clyde swam forward. Floating in front of Nathaniel he whipped the medallion from around his neck and held it at arm's length. The Curo glow around the King immediately dulled. Nathaniel looked up and recoiled as if slapped. Clyde averted his gaze looking to his tail fin. He might have just lost his job, but at this rate, it was the only option he had left. Nathaniel would have never allowed someone so close to his pearls. Let alone just sit their stunned and immobile if they were seized.

"Come on. Princess Kayla will be waiting for us." Clyde extended his arm and half carrying Nathaniel, escorted him to one of the meeting rooms.

"Princess Kayla, thank you for meeting with us," Clyde said politely as he settled Nathaniel down in his chair. Kayla instantly noted the lack of her Dad's medallion. About to say something she caught Clyde's eye. He shook his head minutely and Kayla dropped it. Clyde had always been a loyal friend to her. He was a straight-talking mer who knew how to get to the point but also possessed an excellent sense of humour.

"Kayla. We have some sensitive information to discuss with you concerning your sister."

"April's dead," Kayla said devoid of emotion while Nathaniel stiffened at her words.

"We have reason to believe that April is alive," Clyde continued,

"No, she isn't," Kayla stubbornly interjected. "I refuse to give into whimsical hope again. Is that all you wish to discuss, if so I apologise for excusing myself."

"Okay, regardless of your present convictions, the information you may have for us would've been transmitted to you when you were younger."

"Transmitted?" Clyde had Kayla's attention now.

"Yes, as you know the Queen, your Mother was an excellent one for concealing information and choosing to reveal only what was necessary."

"Umm hmm," Kayla said. She was losing interest already. She did not want to be probed about her Mum.

"Kayla," Nathaniel said. Kayla's eyes flicked up to her Dad. The pain he was in was evident.

"We found something in your Mum's private journal." Nathaniel winced as if the act of talking about Freya was a blow to his chest. Clyde moved to float behind Nathaniel and nodded at Kayla to sit back down.

"Your Mum wrote about a time with April, a time when she was scared of her."

"Scared of April?" Kayla interjected

Nathaniel made no motion to answer Kayla's question, his eyes staring impassively ahead. Clyde hurried to keep the discussion moving before either of the royals refused to continue.

"Kayla do you ever remember your Mum telling you the Tale of the Twins?"

"Twins? As in the mertale?"

"Yes."

"Ummm, I remember it, but not as it being a special story."

"Did your Mum ever confide in you about April? Or April about your Mum?" Nathaniel asked

"April always said Mum liked me more than her. But, Mum never said it. She always told me that April was very special."

"Did she say anything else?" Clyde probed.

Kayla thought back to her memories of her Mum, something she had been shielding herself from doing to avoid becoming overwhelmed with emotion. As she looked back through her memories the powerful light of her Mum shone through.

"I remember, on Mum's first visit to Yelta, she told me I would need to protect April. Which was odd as growing up, Mum was always telling me to be careful around her as April didn't know her own strength," Kayla said.

Nathaniel raised his head and looked over at Clyde. Clyde nodded once.

"Kayla, did your Mum ever tell you about your brother and sister?"

"No." Kayla paused and her eyebrows rose. "I don't have a brother," she said slowly. She looked to her Dad for an indication of where this was going. He had retreated further into his seat. His great frame becoming one with the decorative pillows.

"We have reason to believe that the Tale of the Twins was not merely a tale but founded on fact, as many tales are. And that the very same phenomenon occurred when your parents gave birth to twins."

"Twins? When did Mum and Dad have twins?" Kayla pushed up out of her seat as she scoured her brain for the Tale of the Twins. She tried to recall the details.

"Before April was born, your Mum and I had twins, Anthony and Julia."

"And you never told us!" Kayla demanded her tail twitching.

"They died when April was very young and it pained your Mum to talk about them so we didn't," Nathaniel tried to explain. His body was shaking now and the faint blue glow around his hands was growing stronger. Clyde leant forward shooting a wary look at Nathaniel.

"The Queen believed, that like in the mertale, the powers of the royal firstborn couldn't be divided," Clyde said.

"So, the twins gave April their power?" Kayla asked looking from Clyde to her Dad.

"She absorbed it," Nathaniel said. Clyde turned to his majesty in shock.

"April has double the power of a normal first born to the throne," Nathaniel continued while Clyde stared on in shock.

"No," Kayla turned to her Dad slowly. She was losing the ability to be shocked by information anymore.

"We think April is alive and that her full powers are about to manifest earlier than they should."

"But April's dead," Kayla said.

Clyde smiled with compassion at the young Princess. The control and manner in which she conducted herself often made him forget how young she was.

"I'm going back to Yelta," Kayla declared. She waited for Clyde or her Dad to protest.

"I've almost fully adapted to my new... situation and with continued physio I will be back to normal. Clyde could you arrange transport for myself and Fallon, my physio, to Yelta tomorrow."

"Yes, Your Highness." Clyde bowed respectfully. He acknowledged when he was defeated. There was no point in distressing Kayla any further. She swept from the room without a backward glance.

Clyde looked hesitantly at Nathaniel. The King sunk further into his chair and was staring through the wall opposite him. Clyde didn't know how to proceed. He raised himself out of his chair and floated momentarily.

"Your Majesty," Clyde hesitantly asked, "I'm sorry if I overstepped my mark. But, I think you need help."

"My medallion."

Nathaniel held out his hand without looking up. Swimming forward, Clyde dropped the medallion into the King's hand. Nathaniel's palm closed slowly over it, his gaze straight ahead.

"That is all. We can meet tomorrow and discuss the implications of April's power later," Nathaniel said dismissing him. As Clyde swam for the door he looked back and saw the blue glow move from His Majesty's hand and slowly make its way up his arm and toward his heart. To the guards outside the door, Clyde said, "Make sure the King is watched tonight."

CHAPTER 37

"Fallon, pack your bags, we're leaving," Kayla said swimming into the guest suite Fallon was staying in.

Fallon looked up from her book as Kayla swam up and down the length of her room.

"Are you ready to leave?" she asked following Kayla's progress with her eyes.

"Yes," Kayla said stopping. "I have to be."

Fallon nodded and moved off the bed to start folding her clothes into her suitcase.

"Do you want to leave?" she asked.

"I want to start the war and end it," Kayla said momentarily sitting down on the end of the bed then springing up again to resume her swimming.

"But, can't you do that from here, helping your Dad?" Fallon asked slowly.

"The pearls dictate that a member of the royal bloodline must be head of the army," Kayla sighed.

"Oh," Fallon said but Kayla quickly continued.

"The pearls want someone in power who will protect their interests. They want someone who has access to the mer who can wield all the pearls."

Fallon turned around her eyebrows raised. "The pearls want you to rule the army."

"Yes, I know it sounds ridiculous," Kayla said gesticulating with her arms. "But, in the past the 'pearls didn't approve' whenever someone else tried to lead the meritia," she said making air quotes.

"Storms raged for weeks on end, the pearl caves refused to shine for the next generation of mer."

"So the pearls are alive?" Fallon said.

"Some mer believe they are," Kayla said swimming away from Fallon again.

"Do you believe they are?" She asked staring at her across the room.

"I don't know what to believe in anymore," Kayla said quietly.

CHAPTER 38

"So, what do you think the darkness is?" Megan asked Connor at breakfast that morning.

"I'm not sure. But April can't control it, whatever it is," he said.

Megan nodded. She prodded her plate of scrambled eggs that she had prepared for them. She snuck a look at Connor while he ate his way through his plate of food. He really was cute she thought.

"It's scary isn't it, but also kind of fascinating," Connor said.

Megan blushed and turned her attention back to their conversation.

"Yeah, mer powers are intriguing aren't they, and to think we all used to have powers," Megan said.

"After seeing April I'm not sure I would want them."

"Wouldn't you? I would love to have powers. I think the Tempus pearl sounds really cool. But, then again, they're really rare nowadays," Megan said.

"The ability to control the weather, yeah, April has that." Connor brought the conversation back to his favourite subject.

"Yes, April has all the pearl powers, doesn't she?" Megan asked.

"I presume so," Connor said.

"I thought so because she is next in line to the throne."

"Odd, isn't it, that April's a Princess."

"It is odd," Megan agreed. She cupped her coffee and looked up at Connor. "Do you think it's safe to be around her?"

"Safe? Of course, it is," Connor said indignantly. "It's April." He slid his plate away from him and went to get more coffee.

"April," Connor said rather flustered as April appeared on the staircase. His coffee left forgotten, he went to move towards her. But when Alex followed closely behind Connor stopped. Standing in the middle of the kitchen now unsure of what to do he reached for a bar stool and hurriedly pulled it out.

"Here you go, how are you feeling this morning?" Connor asked. He ignored his previous seat and sat down in the available chair next to April's.

"I'm feeling fine this morning Connor, thank you," April said. She stretched out her arms in front of her. They were bare this morning. No traces of the black energy were left. Megan eyed April's hands as she silently ate her eggs and toast.

"That's so good to hear. Megan, can you make April some breakfast please?" Connor said not bothering to look at Megan as he requested her service. "I was worried about you April."

Megan looked up from her plate and glanced at Connor but his full attention was on April. April smiled apologetically at Megan. Megan averted her gaze and moved from the kitchen island over to the hob.

"Wait why were you worried about April?" Alex said grabbing an apple from the fruit bowl in front of him. He bit down into it with gusto.

"Because of last night. Didn't April tell you?" Connor said. He didn't try very hard to keep the smug tone out of his voice.

"April?" Alex asked through a mouthful of apple.

"Oh yes, I forgot after you told me the news about my pearls!" April said.

"What news?" Connor asked. April continued addressing Alex while swinging on her stool.

"Some sort of dark light energy consumed me. I had some sort of vision or nightmare. I'm not sure. Connor and Megan found me."

"That's the understatement of the century, she was wrapped in darkness," Connor interjected, "Swathed in it, and it seemed to be coming out of her."

April shot an annoyed look at Connor.

"What?" he said indignantly.

"Don't be alarmist!" April said. Alex opened his mouth to comment but April cut him off, "anyway, Alex has some exciting news!"

Alex paused to check it was his turn to speak again.

"Here you go." Megan walked over and placed two large plates of food in front of April and Alex before settling herself opposite Connor.

"Thanks," Alex and April said in unison.

"During my meeting yesterday they accidentally let slip where the laboratories are. The main one is three levels down, almost directly below here," Alex said.

"We're going to get my pearls," April said with a beaming grin. Connor noted that April was glowing a faint white again.

"And how are we going to do that?" Connor asked.

"Well, I've been thinking about this," Alex said. He whipped out his phone and placed it on the counter. "I was running searches through the information we took from Dad's study and I think I've found the software they're using for access rights."

Connor and April waited expectantly for Alex to continue.

"I think I can make one."

~

Alex spent the afternoon coding a card that would grant unlimited access to Rushton. To do this he commandeered the entirety of the kitchen island. Utterly engrossed in his work he only looked up when in need of a fresh cup of coffee. April walked past him to get a snack out of the fridge. The notes covering the counter made no sense to her. She grabbed a freshly baked chocolate cake from last night. Cutting it up into slices, she placed a plate on Alex's island. He gave her a smile and a quick thank you before diving back into his work. April carried the other plates back to where she, Connor and Megan were sitting.

Between the three of them, Connor divided up the information scanned from his Dad's books and the information Alex downloaded. If April was going to leave as soon as she found her pearls, then she needed to learn anything of use now. They were sitting on their respective couches facing towards the magnificent window. Connor passed her a large rectangular pad that reminded her of one of her Iris pads. She started to scroll through it while skim reading the first of the many documents Connor had assigned her. Her section started with the financial details of the laboratory. She scrolled through record upon record of all the transactions made. She swiped through them uninterestedly. Catering, staff, protection, technology, flowers, and maintenance - none of this was of use to her. She only wanted useful information - information about Ethan, her pearls or the war.

She started scrolling faster through the invoices and records. A purple one was the only one of note as it stood out compared to the dullness of the others. 'Socrates Summer Gardens' supplied the government with all their flower needs from Devil's Helmet to Daffodil's. What odd names April thought, though not as bizarre as the toilet roll supply company 'From me to Loo'. April made her way through the rest of the invoices until she reached her next file. The opening layer read confidential. She skim-read the pre-amble of the documents until she reached the next layer. The file split into two sections, 'Mer' and 'Human'. April clicked into the mer database. It was a contents page, she scrolled down alphabetically through hundreds of names. She reached the bottom and saw another folder 'Of Interest' she clicked into it and saw records for her parents, Ethan's parents, Demetrius, Clyde, herself, Tate head of the pearl shamans... the list went on. Every one of 'importance' was listed. Fascinated April clicked on her name.

Name: April Rose Meridia
D.O.B: 30/03/1993
Genetic Status: Mer
Position: First in line to the throne
Pearls: Essentia, Commutavi, Factus, Curo, Assurgere, Communico, Tempus, Tenebrasco, Iris

The information on her was scant, she sagged back into the couch in relief, unaware she was leaning forward. She clicked into her Dad's profile. The information on him was far more comprehensive. Feeling as if she was intruding she clicked out of the file. She backtracked to the human folder and clicked in. Scrolling down to the bottom she found two files. One titled 'Of Interest' the other as 'Classified' April clicked into the classified folder and found a handful of names. She scrolled through and saw one woman with the surname May. She opened up the profile.

Name: Salacia Alexandra May
D.O.B: 19/09/1947
D.O.D: 22/08/2000
Genetic Status: Suspected Mer
Position: Civilian

April read through the profile of Salacia. The woman lived as a human but it was suspected she was a mera. The profile ended 'research terminated due to loss of subject.' April clicked out of the profile and went through the others. James Ross, Kelly Underwood, and Lucinda Harris, all these people were mer masquerading as legged. Reading through the profiles she was gripped. But, the final line on Lucinda's profile gave her goose bumps, it read 'subject lost to research.' What research was this April wondered. The profile gave no specific details. While she sat and contemplated the profiles she suddenly remembered why she was interested in Salacia.

"Connor, are you related to a Salacia May?" April asked. Connor looked up from his own reading quickly.

"Umm yes, that's my Mum," he said slowly with a small smile.

"What?" April said sitting up. She put the pad to one side. "Salacia May is your Mum, I thought she was called Sally?"

"Yes," Connor said shifting on the couch. She could see he was getting agitated. "Salacia May is my Mum, my Dad called her Sally, why?"

"I don't know what to say," she said. April picked up the pad and came and sat next to him. She passed him the pad and let him read it for himself.

"No," Connor said shaking his head. "No, this can't be right." He clicked out of the profile and clicked through some others. He searched through his own and Alex's too.

"No," he repeated again.

"Connor?" April said warily. She moved across the couch to give him some space.

"So you're telling me that my Mum was a mermaid," Connor said sarcastically.

"A mera," April corrected him, then quickly changed her tone "No, I'm not telling you, this profile is."

Connor looked down at the profile again.

"When did you lose your Mum?" April asked.

"It was a long time ago, I barely remember her."

"How did she die?"

"It was an accident, her plane crashed in the middle of the ocean."

"Oh," April said. She didn't know how to respond. "I'm sorry Connor." April received a small smile from his freckled face but he quickly looked back down towards the profile.

"But how could I not know, we not know?" Connor said.

Megan watched the conversation unfold and gathered what April had stumbled upon.

"Think about it, April hid that she was a mera from you," Megan said calmly. She walked over and placed her hand on his shoulder. Connor remained silent and stared down at the ground. Then without speaking he was up and striding over to Alex.

"Did you know about this?" he demanded, thrusting the tablet in Alex's face. Alex hurriedly took his headphones off.

"Pardon," Alex said raising his left eyebrow. He'd never seen Connor so flustered. His brother was white in the face, his freckles standing out more than usual.

"Did you know that Mum was a mermaid?" Connor said.

Alex stared blankly at his brother. He had clearly lost it. He took the tablet off him and started reading the information. His hand cupped the back of his head.

"I didn't know Connor," Alex said eventually looking up. "I swear."

April and Megan rushed over to join the brothers at the kitchen table.

"Are... are you two okay?" April asked tentatively. She walked around and took the seat next to Alex. He was pale underneath his tan. Connor sat too and put his head in his hands.

"More secrets great..." he said bitterly.

"I suppose it makes sense," Alex said. "All the stories, her insistence on being by the ocean."

"Yeah, and now Dad's hatred of mermaids," Connor said. April let the mermaid remark slide this time. She looked intently at Connor.

"You don't think your Dad actually hates the mer?" she asked "I presumed this was some sort of power struggle or desire for resources." No one answered her. The calm of their afternoon was now replaced with a tense silence. Megan flicked her eyes between the two boys.

"Does this mean, that you two are mer?" she asked.

"No," Connor said immediately. "No," he repeated again in shock.

April and Megan stared at the brothers. Their faces were white. Even Alex's joking demeanour was gone. Instead, he sat frozen.

"You could be," April started slowly, talking as she would to a pair of wild and scared seahorses. "If your Mum was a mera the chances are that you two are mer." April stopped to let the information sink in. She reached up and gently patted Alex's back as he did for her. She was rewarded with a small smile.

"I suppose, it would be cool," Alex said.

"It would be super cool," April agreed glad that Alex seemed to be recovering from his shock.

"Cool, it's preposterous. I would know if I was a mermaid," Connor said.

"Mer," April corrected. Connor glowered at her. Megan placed her hand on Connor's arm.

"I know this is frightening, but just think, April hid that she was a mera as did your Mum. How would you know otherwise?"

Connor stewed in silence.

"What about my tongue then?" he said with relish.

"Well, as you're only half a mer that makes sense. Not all mer have blue or green tongues," April stated and was rewarded with another dark look from Connor.

"There is no point arguing about it anyway. It's not like we can prove it," Alex said.

April looked down at her wrist. She still wore Ethan's watch as it reminded her of home.

"Actually, I think we can."

CHAPTER 39

April stood in the middle of the guest suite's wet room. She was filling it with warm water from the shower and adding to it with her own powers. Currently, the water reached up to her calves. The edge of the room glowed a faint white with Factus energy to stop the water from running out of the room. April was almost certain this would work. Her mind raced ahead, if Alex and Connor were mer then they could come with her. They could help her relay President May's plan to her Dad and start to renegotiate peace. This hopeful thought lessened her feeling of dread. The decision to free Ethan and get her pearls meant the next step was to leave. But, April didn't want to be alone. After the news of her Mum and losing control over her powers, April needed to be kept occupied. Whenever she was alone her thoughts drifted back to the unsolvable questions swirling in her mind – the guilt, the anxiety and the pain. Alex and Connor stopped those thoughts. They distracted her.

A memory floated through her brain. She was young, a tiny merita. Above her a rainbow was shining in the sky. Sitting in a hot spring pool she played with the little manatee toy she took everywhere with her. "Come on Maxi let's storm the castle! But oh no, it's raining!" April looked up, her Tempus pearl glowed and it started to rain. She darted Maxi under the sea to protect him and they swam round and round to reach the cluster of rocks she was pretending was the castle.

"April! Stop this rain at once," Freya called out.

"Sorry Mummy," April said petulantly and the rain immediately ceased.

"Really, I don't know what to do with her," Freya said.

"Don't worry your highness. This holiday will distract her," Perdita said.

"April!" Connor called. April blinked and was brought back into the real world. "April is the water almost ready?" Connor shouted from downstairs.

"Almost," she called back. What had her Mum been distracting her from April wondered. She tried not to think about the fact that she would never be able to ask her.

"Woah! What's going on here?" Alex said as he stood hesitantly outside the door. The door was open but in front of him was a knee-high wall of water. It stopped perfectly at the edge of the door as if undulating against a glass wall.

"Come in, it's not going to hurt you."

Connor arrived at this moment with Megan in tow. All three dressed in swimming attire.

"This is cool," Megan said. She prodded the water before walking into the room.

"Ohh! It's nice and warm," she giggled.

Connor and Alex followed her. They stood awkwardly in the wet room while the water slowly rose up across the white tiled walls. Connor folded his arms as he shuffled further into the room.

"What are we doing?" he asked.

"We're going to test if you two can turn into mer," April said excitedly. She flung her arms into the air and wielded an arc of water to frame her as she said the words.

"Show off," Alex laughed and he reached down and splashed her with some water. April flicked her wrist and sent a wave of water crashing into Alex. He stumbled backwards.

"Right who would like to go first?" April said smiling first to Connor then Alex.

"I will," Connor said. His took a step towards April and eyed the water nervously.

"Excellent."

April stepped forward and undid Ethan's watch from her wrist. As she did she shivered involuntarily. The second the pearls left her skin she missed their energy. She fastened the watch to Connor's wrist and twisted it round so he could see the pearls. Connor felt the hair lift on the back of his neck. It could be the pearls but it could also be April's proximity. He tried not to let his nerves show and so gave her a little smile.

"Right so this is Ethan's watch. And as you can see he has three pearls. And this here is an Iris messaging pad, but the poison in the water around here means it's useless," April said in a rush eager to find out if Connor and Alex were mer. "This is his Assurgere pearl," she said pointing to a dark green pearl at the top of Ethan's watch face. "It controls the growth of plants. This one is his Essentia pearl." She moved her finger to four on the watch and pointed to a pale rose pink pearl. "Every mer has an Essentia pearl. It monitors the life source of the wearer and by a wielder can be used to monitor the life source of pretty much anything." April moved her finger to the final pearl that gleamed a bright violet at eight.

"And this one is the Commutavi pearl. Legend has it that in times past only the Royals could transform in and out of the mer and legged form. But, after the Battle of Kara only one living member of the royal family survived. He felt lonely transforming on his own so he combined the powers of the Essentia and Curo pearls and created a new pearl. He called it the Commutavi pearl and it allowed other mer to transform with him."

Alex, Connor and Megan followed her every word. They remained in silence when she stopped with only the sound of the water splashing down from the shower around them.

"Any questions?" April asked letting go of the watch and swinging her arms.

"Do you need this pearl to transform?" Megan asked.

"Yes and no. I don't need a pearl to transform and nowadays nor do many others. But some mer need the extra energy to help them transform," April said.

"So, anyone with one of these Commutavi pearls could transform?" Connor asked. He was holding his wrist at an odd distance away from his body.

"Well not anyone. You need to have the inherent ability to transform. That's why legged can't transform."

"This is fascinating," Megan said. "I wish I could transform."

"So how do I transform then?" Connor asked cutting across Megan.

"Well, I'm not entirely sure. I just think, I want to transform now and I do."

"Excellent," Connor rolled his eyes. "I want to transform," he said.

Alex punched Connor in the arm. "Stop being an idiot."

"You have to really want it or it won't work," April said. The water was now lapping around her waist. She looked down and imagined herself swimming in the water. A glow of violet wrapped around her waist.

"Wow!"

"Oh my!"

"So, there you see, it's as simple as that," April said. Fortunately, the wet room was large enough that she could swim a couple of laps. She couldn't help but smile at the joy of swimming again. Reluctantly she returned to the surface. She wielded a water-dense bubble for herself and perched upon it so she was head height with everyone else.

Alex, Connor and Megan watched avidly.

"Your tail! It's beautiful April," Megan said. She was mesmerised by April's tail as it glistened like a diamond and bounced the light off against the white tiles.

"Thank you, you should see my best friend Setha's tail. It's ruby red and is truly exquisite. I wonder what colour your tails will be," she said grinning.

"Right, it's my turn now. Give me the watch," Alex said and made to grab the watch.

"No. I haven't had a proper go yet," Connor said keeping the watch out of reach. "April can you help me? Please." Connor was still pale from the shock of finding out that his Mum was a mera. April smiled at him kindly.

"Okay, I will access the Commutavi energy so it's easier for you to wield."

"Okay."

"Just believe in yourself."

Connor hesitantly closed his eyes. He felt ridiculous. "I want to be a mer," he muttered so quietly no one could hear. This is stupid he thought. About to open his eyes and complain he heard a splash.

"Alex!" April exclaimed. She widened her bubble and dragged him up onto it. Alex sat there in stunned silence.

"Oh my," Megan said. She clapped her hands over her mouth.

"What?" Connor said. "How did you do that? You don't even have the pearls."

Alex was staring down at his tail. He went to make the motion of flexing his feet and his fin flicked upwards, the shock almost sent him off the back of April's bubble.

"I, I don't know. I did what April said. I felt a warm energy and I… I followed it." Alex said in a daze still staring at his tail. He leant down and gingerly stroked his scales. They were surprisingly soft. He raised his tail as he would his legs and marvelled. His scales were a deep blue, almost black in colour. Next to April's tail it almost looked like a yin and yang symbol shimmering in the water.

"Alex…" April said lost for words. She leant over and hugged him.

"Do you want to try and swim?"

"Umm, I suppose so." Alex tentatively slipped off April's bubble into the water.

"What do I do?" he said struggling to keep his head above water.

"Go underwater, and move your tail. Almost like flexing." April slipped off the bubble to join him. Megan stepped out of the way as April glided through the water. Connor remained rooted to the spot.

"Alex," April said.

"What you're talking underwater. I'm talking underwater!" Alex shook his head.

April laughed and a stream of bubbles issued from her mouth.

"Did you think mer didn't talk underwater? Right, now swim."

Alex's concentrating face returned. He looked just as he had while creating the access cards. He pushed back with his tail and was suddenly moving.

"This is insane. Where do I put my arms?"

April laughed again and followed him, "Anywhere you want!"

"Look at them go," Megan said. Her eyes were transfixed on April and Alex swimming underwater. Their tails were extraordinary. The light glinted off them as they moved and turned. April was mesmerising to watch, she swam with far more confidence than she walked. Alex looked less graceful, but Megan could see after a few laps he was getting the hang of it.

"It's so cool," Megan said trying to get Connor to talk. "I wish I could join them."

"I suppose so," Connor said. He slowly moved to the sidewall to join Megan. April broke through the surface and slipped back onto her floating bubble. Alex followed and tried to join her. He swam towards the bubble and missed by about a metre. Megan laughed and waded over to help April hoist him up.

"That was amazing," Alex said. He sat with a huge grin on his face. Megan stepped back smiling.

"This is so cool. You're so lucky Alex. How does it feel being a mer?" Megan said.

"It's surreal." Alex continued smiling like an idiot. April beamed and lightly splashed him with water.

"Do you want another go Connor?" April said turning her attention to him. Connor was still stood pressed up against the wall.

"No thanks. We should get back to planning," Connor said. He slowly unfolded his arms.

"Are you sure?" April said.

"It's fine."

"Connor." April made to swim after him. He shrugged and turned towards the door.

"I'll go and get us some towels and robes," Connor walked out the door without looking back. April stared after him worried. His shoulders were tensed and his hands were deep in his trunk pockets. Megan and Alex seemed unfazed as they continued to discuss how fascinating the mer experience was. April stared after her friend; unfortunately, disappointment was not something Curo energy could heal.

CHAPTER 40

Titan and Tarzan dashed ahead of Nathaniel as he floated through the palace gardens. Clyde had taken his medallion away again. Without discussion, they came to the mutual decision not to talk about it. Nathaniel stopped and floated up within the willow coral. The smooth tendrils danced around him as he swam under their shade. The darkness soothed his headache. He proceeded on his swim to follow his seahorses along the path to the mother of pearl pavilion. Titan and Tarzan beat him there. They were rolling on the floor of the pavilion in raptures of joy as an old mer bowed down and rubbed their bellies. The man was an impressive figure with an emerald green tail. He wore a well-cut blazer and metallic wrist cuffs inlaid with pearls that flashed in the water. He looked up with a smile until he saw Nathaniel and his eyes clouded over.

Nathaniel swam up the slope into the pavilion and clasped hands with his Father-in-law.

"Good afternoon Perch, I'm terribly sorry for your loss. Where is Clarry?"

"My Nate, you never lost the formalities, did you? Come and sit, Clarry is on her way with some cakes from the kitchen."

Nathaniel did as he was told and sat on the bench running along the edge of the pavilion's inner wall. Titan swam over and rested his head on Nathaniel's tail.

"How are you holding up without Freya?" Perch said. He was not a man to wait for the tide. Nathaniel winced at her name. If Nathaniel struggled around Kayla because she reminded him of Freya, Perch was on another level. Freya shared so many of her Father's mannerisms.

"I'm managing as best I can," Nathaniel said tight-lipped. Perch opened his mouth seemingly to disagree when his wife interrupted him.

"Nate," Clarry called as she swam into the pavilion. Floating a tray of cakes next to her she swooped down and embraced Nathaniel in a hug. As she came away Nathaniel could see unshed tears in her eyes. She straightened herself up and smoothed down her cardigan before reaching to her floating tray of cakes.

"Here, I asked the kitchen for your favourite," she said holding the tray expectantly in front of him. Nathaniel took the cake and ate in silence. The Sebae cake was cooked to perfection, but he could barely taste it. Nathaniel rubbed his forehead as the headache from his Curo withdrawal started to flare up again. He had failed to read the memo about why his in-laws were visiting him and was only reminded of the engagement this lunchtime. Fortunately, his Father-in-law was guaranteed to take charge. That his daughter married the ruler of the seven seas never seemed to faze Perch.

"We're here Nate to discuss two things. Freya's Reflexus arrangements and April," Perch started.

"Oh Perch, we don't need to get straight down to business," Clarry said reproachfully. Her facial expression displayed a calm façade but her eyes were flashing at her husband.

"It's alright Clarry," Nathaniel said.

"Where exactly is my Grand-daughter Nathaniel?" Perch said. A dark glimmer crossed over his grey eyes. April always said she got her colour changing eyes from her Grandfather. Perch had always had a particular fondness for April and her impulsiveness.

"I presume you mean April?" Nathaniel said.

"Yes, though we aren't best pleased that you're letting Kayla wander around leading the meritia," Perch said.

"Now Perch."

"No Clarry, this has gone on long enough. You are the King, you lost your wife but your mer and your daughters need you," Perch said. Tarzan slunk away from him and came to rest at the fin of Clarry's tail.

"You do not get the luxury of falling apart."

Nathaniel sat in silence. Anger bristled through him. But, it was self-resentment. Perch was only reiterating what he knew. His Curo indulgence since Freya's death needed to stop.

"I know," he said quietly but so they both could hear him. "I know," he swallowed his pride and admitted something he previously only admitted to his wife.

"I need help."

Nathaniel spent the rest of the afternoon with his in-laws sorting through his mess. Perch was a former Prime Minister and was independently wealthy. His knowledge and influence was not something Nathaniel could afford to lose. Besides, working with him gave him a piece of his wife back. Clarry set to work planning the Reflexus. The date was set for two weeks' time. Perch hoped that by then April would be found and she could perform the Reflexus ceremony.

"I can't believe you let things go so long without looking for your own daughter," Perch said. He managed to keep his tone of disappointment and frustration to a minimum.

Nathaniel glowered again, "Of course I looked for her. I stretched my Essentia powers to the limit trying to find her. But, it's as if she is out of reach."

"She must be separated from her pearls," Clarry said. "There is no way someone could hold her against her will if she had them."

"Yes, I will set up another search for her pearls as well," Perch said tapping into his Iris pad.

"How come you aren't more worried?" Clarry asked.

"Because April is a survivor. When Freya died I knew...I could feel her presence leave me. But, with April I know she is still there...just currently she is out of reach."

"Your Majesty." A timid porter appeared at the eastern entrance of the pavilion. Nathaniel nodded for him to continue.

"Your Jet Stream is waiting for you at the front gates. Your appointment with the PSOC is in forty minutes."

"Thank you," Nathaniel smiled kindly and nodded for the porter to leave.

"Right, then it looks like you best be off," Perch said swimming into an upright position.

"Yes, thank you both for your help today," Nathaniel said straightening his shoulders. Clarry gave him a final goodbye hug.

"We'll make our way out after a swim around the palace beds."

"I'll keep you updated Nate," Perch said as he clasped Nathaniel's hand and stared into his eyes. Nathaniel nodded his thanks and averted his gaze. He quickly made his way through the archway and swam towards the palace's main gates.

Without saying a word Clyde handed over Nathaniel's medallion as the King smoothed his hair in the hall's ostentatiously large mirror. A small school of yellow fish swam past him and made their way out through the opposite window. Oh, to be a single-minded fish he thought wistfully. He placed his medallion back over his neck and felt a rush of warmth. It was intoxicating. Ignoring the pull of his Curo pearl he swam out the door with Clyde in his wake.

They travelled in the Jet Stream in silence. The giant white orb moved swiftly through the ocean. It was a gentle form of transport and one that provided great luxury with its spongy seating. Nathaniel tried to dismiss the guilt Perch impressed upon him. It was two weeks since April went missing. He should have done more. It was amazing the press hadn't caught wind of this. If April had been captured or if she was in danger he would never forgive himself. But, somehow, he just knew she was okay. He and April shared a connection. He couldn't explain it but he knew that wherever April was she was being well looked after.

"Your Majesty," Clyde said hesitantly breaking Nathaniel out of his reverie.

"I wanted to discuss something delicate with you," Clyde hesitated before continuing. "We would like you to make a formal statement. I have a draft drawn up. Just something to show the mer that you're in control."

"Okay, do you have it on you?" Nathaniel said reaching out.

"Yes." Clyde passed his Iris pad to Nathaniel to read. "I will send it to you too."

Nathaniel started to read the speech. It was all very standard. He was offering protection, extra security and answers. He stopped reading when he noticed that Clyde was still bouncing his tail up and down.

"Clyde?" Nathaniel asked rubbing his forehead.

"Yes, well there is something else."

Nathaniel stared at him pointedly.

"I have received word of a…well an uprising Your Majesty."

"An uprising?"

"Yes, some feel you aren't fit to lead. That you misread the signs of peace, that you were conned."

"Who?"

"It appears Gregor is the leader."

"That treasonous viper," Nathaniel swore. He reigned in his temper to avoid unleashing a storm in the Jet Stream.

"How would you like to act?" Clyde asked tentatively.

"We do nothing. Keep me updated. For now, the best we can do is prove them wrong."

CHAPTER 41

"Your Majesty we've arrived," the Jet Stream steward informed them. Nathaniel nodded and swam towards the exit. He swam to the surface and entered the transformation bubble. He transformed quickly and changed into his legged clothes. He noted that the last time he used his Commutavi pearl he was fleeing a bombsite. Walking through the steamer he entered into PSOC. It was a private island facility. A huge glass dome covered the centre of the island; a tunnel connected it to the ocean. Inside were pools each replicating different seas and ocean cultures. Nathaniel walked his way past the many pools and inhaled their different scents. His current term in Hanaria was coming to an end. It would be refreshing to leave the palace that Freya loved so much. The unique scents of the different oceans brought up memories of his experiences in each sea. Each community was so lively and passionate about their specific eco-system. Nathaniel was proud to lead and support every one of them.

PSOC monitored the levels of different chemicals in each of the seas and oceans. They tested the waters daily, checked if any new diseases were spreading, and monitored the fluctuations in temperature and bacteria cultures. It was here the poisonous substance above the Hanarian Hospital was sent for tests to find or cultivate a cure. He was encouraged to send an informant to the PSOC. But, he wanted to know exactly what was plaguing the mer. And he felt that some time away from the sea might help him. The pearls' pull was less intense on land.

"Your Majesty, pleasure to meet you." A woman in a lab coat greeted Nathaniel and made a low sweeping bow before straightening up with her clipboard. Her poker straight brown hair hung just above her shoulders.

"Thank you, it's a pleasure to meet you Professor Dophia. I read your research regarding starfish mating practices and it was absolutely fascinating."

Professor Dophia blushed slightly but kept her composure.

"Thank you. Your Majesty, shall we head to the lab table and I can show you what we're working with?"

Without waiting for a response Dophia moved further into the dome.

"I had everything prepared up here so you don't need to go into the laboratories," she explained.

Dophia stood at a large metallic table surrounded on all sides by different water cultures. She moved around to the left until she was standing in front of different petri dishes each containing what looked like skin samples. Nathaniel recoiled on approach as a noxious smell reached his nose. He stopped next to Dophia and leant over a small tank on the table. It was full of a dark purple liquid that looked thick to touch. The fumes coming from it made him wrinkle his nose.

"Sorry, Your Majesty." Dophia hurried to cover the tank in front of them.

"Though that actually confirms one of our theories." She reached around the tank and arranged her petri dishes in a line.

"You see these markings?" she said. She traced the hexagonal rashes burnt into the samples. Each petri dish contained a rash of a different colour ranging from pale pink to dark purple like the colour of the poison.

"Each of these synthetic skin samples were given the same dose of poison. But, as you can see they each reacted differently," Dophia said.

Nathaniel leaned in closer to inspect them.

"At first we couldn't identify a correlating genetic factor. But, then we looked into the skin samples backgrounds." Dophia pressed a button and an Iris board rose out of the table. It showed the mer background data for each of the eight petri dishes.

"You see Your Majesty, this poison is attacking mer based on the strength of their pearl powers. The colour of the rash indicates how many pearls they can wield, and the strength of irritation indicates the power of the wielder."

Nathaniel looked on in horrified fascination. This poison was sophisticated. It was designed to target the most powerful of the mer.

"Take petri dish two and seven." She brought both dishes up on the Iris screen and tapped them.

"Look at their transformation. Both of these mer can control the Curo pearl, but number two's power is far greater."

Nathaniel watched the playback of the poison being dripped onto the samples. Both skin samples coloured the same pinkish colour but whereas number seven's stayed in a relatively neat line, number two's spread out across the skin creating a thicker hexagonal lined rash. It was mesmerizing to watch it grow.

"Could you smell the concentrated poison before?" Dophia asked.

Nathaniel nodded not taking his eyes off the screen.

"Fascinating, up until now, we thought it was odourless. But, then no one here has anywhere near your pearl range or power."

"And have you created an antitoxin?" Nathaniel asked eagerly.

"We've run several tests and we think we've created one. It takes over an hour to disseminate through the water. Obviously, we haven't had time yet to see if there are any adverse reactions. But, we are fairly certain that it should be safe." She flicked the Iris Pad onto a different video clip, this time demonstrating a pool of water with the poison being poured in. The time frame sped up and Nathaniel could see the poison in the water first fade then slowly recede until there was nothing left.

"And how do you plan on administering this to an ocean?' Nathaniel asked.

"With the poison you isolated from the tubes we can easily administer a dose large enough to purify it. In cases like the Hanarian hospital, we would hope to quarantine the area with Factus wielders and then administer the antidote. Until it was deemed safe, the water would remain held in isolation."

"Thank you very much Dophia, you and your team must have been hard pressed to turn this around so promptly," Nathaniel said. He turned to her with one of the first genuine smiles he had given in weeks. It lifted his face so he no longer looked so drained.

"It's no problem, Your Majesty. Is there anything else you'd like to know?" she asked returning his smile.

"Do you know how a poison like this would have been created?"

"It is certainly man-made. Our most likely guess is that test subjects would have been needed. This is a chemically engineered poison which would have taken lots of trial and error.'"

"Thank you," Nathaniel nodded slowly. He looked down at his Iris cuff. He needed to move onto his next meeting.

"The poison is the same one that has poisoned the waters around different US government properties. So, presumably, it was created by them," Dophia said. She refrained from naming who them was.

Nathaniel's mouth set in a hard line. The evidence for who was the powerhouse behind the mer attacks was all pointing in one direction.

CHAPTER 42

Setha swam into her bedroom and took in all the clamcases around her.

"Mum," Setha called. "What's going on?" She moved into her room and floated above the mess. Roxana appeared behind her.

"I'm packing."

"I can see that, but why?" Setha asked glaring at her.

"It's time you moved back home," Roxana said grabbing a bag and moving it into a pile.

"I am home," Setha said her voice rising.

Roxana sagged for a moment and then swam to her full height.

"This has gone on long enough. It's time for you to return to your real life."

"My real life," Setha said shouting now, "So the last four years have been what?"

Roxana stared at her daughter clutching a pillow in her hands. She opened her mouth to speak but Setha cut in first.

"You're just guilty you weren't here for Dad when I was," she shouted.

"Setha."

"No," Setha said, "Just no." She swam from the room, dashed down the spiral and out the front door. Setha kept on swimming, putting on a burst of her Factus energy to propel her away. Without thinking she headed for the Floating Labyrinth. Her tail burned from the exertion and her breath caught in her throat but still, she pushed on. She couldn't cope with losing her Dad, her best friend and now her home. Setha focused all her attention on swimming.

Finally, she reached the mass of tangled weeds. The Floating Labyrinth was a hub of sargassum seaweed that floated on the outskirts of Hanaria. Thousands of fish made their home in its mass. The Floating Labyrinth stretched out for over a mile and the edges closest to Hanaria were well known picnic spots for the mer community. She shot towards the closest opening. Pushing the seaweed apart she found a hole close to the surface. Her Factus powers pulsed white energy across her tail, a sign that she had wielded her powers to their limit. Setha closed her eyes and sunk into the opening. No sooner had her tail curled beneath her, a thundering noise startled her. The sea was churning and the labyrinth rocked with the swell. Setha froze in panic fearing another attack. She looked up and broke into a smile.

Above her a pod of at least five hundred Spinner Dolphins were racing through the water. They were leaping up and down in the surf then spinning high in the air before diving back under. There was a certain harmony in their chaotic progress. Setha stretched out in her cocoon hoping to get a photo of the pod. April would be gutted to know she was missing this. But, April was still nowhere to be found, neither was Ethan. None of her other friends mattered in comparison to them. Sshe spent so much time with her Dad, or April, or at school that she didn't know what to do with herself now they were gone. She twirled a piece of seaweed in her hand. It was like a long strand of dark green hair. It was deliciously slippery to play with but wasn't a sufficient distraction.

She couldn't face her Mum again. She didn't want to leave. Her friends, home and Grandmother were all here. She even planned to go to college in Hanaria at the end of summer. The calm life of Hanaria suited her. And now, it was where she would always feel closest to her Dad. Setha shot a stream of hot water through the loop she had been creating with the seaweed. She felt numb inside. For years she had prepared for the loss of her Dad. Yet, his death had been so unpredictable she didn't feel like she got to say goodbye. And now, she felt more estranged from her Mum than ever.

On a sudden impulse, she pushed up from her nest and dashed to the surface with the pod of dolphins. Propelling herself through the sky she felt free. The pod welcomed her and started to squeal in delight. This was true freedom she thought. The sun was shining and it warmed her skin as she dashed across the surface. As she sped up to keep pace with the dolphins, the cool wind brought a blush across her cheeks. The 500 hundred strong pod radiated strength and determination. As she swam with them the numbness of her heart started to thaw. She burst through the water and span as the dolphins did before plunging back down into the sea. She swam with them building up speed. Groups were starting to show off around her. They performed miraculous spins some rotating four times in the air before diving back down.

Racing forwards again Setha breached the surface. Focusing her Factus energy she flipped high in the air. Her hair whipped out behind her and she made a perfect arc in the sky. With her ruby red tail she appeared like a flame dancing above the water. She dove back down into the sea and let herself sink in a flurry of bubbles. Her breath was ragged from the exhilaration. The pod members closest to her swam down and circled her in farewell before continuing off on their voyage. She wished she could understand what they were saying. But she waved goodbye hoping they understood. Setha floated where she was with a smile on her face as she caught her breath. Everything would be okay she thought.

The ride home on the ray bus was uneventful. She was still buzzing from swimming with the pod. Getting off at her stop she swam towards her Grandmother's house excited to tell someone about the Spinners. As she reached the house she noticed a Moving Shell stopped outside. Setha averted her gaze from it. The large house was detached and offered a level of privacy Setha would miss in her Mum's busy apartment block in Bolalia. She swam towards the door and let herself in.

"Setha honey, where have you been?" Roxana immediately accosted her as she swam through the door. She enveloped Setha in a hug before pushing her back to survey her.

"I'm fine Mum, I was just at the Floating Labyrinth," Setha said.

"Thank goodness! I was worried sick! We need to leave here immediately," Roxanna said. She dashed into the kitchen and started piling things haphazardly into a bag.

"What? Why? April is still missing and what about Grandma?"

"April probably has hundreds of mer dedicated to the cause of finding her. Don't you worry, and I offered for Jocelyn to come with us but she refuses."

"Mum, she's my best friend."

"Yes, and you can visit her when all this is over."

"All what?" Setha asked incredulously. Her Mum was acting weird even for her. She was now piling her Grandma's crab cakes into a tub before forcing them into her overly stuffed handbag.

"These poison attacks. There was another one this afternoon."

"What?"

"Right over the Palace, of course, the King was there so he was able to contain it."

"Did anyone get hurt?" Setha asked in shock.

"No, fortunately not. It's all over the news. The government has created an antidote."

Setha sat down at the kitchen table and watched her Mum continue to rush around the kitchen.

"Anyway, I have packed your room up for you. We're leaving tonight. There is an overnight Jet Stream to Bolalia."

"Mum." Setha pushed herself up from the table. "We can't leave!"

"We can and we are. Don't argue with me." Roxana crossed through into the dining area.

"Your Grandma is taking us out for dinner in an hour and then we're leaving."

Roxana stared at her daughter through the doorway. When Setha didn't challenge her she swam from the room, her normally styled hair in disarray. Setha looked after her Mum in bewilderment. She swam up to her bedroom but halted in her doorway. Everything was gone. Only her Grandmother's furniture remained. Setha swam back downstairs in search of her Iris pad. She started typing another message to April.

CHAPTER 43

"Let's go over this one last time."

Megan started detailing the plan once more and April tried to keep her attention focused. But, they had been sitting around the coffee table for hours and her brain had exhausted all the logistics. All she could think about now was getting down there, saving Ethan and finding her pearls. They had discussed the different options, and the pros and cons for each, going back and forth for hours.

"Connor will stand guard outside each room as Alex and April look for Ethan and her pearls. Connor is that okay? I just feel you're the best at thinking on your feet for an excuse," Megan said. Her blushing around him had yet to stop.

"Yes. That's fine. And you'll be up here to field any questions about where we are," Connor said. He moved on before Megan could answer him. "Alex, are you certain your card works?"

April rolled her eyes. This question must have been asked at least twenty times by now.

"I'm positive, and if it doesn't then we can pretend we're lost and I will work on it until it does work," Alex said with slightly more bite than he had the other times.

"And then, if all is successful you take April and Ethan to the port where they can grab a boat and return to the sea," Megan said.

"Exactly," April chipped in. "So, we're ready to go!" She pushed up off the couch and wandered into the kitchen. She fiddled with a thread that had come loose on the denim shorts she was wearing. Mooching around the kitchen she settled on the fruit bowl and rummaged around until she found a juicy green apple she liked. She bit into it harder than was necessary.

The weight of what she had done was starting to dawn on her. She had been missing for over two weeks now. Why on earth hadn't she tried harder to make it back home beforehand? Her security team were going to be fuming. At least now she had the chance to get her pearls back and save Ethan. But, still. What had she been thinking? April leant against the kitchen island and looked over at Megan, Connor and Alex still huddled over the table discussing the details of the plan. Her chest tightened. She was going to miss these leggeds.

"Guys, what is going to happen to you when Ethan and I escape with my pearls?" April said.

"Don't worry, we're going to feign ignorance. Pretend that you've been playing us this entire time," Alex said.

"Are you sure that will work?"

"Yes, positive. Dad doesn't think much of us anyway," Connor answered. He looked back down at the papers in front of him.

"Right, so tomorrow it is," Megan said.

"Yup," Connor said despondently.

They all fell into silence. Alex started shuffling his papers together and organising the table again. April looked around at her friends. She wanted to do something to say thank you to them. She wanted one final evening together where they could pretend they didn't have anything to worry about.

"We should do something fun tonight," April said.

"Fun? Like what?" Connor replied. He was not making this any easier for her.

"I don't know," she said. "What do you guys do around here for fun?" She was met with silence.

"Are there any human things you want to do April?" Megan asked "You know, for your last night masquerading as one and all."

April felt the clenching return in her chest.

"Umm we could make pizzas," April blurted out.

Alex immediately started laughing and even Connor cracked a grin.

"Pizzas?" Alex asked.

"Yeah, I've never had a pizza. It doesn't really work underwater"

"What, no way!" Megan said.

"I took a pizza making course once." Everyone turned and stared at Alex.

"You did what?" Connor asked dumbfounded.
"I happen to like cooking. It relaxes me."
April smiled. "Pizzas then?"

CHAPTER 44

The oven beeped and April opened the door. She reached to slide the pizza onto her plate having been warned by Connor several times that it was very hot. Licking her fingers, she moved over to the island. Alex and Corner were rolling out their dough in preparation while Megan was neatly arranging her ingredients on her pizza.

"You know what I don't get April?" Alex said while attempting to throw his dough in the air.

"Umm hmm," she murmured her mouth full of pizza.

"Well, how do mermai…I mean mer, speak underwater, how do you breathe for that matter?" Alex asked.

"Seriously?" April said sounding surprised.

"Yes," Alex said indignantly.

"Don't you learn these things in school?"

"Nope," Alex said. Megan and Connor both shook their heads.

"Well, do you remember I told you about the pearls and the powers they have. This one," April shook Ethan's watch around on her wrist and pointed at the rose-coloured pearl. "The Essentia pearl monitors the life of the wearer. Legend has it that when the first person transformed into mer form the Essentia pearl realised they couldn't breathe underwater. So, it provided them with a spirit to accompany them. When we transform there is a thin layer of air surrounding us. Mer use far more of their lung capacity than leggeds so we don't need to breathe as often and the Essentia power keeps rejuvenating so you never run out."

Alex stared at her. Connor's face was devoid of expression also. Megan's however, was lit up.

"That makes so much more sense than the books explanation. So, you don't need the pearl you just need the Essentia power?"

"Pretty much, I think some people compare it to chakras. Essentia is within us all even if we don't realise it."

Megan nodded her head vehemently. "So, this is why you don't have gills?"

"Of course, I'm a mammal, not a fish!"

The boys continued to stare in silence.

"I'm not sure I get it," Connor eventually said.

"Okay, imagine you've put on sun cream all over."

"Sun cream?"

"Yes, so you can't see the sun cream as it has sunk in and is now part of you. But, you know it's there. And this sun cream lasts forever. So, wherever you go you will never burn."

"You've lost me."

April frowned.

"How about this," Megan piped up. "It's like you're in a bubble, but a very tight-fitting bubble that is specifically designed to the shape of you."

"Close enough," April said.

"Does everyone have the Essentia power then?" Alex asked.

"They do, and the power of Commutavi. But while everyone has the Essentia power, not everyone can wield it," April said.

"Then why do you need the pearls?" Connor asked.

"Well, if you believe the legends the pearls are the source of our powers and so it is symbolic to carry them. Plus, they are full of magical energy and if you can access the energy then your powers are heightened. They're like magical catalysts."

~

Everyone in bed asleep, April snuck back downstairs. She made her way carefully down the stairs hugging the wall as she went. Setting her foot down silently on the bottom step she sighed with relief that she was alone. She made her way into the lounge and summoning her Tempus powers she wielded a soft wind to part the heavy curtains. As they parted a stream of light flooded the room. She knew it. It was a full moon that had been calling her. Sinking to the floor she sat cross-legged and stared up at the moon. Her palms relaxed down onto her knees and she let out a deep sigh. The power of the moon flooded through her.

Connor watched from the stairs. From this vantage point, April looked every bit the all-powerful mer Princess. The ebb and flow of the sea crashing against the cliffside moved in time with her breath. It was mesmerising to watch. He took a careful step forward and moved down into the lounge to join her. As he approached he could see that she was glowing a myriad of colours. It was as if her powers were dancing around her.

"I can feel them."

Connor stepped back in shock.

"I can feel my pearls," April said. Connor sat down beside her keeping a respectful distance. April turned her head to face him.

"They're calling me."

"Don't worry April. We'll get them back tomorrow. You'll be reunited with your pearls and have access to your full powers," he said with a rush.

"All my power," April repeated quietly. She turned her focus back to the moon. Connor stared at her. It was as if she was in a trance.

"April," he started tentatively, "I, I don't want you to leave."

April closed her eyes momentarily. She wielded her Curo powers over to Connor. A glow of blue surrounded his chest and Connor looked down in amazement. He instantly felt rested, warm and safe. He looked back up at April to see her smiling at him.

"I know, I don't want to leave. But, I must."

"You could stay, we could figure this out together."

"I can't. I need to help the mer. I need to get some answers about my powers from the shamans."

Silence settled over them. Connor shifted his focus to the moon to see if he could feel whatever it was April was channelling. Connor put his head in his hands and tried to summon the courage to tell April how he felt. He couldn't lose her.

"I wish I could come with you," he said softly.

"Then why don't you?" April said turning rapidly towards him. All the colours faded around her. Connor lifted his head out of his hands.

"Because I can't April. You saw," he said and touched his head to the window "I just can't."

"You can, you just don't believe," she said. Her words brought a light breeze around her lifting the hair off her shoulders. "Sorry," she said and the breeze disappeared as suddenly as it came.

Connor sat still, goose bumps rose over his arms from the sudden cold. His eyes grew wide as he looked on bewildered.

"I'm going back to bed now," April stood up and walked towards the stairs. Connor waited for her to turn back to him. His eyes followed her as she walked up the stairs. But, not once did her footsteps falter.

CHAPTER 45

April patted her bag once more. Then, for what felt like the hundredth time, she opened the airtight plastic bag to check she had all the documents and equipment she needed. After a thorough inspection, she pushed herself off of the couch and moved to the window. There she paced up and down moving from one corner of the room to the other. In the midst of her fifth lap, she was startled by a noise. She jumped and turned towards the sound.

"Good morning," a man sarcastically drawled at her. April's eyes widened in shock at the man in front of her.

"Good morning. Freddie, right?" April said brightly. She composed her features so she looked at ease.

"Yes, I'm afraid we haven't had the pleasure of meeting. Alex has been keeping you all to himself," Freddie said smirking.

He was charming like Alex, but there was something about him that made April uncomfortable. She hugged her arms around her waist.

"Yup, so many things to see here. We've been busy."

"I bet you have," Freddie winked at her. April's hands tightened into fists. The way he looked at her made the hairs stand up on the back of her neck.

"Are you looking for Alex or Connor? I thought they were with you for breakfast?" April said. She slowly moved towards the kitchen area.

"We were. Connor mentioned something about wanting to get more involved. So, Dad decided to involve them."

"Ah okay," April said. She attempted to sound light and breezy. Alex and Connor were supposed to be laying the foundations of an excuse for their later wanderings around Rushton and find a way to keep their Dad and Freddie occupied for the afternoon. This was the opposite of that plan.

"You seem uncomfortable April," Freddie said. He walked over to the other side of the kitchen island. "You'll see my brothers shortly."

"I'm fine, just feeling a little weary, I might go and have a nap."

April started to make her way towards the back staircase so she wouldn't have to pass Freddie.

"Nice watch you're wearing."

April stopped. She whipped around to face Freddie. He stood with a smug grin on his face.

"What do you want?"

"I want you."

Before April could react a flash of blue electricity wrapped its way around her body. The pain scorched through her and she screamed in agony then passed out cold.

~

"Dad, this is really cool of you. But, aren't you too busy for this?" Connor asked.

"Busy, no we haven't spent proper time together in weeks. It's Saturday, let me show you what we do here."

Connor shot Alex a look behind their Dad's back. He was acting far happier than he usually did when he was around them. He was dressed rather casually for him too. The linen white trousers with loafers was a disturbing image on their usually austere Dad. They descended several levels into the cliff and then walked down a seemingly never-ending stretch of white corridors. Darius gestured at doors referencing whose office that was or what that room contained. However, nothing made him stop his march.

"Have there been any further terrorist attacks on land?" Alex asked. Maybe he could at least cajole some useful information out of his Dad.

"Since the attack on Shell Island, nothing," Darius said calmly. He didn't seem affected by the loss of his wife's favourite home.

"I thought you said mer didn't have aircraft?" Connor asked.

"Umm hmm," Darius replied without bothering to turn around.
"Then how come the island was in flames? The news said it was bombed."

"They have their powers Connor," Darius said, but the prior cheer in his voice had turned cold.

"Maybe, or maybe it wasn't the mer? It could have been human terrorists who bombed the island."

"Perhaps," Darius said curtly. He finally reached the end of the corridor. He tapped the access button on his control cuff and the door opened. The room was similar to the lounge several floors up in the brothers living quarters with a window taking up one side of the room. The view was just a couple of hundred metres lower.

"This boys, is Lydia's private research lab. She is working here with Frederick."

"Very interesting," Alex said trying not to roll his eyes. Being around his Dad always put him in a bad mood. "And what are we doing here?"

"I thought you wanted to get involved?" Darius said. A small smile had crept back onto his features. Alex was almost too nervous to respond for fear his Dad would actually try to involve them.

"We do... what are you showing us?"

Darius moved over to the windows, he stood in the centre and looked out across the sea.

"Today boys, we are about to make a discovery. For years humans have been searching for the answer of how to access the powers of the pearls."

Alex and Connor shared another look. They hesitantly looked around to try and see where their Dad was going with his speech. Everything was so white and pristine; no clues were left on the laboratory surfaces.

"But, we have taken the testing further than any other team have, and we think we've cracked it."

Darius turned and walked towards a door to the right. He walked through and Alex and Connor slowly followed him. They walked into a solid metal chamber. Immediately in front of them were two examining tables. Freddie was standing in the middle grinning at their Dad. Either side of him two people were strapped down. As Alex and Connor took a step closer they both blanched. Unconscious and lashed to the table by blue lasers was April. Her body splayed out like a star. The pale blue dress she was wearing earlier was now soaked through with sweat. Across her body a hexagonal rash was spreading. The two brothers stood in shock.

"Surprised?" Freddie asked coolly.

"What are you doing?" Connor demanded.

"Your brother was duped," Darius replied with infuriating condescension. "He was taken in once more by a pretty face."

Alex gripped his fists. Connor grabbed his arm to stop him.

"Your latest hook-up has been playing you Alex, this is Princess April Meridia, a mera," the contempt dripped from Darius' voice.

The body on the left thrashed his arms. Alex flicked his attention over. A young man was lashed down in the same way as April. But, a laser across his mouth stopped him from speaking. This must be Ethan, Alex thought. Alex scanned the room quickly while his Dad continued to mock him. A lifetime of military education kicked into action. Alex manoeuvred himself to the left of Connor, positioning himself closer to Ethan. Alex stared at him and nodded minutely in the hope that he would realise he was here to help.

"Now that the mera is detained we have a unique opportunity," Freddie said.

Freddie twisted his own cuff and electricity spiked through the lasers lashing April and Ethan down. April was jolted to consciousness. Ethan thrashed against the table and then lay shaking. Darius unlocked a cabinet with his own cuff and wheeled out a strange contraption. It consisted of two metal basins filtering into a small glowing metal dome. Darius wheeled the dome to stand between the two lab tables. Connor and Alex gasped in shock. In one basin lay the watch April always wore and in the other was the most exquisite necklace either of them had ever seen. From its position in the basin, the gemstones spaced between the pearls glimmered. But, it was the pearls that demanded attention; they radiated power as they pulsed in different colours.

Connor stared at April. She looked so helpless restrained on the cool metal surface. He followed the path of her eyes as she scanned the room. As her eyes locked on his, the pain he saw made him recoil. But, he didn't look away. His eyes were tethered to her like a lifeline. Taking an infinitely small step forward his arm started to reach for April.

"These pearls and the raw power possessed within them… it's like nothing we've encountered before," Darius started talking. "But we needed a sufficient test subject to tap into their powers."

Alex flicked the key card out from under his sleeve while his Dad was distracted. He was sick Alex thought. Why would anyone ever be compelled to hurt someone in this way, to experiment on them as if they were less than a sentient being. Freddie was busy with the dome, placing it over the two sets of pearls. Alex casually placed a hand on Ethan's table looking curiously at the laser restraints. He hoped this would work. With a flick of the card he swiped over the connection point and Ethan's arm was free. Alex mentally high fived himself, he slowly moved round to release Ethan's left side. Alex steeled himself then swiped the card. The second the restraints were lifted Ethan sprang up. Freddie finally noticed what Alex was doing.

"You," Freddie glared at Alex. Before he could get out another word Ethan barrelled into him pinning Freddie against the wall.

"Help April," he shouted. Alex turned to free April and was sent reeling backwards. Standing up he rubbed his jaw and grimaced.

"How dare you," Darius said bearing over him. Alex had never been scared of his Dad. The moment he saw April strapped down he lost any remaining respect for his Dad. Now, he loathed him. Years of anger surged through Alex as he charged towards his Dad. The grimace slipped from President May's face as Alex pinned him to the ground.

"Connor, get the card," Alex shouted. He continued to wrestle his Dad.

"Why are you doing this?" he demanded through their struggle.

"Get off me," Darius commanded. The strain to remove his son was turning his face red with anger. Sweat dripped down his forehead.

"You bombed the Peace Treaty. Why?"

A cruel smile twisted across Darius' face.

"Don't you have all the answers Alex? I thought you were supposed to be the intelligent one."

Alex slackened his grip for a moment. Darius seized his chance and span Alex around him until he had his head pinned to the floor.

"You ungrateful child."

"You're nothing more than a terrorist," Alex spat out.

"You don't know the meaning of the word. I'm helping the human race. The mer are a menace. They need to be controlled, their unchecked powers are a threat to us all," Darius rasped.

Alex stared up at his Dad glaring down at him. Pure hatred shimmered in his eyes, but something else he couldn't place.

Rational thinking had been replaced with what looked like cold hard revenge.

"You're wrong, you should be working with them," Alex managed to say but the pressure on his chest and head was starting to choke him. Darius let out one short sharp laugh.

"Hah, my research is necessary. Everyone else is too afraid. They talk about the injustice, but no one has actually tried to readdress the balance. I've been waiting for this opportunity for years."

Darius turned to survey the room around him. Connor was rushing to Ethan's aid to try to subdue Freddie. Darius' eyes lingered over April's form.

"Your little friend is the final piece," Darius' eyes lit up as he said these words. Alex's mouth twisted in disgust at his Dad's expression.

"You knew all along," he choked out.

"Yes," Darius tapped his wrist cuff and sent a shot of electricity through Alex's chest tethering him to the floor.

Alex's screams sent Connor rushing from Ethan back to his brother. He flung himself at Darius but his Dad was too quick. Darius twisted his torso and caught Connor mid-air and hurled him over his head.

Ethan and Freddie were still fighting in the corner of the room. Not used to fighting on land Ethan was outmatched. He turned to see where Connor had gone. He saw Alex pinned to the ground and Connor lying slumped against the wall. Momentarily forgetting Freddie, he surged forward to throw Darius off of Alex. Freddie lunged at him and sent them both sprawling to the ground. As they fell Freddie's head glanced off the corner of the table. He fell to the ground where he lay perfectly still. Ethan heaved himself up and noticed blood trickling from Freddie's head. Without stopping to help he barrelled forward and knocked Darius from on top of Alex. The blue laser instantly vanished. Alex knelt and caught his breath.

"Thanks," he choked out.

"I'll check on him," Ethan pointed at Connor curled into a ball against the wall. "You free April."

Ethan gave Alex a tight smile and offered his hand to help pull him to standing. Alex looked at the proffered hand for a split second before taking it gratefully.

The two-stood face to face, they were built like for like with the only difference being Ethan's brown hair to Alex's blonde. Their eyes connected for a moment.

CHAPTER 46

April's eyes were wide open. Panic was etched across her face. Alex could make out tear marks streaked down her cheeks. Across her body were dark red hexagons that seemed to be growing. He whipped out his back-up key card and quickly released April's mouth. She gulped in as she was released.

"Alex," her voice broke in a sob.

"Don't worry April, we're getting you out of here," Alex ran around to the other side and released her.

"Come on, it's going to be okay," Alex said. He helped to raise her into a seated position then draped her arm over his shoulder. Carefully, he slid her legs to the ground.

"Are you okay to stand?" he asked. April nodded once. She took a careful step forwards. Alex looked back to see that Ethan was helping Connor to stand. He looked pale with shock but otherwise okay.

"Let's move," he called over to the two of them.

"What about Dad and Freddie?" Connor said.

"Leave them," Alex shook his head in disgust. "They'll be fine. The security detail is probably already on its way."

"We'd better move then," Ethan said as he caught up with April and Alex.

April was slowly making her way towards the door in evident pain. Ethan swooped his shoulder under April's other arm.

"What did they do to you?" Ethan asked. His eyes scanned over the rash covering her body.

"I don't know," April said. "Freddie came to the apartment, and then next thing I remember I woke up here and my body felt like it was on fire." April shuddered. Ethan gripped April's hand in support before turning his attention to Alex.

"How long do we have until security get here?"

"About three minutes, if that," Alex replied.

"How are we going to escape? We can't get to the tunnel now," Connor said.

"We're going to have to," Alex said gritting his teeth.

As the boys talked tactics, April concentrated on trying to walk. She breathed deeply and focused on the warm glow that flickered in her heart. She exhaled and a sky-blue glow started to spread over her. She breathed again and wielded her Curo power over first Ethan, then Alex, then let it travel backwards to Connor. Connor gasped in shock behind them.

"April, your pearls."

The group were now back in the laboratory that Ethan had spent so much of his time as a prisoner. Connor turned and driven by the Curo energy sprinted into the metal room.

"Connor," April and Alex shouted in alarm. The Curo power empowered them all and they ran after him. Connor made it to the basin with April's pearls in. He removed the dome Freddie had fastened over and scooped up the pearls. They were deliciously cool in his hands and radiated power.

"Got them," he smiled at the door. April and Alex were standing in the doorway and he saw their facial expressions drop before he heard their cries.

"Connor!" they shouted as the metal door slammed shut in front of them. April beat her fists on the door.

"Connor," she screamed again. Alex moved her aside and tried his key card to unlock the door. A red light flashed denying access. He tried again, "Come on," he muttered in frustration. The little red light taunted him. April looked on in growing irritation.

"It's not working Alex!"

Her hair started to crackle with energy. She tilted her head to the ceiling as her eyes momentarily rolled back into her head. Static electricity gathered around her and her fingertips turned a deep navy. Alex took a step back from the door in bewilderment.

"April," Ethan shouted in shock. "No, it's metal the conduction would kill him."

April span round and her Tempus energy crackled in the air. Alex looked between the two.

"April," Ethan said once more, this time in a more soothing tone. Slowly, she dropped her gaze back to a normal level and her hair settled back onto her shoulders.

"We have to do something?" she said turning to the door.

Connor recoiled as if slapped when the door slammed shut. The pearls clutched in his hand seemed to hum in frustration. He hadn't thought, he just ran. And now... now he was trapped. He looked across the room and saw Freddie still slumped across the floor. His head was resting in a pool of his own blood. Connor ran over to the door to try and open it. But, it remained solidly shut. He whipped his key card and swiped it against the door.

"Nice of you to return Connor."

Connor span around. Darius was propping himself up against the laboratory table leg and slowly heaving himself to standing. Connor spun around and frantically tried the handle and key card again.

"That's not going to work," Darius said coolly. Finally pulling himself fully to standing, he raised his command cuff to his mouth and pressed his intercom.

"Release the poison."

Connor watched from the door as his Dad calmly gave the order to poison his facility.

"What are you doing? You could kill us all!" Connor cried desperately.

"Not all of us," Darius said. The gleam in his eye was cool and calculated. "What are you going to do Connor, try and stop me?"

Connor jolted his body forward to confront his Dad but then recoiled. His Dad laughed callously.

"You always were the weak one," Darius said. "Now check on your brother."

Connor stood rooted to the spot for a moment. His eyes flickered across the room. His heart was pounding in his chest and his body ached all over. He was paralysed with indecision.

"Now," Darius barked and Connor caved. He moved to his brother and fell to his knees in front of him. He checked his breathing and his pulse. Determining that Freddie would survive he put him in the recovery position and then leant against the wall. Connor rested his head in his hands in defeat. He hoped that against the odds Alex would find a way for April to escape.

~

"Alex. We can't leave Connor," April said. Her expression was deadpan. She wasn't going to leave her friend.

"April, we don't have a choice," Alex said. He ran over to the entrance door and locked it, sealing themselves in so they had time to formulate a plan.

"Connor would want us to leave."

April held her ground by the door. She wasn't ready to give up. She tried the handle again in frustration. Rattling it until her patience was spent, she struck out at it.

"April, that isn't helping. We need to focus," Alex said. He was rewarded with a glare.

"Can you feel something?" Ethan said warily. The other two turned to him in confusion. Then April reached up to scratch her arm, a slow tingling sensation was working its way across her body. She looked down at her arms and the dark hexagons were starting to rim with a faint red outline. She looked over at Ethan and saw the same spreading across his broad shoulders.

"I feel a bit tingly..." Alex said cautiously.

"It's the poison," Ethan said.

"We need to get you out of here," Alex said. As he spoke a siren started wailing through the room. "They must know we're in here."

"What's the protocol here for emergencies?" Ethan asked.

"Well, there are several options, none of them are good."

The boys continued to discuss while April turned away from the door. She muttered an almost silent goodbye to Connor. Her heart ached at the image of his face as the door slammed shut. He was trapped because he tried to help her. Guilt wracked her body. She would come back for him. Walking over to the window wall she was struck by how similar it was to the one back in the apartment. She looked out and saw that it overlooked the same craggy rock face as above. Breathing in slowly she focused her energy on her Factus and Tempus powers, she breathed out and an icy mist issued from her mouth. She placed her hand on the window and pushed the white and navy glow from her hands sending a frost across the glass.

It spread out like a snowflake crystallising and spiralling out in an octagonal circle. For a moment, she stared and appreciated the frost she was creating. Pushing harder she sent the temperature plummeting. The boys' breath started to come out in little puffs of hot air. The window groaned in place as it tried to spill out of the framework's confines. A sharp crack sounded across the glass. Footsteps could be heard pounding down the corridor but April focused on her task. The crack scissored across the glass making an odd creaking noise at first. Then in a final surrender, it splintered out in a hundred directions.

The window hovered for a split second and then fractured into a thousand pieces. Starting from the top the glass started to rain down into the sea. The window gone, fresh air blew into the room and the rash on April's skin started to recede. Ethan and Alex stared on in bewilderment. Ethan took a step towards the now windowless wall and took his first breath of fresh air in over two weeks. He looked out across the sea and had to resist the urge to dive straight down into the water below. To hell with the rocks - he wanted to be free.

"April, do you have a plan?" Alex asked uncertainly. April nodded.

"Will the door hold?" she asked.

"We probably have a minute or two before they're able to override it. Dad and Freddie have the master cards."

April had lost her pearls. A tugging in her heart wanted her to go back to that door and blast it down so she could be reunited with them. But, that would hurt Connor. She couldn't move her focus from the sea or she would lose her control. The pearls' call was so powerful. However, the call of the ocean was almost equally as strong. She so longed to be back in the sea. To be free and swimming and as far away from this place as possible was her foremost wish. She stepped forward so her toes almost touched the edge of the now open wall. They couldn't dive it would be too dangerous. Between the poison and the rocks, it wasn't worth the risk. But, perhaps there was another way.

Beyond the rocks, about two hundred metres offshore, she focused her gaze. Her body glowed a brilliant white as she raised her hands. She moulded the sea to her will and a tower of water rose at her Factus command. She then pulled and twisted her arms towards her. Under her guide, the water grew and grew as it reached up and over the rocks. The tower of water stretched until it came to a rest at April's feet. The sight was glorious. A thundering bridge of water now connected them down to the sea.

"Do you want us to walk on water?" Alex asked tentatively. A loud thump on the door sounded behind them.

"I was thinking we could slide down," April said with a gleam in her eyes. She held her hands up in front of her as if holding an imaginary ball and then gave them a sharp twist. The water corresponded to her movement as it had done all those years ago when she made a slide from her land palace window into the surf. The calm bridge now roared to life. It funnelled itself out in the centre while constantly spinning around the outside. April wielded a wave to continuously flow down the slide. Her whole body pulsed white with Factus energy.

"I see you haven't lost your flair for the dramatics," Ethan said raising his eyebrows. The door shook once more, and one of the hinges came loose. The top corner was now open. A gun appeared at the mouth and started firing at random.

"Go," Alex shouted. April nodded at Ethan and he jumped into the slide. He couldn't help himself as he let out a "whoop" on his way down.

"Alex, I'm not leaving you. You'll be safe with us, I promise."

Alex paused for a moment. The shots fell short of their position but it wouldn't be long before the door broke down and they would be trapped.

"I suppose I don't have a choice," Alex stepped gingerly into the whirling tube of water. Shocked that it supported his weight he pushed off with his hands exactly how he would at a waterpark. April quickly followed. The door opened just as she disappeared down her funnel.

The whirling tunnel was surprisingly cold. She transformed as she slid. Her legs glowed a stunning violet with Commutavi power and then as the glow subsided her diamond tail glistened beneath her. Despite the danger, a grin spread across her face. April redirected the water and let it carry her upwards. She flew up into the air and for a moment it felt like she was flying. Twisting in mid-air she turned and dived down into the water.

The cool water engulfed her and she spent a brief moment under the surface composing herself. She vibrated the water around her to warm up their surroundings. The burning rashes on her arms were soothed by the water. Combined with her healing from earlier they were beginning to fade. About to search for Alex and Ethan a bullet suddenly shot past her. She whipped round in shock. Realising the shooting was coming from above her she sped up through the water. She looked around frantically and saw Ethan supporting Alex behind her. She threw a wall of water up the side of the cliff. It raced up towards the window then froze creating a barrier between them and the shooters. April's head throbbed as she wielded the poisoned water below the cliff's edge.

"Ethan, hold Alex," April shouted. She dived down into the water and swam towards them. The bullets echoed as they ricocheted off the ice wall.

"The ice won't hold for long," April said as a loud crack sounded above them. Alex and Ethan looked shaken but fine.

"What's the plan?" Ethan asked. He had Alex propped over his shoulder holding him afloat.

"Alex, you need to transform," April said. His face looked white with panic. "You can do this, I'll help you."

Alex closed his eyes to focus. The pressure to transform was too much. But, then suddenly heat seeped across his legs. He felt rather than saw a colour that reminded him of April, as if her spirit was wrapped around him helping him transform. He kicked his tail in amazement.

"Woah," Ethan said. He removed his arm from Alex awkwardly and let him support himself.

"I did it," he said in awe. Alex looked down through the sea and tried to assess his tail through the purple Commutavi glow. The same sense of fascination and power filled him. It felt natural; it felt right being in the sea.

"We'll explain later. We need to get out of here," April said.

"Where?" Ethan asked.

"We'll head towards Hanaria and hopefully someone will find us along the way."

Ethan nodded. He turned to Alex, "Have you swum at full speed before?'"

About to respond, Alex was cut off as the ice shattered. From the sea, the spectacle held a deadly beauty. It fell as if in slow motion. But, as the ice disappeared a line of soldiers stepped forward. They raised their guns in synchronisation and opened fire.

"Take my hand. April go!" Ethan shouted. April didn't stop to turn she propelled up into the air and dived down shooting off. Ethan tugged Alex down.

"Don't let go."

Ethan held Alex's hand and kicked out with his tail hard. Together they sped off after April.

CHAPTER 47

Darius unlocked the door as he heard his troops running into the lab. He halted in shock. A torrent of water was swirling into the room. He stepped towards it and the water instinctively retracted away from him and reduced back into the ocean. A few of the soldiers ran over to ask if he was okay. Darius ignored them.

"Fire," he said simply.

"No!" Connor shouted. Darius pulled him back by the scruff of the neck as Connor tried to surge past him.

"You can't..." Connor was cut off mid-sentence as a deep rumbling sound echoed throughout the room. Everyone stopped for a second and looked around in disbelief. Then before their eyes, a wall of water loomed ahead of them covering the windowless wall. The roar of the water was deafening. Connor prepared to run. But suddenly the noise stopped. The room was plunged into darkness as the water solidified into ice and blocked out the natural light.

"Don't just stand there. Shoot," Darius commanded. As each line ran out of ammunition another stepped forward to open fire. Connor stared in horror.

"What about Alex?" Connor asked.

"He made his decision. He'll see I was right," Darius said without bothering to turn and address Connor. "Send someone to check on Frederick."

Connor opened his mouth to protest but closed it. Considering all that he had done his Dad was being surprisingly tolerant. He didn't want to push him now. The security team were first aid trained so Connor grabbed one standing by the door and led her to where

Freddie lay. The guard knelt immediately and started checking over his body. She stopped periodically to ask questions. How did he fall? How long had he been out cold? Connor leant against a wall and replied numbly. He avoided looking down at where his brother lay unconscious.

The earlier events kept flashing through his mind. It all seemed so surreal. How could this have happened? He promised to protect April, to help her. Instead, she had been captured, tortured and shot at. Connor reached into his pocket and pulled out her pearl necklace. He carefully caressed each pearl and gem. The smooth, cool stones soothed him. He hoped April was okay, and Alex. A sudden loud crack brought his attention back to the room. He ran into the laboratory just as the ice gave way and shattered. He stood in awe as the ice tumbled down in a million shards. As soon as the way was clear a new line of guards stepped forward and opened fire on the sea. Connor turned away instinctively.

"Pathetic," Darius said staring at his son.

CHAPTER 48

"Perch," Nathaniel said as a greeting. His Iris pad was on his desk as he swam up and down in agitation. "I felt her. She's in danger. But, April's alive. She's consciously using her powers. The pearls are angry for some reason."

Perch hesitated for a fraction of a second before responding. He didn't understand the pearls, part of him thought it was all a load of nonsense and natural selection.

"Where is my heading?" he eventually responded.

"Head to the Periculi Gemini Cliffs. April will be travelling away from them, so spread your search wide."

"Okay, I will update you on our progress."

"Thank you," Nathaniel said and tapped out of the call.

His pearls were vibrating in anticipation. A power was surging through him. He hadn't felt this sort of power since April was first born. The pearls had a plan. He could feel it but for now, they weren't ready to share it with him. Nathaniel swam around his office one last time. He looked at his Iris pad lying on the desk. He had to make the call. He floated in indecision. It would only take a moment.

"Call Kayla," he said. The Iris pad started ringing. He drifted down into his black sea silk chair. He let its comfort absorb him.

"Dad?" an irate voice called out.

"Kayla. How are you?"

"I'm good thank you."

The hostility in her voice made him recoil.

"Kayla, the pearls are stirring. They're sending me flashes of information. Your sister is using her powers. She's alive. Your Grandfather is off to find her now."

"I… I don't …. No."

"Yes Kayla. If you listened to your Essentia pearl you would know it's true."

Kayla hesitated, "I don't believe in the pearls Dad. It's just a load of superstitious nonsense."

Nathaniel leant his forehead against his hands. Kayla always had been stubborn, much like her Mother.

"Please, just come home."

"Dad."

"You can see the poison neutralisers for yourself and discuss your plans with the Hanarian government."

He heard Kayla sigh.

"Okay, I'll come tomorrow. Have Clyde draw up a schedule."

"Okay. Thank…" But Kayla had already hung up.

Nathaniel leant back in his chair and looked across his study. In a palace full of servants and advisors he had never felt more alone. He called for Titan and Tarzan. The two came whizzing into the room. Nathaniel leaned up and patted them as they darted above his head.

"Let's go for a swim."

The two seahorses dashed immediately to the window and swam around each other in dizzying circles. Nathaniel swam to join them. He swam out of the window and shot off. Titan and Tarzan zoomed after him. Nothing was left but a trail of bubbles.

CHAPTER 49

April slowed as she approached a small coral reef out in the middle of the ocean. It would be a good place to rest she thought. The coral encircled an underwater volcano. It was a safe haven for a menagerie of exotic coral fish. She slipped through the shoals and came to rest on one of the few bare rocks amongst the reef. Ethan steered Alex carefully behind him. Many corals were poisonous to mer and others were just plain painful if you caught yourself on them. April looked up and marvelled at the colours all around her. The moon was only just shy of being full and its bright light shone down into the shallow waters. The light reflected off the scales of the hundreds of fish and sent shafts of colour spilling in all directions. From where she sat it looked like a choreographed dance.

The fish had fallen into a rhythm. They swam this way and that heading into the safety of the corals before the sunset. Then the sea would be plunged into darkness with only the moon's glow to guide them. It was a pleasant change from the stark white and black décor of Rushton. These waters were relatively safe because the deathly Musto coral deterred larger predators.

Ethan had successfully gotten Alex to the rock and the two sank down next to April. Their tails hanging off the edge, they leant back and joined April watching the fish darting home.

"It's beautiful," Alex said. He still wasn't used to speaking under water. With every word, he felt he was going to swallow water. And yet, he didn't.

"It is, isn't it?" April said. She let herself melt slowly down into the rock and cushioned her head under her arms.

"I can't believe that just happened," April said.

"I know," Alex replied "My Dad, he knew all along. He brought you here on purpose."

April shuddered. She closed her eyes momentarily and saw Freddie looming over her.

"What happened to you Ethan? How long have you been there?"

"Since the Peace Treaty," Ethan said rolling onto his side. Alex averted his gaze and looked to April.

"I was captured after the explosion. Lydia and Frederick have been experimenting on me. They wanted me to tap into your pearls' power. Then, when that didn't work they started testing the poison on me."

"I'm so sorry," April said. "I should have come for you sooner."

"It's fine, I'm fine, at least they never got access to your powers."

"It's disgusting though," Alex said. "What they were doing to you, what they were going to do."

"I think, Lydia and Frederick were trying to make the pearls' powers accessible to everyone," Ethan said. "They healed me with Curo energy they had already harvested."

"What?" April said pushing herself up off the rock. "That's impossible."

"Apparently not, but their process sounds long and painful for such small results. They want to refine it."

"I think that's only half the story. The way my Dad and Freddie were talking tonight. They want to control the mer," Alex said with disgust.

"Control, but how?" April asked. The small sense of security she felt on her rock vanished.

"I don't know."

The three lapsed into silence, each pondering the events that had led them to their rock.

"What's the plan April?" Ethan asked.

"I think we should rest here for an hour or so and then push on?"

Ethan nodded, "Alex, can you manage another swim?"

Alex bristled at the implication. "Yup," he said tightly "I don't think I could sleep even if I tried."

Alex knew he should be worried or at least concerned about what he had just done. But, somehow the emotion eluded him. Instead, all he felt was excitement. Leaving had been the first major action in his life that didn't fall neatly into his Dad's plan. For once he felt entirely free. It might have just been the water but he actually felt lighter. His body and mind were released. It was as if he had been holding his breath for years without knowing, and now he had finally learnt how to exhale.

April, beside him, did not look nearly so relaxed. Her fingers were subconsciously tapping the rock. She was so close to home, yet now it was happening she didn't feel excited. Panic was flooding through her. What was the next step? She wasn't ready to confront all the pain that was awaiting her.

A fish swam across April's stomach and she jumped up in alarm. Her hair flung up so it was standing on end horizontally.

"April?" Ethan asked.

"Don't worry, April," Alex said. He sat up and put his arm around her. "At least we're all free now."

"We are," Ethan said and hesitantly dropped his arm around April's shoulder too.

"Connor isn't though," April said quietly. The look on Connor's face haunted April. She dreaded to think how Darius would punish him. Her mind turned to Megan too. She had been sent to help tidy the President's rooms that morning and April hadn't seen her since. April hoped Megan wasn't implicated in their escape. She had grown to like Megan and her fascination with mer. She would go back for them both. After searching for her pearls for so long, she realised that they weren't the point. She could get new pearls. But, she couldn't replace her friends. She had gained Ethan but lost Connor and Megan.

After returning home she would head to a pearl cave and welcome a new set of pearls. Then she could find Connor and Megan and Darius would feel her wrath. As memories of Darius and how she had been strapped down flashed through her memory April's fingers closed into a fist. The black light flickered across her fingers.

Her vision blurred and suddenly she was back in the hole in the ground, a crying young merita. Instead of being consumed by the memory it was as if she was looking on. She recognised the substance covering the walls now. The hole was lined with sea-worn Tenebrasco pearls. The darkness was emanating from her merita self. She heard her Mum's voice above her. Both Aprils turned to look up searching for their Mum.

"Are you certain?" Freya asked.

"Yes, Your Majesty. April can wield the Tenebrasco pearls."

"But how?"

"I don't know for sure. The extra energy from Julia and Anthony must be key."

"What should I do?"

"For now. I would protect April. Limit her experimentation and teach her control. We don't understand these powers enough to know how they will manifest."

"Thank you, Shaman Tate. That will be all."

April had one fleeting look at her Mum, leaning down to remove the bars sealing young April into the hole, when her vision cleared and she was back on the rock with Alex and Ethan. They were still talking, unaware of April's temporary blackout. Her eyes welled up at the image of her Mum. She missed her more than she could admit. April swallowed back a sob, her sadness turned to anger. Why had her Mum kept so much from her? April had been five when her Mum found out she could wield the Tenebrasco pearls. Yet, she never told her. All this confusion, all the distance, it could have been avoided, and now it was too late.

April wracked her brain, trying to recall the other details from her pearl flash back. Shaman Tate had been there, another mer who hid the truth. She wondered if her Dad knew. But, April quickly banished the thought. Her Dad would have told her. Another detail floated to April's mind. Anthony and Julia. The names were oddly familiar as if they were friends from a long time ago.

Her own ignorance of her powers was hindering her. All those years of ignoring her pearl studies and her powers - she wondered if it was her Mum's subtle influence. Perhaps her Mum's distance was out of fear. No one knew what the Tenebrasco power was, just that it was powerful and if left unchecked, destructive. April thought back over her pearl memory surges and the flickers of black magic. Slowly it all started to piece together. April wracked her memory. Each time she had been afraid of the darkness, but what if the Tenebrasco pearls were trying to communicate with her. Did they want her to know that she possessed their powers? April threaded her fingers through her hair in thought. She wondered if that was the only message they wanted to tell her.

April flexed her hand out in front of her and released a stream of darkness. The dark light leeched out like tentacles, it sucked the light from the surrounding area. The fish scattered and the coral receded.

"April?" Ethan shouted. He whirled around thinking the darkness was coming for her.

She curled her fingers into a fist and the darkness retracted into her.

"I can wield it," she said in awe. "The Tenebrasco energy, I can control it," she clarified.

"Tenebrasco? That's the black one right?" Alex asked.

"Yes," Ethan replied. "And up until now, no one could wield it." His face was ashen.

"Why?" Alex said, not realising the oddity of the situation.

"We thought the power died out," April said.

"I see," Alex said, "And yet, you can control it?" His eyes focused on April.

"I think so," April said looking towards her hands again. "Before it felt like the darkness was consuming me. It was leading me somewhere. But now, it's like I have a hold on it or at least part of it?" April shook her head in confusion. "I need to talk to Shaman Tate," she said more to herself than Alex and Ethan.

"We should have taken your power surges more seriously," Ethan said suddenly, "You're only nineteen, even I haven't started the Kallion."

"I know," April said reproachfully. "I just thought it was an heir thing."

"An heir thing?" Alex asked.

"All mer have access to their full range of powers on their 25th birthday. Two to three years before their powers mature they go through the Kallion. During this time mer experience a loss of control, a heightening of powers then eventually, on your 25th birthday, a calm settles over you and your powers are fully matured," Ethan said while moving his hands through the water.

"I see."

"But, for the heir to the throne, it can be really dangerous," Ethan said. "On the eve of the heir's birthday, they lose complete control. It is said that the wielder of a Tenebrasco pearl could control the heir and wield them to their own uses."

April turned to look at Alex to see him watching her fascinated. She did not appreciate Ethan's tone.

"I just thought my weird pearl memory surges was the Kallion starting early," she tried to explain.

"And now?" Alex asked.

"Now, I think the pearls, the Tenebrasco pearls were trying to communicate with me."

"Okay," Alex said trying to catch up on the pearl lore. "Do you know why the pearls want to talk to you?"

"To tell me about my power and maybe something else, I don't know," April finished.

Alex smiled at her reassuringly. She managed to give him a small smile back.

The confidence she felt at finding some element of control dwindled as quickly as it appeared.

"What's the power?" Ethan asked. His face was impassive.

"I'm not sure," April answered. She tried not to be defensive at Ethan's reaction. "It feels like I'm absorbing the power of the light, like borrowing energy from my surroundings."

"Like darkness feeding off the light," Alex said.

"I suppose so," April swam up from the rock. She was done with waiting around. She kicked her tail to keep her suspended.

"Are you guys ready to head off again?"

Alex swam up beside her. Sensing that April was done talking he said, "Ready when you are."

He smiled and ignored the fact that they were supposed to be resting for the hour. "I still can't believe I'm a mer. All those years training to fight on land I never once thought to learn any underwater skills."

Ethan ignored him. "Off we go then," he nodded at April and Alex, and with a powerful kick spurred off.

April looked after him despondently. April grabbed Alex's hand.

"Ready?" She asked with a tight smile. Before he could answer she dragged Alex off after Ethan with a strong thrust of her tail.

CHAPTER 50

Connor sat on the couch with a cup of hot chocolate untouched on the table in front of him. In his lap, he held April's pearls. His fingers caressed each one of them in turn. The necklace must cost a fortune he thought. Diamonds, emeralds, rubies, sapphires and onyx stones, the list of precious jewels went on. But, it was only the pearls he cared for. Their intermittent glowing captivated his interest for hours on end. When sleep eluded him last night, he wrapped the necklace around his hand for comfort. It served as a small reminder that he hadn't made April up. Could it really have only been two nights ago she was sat here in a pool of moonlight. He would give anything to be back with her alone. Instead, he had Freddie for company.

Freddie had been moved back into the brother's quarters. He was suffering from a concussion after the blow to his head. For now, he was supposed to be resting. His presence in the apartment only served to make Connor's mood worse. He missed April, he even missed Alex, he would give anything to be with them now. His Dad had put him under house arrest. There was no more wandering around Rushton. He was confined to this apartment. His Dad had all but washed his hands of him. When he passed through to check on Freddie it was as if Connor didn't exist. He thought his Dad would at least demand the necklace back. But, no one seemed concerned that he had it.

Megan walked into the lounge from the kitchen carrying a tray of fruit. She moved silently across the dark wooden floor. Sudden noises startled Connor. Standing in front of him she saw the dark circles under his eyes had not improved.

"Connor," she said tentatively. "Would you like some fruit?"

Connor nodded minutely. She placed the tray down and came to sit beside him. She sat in the corner of the couch facing him. His head didn't turn to acknowledge her. The fruit was a cover in case someone else wandered into the lounge. She reached forward and placed April's strange black stone in his hand. It pained her to see how much he cared for April compared to the way he treated her. But, still, she wanted to help him. His hands gripped the stone and he stroked it like April used to.

"I thought you would like this," she said timidly. "I found April's waterproof bag with all her information in. The stone was inside."

Connor looked up at Megan and gave her a small smile of thanks before resuming his staring at the stone.

"Connor, I was continuing our research," Megan said. Connor still stared absently down at the necklace and stone in his lap. Megan ploughed on hoping to pique his interest.

"I was interested in Lydia's mer research."

Connor's head lifted slightly at the information. Megan took this as a good sign.

"I was reading through some different reports, and the reports on the deaths of some of the test subjects, don't add up," Megan said.

She grabbed the tablet from the fruit tray and started pulling up different reports.

"Look, this one here states that they were lost to research. But this one," she said flicking to another screen. "Says they were lost during transportation."

She finally had Connor's interest as his eyes scanned the documents with her.

"Then I looked into reports of their plane crash. The plane crashed over the ocean. But the mechanical report says there was no failure in the system, no fuel shortage, no nothing. It's as if it crashed of its own accord."

She knew it sounded far-fetched, but she hoped Connor was seeing where she was going with this.

"Then look here, the dates don't match up either. On some documents, there is a definite date, on others, it is just left blank. The date is the date of the crash though," she trailed off.

"You don't think they're dead?" he asked. His voice sounded sceptical even to himself.

"I don't. I really don't," she said glad that Connor wasn't shooting her down. "I think somehow they escaped. And if they escaped, then maybe we can find them. They might be able to tell us what your Dad, Frederick and Lydia are really up to," Megan said. "We could find your Mum."

Connor paused frowning. Megan waited patiently holding herself back from saying more. Then suddenly, Connor leant forward and grabbed Megan in a hug. He released her quickly; unsure of what had overcome him. He noticed a slight blush spread across her face and was sure a matching one was spreading over his.

"Do you know where the plane crashed?" he asked, composing himself once more. His appetite was back and he leant forward and grabbed an apple from the plate.

"That's another thing, the heading was for Shell Island. The plane crashed just off the shore."

"That's what Alex and I were told as children."

"What?"

"That our Mum died on the way to meeting us at Shell Island."

"It makes sense then."

"Do you think we should start there?" Connor asked eagerly.

"The whole island has been blown up... but I suppose we have nothing else to go on," Megan said.

"To Shell Island then," Connor said, a glimmer in his eye. His newfound enthusiasm was infectious and Megan started smiling too. Connor leant over and started asking Megan questions about the different reports. Reading through them he felt he had a purpose. He didn't hold out much hope that his Mum was alive but this felt like the next step to being reunited with April.

CHAPTER 51

Perch tapped his Iris pad to bring up a map of the currents. He held it in the sea, floating in a circle to check he was hovering at the exact coordinate. This was the spot he thought. He had been tracking the natural sea trails from the Periculi Gemini through to Hanaria. This was the end of the route he would have taken. From here it was a gentle swim into Hanaria with warm untroubled waters ahead. He had sent squads off to all likely route options but here was where he stationed himself. Perch was not a gambling man. He did not take risks. But, if he were going to bet on where his granddaughter would appear. Here it would be.

He turned to monitor his staff setting up his deck for him. They grew the underwater floating island to the size of a decent patio. Set up some chairs, a comfy couch, a desk and a coffee table. As they finished he swam over to take up a seat at the desk. The precision in the detail of the circular slabs forming the floor of his hovering island impressed even him. He nodded to his crew to signal a job well done and off they swam to set up their own quarters. Perch opened up the daily news and sat and waited.

~

"April, what is that?" Alex said. The stream of bubbles muffled his words as they swam at full speed.

"Pardon?" April said.

"What is that?" he repeated slowly.

April pulled them to a halt. "What are you saying?"

Ethan slowed to float behind them. "Why are we stopping?"

"Alex was trying to talk again."

Alex rolled his eyes, he had not been trying to talk, he was talking and the bubbles were merely getting in the way. He ignored April's statement and pointed slightly to the left of their course. He was exhausted. They all were and tensions were starting to run high.

"What is that?" he asked again. "It looks like a floating study."

April squinted in that direction. "It does," she said slowly. She was exhausted and thought her mind might be playing tricks on her.

"Nothing should be out here for miles," Ethan said matter of fact.

Alex restrained himself from rolling his eyes again. "Well, there it is," he gestured.

"It might be..." April said, she reached out with her Essentia powers then dashed forward. Alex and Ethan shared confused looks then quickly chased after her.

April stopped fifty metres away from the floating study. The final spurt of energy had drained her. The mer at the desk looked up at her over his Iris pad.

"Perch," she said. A flicker of recognition passed over the mer's face as he swam upwards. The two shot towards each other and met halfway in a hug. Alex and Ethan hurried after April and floated behind her. Perch ended the hug and held his Granddaughter at arm's length. He stroked a strand of her matted hair back behind her ear.

"April. Welcome home," he said bringing her back into a hug. Perch's Essentia pearl glowed in response. Eventually, the two parted.

"Perch, you know Ethan and this is Alex. He looked after me," April said as an introduction. The oddity of the situation caused her to turn first to formalities.

"Perch," Perch introduced himself extending a hand to Alex. "Thank you for helping my granddaughter. You have done my family a great service."

Alex took the proffered hand saying, "Nice to meet you, sir it was no problem, your Granddaughter is a young lady who has helped me far more than I have helped her."

Perch nodded and turned to Ethan. "Good to see you alive and well."

"Thank you, sir," Ethan replied.

"What are you doing here?" April asked.

"Looking for you of course. Your Father sensed you using your powers and so I stationed my mer at points between potential courses from Periculi Gemini to Hanaria," Perch said perfunctorily.

"Come," he gestured. Perch swam them back to his floating study. They settled themselves on the couches. The group formed an oddly homely scene floating in the middle of the ocean.

"I'll message your Father and then we'll head back into Hanaria and to the palace."

April let her body sink into the couch. She saw Alex gingerly rest his tail on the coffee table and then seem to think better of it and let it sink to the floor. She giggled in response. A huge weight lifted off of her shoulders.

"We finally made it," she said gleefully.

"We have," Ethan replied, "It feels so good to be rid of that facility and that awful woman." He stretched out and closed his eyes. He just wanted to sleep.

"The ocean is so big," Alex commented looking side to side.

They were deep enough down that you couldn't see the surface, but not deep enough to see the seabed.

"It's like time has stopped," Alex said.

Moments later a large Jet Stream cut through the water as if appearing out of nowhere. It pulled up alongside the platform.

"I couldn't get hold of your Father, but we can give him the good news soon enough unless Clyde gets to him first."

He swam forward and passed Ethan an Iris pad saying, "Here, it's best you contact your parents yourself."

Ethan smiled in thanks. One of Perch's attendants came and opened the doors to the Jet Stream and ushered everyone inside. Ethan swam to a seat and immediately called his parents. April and Alex chose seats across the Jet Stream to give him some privacy.

The Jet Stream journey shot by, April spent her time explaining the wonders of Hanaria to Alex. Her fatigue had left her now that she was so close to home. Her dress was sweat-stained and her skin was mottled with different shades of red from the poison rash, but she still had a smile on her face.

"The whole city rests on a giant floating platform, like the one we were just on. That way the city can be kept at an optimum distance from the surface," April said to Alex.

She was giddy with excitement at finally returning home. April couldn't wait to see her Dad, her sister, Setha and all her favourite members of the household. She tried to keep the less joyful tidings out of her mind: the loss of her Mum, the absence of her pearls and the awakening of the Tenebrasco darkness. She didn't relish explaining what had happened to her or informing the mer that the legged in power wanted war. April wanted life to go back to the way it was. But, then she looked across to Alex staring in awe out the window. Not everything had been bad she thought.

The Jet Stream pulled up to the station just outside the city by the Floating Labyrinth. Large craft weren't allowed into Hanaria unless for emergencies. Perch didn't want to draw attention to April's return so he had arranged for them to stop just shy of the surface. April swam from the Jet Stream and floated above the city looking down at the sea life below. Alex swam up beside her.

"It's beautiful," he said. His eyes trained on the teeming city below.

"That's home," Ethan said swimming up beside them.

"I'm home," April said. Finally, she had made it home. It felt as if more than two weeks had passed since she had been preparing for the Peace Treaty. So many things had happened. She felt as if she had changed. April was ready now. Ready to take on the responsibility of her position. She was ready to become the pearl wielder the mer needed to bring peace to the legged and the mer.

A smaller Jet Stream appeared and the doors opened before the vehicle stopped. Ethan dashed forward into the arms of his parents. They immediately moved him into their own private Jet Stream. Perch and his men moved over to the Vale's to explain how they had found him. Ethan barely had a chance to wave goodbye before he was bundled into the back of the Vale Jet Stream and then he was gone. April turned to Alex.

"Can you cope with one final swim?" she asked.

He nodded. April ignored her Grandfather's insistence that they take another vehicle to the palace. It was not far away and she wanted Alex to see Hanaria. Alex swam alongside her but they were both too exhausted to talk. He looked down and marvelled at the city below. He could see the palace. It looked like something straight out of a fairy tale. Tall turrets, large windows, intricate architectural embellishments and the whole building glistened a light metallic blue. It was a magical world, one he couldn't imagine living without now he had seen it.

CHAPTER 52

They neared the palace and without thinking, April went to swim straight to the front doors by passing over the entrance gates. She was quickly stopped by an angry mer.

"All visitors must report to the front gate," he said.

April swam down to the front gate as asked.

"He'll be feeling foolish shortly," Alex joked.

They presented themselves to the gate.

"What is your business at the palace today?" the guard asked not bothering to look up from his Iris screen.

"I'm returning to see my Father, King Nathaniel, ruler of the seven seas," April said. The guard looked up. His face went bright red.

"Princess April, right this way," he said hurriedly opening the gates.

Tapping on his Iris screen he called up to the palace, "Inform the King, his daughter has been found."

"Thank you," April said, if she wasn't so exhausted she would have made the point that she had not been found, she had returned herself.

"Should I go somewhere while you see your Dad?" Alex asked. He was suddenly very anxious about meeting the 'ruler of the seven seas' as April put it.

"No, where would you go?" April asked.

"You have a point."

The doors suddenly burst open. Two giant seahorses raced towards them. Alex faltered in apprehension.

"Titan, Tarzan," April called. They whirled around her then darted over to Alex who tentatively patted them.

"Dad," April said. She dashed forward.

"April."

A warm pink light glowed around April and the King as they hugged in the doorway. Clyde slipped out of the doorway and moved over to Alex.

"Hello, Alex I assume. Perch called to inform us of your arrival." Clyde extended his hand. "I'm Clyde, would you like me to show you to your rooms."

Alex shook his hand and nodded. "Thank you."

"I'll be back in a bit, I just need to talk to my Dad," April said.

"Thank you for helping my daughter," Nathaniel said and he grasped Alex's hands.

"It was no problem, Your Majesty," Alex said and tried to bob a bow.

Nathaniel and April swam off and Alex was left awkwardly in the palace hall.

"Let's head to your rooms," Clyde said kindly.

"Yes please."

His tail was starting to seize up after all the swimming. He didn't even have the energy to marvel that he was in an underwater palace.

"I will send up some food as well," Clyde said as he led them up a spiral slope. "You must be starving after swimming all that way."

"Yes. It was quite a long swim, especially as it was my first time," Alex said, following slowly behind him.

"Your first time?"

Alex internally berated himself. April may be his friend but that didn't mean all mer were friendly to humans. "I mean, my first swim in these waters."

Clyde smiled politely.

"Here is your room." He opened a gilt door.

Alex swam through and was surprised by how normal the bedroom looked. The walls of the room were inlaid with little white shells. The large bay window looked out over the front beds of the palace. Alex swam over to the bed and sunk into the large squashy mattress. He closed his eyes and in a matter of moments was asleep.

~

April sat with her Dad in her Mum's library.

"I'm so sorry I didn't find you April."

"It's okay Dad. I'm fine. I was fine. Alex and Connor looked after me. You needed to be here."

Nathaniel beamed at his daughter.

"I miss your Mum terribly, but having you back I can't help but feel like celebrating."

"What about Kayla?" April asked smiling at him too.

"Your sister is not taking things well," Nathaniel said not wanting to go into details.

"When is she coming to Hanaria?" April asked.

"Tomorrow."

"Okay, tomorrow we can talk and fix this mess together."

Nathaniel smiled, April was always the optimist.

"We can, you must be exhausted though."

At that moment April yawned.

"Just a bit."

Nathaniel rose from his chair.

"Go, sleep, we can talk more tomorrow."

He kissed his daughter's forehead and together they swam from the room.

April swam down the corridor. She saw one of the maids and asked them where Alex was.

"He's in the North turret guest room, overlooking the beds Your Highness."

"Thank you."

"It's lovely to have you home safe Princess April."

April smiled and swam off to find Alex. She wanted to check he was okay. She knew first-hand how odd it was being in a strange place. Swimming up the spiral she found his room. She knocked and waited politely.

"Alex," She called.

There was no response so she pushed the door open slowly figuring he was asleep. She swam into the room. He wasn't there. She moved into the lounge area and then the bathroom. But, there was no Alex. She swam to the Iris pad on the desk and dialled Clyde's number.

"Clyde, where's Alex?" she asked as soon as he answered.

"He's in the guest suite in the North turret."

"No, he isn't," April said. "I'm in the North turret and he's not here."

There was a pause on the line.

"I'll ask the staff to keep a look out for him."

April hung up and made her way down the turret spiral.

She didn't have time to relish that she was finally in a safe environment. Something felt wrong. She closed her eyes and connected to her Essentia pearl powers. She spread out her awareness until she could sense the life force of every mer in the palace. Every life force she touched that wasn't Alex brought an increasing sense of panic to her. She opened her eyes and dashed for the central spiral. Swimming as fast as she could she made it to her Dad's suite of rooms. Without knocking she barged in.

"Dad, Alex is missing. He's gone."

"When?" Nathaniel asked. He shot up out of his chair.

"I don't know, while we were talking."

Suddenly the door burst open and Clyde swam into the room.

"Your Majesty, Perch is here to see you," he said breathlessly. A moment later Perch swam into the room. His face was grave.

"Gregor has just contacted the legged President. He wants to unite with them to overturn you as ruler."

"What?" April said stunned.

"How do you know?" Nathaniel asked.

"I've been hacking into his personal Iris account."

"President May can't be trusted. He'll use Gregor to try and destroy us and then turn on him," April said.

"Gregor is more of a fool than I thought he was," Perch said.

"Peace is going to have to wait," Nathaniel spoke gravely. "Contact Yelta. Tell Kayla we're going on the offensive. It's time to stop this war before it spreads any further."

"Do you think Gregor took Alex?" April asked.

"Alex is missing?" Perch asked. April nodded in response.

"I went to find him and he was gone. I can't find his life force in the palace."

"For his sake, I hope Gregor hasn't found him. I shall get my mer on the case."

Perch bowed and swam from the room. Clyde glided after him escorting him out of the palace.

"Dad, I wish Mum were here," April said. The look on her Dad's face said it all. His Iris pad started to ring so she swam from the room. After all she had achieved in the last twenty-four hours she felt like she was back at square one. She wanted to be close to her Mum so she swam back up to the library and out onto her parent's balcony. April looked out over Hanaria. It didn't feel as much like home anymore. She made a silent promise to Alex. She would find him. Without thinking April swam out of the balcony and down towards the nearest entrance to the Great Pearl dining room. Making her way into the room she was unsurprised to see the Great Pearl pulsing a deep black. April floated in front of the pearl. She closed her eyes and relinquished herself to its power. It was time to stop running; it was time to take control.

COMING SOON

Want to know what happens next?

Read on for an excerpt from the highly anticipated Book Two of the Pearl Wielder series…

ESSENTIA

By Hannah Reed

ESSENTIA

April surfaced at the bottom of a great cliff face. She shuddered; the water was a lot cooler than what she was dressed for. She looked around. The area was familiar, but she was sure she had never been there.

"Go deeper," a distinctly soft voice whispered in her mind.

"Deeper," April muttered. She sank back under the waves. The water was relatively shallow with russet rocks jutting out of the cliff. The fish around her glistened a dark silver. They swam up to inspect her as if unused to seeing mer in their parts of water.

"Where is deeper?" she asked them.

The school floated for a second and then darted towards the cliff face. Then suddenly they veered down.

April followed them, pushing past the mounds of seaweed so she didn't lose sight of them. The fish kept swimming and April put on a spurt of speed to keep up. Then suddenly they disappeared. April swam down to where they had seemingly vanished. She shivered in the colder waters looking around in vain for a flash of their silver scales. It was eerie down here she thought and shuddered involuntarily. The water seemed to be moving, sighing even. There was a definite up and down movement as if it were breathing. She projected her Factus energy out to try and create some light. Along the cliff face she could just make out a jagged crack. Swimming forward she could now hear a sucking noise. The sea was rhythmically moving in and out of the slit in the rock face. She followed the dark line deeper.

Eventually, she found an area wide enough to pass through. The noise was even louder here, the cliffs sounded alive. April shot her Factus energy through the opening to check for a dead end but the white light kept on going. April looked around her before entering the cliff face. But there was nowhere else the fish could have gone. She turned back to the cliff and peered inside. Her back tingled and she whipped around expecting someone to be watching her. But, she was alone.

Carefully she started swimming, even with her Factus energy lighting the way, the tunnel was dark. She had to curve her tail to slide through the impossibly narrow crevices.

She winced as she scraped her arm against a particularly jagged piece of rock. Her arms stung from where they were grazed and her scales tugged as they were scraped out of place but she persevered through the tunnel. Eventually she could feel the suction growing stronger. Finally, April pulled herself through and into a cavern of water. It was like a vertical tunnel had been carved through the cliff. A groan sounded below her then suddenly a rush of water dragged her down. Her arms flew in the water and her hair streamed behind her.

"Your Highness."

April swam upright with a jolt.

"Your Highness," a guard repeated, floating awkwardly in front of her. "Your Father has requested that you join him in his study."

"Oh, okay," April said trying to recover her composure. "Thank you very much. Tell him I'll be along shortly."

The guard swam off with a small bow and April turned her attention to the Great Pearl.

April eyed it angrily. She wished the pearls would just talk to her. She wanted to know if these blackouts were dreams or some sort of pearl memory. April pressed her hand against the pearl. The Great Pearl flickered through the colours of the pearls in response. April placed her other hand on the pearl and wielded her Factus and Essentia energy into a ring around it. She lifted the pearl and started to swim it back to the dining room, not bothering to make sure the Great Pearl didn't hit the ceiling. As they reached the dining room the Great Pearl settled itself above the dining table. As if sensing its work was done its outer glow faded. April could just identify an Essentia heartbeat deep at its core.

"Are you not going to tell me anything?" she asked, arms folded. The Great Pearl did nothing in response.

She swam from the dining room and headed to her Dad's study. At the last moment, she ducked down a corridor to grab a jumper from her room. She didn't want to face him after the Reflexus. But, she knew she couldn't put it off forever. She grabbed a pale, pink, fluffy jumper and pulled it over her head. Its heaviness comforted her.

April knocked on her Dad's study door, unsure of the formality of the occasion.

"Come in," he called. April pushed the mother of pearl door open slowly and swam into the study. She paused and let the door swing shut behind her. It felt as if she hadn't been in here for years, yet it had only been two weeks.

"Kayla," She said in shock as her eyes scanned the room and landed on her sister.

"April," Kayla said. She sat in the comfy sea sponge by her Dad's globe of the sea. Kayla span the globe with her tail. Her arms folded, she stared straight ahead.

"Please," Nathaniel said from the window. "We need each other now more than ever. Your Mum wouldn't want you two to fight."

"How do we know what Mum wanted?" Kayla said. "She had her own agenda."

April frowned at her sister's words. Kayla idolised their Mum.

"What's happened to you?"

"I grew up April. I took on some responsibility," Kayla said rising from her chair. "While you were playing damsel in distress, I was busy trying to stop a war from escalating."

"Kayla," Nathaniel raised his voice.

"And you, you talk about not 'breaking down' but here you are addicted to your Curo pearls. I know that Clyde has been taking away your medallion."

"Stop, this," April said.

"You just swam back here like everything's great again now that your back," Kayla shouted. "But it's not!" Kayla floated with her fists locked. All three stared at each other.

ACKNOWLEDGEMENTS

There are several different versions of this acknowledgment – the pithy short version and the theatrical long version. Hopefully this final version is a good mix of the two.

I can't believe I have finally gotten to this point and published my first book. There are so many people who have helped me get to this point and I hope to pay tribute to most of them here.

I must thank my tireless editor Sarah for all her time, effort and dedication to the Pearl Wielder Trilogy. To the hours of editing and debating commas and speech marks, to the months of agonising over a title (I'm still not sure we chose the right one.) Thank you for all your support and hard work.

TV shows like Gossip Girl, 90210 and Avatar: The Legend of Ang, books like Sweet Valley High, the Lioness' Quartet, the Stravaganza series, Hunger Games and Twilight – all these stories helped to shape me as I returned to them time and time again as a fictional sanctuary.

Thank you to Keve Szatmari (check out his work at @szatmari_keve) for giving my book a cover and turning it into a reality. It was a process to get there but we did it – thank you for agreeing to work with me.

This book could have been published several years ago. But, for many reasons it wasn't. One reason it has come to fruition now is because of my boyfriend and best friend Hayden. Although it has been difficult for him as someone who is not a natural reader or a lover of fiction, he has worked relentlessly to support and encourage me.

My beta readers Eleanor, Sophie, Brandon, Krystian and my sister Leanne. Thanks for your honesty (even if hurtful at times!), your advice, your support and your criticism.

Thank you to my friends for your constant questions of 'When are you going to publish your book?' Every time you asked it made me determined that sometime soon I would have an answer for you.

Thank you to my family, especially my Dad – he may have never actually read the book… but he is the first to mention it to random strangers and the one always probing me about when it would be finished and encouraging me to 'just get on with it!'

To everyone who is out their pursuing their dream remember that it is only you who can make your dream come true. And the only way to do that is through hard work, perseverance and courage. Believe in yourself and never forget your dream – you will make yourself proud.

DID YOU ENJOY THE FIRST INSTALMENT OF THE PEARL WIELDER TRILOGY?

Help spread the word to fellow readers
by leaving a review on amazon.

AFRAID OF MISSING ANY UPDATES ABOUT THE PEARL WIELDER TRILOGY?

Follow @hannah.reads on Instagram for regular updates or visit
www.hannahreads.co.uk.

Printed in Great Britain
by Amazon